LOVING THE ALPHA'S DAUGTER

THE VAMPIRE KING'S FEEDER
BOOK TWO

BELLA MOONDRAGON

CONTENTS

THE GOLDEN HOUR

Emory

I close my bedroom door gingerly, trying to make the least amount of noise possible. I do think it's ridiculous that I have to sneak around the castle which I have come to see as my new home. Even when I was a prisoner here, I hadn't had to be this careful with how I moved around. Much has changed since the first time I walked into this ancient and foreboding fortress.

I look around to check if the coast is clear. There have been guards stationed at my door for my protection, but I have spent days learning their blind spots. There is a guard change that gave me two minutes to escape. I walk briskly down the hallway, trying not to make noise and hoping nobody sees me. There are always servants walking around, but if I keep my head down, I might be able to get away scot-free.

This wing of the castle has many twists and turns like a labyrinth. Since this wing is connected to the wing where the royals are, it has been designed to be difficult to navigate for anyone who doesn't know the castle layout. I spent all of yesterday studying the floor plan so I know where to go. After one last turn down a long hallway, there's a door I know leads to the outside. From here, I'll be able to get to the gardens and to sweet freedom.

I reach the door and I grasp the handle when a familiar voice asks, "Where are you going, Emory?"

I have to stifle a scream, putting a hand on my heart, which is beating faster from shock. I turn to see Kane's handsome face with his sharp cheekbones, porcelain skin, dark hair, and those striking pale blue eyes. I don't know if I'll ever get used to how attractive he is. He has a hypnotic beauty that makes me want to keep staring at him... which makes sense, as he's a vampire.

His species can hunt with their superior speed and strength as there is no other creature on earth that could match them, not even wolf shifters. And if they want, they can lure their prey with their deadly beauty. Most vampires nowadays are too impatient to bother tempting their victim, preferring to get blood from feeders. Still, looking at Kane reminds me that vampires are always dangerous even when they haven't lifted a finger yet.

"Emory," he says my name almost in a purr. "Why did you leave your room?"

I refuse to act like a child that has been caught sneaking out by my parents. I am a grown woman. I am almost twenty-one. I can leave my room if I want to.

"I just wanted some fresh air," I explain. "I can feel the cabin fever settling in."

He raises his eyebrows in disbelief. "It's only been a week since the doctor put you on bed rest. Are you that bored already?"

"I'm ready to claw at the walls, Kane."

A week in bed with nothing else to do has been frustrating and mind-numbingly dull. Kane has been away dealing with King Peter and trying his best to stave off a war with the other kingdom. His best friend Rainer has been helping him with that, so that leaves me with few visitors. My maids have tried their best to keep me entertained with card games and books, but I want to go outside.

While I don't mind being indoors, there is an intrinsic part of my being that craves to be in nature. I am a wolf shifter. I revel in the freedom of being surrounded by trees and feeling the earth underneath my feet. Feeling the sun on my skin and breathing in fresh air makes me feel the most alive. Every shifter has the same connection with nature, and any of us would start to get antsy if we are cooped up for too long.

Kane looks exasperated. His blue eyes stare me down, and I refuse to back down. I tilt my chin up defiantly. I know Kane is the boss around here, as he is the literal king of the castle, but I am the new Alpha of the Moonraker pack.

I have my own power.

"Were you going to go outside alone?" he asks. "Where are Helga and Nellie?"

"They're busy, and they don't know I snuck out." I don't want to get my maids into trouble so I add, "They wouldn't have been able to stop me. I was ready to tie up the bed sheets into a rope and scale down the building through the window if I had to."

He smiles at the thought. "You could've fallen and broken your neck."

"Which is why I went with the safer option of just going out the door," I tell him. I haven't let go of the door handle, still intent on escaping even if I have to run screaming from the castle like a madwoman. "If you will excuse me…"

"Emory."

I go still.

Kane's icy blue eyes don't even blink as he moves forward. He carefully pushes me out of the way with the gentlest touch, forcing me to let go of the door handle. I glare at him, ready to give him a piece of my mind. I don't care if he's the fucking vampire king.

"It's locked," he explains before reaching into the pocket of his pants and pulling out a large iron key. He unlocks the door and gestures for me to go outside. "Go on."

I didn't even know the door was locked. That's embarrassing. It would have made my escape plan futile. I don't know how to pick a lock.

My anger dissipates like smoke. I'm too embarrassed and confused. "You're just letting me go?"

He gives me an amused smile. "If you must go outside, I'll go with you. I want to be there just in case you feel faint."

"Oh."

He waits.

Sheepish, I say, "Okay, then."

He offers his hand, and I take it. He laces our fingers together and leads us outside. It's the later part of the day, and the sun will be setting soon. Sunlight can't kill vampires. Kane won't burst into flames, but the sunlight is uncomfortable on sensitive vampire eyes, and that's what makes some of his kind prefer being nocturnal. He's the king–not much can harm him.

I don't have that problem at all. When we reach the gardens, I let go of Kane's hand to spread my arms as wide as I can. I close my eyes and breathe in the fresh air and the smell of earth and flowers. The sunlight warms my skin, and I soak it up like a deprived sunflower.

It's the golden hour, and the world is saturated and beautiful. Kane stands by a tree and watches me. He isn't as ghostly pale in this lighting. He looks even more handsome. It's a little bit annoying. Does he ever look terrible?

"What are you thinking?" he questions.

"Nothing."

I am not going to stroke his ego by complimenting his good looks. He already knows he's hot. Even other vampires aren't immune to his allure. Being a powerful king makes him irresistible to almost everyone.

He moves closer, and I stay still as he reaches me. He tilts my chin up with a finger, and I close my eyes as he kisses me. His lips are soft and warm. I have always thought kissing a vampire would be like kissing a marble statue, cold and unpleasant, but the reality with Kane is different. He deepens the kiss, his tongue lightly touching mine, and I shiver from desire.

I have missed how he tastes–like strawberries and cinnamon, and

I want more. I've missed how he smells. I've missed how his skin feels in my hands. I've missed the weight of his body on top of mine.

I reach for the collar of his shirt, wanting to unbutton it, but his hand stops me. He pulls away from my mouth to kiss the inside of my wrist.

"The doctor said no sex," he reminds me, apologetically.

"He also said bed rest, and yet, here I am," I reply. "We're already breaking the rules. We might as well keep going."

He kisses my other wrist. "Emory, think of the baby."

I sigh, knowing I'm beaten. He has to use the baby card. I have only known I'm pregnant for a little over a week, and I'm already being treated with kid gloves. Ever since I told Kane I was carrying his child, he has been acting like I'm as delicate as a china teacup.

I pull my hands away from him. "I'm strong. I can handle it."

"I know just how strong you are, but vampire pregnancies are notoriously difficult," he says. "My mother had a few miscarriages after I was born. She was unable to have any more children after she had Lex."

"I didn't know that."

Most vampires are unable to have children naturally. They usually grow their numbers by turning humans into vampires. There are a few royal bloodlines that are able to birth children like Kane's family, and no one quite knows how this is possible. Even more unfathomable is Kane getting me pregnant.

I have never heard of a vampire and wolf shifter creating a child before. Wolf shifters can't be turned into vampires. For centuries, we have been told that our two species are completely incompatible. We have managed to defy everything we've been told for generations by falling in love.

"Pregnancies amongst wolf shifters are risky, too," I explain, a hand touching my abdomen in concern. "Women can't shift while pregnant as they could miscarry or induce labor too early. If they get sick during pregnancy, their bodies don't heal as quickly, so it can lead to complications."

I watched Mother help deliver babies for years. So many things can go wrong during labor.

Kane must sense my distress. He cups my face in his warm hands. "Look at me."

I look up into his blue eyes and feel some of my worry melt away. I'm reminded who I'm with. This is a king that has ruled for a long, long time. He doesn't balk at difficult situations.

"We'll talk to the doctor," he says. "If it is a risky pregnancy, we'll take every precaution to make sure you and the baby are safe."

"Will the doctor even know what to do? This baby is going to be part-vampire and part-wolf shifter. Does anyone know what we're dealing with?"

"We can consult with a wolf shifter healer as well. I'll move one into the castle immediately."

"What is the baby going to be?" I ask, trying to picture something unimaginable. "A vampire? A wolf? Something else entirely?"

"It's our baby," he reassures me, his conviction unwavering. "No matter what he or she is, they're ours."

"Ours," I echo.

Our baby.

Ours.

It doesn't matter if the baby comes out with fangs and six arms, I will love them anyway. I have always wanted kids, and now I am getting my dream. And I get to share this with the man I loved. What else matters?

Kane strokes my cheek, his gaze soft and adoring. No one has ever looked at me that way. When I was a child wondering about my mate, I wondered what he would be like. I thought it would be Darius, the son of my father's Beta, but I hadn't and could never love him. Darius is nothing like Kane.

Kane is something I could have never seen coming. I haven't even told him, afraid of what it would mean for both of us. He deserves to know. A part of me aches to tell him and to put into words what I know deep in my bones.

I open my mouth to speak, but he beats me to it.

"Marry me."

THE BEST THING

Kane

This isn't how I imagined proposing to Emory. I have been thinking about the right way and the right time to ask her. This past week, she has been miserable, stuck on bed rest, and I had to run off and deal with an impending war with Scarlett Thunder. I haven't had the time to compose what I want to say in a proposal, but as the two words came out of my mouth, they sum up everything that I want.

"Marry me."

Emory's green eyes widen as she takes in the words. They are the prettiest shade of green I have ever seen, emerald, and framed by long, dark lashes. Her red hair is a deep burgundy in the golden hour. The sight of her makes something in me ache, but I can't put a name to it.

"What?" Her voice is small, unsure. "Did you just...?"

I bury my fingers in her red hair, needing to ground myself. My pulse quickens as doubt makes me consider if she's about to reject me. She has told me she loves me. Does that not guarantee that she will say yes?

"Marry me," I repeat, trying to hide my growing anxiety. "I want you to marry me."

"But…" She blinks, her brows furrowing. "Now?"

I nod. "Yes. Now."

"You're about to go to war with Scarlett Thunder," she points out. "I've just become the Alpha. And then there's the baby…"

"I know."

I want to tell her how I don't fear what is to come when I have her by my side. Nothing feels unmanageable knowing that she will always be there with me. I have never dared to dream of having a marriage with someone I could have a true partnership with. My own parents had an affectionate marriage, but they hadn't been equal. I had resigned myself to a loveless marriage with King Peter's daughter, Opal, before I met Emory and my life changed.

"There's too much." Emory's face crumbles. "I can't deal with everything and add a wedding on top of that. I can't. I don't know how."

Her face has gone pale. Her eyes are wet with unshed tears. Even though I'm disappointed, I don't like to see her in distress. I wipe away her tears with my thumbs.

"It's okay," I murmur. "Everything will be all right."

She sniffs and tries to turn away. I pull her back, needing her in my arms. She buries her face in my shirt, her tears wetting the fabric and neither of us care.

"I'm sorry," she mumbles into my chest. "It's not that I don't want you. I want you so much. I love you. I really do, but everything is just…"

"Messy?" I offer. "Overwhelming?"

"Both." She pulls back to look at me, her green eyes taking me in like she's afraid I'll disappear. "You're not messy or overwhelming. You're the best, actually. I had just been thinking the same thing, that we should get married, but when you said the words, it all came crashing in on me."

I smile, feeling some of that disappointment abate. "You're the best thing that's ever happened to me."

That makes her smile back. She wipes away the last of her tears. She says, "I'm not saying no."

"But you're not saying yes."

"I'm saying not now."

I have to ask as the doubt would gnaw at me. "This is just a question. Do you want to marry me?"

"Yes, I do," she replies, quickly. "I would love to marry you, but now is not the right time."

Relief makes it easier to swallow my disappointment. I have asked at the wrong time, and that's not a failure. I do see her point with my kingdom on the verge of a crisis and her dealing with her own with the Moonraker pack. Add in the pregnancy, and it would overwhelm anyone.

I take her hand, needing to be connected to her. "All right, Emory. I can wait."

Emory

I don't know who to talk to about Kane's proposal. Anyone in Crimson Peak would say I'm a fool for not immediately jumping to say yes to their king's proposal. I'm thinking I might be a fool for not running off to the altar with Kane at the first opportunity, no matter what is currently happening. Considering the nature of our positions in life, there will always be something we have to deal with, so does making Kane wait even make sense?

I'm conflicted, and I have to bite my tongue from saying a word as Helga and Nellie help me get dressed for the day. They don't even know about the pregnancy. Kane and I both agreed not to tell anyone else until I'm past the first trimester. According to the doctor, I won't even be showing until then, so neither of my maids should notice anything.

If they do notice, I will make them swear to secrecy. I trust them to keep the news to themselves until Kane and I are ready to tell the world. It feels nice to have a secret that only belongs to us. This baby is going to be of two worlds, and there are going to be people from both of those worlds that would have something negative to say about the child's existence.

The thought always makes a swell of fierce protectiveness take me over. I won't be meeting this baby for a long time, but I already want to shield them from the world. I've seen how cruel it can be to children. There are parents that don't deserve children, my own father being one of them, and I cannot understand how they can be so heartless toward something so innocent.

I remember that Lola is coming to Castle Graystone that day and smile. She will be moving into the castle to be with me. While Colt is leading the pack in my absence, I still cannot trust anyone not to hurt Lola or use her in any way to get to me. My half-sister Lola holds a part of my heart, and I will do anything for her.

Once I'm ready for the day, we leave my rooms. I stand outside the front of the castle with my maids as a car parks near the castle steps. Darius, the current Beta of the Moonraker pack, is driving. He steps out of the vehicle as his mother, Margaret, helps Lola out of the back. Lola runs to me as soon as her feet hit the ground. My arms envelop her in a hug, and I nearly burst into tears at being able to hold her again.

There had been a time I thought I would never see my sister again. When I took her place as a feeder for King Kane, I thought I wouldn't live long, but it would have been worth it to protect Lola. How my own father treated her was unfathomable to me. Her mother died shortly after she was born, and I have been the one to raise her. I'm the only mother Lola has ever known. She lived her entire life in our family home, but my father had tried to sell her off to King Kane to repay his debts.

I could never imagine trying to sell my own child in that way. I took Lola's place to spare her what I had thought would be a terrible fate. Our father's betrayal had started the ripple effect that would lead to his eventual downfall. Instead of being the respected Alpha Bernard of the Moonraker pack, he sits in a cell in the castle dungeons. My sternum still stings in the place where he tried to tear me apart when I was giving him one last chance for mercy before Kane's armies destroyed him.

"I missed you, Emory," Lola says

"I missed you too, Lola." I pull away to look over at her, checking if she's healthy and find that she looks physically unharmed. "How have you been? Did the Kincaids treat you well?"

"Margaret is very nice. And Darius helped me with my homework."

I look toward Darius and his mother who have been waiting for me to acknowledge them. "Darius, Margaret, thank you for bringing Lola here. And for taking care of her while I was gone."

"Alpha Emory, it wasn't difficult to take care of Lola. She's a precious child," Margaret replies with a smile. "She was better behaved than my own children."

"Ouch," Darius remarks with a laugh. He nods to Emory. "I am glad to be under your command, Alpha Emory."

Darius was the boy I thought would be my mate someday. It had made sense logically as his father had been my father's Beta. Looking at him now, I feel nothing for him except gratitude for his treatment of Lola. He is definitely not my mate, but he would be a good mate for some other girl.

"How are things with the pack?" I ask.

"Colt is doing his best, and I'm helping him as much as I can," Darius answers. "Rebuilding our relationships with the packs around us is going to be a difficult road ahead but not impossible."

"We can't blame them for being cautious after what my father did, starting pointless wars with them for territory. Forgiveness might come in time, but we should focus on rebuilding our pack from within."

"Now that we're no longer having to fund a senseless war, we should be on our way to rebuilding."

"If you don't mind me saying, Alpha Emory, your father ruled the pack as a tyrant. He didn't care for any of us unless it served his own agenda," Margaret remarks. "The fact that you want to focus on rebuilding rather than conquering means you are already doing better than him. Not that the bar was raised that high."

"Thank you, Margaret," I tell her, sincerely. "But I can't do any of it without you. We are and have always been stronger together."

"The lone wolf dies," Margaret starts.

"But the pack survives," Darius concludes.

It's a mantra wolf shifters live by. We are stronger as a community, working together to create and restore our kingdom. A lone wolf hunting on its own is formidable, but a whole pack of us? We can take down large prey more than twice our size if we work together. My father tried to destroy all of that.

Kane has left what punishment I want to bestow upon my father in my hands. Despite everything my father has done, I can't bring myself to make a decision. I can't give the order to have him executed, but I can't let him go free to wreak havoc again. He has been the cause of so much death and strife amongst wolf shifters and vampires. His inflated ego is too dangerous to let loose again.

I won't kill him. No one will feed on him. He might have to rot in the dungeons for the rest of his life. I don't know which fate he would rather have.

Darius and Margaret leave as I bring Lola into the castle. The last time she was in Castle Graystone hadn't been a pleasant experience. I try to make it up to her by telling her about the secret passageways and the ghost stories I've heard from the servants. Lola has always shared Colt's love of horror stories and delights in the spooky tales of grieving dead queens and headless knights. Lola is no longer afraid by the time we reach what will be her bedroom.

I open the door and let her in. Her green eyes widen in surprise as she takes in the large room. It is smaller than mine but still as opulent, with plush rose carpeting and a four-poster bed with a pink canopy. There is also a desk and bookshelves. All the furniture is heavy cherry wood with flowers carved in it. The walls are painted with a variety of white flowers.

"Is this your room?" Lola asks. "It's so pretty."

I smile at her. "My room is next door. This is your room."

Lola smiles widely. "Really?"

"Really." I put a hand on her shoulder. "This is going to be your home now, Lola. I want you to be happy here."

"I'm just happy I'm with you," she tells me. "Margaret was nice, but she's not you."

I swallow back my tears. The pregnancy hormones make me want to weep at every little thing. I give Lola a conspiring smile. "You want to see how soft that bed is?"

"Can I jump on it?"

"I don't see anyone here stopping you."

Lola doesn't need to be told twice. She takes off her shoes and tosses them aside before running and jumping on the bed, testing out the softness of it gingerly at first before bouncing on it until the canopy is shaking. I laugh before climbing up to jump with her- being cautious of my condition. Soon, we are hugging and laughing.

I have my sister back.

THE OBVIOUS SOLUTION

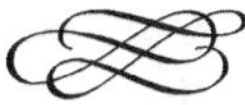

Kane

There are times I wonder if I remember a time before I wasn't constantly at war with a neighbor. I spent over ten years in conflict with Bernard Moonraker for his inability to repay his debts. Now that he is locked up in the dungeon of my castle, I'm dealing with King Peter of Scarlett Thunder because of his unhinged offspring. Bernard had been a nuisance, much like a cockroach that refused to die. King Peter is a whole different kind of asshole, with enough power and resources to actually be a problem for me.

Neither of us has withdrawn our troops from the battlefield. Our men are waiting for word for them to battle to the death. We send messengers back and forth, switching from veiled threats to half-assed attempts at compromising. We are at a stalemate, neither of us willing to back down or be the one to make the first move. Unstoppable force meets immovable objects.

I stare outside the castle window at the gray skies. It looks like it is about to rain. The smell in the air makes me certain of it. If I were to go to the north tower of the castle, I could see the lightning hit the grounds of Scarlett Thunder. Crimson Peak is on higher ground, and we loom over the other kingdom. We have the geographical advantage of being able to see the enemy coming first.

"There's been a new letter from King Peter's messenger," Rainer says. "Shall we see what demands he has for you today?"

I don't turn away from the window. "Open it."

I wait as Rainer does as I say and begins reading the letter. It's the same demands as before. King Peter is willing to overlook all transgressions if I release his son Jacob and marry his daughter Opal. He refuses to believe that I'm not the father of her unborn baby. I have never touched Opal as her personality repulses me.

I turn to look at where Lex is sitting at the table. Slender and blond, he doesn't resemble me at first glance. Lex inherited his coloring from our maternal grandfather, King Alexander, while I took after our father. No one would think we are brothers until you see us beside each other. Only then can you see the slight resemblance in our sharp jawlines and cheekbones.

"He refuses to think Opal isn't anything but the purest of snow," Lex remarks. "Even though anyone who's met her knows there's nothing pure and virginal about her."

"You would know better than anyone," Rainer quips.

Lex gives him a mocking smile. "Of course. I'm the whore, after all."

"You said it, not me."

"Or are you just bitter we never invited you to any of our parties?"

Rainer grimaces. "I would rather not have attended your disgusting orgies. No thank you."

Lex shrugs. "I don't know, Rainer. You might have enjoyed it."

I have to assume my brother is joking or just trying to get under Rainer's skin. Either way, it's working. Not wanting to focus on the topic of what Lex gets up to in the dark of night, I join them at the table. I take the letter from Rainer and shake my head over King Peter's stubbornness.

I look to Lex and nod for him to begin writing a letter down for me. For all his complaints that he doesn't enjoy working, Lex makes a half-decent secretary. He writes fast and has nice handwriting. My response to King Peter is quick and to the point: no.

"He's not going to like that," Rainer says. "Perhaps we could offer him something besides you being trapped in unhappy matrimony with his awful daughter?"

"He only wants blood and gold," I reply. "Neither of which do we have an infinite supply of."

Even if the war with the Moonraker pack hadn't cost me so much, I wouldn't be willing to give him so much money. If this war with King Peter had come a decade or two later, I might have been willing to pay him off, but at the moment, I am in no mood to spend the money I do have on the likes of that tyrant. I have loans with other kingdoms and packs I could come collect early but that might just entice them to join my enemy's side to get rid of me. No one ever said ruling is an easy job.

"We could release Jacob," Lex suggests.

"Absolutely not," Rainer counters. "He's the only bargaining chip we have."

This is true, and I cannot stand Jacob after what he did to Emory. He almost killed her in the library. I came so close to losing her over his terrible sister's jealousy. Jacob will not leave my dungeons unless I have no other choice.

Lex sighs. "What do you want to do, then?"

"We can't give in to King Peter's demands," Rainer says. "He could go back on his word as soon as Jacob is back in his custody. He could still choose to attack us."

"He could still attack us even if we have Jacob," Lex points out. "He already has once. Let's be honest here. King Peter has been looking for a reason to conquer Crimson Peak even before any of us were born."

King Peter has an infamous mutual dislike of my father, King Michael. The details of their rivalry vary with who is asked, but there was a general consensus it might have had to do with my mother, Queen Agatha. The rumor is that King Peter wanted her hand in marriage, but King Michael had beaten him to it. My mother's native kingdom of Cerise Port had been a wealthy land due to their several ports that made them a central trading hub. Whoever she married stood to gain a lot of money, and my father had won that privilege.

"All of this because of spices," Lex mutters. "That old bat would have been at odds with Uncle Cyrus and gone to war with him too."

Our uncle, King Cyrus, is not known for his prowess in battle. Cerise Port is wealthy but not particularly robust with their military. Crimson Peak has been sending down men to help them with that problem for generations. I doubt King Peter would have done anything but suck the kingdom dry of its wealth like a leech.

"Speaking of your uncle, have you talked to King Cyrus about helping with the war? Financially, at least?" Rainer asks.

"I was going to go see him in a few days."

Lex's eyes light up. "Can I come? I love going to visit Cerise Port."

I stare at my brother, exasperated. "Does it have anything to do with Cerise's red light district? I think you've done enough damage in that regard, haven't you?"

Lex coughs uncomfortably. "I should go."

My brother scurries off, and I don't bother asking where he is going. Instead, I reach for the letter Lex has written and hand it to Rainer.

"Have this sent to King Peter," I say. "And don't bother waiting for a response."

I get to my feet. Rainer stands up and follows me. We walk out of the room and down the hallway.

"Do you think your uncle can help?" he asks. "Didn't he already send you money?"

"Hopefully, he'll be willing to send me a little more until I can think of a way to get King Peter off my back."

"Do you think King Peter's planning something terrible?"

"What else would he be doing?"

Rainer leaves to go send the letter, and I continue on to my destination. I largely avoid this wing of the castle. The nobles live here, and I already have to deal with their simpering at dinner every night. The person I want to speak to also stays here, so I can't avoid it.

A guard standing by nods before he opens a door for me. It leads to a suite of rooms with antique dark furniture. I have never been in these rooms, and they are simpler than I expected. Clark sits at a chair with a book in his lap. He looks up from his book, his spectacles gleaming under the light.

Clark was turned later in life, and his hair is mostly gray. Even vampirism hadn't managed to fix his terrible vision completely, and he still needs spectacles to see. As a human, he worked as my father's advisor before finally being given the gift of prolonged life. When I was a child, I used to see Clark as a foreboding, serious character with no sense of humor and no patience for little children.

Still, my father trusted him and sought his counsel for many matters, especially when our kingdom was at war. As much of an asshole as I think Clark is, he has something valuable. *Knowledge.* It's the only reason I didn't have him executed after I saw how he had been mistreating the feeders and letting the guards debase and abuse them.

He puts his book down on a table and gets to his feet slowly. He gives a shallow, mocking bow. "Your Majesty. To what do I owe the honor?"

"Don't be clever with me, Clark. I'm not here to play games."

"I would never dare to suggest a thing, sir."

I resist rolling my eyes and take the seat across from him without a word. He sits down and waits for me to speak. I have vague memories of my father's war council, a select group of a dozen men he had implicitly trusted to help him win wars. I have a war council of only two men I can trust.

"I need a war council."

"About time," Clark states. "I would have advised you to put together one before rallying the troops."

"I would have asked for your advice if you hadn't done what you did to the feeders." I think of what almost happened to Emory because of him.

"Are we really going to go over the rights of feeders, again? You always were more soft-hearted than you needed to be. Your father always worried about you and how you would fare–"

"Enough," I snap. "I didn't come here for a lecture."

"Of course, Your Majesty," Clark amends, glibly. "How may I help you?"

As much as Clark annoys me, he has been my advisor since I became king. It's easy for me to tell him my concerns with the war and how I am at a stalemate with an egotistical king. As I speak, I think of my father who would have already thrown everything he had at Peter. He acted quickly, sometimes too quickly, and I didn't want to find myself backed into a corner as he sometimes did.

Clark removes his spectacles and wipes at the lenses with a handkerchief. "I would think the solution is obvious, sir."

Frustrated, I demand, "And what is that?"

"Give him back his son and marry his daughter. Prevent bloodshed for your people and save your kingdom."

"I can't marry Opal. She's carrying Lex's child."

"Why does it matter?" Clark replies. "As long as it's the same bloodline, your legacy lives on."

"She's awful, a total raging bitch. We would never be happy together."

"You already knew that before, and you were still willing to marry her."

"That was different."

"Before you had your little she-wolf by your side?"

"Careful, Clark," I warn. "You say one bad thing about Emory, and you will spend the next hundred years in the dungeons instead of your comfortable suite."

Clark put on his glasses, his expression grim. "Do you want to know what makes you inherently different from your father?"

"What?"

"Like most royals, he understood that duty comes first. Love is a privilege you are not afforded when you already possess so much power."

I swallow hard. I've known this truth my entire life. My parents didn't hide the facts of this life from me, and I had accepted it for the longest time. That was before I met Emory. I could no more give her up now than I could live without blood. I needed her.

"I won't lose her," I confess in a whisper. "I don't know what I would be without her."

"Better off," Clark concludes. "After all, Kane, she'll age and die like all of her kind. And you'll be alone once again, but this time with a broken heart. And if you're not careful, no kingdom."

SHOCKED, RELIEVED, OVERJOYED

Emory

Lola wants to see the gardens, so we leave Helga and Nellie to unpack Lola's things and we make our way outside. Kane insists I have guards with me at all times so we have two guards following behind us, far enough to give us some privacy but always in sight. I bring Lola to the rose garden. I haven't avoided the place even after that time Opal and her friends tried to attack me there.

I refuse to let Opal and her ilk drive me away from things I enjoy. The rose garden is a truly beautiful place, and I will continue to visit it. I warn Lola not to touch the rose bushes so she won't hurt herself on the thorns. Lola gives the roses a minute of her attention before proceeding to try and climb a tree.

"Be careful," I warn her. "You could fall."

"I'm fine!" she calls out as she climbs up a branch. "I climb trees all the time."

That I can believe. I spent my childhood climbing trees around our family home, and so did my brother Colt. We used to make our mother angry when we would come home covered in mud and with green stains on our clothes. Lola isn't nearly half as messy as we were.

I continue to watch Lola climb the tree, worrying she'll fall and break an arm if I look away for one second. The scent of roses and vanilla makes me turn to see a familiar woman approaching. I have never spoken to Queen Agatha directly and only see her from a distance at dinner time. She is a beautiful woman with gray-streaked dark hair pulled up in an elegant bun and pale blue eyes. I can see where Lex inherited his delicate beauty from.

I expect Queen Agatha would walk past me, not acknowledging my existence except for a nod, but she surprises me by stopping in front of where I sit. I stand and curtsy quickly, looking less elegant than I want.

"The girl is your sister, am I correct?" she asks. "I remember seeing her in the castle that day you arrived."

I don't remember seeing her in the throne room when my father had come to bargain with Kane in what felt like a lifetime ago. I might not have noticed if she was there as I had been preoccupied with trying to keep Lola safe from my father's selfishness, but it's more likely she had a vantage point I hadn't been privy to.

"She is," I answer. "Her name's Lola."

"Half-sister?"

I hesitate, wondering how pack gossip has managed to reach Crimson Peak. I wonder who has been blabbing about my family's business. I will have to reprimand them. Lola has never deserved being treated as less than. The circumstances of her birth were beyond her control. My father had an affair with a scullery maid who passed away. I try my best to make Lola know that she is wanted and a part of the family, but people can be so unreasonably cruel to children for things that aren't even their fault.

"I only ask because you don't look alike," she adds. "I didn't mean to imply anything."

That is true. I have red hair and green eyes from my mother's side of the family. Lola's hair is a dark blonde, and her eyes are a silver gray. Ironically, despite being the child our father values the least, Lola is the only one who inherited his eyes.

"Her mother passed away during childbirth," I explain. "I have taken care of her since."

"Poor thing. It's not easy to grow up without a mother," she muses, watching Lola contemplatively. "I tried my best to keep my boys from being unruly as children with mixed results."

I can't help but ask, "What was Kane like as a child?"

She smiles, and I see where Kane inherited his smile. "He was a sweet boy. He would take in every wounded animal he could find and try to nurse them back to health. My husband worried he'd be too soft, but I saw Kane's caring heart as an asset. Kane was always made aware of his future responsibilities. He wants to take care of his people, and he has done so ever since the crown was placed on his head."

"That does sound like him," I muse. "What was Lex like?"

"Believe it or not, he was quite shy as a boy."

I stifle a laugh of disbelief. "Lex was shy?"

"He was. He would hide behind my skirts instead of having to go play with the other children. He idolized his older brother, wanted to be just like Kane, but he always fell short. It crushed him over time, always being compared to his brother and found lacking."

"Is that why he's the way he is now?"

"That poor boy doesn't know who he is. No one has ever expected anything from him, so he's never had to really try. I had hoped he'd find purpose as a general or a politician, but neither path interested him. Now, he just wanders around, seeking temporary entertainment to pass the time."

The picture the queen paints about her son makes me feel sorry for him. I have wondered growing up what Colt had felt being second to me. My father raised me in the belief that I would take over as Alpha someday, which later turned out to be another one of his lies, but he never publicly declared Colt as his heir until the day I arrived at the castle. If things had gone differently, would Colt have ended up like Lex?

"Have you talked to Lex about this?" I ask.

"He's long past the age of confiding in his mother," she answers. "And I could imagine how embarrassing it would be to admit that you still feel lost even after all these years, perpetually stuck in an in-between place."

"Maybe we could help him," I suggest, genuinely wanting to make a change. "Surely there's something out there that could give him purpose."

I understand having a purpose. I had grown up believing I would be an Alpha, and now I am. I have been like a mother to Lola all these years. Surely, it wouldn't be such a chore to help a vampire find their purpose in life.

"Perhaps. You are welcome to try." Queen Agatha looks thoughtful. "I had been pressuring Kane into giving me a grandchild for years. From what I've been hearing about Opal, I'll be getting my wish even though I'm not sure Peter would let that child ever leave Scarlett Thunder."

"You don't think Opal's child is Kane's, do you?"

She purses her lips in disgust. "No, I heard she had been warming the bed of my other son. Either way, I'm going to be a grandmother."

Kane hasn't told his mother about my pregnancy, which is what we agreed on. I don't know how the queen will react to the news of me carrying her other grandchild. She doesn't seem that terrible. She's actually being nice. Maybe she'll be pleased?

"How would you feel if Kane was a father one day?"

"Shocked. Relieved. Overjoyed," she replies. "Babies are a gift, and Kane does need an heir. Should something happen to him, the throne would go to Lex, and he doesn't have the right temperament to rule a kingdom."

It couldn't hurt to tell one person, could it? Queen Agatha is Kane's mom. She deserves to know. I haven't had the chance to tell my own mother, but I haven't been able to get her on the phone anyway. I'm not sure how she feels about my father being in prison.

"How would you feel if Kane was having a child…with me?"

Queen Agatha goes still. Her pale complexion makes her look almost like a statue. Slowly, she turns to me, her pale blue eyes over-analyzing my face before dropping down to my abdomen. She doesn't say anything, her eyes narrowing as if she's concentrating hard. She seems to find whatever it is she's looking for, and she looks me in the eye again.

"It's very faint, but I can hear a heartbeat."

"You can?"

She nods, smiling softly. "I remember what to watch for from when I was pregnant with the boys."

I put a hand against my abdomen as if I can feel the heartbeat. "Does the baby sound healthy?"

"I believe so," she replies. "Have you had the ultrasound yet?"

"Not yet. We were going to have it next week."

She takes my hand in hers, her skin soft like silk. "Would you tell me how it goes? Please?"

"You're not upset?"

"Why would I be upset, child?"

"Well, because Kane's having a baby with me, and I'm not a vampire."

"Stranger things have happened," she says. "Where I grew up in Cerise Port, you would hear all sorts of stories. I don't know how true those stories are, but I used to hear a folktale about a wolf shifter that had a child with a vampire."

"What happened in the story?"

She blinks. "I don't actually remember. I was very young when my governess would tell me these stories to get me to behave."

That doesn't sound promising. It sounds like the kind of stories my mother would tell my brother and I to scare us into being good.

"Were they scary stories?"

"I'm sure they were greatly exaggerated," she amends, seeing the concern on my face. "You could go check the castle library to see if there's any mention of these folktales, but I would advise you to take them with a grain of salt."

I will take everything with a pound of salt. If the only stories I can hear that relate to my situation only end with blood and tragedy, I might rethink actually looking for these stories. Unfortunately, they might be my only lead to finding out more about my pregnancy. I will have to choose between being armed with knowledge and living in blissful ignorance.

"Thank you for your help," I tell the queen. "Only Kane, the doctor, and I know about the pregnancy besides you, and I've been worried about how risky this will all be."

The queen listens intently as I continue. "I don't know what they would be. A vampire? A wolf? Something in between?"

"A hybrid. I remember that one word from the folktales."

Hybrid. A creature that is a combination of two other types of creatures.

"I'm scared I'll lose the baby. I heard how risky vampire pregnancies are, and I have no idea whether it'll be even more difficult because I'm a wolf shifter," I confess. "I don't want to lose my child. Just the thought of it…"

Queen Agatha squeezes my hand reassuringly. "Babies will come when they want to whether there's war or bad weather. You cannot stress as it will affect your health. You must focus on what you can control, which is taking everything a day at a time."

"I'm trying." I take a deep breath, trying to calm himself. "How do you stay so composed?"

"My child, I have been around a very long time. I've learned the art of appearing unaffected when I want to. It will come with practice. You are young, and you have time to learn."

I nod, feeling better from the queen's wisdom and calm reassurance. She loops our arms together and asks, "Have you had lunch, my dear? We could have a meal in the gazebo."

"There's a gazebo?"

No one has ever told me there was a gazebo in the gardens. Helga and Nellie never mention it.

"Not far from here. My husband had it built for me after our hundredth anniversary."

Hundredth? I forget sometimes how long vampires can live. I can't imagine staying married to someone for that long. It also sounds wildly romantic.

"How long were you and your husband married?"

"Almost two hundred and fifty years."

"Wow," I say. "Were you happy together?"

"Happiness is a fleeting emotion. One can hardly be happy all the time, but Michael and I found contentment with each other. We were quite lucky as arranged marriages went."

"You didn't marry for love?"

"That is not often a luxury for somebody in my position. I was raised to marry a king and bear him heirs. And that's exactly what I did."

It's very different from what I'm used to, with fated mates and the Moon Goddess choosing for us. Yet, my own parents, while they were mates, that didn't signify they would be happy together, only that they couldn't leave each other. I want to ask Queen Agatha how she would feel about Kane proposing to me, but I decide to hold off on that. The queen has many stories to tell me in the meantime, and I am eager to listen and learn. I wave at Lola, and she comes with us to the gazebo for lunch and the start of a new friendship.

BAD COMPANY

Kane

I'm not in the best mood after talking with Clark. As much as I dislike him, he is right about some things. Delivering awful truths has always been something he relishes in. Clark practically snickered as I left his suite, enjoying how his words affected me. I needed to go to my office afterward to get some work done and think about everything he told me. Hours pass by, and I haven't gotten much work done. I'm worried about the war, the baby–everything.

It's time for dinner, and the thought of being surrounded by the nobles exhausts me. I could make an excuse and not show up, but Emory's sister, Lola, is having her first dinner in the castle, and I can't leave them alone with the pit of vipers. Even with Opal and her terrible friends gone, the other nobles aren't much more accepting of anybody they deem beneath them. I just have to suck it up and get through the meal.

I'm late, but nobody will say a word about it. There are perks to being the king. The meal starts when I arrive. They're all seated when I enter the dining room, but they rise from their chairs and bow. It's not until I take my seat at the head of the table that they sit down.

Emory is usually seated to my right. I have insisted on it, wanting to make sure she is close to me and away from the venomous whispers around her. It would be impractical for me to cut out the tongue of every person that says something mean about her, but the urge is there. My bad mood only makes the bloodlust worse.

To my surprise, Emory isn't seated at my right. She's seated at the end of the table next to my mother. Lola is there at Emory's side. The twelve-year-old eyes the room from the large chandelier to the snooty faces of the nobles.

I catch her gaze, and her silver eyes widen in recognition before she turns away. The last time I saw the girl was when her own father tried to sell her off as a feeder to pay his debts. I can't blame her if she associates me with a bad memory. I still remember how she begged not to be taken away, and how she cried when Emory volunteered to take her place.

The two sisters clearly love each other. I am unfamiliar with the feeling as my relationship with my brother has always been complicated. Lex vacillates between being a nuisance and a rival. I have never been able to get myself to count on him like I would Rainer. He has always been too volatile to be fully trusted.

I look to where Lex is seated in the middle of the long table surrounded by nobles he ignores in favor of his meal. I can still picture in my mind him being friends with Opal and her sycophants. All of them brought out the worst in each other by being petty and self-involved. And Lex fit right in, never bothering to ask himself if he could be better than that.

My brother looks almost lonely without his old friends around him. He's not part of the nobility around him but not excluded either. Across the table, our mother is talking to Emory almost warmly.

I gesture for Rainer to move closer so he can hear me ask, "Why is Emory seated next to Mother?"

"Apparently, they ran into each other in the rose garden, and they spent the day together. They had lunch at the gazebo. And Queen Agatha insisted Emory and Lola sit on her end of the table."

"All of this happened today?"

"That's what I've heard from the guards and servants."

I eye my mother warily. I never had to doubt her motives before. She was a formidable figure during my father's reign, helping him keep his power through her own machinations. She took a backseat in court politics after I ascended to the throne, preferring to give me advice when I ask for it.

What is she doing with Emory? Surely, she isn't going to try and hurt the woman I love. My mother might not be the biggest fan of wolf shifters, but she helps maintain diplomatic relations with the wolf packs. And she hadn't been happy with me when the war started with the Moonraker pack.

"Keep an eye on Emory," I tell Rainer. "And have somebody taste her food before she does from now on."

"You don't think the queen would poison her, do you?"

"I wouldn't underestimate her. Her mother, Queen Nerissa, gifted a poisoned hat pin to an enemy once."

Rainer nodded, grimly. "I'll get the food tasters by tomorrow morning."

EMORY

Queen Agatha never runs out of stories. One perk of living for so many years is having an interesting life. Her stories about her childhood in Cerise Port and her subsequent marriage to King Michael that brought her to Crimson Peak are fascinating. I'm so focused on listening to her that I don't immediately notice Lola's discomfort throughout the dinner.

I glance at my sister and find her not eating, moving her food around on her plate. She keeps her head down, her dark blonde hair covering her face. I see the condescending looks from the nobles and know they're the ones to blame. They haven't treated me any better even after I defended the castle while Kane was away with his army. I almost died to keep their home safe, and they don't care at all.

They hide their insults in whispers and pretend I don't exist unless Kane forces them to. Being treated as a ghost is better than being subjected to vicious insults. It's easier for me to ignore, and I have thick skin. Lola is more vulnerable. My sweet sister doesn't deserve their vitriol.

I lean closer to her and tell her quietly, "Ignore them. They're just bored and mean. They have to say bad things to other people to make themselves feel like they're important."

Lola looks up at me and asks, "Why would they need to do that?"

"Look around this room. The only person that has any real power is King Kane." I nod toward where he's seated and conversing with Rainer. "His best friend, Rainer, is the second most powerful because Kane listens to him and values his opinion."

"What about the queen?"

"She's his mother. Her opinion matters as well," I explain, conspiringly. "Only King Kane gets to decide who is important. And he has told me himself that he doesn't care for most of these snooty people."

"Does he value your opinion?"

"I would hope so."

She looks hesitant as she voices out, "Is he nice? He did take you away from me before."

"That wasn't his fault. That was our father's doing. King Kane didn't have to take me over you, but he agreed because he knew what our father tried to do to you was wrong."

"He still took you away."

"Only because I asked him to," I reason. "If you had asked him not to take you, I promise you he would have listened."

"So he's nice?"

I smile. "He is, but that's a secret. He doesn't like it when other people know that."

"Why not?"

"Because some people need to be scared of him so they do what he says."

"Like how our dad was?"

"He's nothing like Bernard. Kane could never be like him."

Lola still looks unconvinced, but she is no longer trying to retreat into herself. I have a feeling it will take time to get my sister to warm up to Kane, but that is expected. After how we were raised to fear and distrust vampires, learning how they could be decent and kind will take time to sink in, but I am hopeful. If I could learn to see the goodness in vampires, my sister can too.

Kane

Dinner finally ends, much to my relief. I go to Emory as she and Lola are leaving the dining room. Lola still looks uncomfortable to see me, and she hides behind Emory as she watches me approach. I try to smile at her to show her I mean her no harm, but the girl holds tightly to her sister as if I am about to snatch Emory away from her. Again.

Emory smiles when she sees me. "Hi."

"Hi." A part of me uncoils at the sight of her, knowing I don't have to use any masks around her. "How was your day?"

"Lola is settling in. She really likes her room and the gardens." Emory turns to her sister. "Right, Lo?"

The little girl nods but still looks at me like she wants me to leave.

"She's not used to being around vampires," Emory explains. "It's going to take some time until she gets used to everything. Remember when I first arrived here?"

"You had a terrible introduction to this world thanks to Clark. I don't blame you for how scared you were."

"I wasn't scared," she argues.

"I saw how you handled yourself with the guards, but you were not that good at hiding your fears around the other vampires. We could smell it on you."

"You could?"

I nod. Seeing the distrust in the little girl's eyes makes me want to leave, so I tell Emory I will see her in the morning. "If you need anything, you know where to find me."

She smiles, knowingly. Memories of us in my room together, our naked bodies tangled up in my sheets would have gotten me hard, but

I willed those thoughts away. Tonight won't be the best time for such things. I wouldn't be good company anyway.

I move and kiss her lightly, still conscious of the gray eyes glaring at me like I am a perpetrator in my own home. "Goodnight."

Emory smiles, softly, melting from my touch. "Goodnight, Kane." She pats Lola's shoulder. "Say good night, Lola."

Lola murmurs a "Night" with no particular enthusiasm. I leave because I want to be back in my room and go to bed. I reach my bedroom door as Lex appears with a bottle of blood in hand. He holds it up like an offering.

"You look like you need a drink."

I open my bedroom door and let him in. This is an old ritual going back to our long ago days of youth. Something would happen, and we would escape to somewhere in the castle to talk it out with a bottle of the best stock. Whatever walls we put up around each other would melt away, and we would talk freely with the silent agreement that what was said during these nights would never be repeated elsewhere.

Lex takes a swig from the bottle and asks, "What crawled up your asshole and died?"

"I talked to Clark today." I accept the bottle from him and swallow a mouthful of blood. It's a nice vintage. "He gave me some advice."

"Why the fuck would you do that? That fossil hasn't had a good idea in a century."

"Like a broken clock, he is right at least twice a day. And all he said was that I was being selfish."

Lex snorts. "You? Selfish? You're the most dutiful person I know. That's why I always look like a dickhead next to you."

"Most royals don't get to marry for love. They marry for the benefit of the kingdom."

"You tried to do that, but Opal is insane. And her father is a colossal prick. Hitching your carriage to that crazy herd of horses wouldn't have done you any good."

"I know, but Emory..."

He gives me a look. "I thought you loved Emory."

"I do. I've never loved anyone like I love her."

"But?"

I drink from the bottle, swallowing twice before handing it back to him. "I'll have to lose her someday whether that's old age or illness. She can't be turned, so I have no way of prolonging her life."

Wolf shifters can't be turned by vampires. Nature made sure that only humans can be turned into vampires. Wolf shifters can't be created, only born. And even if I have the option to turn her, I know Emory won't want to be a vampire.

"So you think you have to give her up?" my brother asks.

I stare at him for a long moment before I admit, "I don't know."

IN YOUR SHADOW

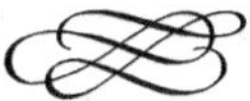

Kane

Lex is quiet as he listens to me talk. He sips from the bottle of blood as I tell him about my fears of losing Emory. I'm in an impossible situation where the laws of nature that govern our world are working against me. Yet, those same rules had bent themselves to make it possible for us to fall in love and then have a child. Could nature bend again to accommodate me?

Lex snorts. "Maybe you are selfish."

I stare at him in disbelief. "Now you're agreeing with me?"

"I'm not judging you. I'm actually kind of proud that for once you're thinking about what you want and not what you think you should be content with."

"Even if it affects our kingdom?"

"Everything you do affects our kingdom. You're a king. Your existence affects our kingdom, so of course for the first time you actually selfishly want something, you want nature to give you a pass. Break the very foundations of our existence so you can be with the woman you love."

When he puts it like that, I sound like a horrible self-indulgent person uncaring about consequences. I'm not an impulsive person. I never have been, but Emory has a way of making me act on my emotions. It scares me knowing what I'm capable of if it comes down to keeping her safe from those that wish her harm.

"Do you know what that makes you, brother?" Lex continues. "Just like everybody else. You're flawed and greedy, and you can't help yourself because now you want something more than anything in this world."

"I just want to keep her," I say. "I need her."

"You already have her. You have the love of a good woman," he tells me. "Not to mention that you're a handsome, powerful king who is respected by his people. And despite all the recent troubles of an impending war, you are still remarkably lucky."

"I don't feel lucky. I never have."

"I know, and that's what makes being your brother so frustrating." He sighs before continuing, "Do you have any idea what it's like living in your shadow? Always second best—the spare? I have lived my whole life knowing I'll never measure up to you, and here you are worrying about a future that hasn't even come to pass yet."

"I'm afraid because I have no control over any of this. Despite all my supposed power, I have my limits."

"No one can control death, not even us. Everyone dies eventually. We just take longer than the other species. We could die in battle or any number of other ways. And as for Emory, it doesn't even have to be old age. She could die from an illness or an accident. You can't control her fate and you shouldn't try that."

"Why not?"

"Because my brother, my king, you will destroy everything you have in the process."

I take the bottle from him, realizing that we're halfway through it. "When did you get so wise?"

"Maybe I'm finally growing up," he says, bitterly. "Impending fatherhood is taking its effect."

I'm still wrapping my head around the fact my brother is going to be a father. The fact that it has to be with Opal is unfortunate, but it will still be our blood. My own impending fatherhood looms over me. Hope and dread settles in my belly like stones.

"Do you think this is what our father felt when we were born?" I ponder. "Do you think he was scared if he was going to be a good dad?"

"King Michael? Nervous about anything?" Lex snorts. "No way. He wasn't afraid of anything, especially by the time I was born. Babies were old news."

"He might have just been good at pretending to never be scared, but deep down he was terrified every minute of every day."

"Is that how you feel?"

I shrug, avoiding answering that question. Instead, I say, "I wanted to be just like him. He was like a legendary king from the myths. When he walked into the room, no one else mattered. Just him."

"I remember. I wanted to be like him too," Lex agrees. "I failed more than anything. I think that's why he didn't like me."

I shove him on the shoulder. "Don't be ridiculous. He liked you. He let you get away with so much more than I could."

"That's because he expected things from you. He didn't care what I did. I was just the spare. Still am." Lex gestures more wildly which is how I know he's getting agitated. "He spent time with you. He taught you how to run a kingdom and how to fight battles. Me? I was an afterthought."

"Every moment I had with him was about training me to be his replacement. I had to remember that the only way I could be king was through his death. Every time he looked at me, it's like he saw his own mortality staring back at him."

"I think that's just what being a parent is about. You teach your kids as best as you can, and they hopefully learn enough to survive. And then you die."

"That's morbid."

It's a dark thought, but not completely untrue.

For the first time, I look at my brother and see shades of the better man he could be. Maybe he is growing up. Fatherhood might do him good. Lex has always been lost, craving a place in the world. He always wanted mine despite how unqualified he is to actually rule.

Curious, I ask, "If you had my throne, say you had been born first, what would you do with it?"

"Abdicate and give the job to somebody else."

"Why?"

"Look at me. I'm not king material. I may be pretty and would look amazing with your crown on my head, but it'd all be style over substance. You were born for this. You were made for this."

"And what about you, my brother? What were you made for?"

He smiles, guile hiding what he may truly feel. "Absolutely nothing. I'm the fuck-up, remember?"

Emory

I wake up bright and early. I have a lot I want to do today, so after I have breakfast with Lola in the kitchenette of my bedroom, we make our way to the castle library. The last time I was here, I had almost died when Jacob and Opal attacked me. Fear blooms in my belly as we enter the library, and I look around as if waiting for one of them to appear.

Instead, Lola sees my distress and holds my hand. "Are you okay, Em?"

I smile at her, trying to hide how I feel. "I'm all right. I'm just a little tired."

"You look scared."

"I just remembered something unpleasant that happened here, but it's over now. I'm safe. We're safe," I tell her, more to reassure myself.

I know I'm safe. Jacob is in the dungeon, and Opal is all the way in Scarlett Thunder. There are guards hovering nearby to come to my aid if I need them. Nellie is with us, too. She follows closely behind us.

"Nellie, do you know which section in the library we can find books on folktales?" I ask.

"I'm not that familiar with the library, Princess," she answers. "You can ask the librarian for help."

"I didn't know there was a librarian."

Nellie points to a desk to the right where a vampire with short brown hair is sitting. "That's Willow. She's the new librarian."

"What happened to the old librarian?"

"Unfortunately, the interim librarian was killed by Opal and Jacob that night they hurt you. The librarian before that was killed by King Michael."

Anger shoots through me at the revelation. An innocent person died because those two heartless assholes don't care for anyone but themselves. And what has it all been for? Just to get rid of potential witnesses to their terrible behavior? I don't even ask about the other librarian. I'm too focused on what happened the night I was attacked.

I have to resist the urge to run down to the dungeon and kick Jacob's broken leg.

I try to focus on the task at hand. I go over to where the new librarian is reading a book at her desk. Upon getting closer, I can see how pretty she is, with pale blue eyes and a face like a porcelain doll. Her hair is a warm, chestnut brown that reaches her shoulders, and she's wearing a blue dress with a high collar.

"Hi," I say. "I'm Emory. We've never met."

"No, but I've heard of you through reputation," she replies, setting her book down. "I'm Willow." She smiles, and I return the gesture.

"It's nice to meet you. I need your help looking for some books in the library."

"What topic would that be?"

"I'm looking for folktales, particularly about wolf shifters."

She gets to her feet and signals for me to follow her. We go up the stairs to the second floor of the library. She leads us to a particular section and starts pulling books off the shelves, handing them to me. Soon, I have a tall pile of books in my arms that I need to split with Nellie so I don't drop them.

"We have a limited collection when it comes to wolf shifters due to the enmity between our species and wolf shifters' aversion to documenting much about themselves." Willow explains. "I'm not sure how much information you can glean from those books as they are mostly written for children."

"I can work with this. Thank you for your help, Willow."

"I'll be at my desk if you need anything."

The brunette vampire returns to her desk, and we claim a table nearby. Lola and Nellie help me research about shifter and vampire hybrids. Neither of them know why I'm so interested in the topic beyond simple curiosity. The faster I can find answers, the faster I can get peace of mind over my pregnancy and my unborn child.

We read quietly for an hour, skimming through every book and finding old folktales about wolves terrorizing villages and slaughtering random townsfolk who make the bad choice to enter the forest on their own. They all have the similar themes of not trusting wolves and keeping away from the forest. Nellie finds a promising story about a she-wolf that nurses twin boys who have lost their mother. The twins go on to find two separate wolf packs, both of which are still around. One of them is my own.

Lola reads through a book of fairy tales she shows me a story about a woman that's impregnated by a wolf. The story is written in a language I don't recognize. I can only try to guess through the illustrations in the book what the story is about. All I can put together is that a woman gives birth to a baby that could shift into a monstrous, bloodthirsty beast. It slaughters entire villages on its own, insatiable for blood and carnage.

"What does this mean, Nellie?" I ask.

"I'm sorry. I don't know that language."

At the sound of familiar footsteps, I look up to see Rainer's smiling face. He makes a beeline toward us. "Hey, Em. Nellie. Em's sister."

Lola goes pink, looking more shy than afraid as Rainer gives her a charming grin. "Hi."

My sister could barely look at Kane without being scared. Rainer is the first vampire besides my maids that Lola doesn't try to hide from. It couldn't be because she has a crush on him. Lola is way too young for crushes. But he is charming, and everyone seems to like him.

"What are you looking at?" Rainer asks, as he looks down at the book I'm reading. "*The Curse of the Blood Wolf.*"

I look at him in surprise. "You know this language?"

"It's a dead language. People stopped using it a hundred years ago or so."

"What is a blood wolf?"

There are notes in that dead language that might give me more clues. Rainer reads through them and translates it for me.

"The blood wolf is a hybrid, made from two different monsters, both violent and bloodthirsty, the *loup-garou* and the *vampyr*. It craves blood constantly and can never be appeased. It's a being so powerful that the native tribes start worshiping it as a god. It's not until a coven of witches stand up against the blood wolf and put it down with a spell that the land is freed of its evil."

He looks up at me, and I swallow hard. What have we done?

MICE AND MEN

Emory

I can't move as Rainer continues to translate the story about the hybrid. It is nothing but a terrifying monster, a mindless killing machine. My breath quickens as panic sets in, making me want to run away. I want to hide under the blankets of my bed and shut the world out. I don't want to believe my baby could turn into the beast in the story with no ability to reason and only an insatiable urge to kill.

I touch my abdomen with my fingers, feeling protective and terrified of the life inside of me. Perhaps I could teach them to be good. Even if they have these bloodthirsty urges, I can guide them to control themselves so they won't hurt other people. Humans thought that wolf shifters are like the werewolves in myths that were mindlessly violent, but we aren't like that at all. I could make sure my child learns they don't have to be anything other than what they want to be and not just what their base urges lead them to.

"Are you all right, Emory?" Rainer asks. "You're looking kind of pale. And that's saying something coming from me."

I check my watch to see it's lunch time, and it gives me the perfect excuse. "I think I'm just hungry. We should go have lunch."

"That's why I came to get you, actually. Queen Agatha is inviting you to have lunch with her again today. You and your sister are both invited, of course."

"We shouldn't keep her waiting, then."

We all stand up to start putting the books away. Willow comes over with a book trolley to collect the books from us. Rainer scoops up half the books on the table and hands them individually to Willow.

"Long time no see, gorgeous," he says with a salacious grin. "Where have you been hiding all this time?"

"None of your business, Rainer," she replies with a cold glare. "If you have no further need of assistance, I suggest you leave the library."

"I do need assistance with something." He wiggles his eyebrows at her in an attempt to be funny and suggestive.

She is not amused. "If it has nothing to do with any books in this library, then I can't help you. Please leave."

"Willow, come on...."

She turns and walks away with the trolley before Rainer can say anything else. He lets out a defeated sigh and we all leave the library together.

"How do you know Willow?" I ask, curiously.

"We know each other from a long time ago. I thought she had left the castle. I didn't know she was still around or had come back."

"You have a history together?"

He shrugs nonchalantly. "You could say that. We're old acquaintances at best."

I could asked him more questions, but my mind is too preoccupied with the story of the blood wolf and what that could mean for all of us.

Kane

King Peter did not send a letter back this time. Instead, he sent a messenger. This is the same one I had seen for the past few weeks, the smooth-talking man who has a talent for spinning King Peter's angry vitriolic words into something bearable. He looks like an ordinary vampire with the same pale skin and icy blue eyes as most of the rest of us. His hair is cut short and slicked back.

King Peter seems to trust this messenger the most because he's promoted him to the status of a diplomat.

He bows low. "Your Majesty, I am now *Lord* Alistair. Vampire King Peter has sent me to be his representative so we can work on a peaceful resolution to the misunderstanding between our two kingdoms."

"Misunderstanding?" I repeat with a scoff. "That's what you want to call it? You tried to invade my land, and your troops are still camped at my doorstep ready to draw blood."

"The situation may have regretfully escalated, but not to the lengths that it can't be remedied. King Peter believes we can put this all behind us and renew the friendship between our kingdoms again."

"And what would he want in return?" Rainer challenges, his arms crossed over his chest as he stares down at Alistair's pointy face. "He does seem to enjoy making demands."

Alistair gives a bland smile. "I trust you may understand that King Peter has been distraught over the welfare of his children. He cares for them deeply. All he asks is that you allow his son, Prince Jacob, to return home where he belongs."

"No way," Rainer counters. "We're not letting him go so you feel comfortable attacking us with nothing to lose."

"My king has learned of his son's injuries and only wants to have him treated by his royal physician. Surely, we can all understand that everyone is deserving of compassion and should be treated accordingly."

I look down from my seat on the throne at Alistair's face, which does remind me of a weasel, and contemplate my next move. I know I can't let Jacob go—not until we have assurance that King Peter will not attack us once his heir is back in his grasp. I need to buy us time.

"I will send my own doctor to heal Jacob's injuries and to make sure he is well taken care of," I offer. "He will continue to stay in the castle as he heals."

Alistair's pale blue eyes blink before he starts, "Surely, Prince Jacob would be better healing at home than here–"

"Surely, we can provide adequate care for him here," I cut him off. "I have a competent doctor in the castle, and I assure you that Jacob will be getting the care he needs."

Knowing he's beaten, Alistair gives another dry smile and bows low. "Thank you for your compassion, Your Majesty. I will inform King Peter of your merciful consideration with and take my leave for the evening. I will let His Majesty know of the situation."

I dismiss him, and the weasel scurries off. He will be staying in the castle in a bedroom furthest away from mine. I have many servants and guards watching his every movement should he try anything. I even double the security in the dungeons.

"I don't like that guy," Rainer remarks. "He reminds me of a rat sniffing for cheese."

I stand from my throne and step down the podium stairs. "The cheese being my downfall, I take it."

"I expect him to scurry around like a little rodent for his master."

That makes me smirk in amusement. "Perhaps you should prepare some mouse traps."

Rainer's eyes light up in delight. "That would be entertaining and useful. Good idea."

"Just make sure you don't get him injured. I already have enough trouble to deal with."

Rainer salutes me before walking away from the throne room. I decide to look for Emory. I go to her bedroom and only find Helga who tells me that the princess should be having lunch with my mother. This new development still concerns me.

I go outside toward the gazebo and find my mother and Emory having a pleasant lunch of tea and pastries. Lola is there eating colorful macaroons. My usually stoic mother is laughing at a story Emory is telling her. I don't remember seeing the queen laugh like that in years.

My mother notices me first as I approach the gazebo. "Hello, darling. What are you doing here?"

I walk over to her and kiss her on her cold cheek. The familiar scent of roses and vanilla remind me of my childhood. "I was about to ask you the same question."

"I'm having lunch with Emory and Lola. We were discussing her childhoods. She was telling me this amusing story of the time she played a prank on her brother."

I turn to her, eyebrows rising in question. She explains, "I used to scare my younger brother by hiding in his closet and pretending to be a vampire about to bite him and bleed him dry."

"We're the bogeyman in your childhood stories?"

"I'm sure we were the bogeyman in your world," she replies. "How did you scare vampire children into behaving?"

"We don't."

That's not true. I heard plenty of stories involving terrifying 'werewolves' while growing up. Terrifying children to stop misbehaving is a universal thing amongst all sentient species. When it comes down to it, we are all more similar than what we would want to admit.

"Don't lie to the girl, Kane," my mother chides. "You used to chase your brother pretending to be the big bad wolf."

Emory gives me a knowing look, smug in her righteousness. I have to resist the urge to kiss that look off her face. I will have to do that later. I won't kiss her in front of my mother–not yet anyway.

"Have you eaten, Kane?" my mother asks. "Darling, you must eat. You're getting far too thin these days."

"I'm fine, mother."

"Come take a seat. We have those butter biscuits you enjoy."

I take the empty seat beside Emory. Food will do nothing to put meat on my bones. Only blood will do that. But they do taste good, so I help myself to a cup of blood and the butter biscuits, leaving the macaroons to Lola. I pour the blood into my cup carefully and stir it with a spoon.

My mother takes a sip of her blood. "There's a matter of importance I need to discuss with you, Kane."

"About what?"

"We should renovate the nursery in the castle as it's been some time since we had a baby to take care of. And we'll need to purchase with all the things you'll be needing to take care of the child. Your old things won't do at all."

I stare at my mother in shock, trying to comprehend what she's saying. I try to play dumb. "What do you mean? What baby?"

She puts down her cup to give me an exasperated look. "Are we really doing this, Kane? You are far too old to be pretending like you don't know exactly what I'm talking about."

"I truly don't know what you're going on about, Mother." From my peripheral vision, I can see Emory's guilty face. Turning to her, I stare at her in disbelief and betrayal.

She swallows hard. "She knows."

Turning to face her, my eyes widen. "You told her? How could you?'

She winces. "It just slipped out. It felt wrong not to tell your mom. Besides, she sort of already knew."

"Did she tell you how much she wants grandkids? She's been using that line on me for years."

"You're being dramatic, Kane," my mother rebukes. "Emory simply wanted to share the good news with me, the *grandmother* of your unborn child. It's not as if I couldn't hear the heartbeat."

She says 'grandmother' with such relish. She can't even hide her glee at the news even if she wants to.

"We were going to wait until Emory was past her first trimester to tell anyone. You know how risky pregnancies are for our kind."

"I am very aware, which is why Emory needs to have a support system. You are far too busy to be here every moment of the day. Emory could use all the help she can get before and after that baby comes."

I resist the urge to stab myself in the eye with a butter knife out of frustration. I mistakenly thought my mother was trying to poison Emory out of disapproval of our relationship. Instead, my mother approves wholeheartedly and is practically frothing at the mouth at finally becoming a grandmother. This shouldn't be a surprise as my mother has been nagging me about having an heir for decades.

"The baby might need a particular sort of care considering their parentage," my mother continues. "With the baby being half-vampire and half-wolf shifter, it's certainly going to be a handful."

A movement in the corner of my eye makes me turn to see the weasel of a diplomat standing nearby and listening to our conversation. Before I can get to my feet and run after him, Alistair is already rushing back to the castle. I don't know how much he heard, but it was likely more than enough. He will no doubt share the news about Emory's pregnancy with King Peter as soon as he can get his hands on a phone.

Emory notices I am truly upset and worriedly asks, "What's wrong?"

I grab a biscuit off a plate and take a bite. "King Peter's rat just found some cheese."

PREGNANCY WOES

Emory

I try to sit still as Dr. Joe Martin looks over my vitals. Kane is busy dealing with the diplomat from Scarlett Thunder to be with me for the check-up. He feels terrible about it, but I told him it isn't a big deal. I know he's stressed enough dealing with this stalemate with King Peter, and I don't want to add on to his load.

Besides, I'm not alone. Lola is here trying to sit still on a stool nearby. My maids, Helga and Nellie are in the room with us trying not to hover. After Lord Alistair found out about my pregnancy and informed King Peter about it, Kane and I decided to let our friends in the castle know. We need the support of those closest to us more than ever.

We know that King Peter won't be sitting on this information for long and will probably be spreading it to the other kingdoms to curry favor for his cause against Kane. We can't keep this information to ourselves any longer, so all we can do is try to mitigate the upcoming wave of opinions that is coming our way.

We haven't sworn our friends to secrecy, but we know they aren't blabbing to others about what they know. Helga and Nellie have become my biggest supporters, concerned and overjoyed at me carrying Kane's child and heir. Along with most people in the king-dom, they have been waiting for him to finally reproduce–even if it is with a wolf shifter.

"Have you been sleeping well?" Dr. Martin asks. "Your blood pressure is higher than normal."

"I've been having trouble sleeping. I seem to only get morning sickness in the evenings, usually late."

"It's not that uncommon with vampire babies. I recall Queen Agatha had similar symptoms when she was pregnant with the king and his brother."

"I also get really queasy around strong smells. Garlic makes me want to barf."

He nods and makes a note on his clipboard. "That's also common. Your wolf shifter senses might be even more heightened as the pregnancy goes along." He looks up and asks, "Are you also feeling ill at the smell of blood?"

"No," I reply. "I like my meat rarer now."

I prefer my meat to be practically raw, which might have been unhealthy if I wasn't a wolf shifter but I won't get sick from it. My dinner last night could probably moo at me with how rare it was.

"The baby will be craving blood. Preferably fresh."

My eyes widen slightly as I realize what he is getting at. "I have to drink blood?"

"You will only need to consume it in small amounts. We can have the staff serve you a small cup of blood during dinner."

The thought of me drinking blood would have thoroughly grossed me out months ago, but I don't feel the same way now. I have a craving for it like I would with a good steak or even ice cream.

"This is good for the baby?"

"Healthy vampire babies need blood."

"All right. I'll do it for the baby."

He prescribes prenatal vitamins to me then instructs Helga and Nellie about the best food for me to eat. Lola is bored during the entire appointment and is happy to leave once it's over.

"Are wolf shifter babies the same?" Lola asks me as we walk back to our rooms. "Are pregnancies this difficult with our kind?"

"It can be rather complicated," I answer honestly. "There's the risk of miscarriage if the mother shifts into her wolf form during the pregnancy."

"That won't be a problem with you."

Lola knows I haven't met my wolf yet. Wolf shifters don't change into their wolf forms until their twenty-first birthday, and my birthday is still months away. That will be a problem I would have to deal with when it comes because I won't be able to stop myself from shifting for the first time on my birthday, but I don't want to think about that now. Being pregnant already scares me enough as it is.

"Not now, Lo," I tell her. "It'll all be okay though."

"Did my mom have a difficult pregnancy with me?"

That makes me pause. Lola rarely asks about her mother. It is a touchy subject due to how other people, including our very own family, treated her differently because of who her mother was. I never really tried to ask about the scullery maid that had given birth to Lola as Bernard had tried to erase her presence in the castle as if she never existed. My mother had been upset about his infidelity, and he had tried to make it up to her by making everyone in our home never mention Lola's mother as if it could negate the shame of what he had done.

I never saw Lola as something to be ashamed of. She is my heart and some of the best parts of me. I look at her, and I see none of Bernard's cruelty and selfishness. I see a happy little girl who just wants to live a normal life.

"I don't know," I finally reply. "I never really knew her."

Lola goes quiet. I can see the play of emotions on her face as she takes this information in. We reach the door of her bedroom, and she hesitates before going inside.

"Did your mom have a difficult pregnancy with you?"

"I've never asked her, and she's never told me."

"Maybe you should talk to her about it?" she suggests. "Just in case anything isn't normal with the pregnancy."

"Normal?" I echo.

Lola looks worried. "There were also those stories in the library about hybrids. I just want to make sure you're going to be okay."

I reach over to touch the apple of her cheek gently. "Of course I'll be okay, Lo."

"I hope so." She surprises me by hugging me, her arms wrapping around my middle. "I don't want to lose you again, Emory."

I pat her shoulder, trying to hold back the swell of emotion that threatens to make me cry. All the pregnancy hormones make me want to burst into tears at every little thing. The lack of sleep doesn't help. All I want to do is have a good cry and take a long nap.

"I'm not going anywhere, Lola," I say. "I promise."

Lola goes into her room after that. I give in and take a lengthy nap in my room. The baby doesn't seem to bother making me want to puke my guts out when the sun is up which is a much needed relief. Nellie looks guilty as she has to wake me for lunch. I begrudgingly get up, and my maids help me change into a green sundress and strappy sandals.

Having lunch with Queen Agatha has become part of my routine. She has a spread of delicious food waiting in the gazebo every day for us. The queen has been kind enough to have food Lola especially likes. And after that incident with garlic bread and me puking into her prized rose bushes, she makes sure to not have any food that would set off my oversensitive nose. Vampires don't really care for garlic anyway.

Queen Agatha smiles when we arrive at the gazebo. "You're looking better today, Emory. Have you been able to rest?"

"I took a nap," I reply. "The baby lets me sleep before sundown."

She takes a sip of her blood. "That's good. You should try these meat pies the cook worked on today. There's no garlic and onions in them."

I pick up one of the meat pies from the platter. It is the size of my palm. I place it on my plate and slice through it with a butter knife. Spearing it with a fork, I take a small bite. I taste butter, meat, and pastry. It isn't bland, but it's not too flavorful. I'm able to swallow without an issue.

"That's really good."

The Queen pours a cup of tea for me, pouring a small amount of milk in and stirring. She slides the cup toward me and asks, "How did the check-up with Dr. Martin go?"

"It was fine. He said there doesn't seem to be anything unusual with the pregnancy."

"That is a relief to hear. Have you told Kane?"

"Not yet. He's been in meetings all day."

"No doubt dealing with that obvious mole Peter has sent to bother us."

Seeing Lord Alistair scurrying about the castle is a common occurrence. More than once, he has tried to go into areas he is not allowed in only to be deterred by a guard or servant. He has even tried to bribe whoever caught him in the act, but Kane fires whoever gives in and replaces them immediately. Kane complains about how easy it seems to bribe people in the castle, and it's becoming an epidemic.

Kane

"We could just kill him," Lex suggests not for the first time. "And then deal with the consequences later."

"And this is why you're not ruling this kingdom," Rainer quips. "We're trying to keep King Peter from attacking us, not give him another reason to give the marching orders."

Lex gives him an annoyed look. "How do you propose we deal with Alistair? He tried to bribe his way into the dungeons this morning."

"Well, fuck. If he sneaks Jacob out of the castle–"

"I doubled the security guarding Jacob," I cut in. "I also have the servants collecting any letters he has that might be interesting."

"It's still not enough, Kane," Rainer points out. "Peter already knows about Emory's pregnancy."

I sigh and lean back in my seat. The stress migraine I have been fighting off all day makes me feel like my brain is going to explode. I slide King Peter's latest letter across the table for Rainer and Lex to read.

As soon as King Peter found out about the baby, he proceeded to threaten me with telling all the vampire kingdoms about it. In his eyes, I not only got his precious daughter pregnant and refuse to claim her spawn as my own, I have defiled her honor even more by getting another woman pregnant. And it's a wolf shifter to boot.

"He wants you to declare Emory's baby is a bastard that will never inherit your throne and that Opal's baby is your rightful heir?" Rainer looks furious and astounded. "Is he insane? You can't agree to this!"

"I already told him no."

I don't care what King Peter threatens me with. I will never forsake Emory and our child. He can just add this onto my list of perceived sins against him and his family. I'm quickly losing my last vestiges of patience with this man.

"He wants a hostage," I continue. "Since I won't let Jacob go, he wants his own leverage."

Political hostages are an old practice dating back to my grandfather's time. A royal child from another kingdom would come to stay with the kingdom they're warring with to ensure peace at the cost of that child's life. A political hostage would be treated well and raised among the other kingdom's royal children but would never truly be a part of the family.

My mother's brother, King Cyrus, had been a political hostage for another kingdom when he was a child and was only released as an adult after his father died, and he became the new king of Cerise Point. My mother told us how it had been a lonely and unhappy time for my uncle. My father managed to secure peace with our neighbors so that neither I nor Lex had needed to be hostages.

"Who would you even send?" Rainer questions. "Your child is still in the womb. Does he want you to send Emory?"

"Absolutely not," I tell him resolutely.

I will burn down Scarlett Thunder before letting them get their grubby hands on Emory.

"You can't send Mother. She hates him," Lex points out.

I can't look at my brother. "I know." He was in King Peter's possession once and managed to trick the king into thinking he was more useful here, but now, well… maybe there's another option.

There's a silence as the only option is blatantly obvious to all of us. I have no children to send. What I do have is a brother. The spare.

"You want to send me," Lex concludes.

BE THE HERO

Kane

Guilt burns in my chest. I have no desire to give in to King Peter's demands, especially if it endangered my family. Despite all that has happened between us, Lex is my brother. I should not give him up.

"I don't want to send you as a hostage," I tell my brother. "I'm going to refuse King Peter, and he can deal with it–"

"Stop," Lex interrupts me. "You're just prolonging the inevitable."

"Lex–"

"King Peter will never stop. This man is looking for any excuse to come after you. If you're seen refusing to concede on old traditions, you're going to look worse in the eyes of the other vampire kingdoms."

"I don't care what they think."

"You should. You used to. That's what made you a good king. You thought about what was best for your kingdom above all else." Lex sighs, looking wearier than I've ever seen him. "And it's my turn to be the same way. I've been selfish long enough."

"Lex, if you become a hostage, I can't protect you," I point out. "King Peter could decide not to honor the agreement and have you tortured and executed before I can even try to help you."

"That's the point of this. It's a big game of chicken," he replies. "You have no one else you can send. Anybody else besides me, Mother, and Emory aren't important enough. It has to be me."

I stare at my brother. His face is as familiar to me as my own. I remember the boy he was, always following me around the castle. I've seen the man he became, stuck in a perpetual adolescence with no real purpose. Today, I can see glimpses of a better man he could become, and I feel a swell of pride.

"If you're sure…"

Lex nods, his expression serious. "I am. Let me serve my kingdom in the only way I can."

"There's a chance you might not come back."

My little brother has worried, frustrated, and at times, consoled me. If he never returns, what would my life be like? I can't quite picture it.

"I know," Lex declares. "But that's part of the risk, and I've always liked my odds."

EMORY

I call Colt once a week to keep up to date with Moonraker pack and what's happening there. Colt seems to be putting out fires when he isn't bogged down by the day-to-day minutiae of running a pack. He complains to me about the amount of paperwork he has to go through, and he can see why our father hadn't bothered with this and instead dumped it on his Beta to take care of. Jace Kincaid had been an Alpha in anything by name with the amount of work he had done behind the scenes to keep the pack running.

"Darius suggested hiring an accountant to help us with all of this," Colt says. "His dad had hired one off the books who he paid out of his own pocket which is really unfair."

"I agree. That shouldn't have been Jace's responsibility. We should hire an account, officially on the books. Maybe Jace can suggest a good one."

"I'll talk to him about it. I cannot get my head around all these numbers. I barely passed algebra in school."

"Hire a professional and stop worrying about it."

"Will do, boss." He snorts. "Sorry. I mean *Alpha*."

"I don't know if I'll ever get used to being called Alpha. I was brought up to be one, but it's different to actually be called that. And then, with the stunt that bastard pulled...."

"That's Father," we both say in conclusion. I roll my eyes.

"He's such an asshole," Colt states. "The more of his mistakes and damage to this pack I uncover, the angrier at him I get. I can't get my head around the kind of person he was pretending to be and who he really is."

"He fooled all of us."

I loved my father. I worshiped the ground he walked on. He was this hero Alpha trying to fight off the evil vampires who were trying to hurt our pack, but it had all been lies upon lies. In reality, he is a greedy coward who only ever cares about himself. The man and father I thought he was had never existed.

"The worst part is not all of it was bad." Colt's voice is wistful. "When we were little kids, he'd play with us and take us camping."

"I remember."

I close my eyes, and memories of Bernard taking us camping and teaching us about the stars at night make me want to weep and throw something. Monsters aren't supposed to make you feel loved. Even if it had been lies, they had felt real at that time. And I can't remove them from my memories.

I don't want to talk to Bernard. I don't want to see him. He's rotting in the dungeon beneath my feet, and I try to pretend like he isn't there at all. The person I want to talk to is my mom.

"Every time I try to call Mom, she doesn't pick up," I say. "Is she upset with me?"

"No." There's a pause before he concedes, "She's upset about the situation. Everything that happened with Father is confusing for her."

Hurt blooms in my chest, but it comes out more like anger.

"What's confusing? He almost destroyed all of us for his own ego. Why is she upset with me? She should be upset with him!"

"I know," Colt tries to appease me. "But he's her mate, and you know what that means."

I do know what that means. I witnessed it growing up, and I feel it now with Kane. My mother endured so much because of Bernard, but she never left him because being mates are not something you can throw away. It's for life and there's no way out except death.

I sigh in frustration. "I just want to talk to her. Why can't she just pick up the phone?"

"She..." Colt lets out a ragged breath. "She said that she won't speak to you until you release Father."

"I can't do that. You know I can't do that." I refuse immediately. "After everything Bernard has done, we can't trust him not to try and start a war again as soon as he's free. He's too dangerous."

Bernard had tried to kill me, his own daughter, for getting in his way and exposing him for the terrible person that he is. I shudder to think what he will do if he ever gets out of the dungeons.

"Could you talk to Mom?" I ask. "Just try to persuade her to talk to me. I really need to talk to her about something."

"About what?"

"I'm not ready to tell you that yet. Just help me out with Mom, please."

"I'll try, but I can't promise she'll listen."

I thank my brother for all of his help. I'm truly surprised he isn't more upset that he's no longer going to be the Alpha. The call ends soon after that. I hang up the phone and cover my face with my hands, feeling weary and overwrought. My own mother doesn't want to talk to me because my terrible father is my prisoner. When did my life become this tragedy?

All I want is to talk to my mom about my pregnancy. I want to hear her advice on what to do and for her to share what her own pregnancies had been like. When I was younger, I would talk to her about anything, and she'd make everything better somehow. I want that.

Lex

I have never lived outside of Crimson Peak. I stayed in other kingdoms for short periods of time as a guest or a tourist. Being a political hostage means I could be living in Scarlett Thunder for decades or even centuries. If worse came to worst, I could never even come back.

My bags are packed. I have my entire life squeezed into half a dozen trunks. The items I will leave behind have been deemed unnecessary to be brought along into my new life. I've spent the day walking around the castle and the grounds, looking at my home for what might be the last time.

Only a few people have been informed of my departure. My mother makes a show of being quietly dignified before giving in to a few tears and hugging me. She is reminded of her brother being sent off to a similar life, and now she has to see her own son have the same fate. Uncle Cyrus was lucky. He came back.

"Don't let them break you," she murmurs into my coat. "You are, and have always been, stronger than you know."

We say our farewells, and she retreats to the rose garden where she has always found solace.

Emory is sleeping so she hasn't been informed. I asked specifically for her to learn once I've left. I still harbor guilt for my past actions against her, and I feel it's better this way. I won't blame her if she's relieved to see me go.

Kane is more maudlin than I expected. My big, strong brother looks like I just shot his dog. Guilt is written all over his face. I can't stand it.

"Don't look at me like that," I tell him. "I'm not dead yet."

"Don't be stupid when you're there," he replies. "I mean it, Lex. You have to be careful if you want to survive in King Peter's court. Just like you were the last time you were there."

"I can be clever when I want to be." I give him a pointed look, both of us remembering I managed to get home last time I was there.

He sighs deeply. "Lex, it's not too late to back out of this—"

"You don't get to take this away from me," I counter. "Let me be a hero for once in my goddamn life, Kane."

He looks furious and devastated as he grabs me hard and pulls me into a hug that makes my bones rattle. I don't remember the last time we hugged. I think we haven't hugged since we were little children.

"You little shit," he hisses angrily into my ear. "If you get yourself killed, I'm going to actually have to go to war with Scarlett Thunder. I love you, you fucking idiot."

That makes me laugh. "I love you too, brother."

I'm not going to cry. I'm not sad, not really. I know deep down I'm doing the right thing. Centuries from now, when the history books are written, I want to be remembered for doing something good for my kingdom. The whole mess with Opal and Scarlett Thunder is partially my fault. I should be the one to fix it.

In a black SUV, I'm escorted by a handful of guards to Castle Blackmoor. It isn't as large as Castle Graystone but makes up for it with a moat and more spires. I look at the dark fortress from the car window and try not to show my hesitation. Rainer is one of the guards, and he will never let me forget it if I look scared.

"You should know that, if you betray us, I will hunt you down," he says. "Kane may trust you, but I don't."

I give him a bland smile. "No need for threats. I'm already walking into my tomb."

"Don't be dramatic. King Peter won't kill you."

I raise both eyebrows at him. "We'll just have to see if that's true or not."

I exit the car, slamming the door behind me. This is as far as my escorts can go. Scarlett Thunder's guards allow me into the castle while servants carry in my belongings. I walk down the long hallways flanked by the guards preventing me from running away even if I try. The castle is made of black brick and decorated with dark wood furniture that makes me feel like I'm in a mausoleum.

I'm shown to the throne room where King Peter is seated on his high throne. He looks down at me haughtily. His pale blue eyes glare at me like I'm a cockroach he's considering crushing underneath his shoe.

"Lex," he intones. "Welcome back to Scarlett Thunder."

JUST LIKE US

Kane

I try not to focus on the worst case scenarios of my brother being held as a political hostage by Scarlett Thunder. I need to hope that King Peter will keep his word not to harm Lex, and I have to trust Lex not to get himself killed before this conflict with Scarlett Thunder is over. This is a test of honor for both King Peter and I, to show we can be trusted to keep our promises. The stakes are dire; a monarch whose word has no weight makes diplomacy with other kingdoms a near impossibility.

I feel helpless, which is not an emotion I've ever cared for. Shame colors my view of everything, and I can't help comparing myself to my father. King Michael never had to send away any of his family to become hostages. He wouldn't have given in to King Peter's demands no matter what the consequences were. He would have resolved things by now.

What have I done? I have just sent my only brother off alone to fight for his survival in a den of vipers. My little brother who has never been to war who has spent his long life chasing every pleasure he could get his hands on. I fear that he is too soft and will break without an ally in a foreign court.

I watch the view outside the window from the throne room, my thoughts muddled with worry and frustration. Rainer has returned from escorting Lex to Castle Blackmoor. My best friend arrives with no fanfare. He steps into the throne room and approaches me without hesitation.

Rainer only bows to me when we have an audience. I have long dissuaded him from the pomp of courtly manners. I have known him too long to expect him to act as nothing but my closest friend and confidant. We have known each other for so long now, he can practically guess what I'm thinking most of the time.

"How was he?" I ask.

"Lex was his usual charming self," Rainer replies. "He didn't even look the least bit scared at the concept of being a political prisoner."

"You know as well as I do that my brother is good at hiding his true emotions," I remind him. "If Lex was scared, he would never show it around you."

Rainer looks thoughtful. "It's strange. No matter how many years pass, I still see Lex as that little boy that cried over every little thing, clutching at Queen Agatha's skirts for protection."

"Lex hasn't been that boy in a long time."

"Are you sure?" Rainer questions. "Hasn't his impulsiveness brought us to the situation we are currently in?"

"It's King Peter's offspring that are to blame for the situation we are in. He raised them to be cruel and thoughtless. Lex's... activities in the bedroom may not have helped the situation, but it wouldn't be fair to drop all the blame at his feet."

Rainer shakes his head. "You still do that."

"I still do what?"

"Protect him even when he doesn't deserve it. You used to take the blame for his messes when you were children and get punished for it, didn't you?"

"I did. He was smaller than me, and punishment never worked well on Lex. I didn't mind taking the punishments."

"As you've said, Lex isn't that little boy anymore," Rainer points out. "Maybe you should let him be a man and take accountability for his actions."

"He has taken accountability for his actions. He practically volunteered to be a hostage. That is the most selfless thing he's ever done."

Rainer snorts. "Lex is not selfless. Everything he does is for his own self-interest. And he'll never change. You're giving him waaay too much credit."

I cannot change Rainer's opinion of Lex. He knows my brother far too well for me to even try. Numerous mistakes over the centuries have cemented what Rainer thinks of Lex. There've been times when I've wished the two of them could get along, but without Lex here now, it really doesn't matter.

"I trust Lex," I tell him. "You may not see his potential to be more than what he has been, but I do. I want to have faith in his growth."

"Growth?" Rainer repeats with a scoff. "Like that time he insulted the ambassador of Ruby Rivers by admitting to the man's face that he slept with his wife, and she wasn't good in bed?"

"That was a long time ago." Why I'm defending him, I'm not sure.

"Or the time he stole a carriage that belonged to the Queen of Sardania and crashed it into a tree?"

"He'd been distracted by her beautiful daughter. And he had made sure to profusely apologize to Queen Olga after it happened."

Rainer gives me a challenging look. "How about when he pulled a prank by forging your handwriting and sent a letter to your lead farmer Cyrus asking for a hundred geese that he put in this very room?"

I grimace at the memory. Geese are more aggressive than anyone talks about. It took all the servants hours to gather the geese and get them out of the castle. All the while, Lex hid away in a tower and laughed at the chaos he'd created.

"It was childish, but there was no real harm done," I say.

"No real harm?" Rainer raises his dark eyebrows in disbelief. "Do you remember that time your father almost killed him for almost accidentally creating another vampire?"

"That was centuries ago. And my father punished Lex for that."

"What about when Emory was attacked in the library? He stood and watched as Opal and Jacob fed on her and threw her down the stairwell?"

The familiar anger at what Emory endured under my nose bubbles up. I am angry at Jacob and Opal but not more than I am at myself. I should have protected her better. It's a mistake I intend never to make again.

"Lex is the only reason Emory is still alive," I remind Rainer. "If he hadn't gotten help, she would have bled out."

"If he had grown a pair and told you what those two assholes had planned, Emory wouldn't have needed to get hurt."

"He claims he didn't know they were going to do that. Besides, there's no changing what happened. I trust Lex to do the right thing this time. He has proven himself loyal before by giving King Peter false information to help us."

"And what makes you think that when this little act of his gets boring that he won't sell you out so he can be king instead?"

I remember what Lex's words. *Do you have any idea what it's like living in your shadow?*

"Nothing," I answer. "But I choose to believe he won't betray me."

Lex

"You are lucky," King Peter declares. "You get to live in luxury. Your whims will be catered to as what benefits your station. And yet my son… he is treated worse than an animal."

I stand still as King Peter circles me in the throne room. He's angry, and I am his chosen target. I can't truly fight back without risking my head being separated from my neck. I choose to keep quiet and let him air out his grievances.

"I had thought Kane would send your mother or that mongrel he's gotten pregnant. And yet, he sends you? How does it feel to know you are less valued than a werewolf bitch?"

I bite the inside of my cheek so as not to retort. King Peter wants to diminish my ego because he wants to hurt my brother. I'm the closest thing to my brother he can reach. I tell myself that his words don't matter, and they are the rantings of an old man.

"Is this what has become of the sons of the great King Michael of Crimson Peak?" he continues. "One fornicates with wolves, and the other is a sniveling little coward. Michael is fortunate he's dead so he doesn't have to witness the fall of his bloodline."

"Don't bring my father into this," I say, unable to hold my tongue anymore.

"Why shouldn't I? You are in my home. You have no power here, Lex. From now on, you wake up each morning alive and well because I decided to be merciful and not end your pathetic life."

These are empty threats. Part of the deal of me being a hostage is he can't harm me, not physically anyway. He can call me awful names every minute of my time here, but he cannot have me killed. King Peter is a lot of things, but he's not an idiot. Nobody rules for this long by being one.

He has always been vain. I know that.

Kane told me I had to be smart. I have always been better at playing games than him.

If I play my cards right, I might just survive this.

I bow deeply and rise up slowly. "Of course, Your Majesty. I am eternally grateful for your generosity."

King Peter turns away in disgust. "I have no patience for your groveling. Get out of my sight."

I bow to him, not as deeply this time. The guards escort me from the throne room and to another wing of the castle. They bring me to a suite of rooms, smaller than I'm used to, but it still contains a kitchenette, an ensuite bathroom, and a bedroom with a large four-poster bed. The furniture is all heavy, dark wood with the walls painted a deep green.

The guards close the door behind them but don't lock it. I know they are waiting outside the door, making sure I either can't leave the rooms without them following me. I don't plan to leave the suite at all.

My trunks have been brought into the castle and placed in the middle of the bedroom. I go to the window to see the view of the grounds. I'm on the opposite end of the castle where I can't see Crimson Peak in the distance.

A deep longing threatens to overcome me. I've rarely been homesick. There have been times I visited faraway kingdoms in a futile attempt to escape my identity, trying to be known as somebody else besides King Kane's brother. In this dark room in this miserable castle, I miss my home.

The door opens, and I turn to see Opal has entered the room. Objectively, I see her pretty face with her long, dark hair and milk pale skin and know there have been plenty of men that have succumb to her physical perfection. I know what truly lies underneath the expensive gowns and coifed hair. I feel nothing but disgust at the sight of her.

"Lex," she croons, moving closer to me. "I've missed you."

Her cold hands grab for my clothes to remove them. I catch her hands and stop her.

"I haven't missed you," I tell her bluntly. "Not after everything you've done, Opal."

"What I've done?" she challenges with an ugly scowl. "What about what you and your brother have done? Using me and tossing me aside now that you have that werewolf slut to play with?"

"You don't even compare to Emory. She has more heart in her pinky finger than you do in your entire body."

"How dare you!" she shrieks. "I am a princess, the daughter of a king! I'm not lesser than some common wolf whore Kane plucked off the streets! And I'm carrying a royal child!"

I push her away from me, not wanting her in my personal space. "Believe what you want, Opal."

"Don't you fucking patronize me, Lex! If anyone doesn't matter here, it's you. If you were to die in this castle, nobody would care! You're the spare and you always have been! You're nothing!"

I give her a bland smile, knowing she's lashing out because my words have affected her more than she wants them to.

"I may be just the spare, but do you know what you are, Opal?

You're a broodmare that your father sold off to the highest bidder as soon as he could because, in the end, we're both disposable."

"I'm nothing like you! I am not disposable!"

"You're exactly like me," I declare. "And that means our child we'll be a monster just like us."

HOW A WITCH BECAME A VAMPIRE

Lola

I'm not used to living in such a big place. The castle is too big. I don't know why people want to live here when it takes forever to get from one room to another. I know vampires move fast, so it might not be a problem for them, but I have short legs and climbing all the stairs is not fun.

Emory doesn't agree that they need to install elevators in the castle, but she's taller than me and doesn't understand how hard it is. I don't like being out of breath because I want to go to her room or visit the library. I like the library a lot because most of the vampires seem to avoid it, and the librarian is really nice. Miss Willow is usually the only person at the library, and she recommends books to me and even sits down and talks to me if I ask her questions.

She's seated at her desk and looks up when I come near here. She gives me a soft smile in greeting. Miss Willow is pretty, and she's not mean like some of the other vampires. She doesn't say nasty things about me behind my back.

"Hello, Lola," she says. "Have you finished the book you checked out already?"

I hand her the book I'm holding, and she takes it carefully. "I read through it last night after Emory told me to go to sleep. I just had to know how the story ended."

She smiles and places the book on the trolley. I follow her as she pushes the cart toward the shelves to the right to put away my book and a few others.

"You read fast for your age," she comments.

"I didn't have much to do at home so I would read a lot," I tell her. "Luna Helen didn't let me watch spend much time with the other children. She said I didn't need to have friends."

"Who's Luna Helen?"

"Emory's mom. She doesn't like me very much."

Miss Willow's eyebrows furrow. She looks concerned. "Why do you think she doesn't like you?"

"Well, it's because my dad is mated to her, and he had me with my real mom, so Luna Helen sees me as a 'tragedy.'"

"She said that to you?" Miss Willow asks. She looks upset. "She told you that you're a tragedy."

I shrug. "Emory always told me that people who are hurt will hurt other people to make themselves feel better. I think Luna Helen was really hurt by my dad, and that's why she was mean to me."

"She still shouldn't have been mean to you. It's not your fault what your father did."

"Yeah, but nobody ever blamed my dad for anything before cause he was the Alpha. Now that Emory's the Alpha, everyone is angry at my dad. He did a lot of bad things."

"They should blame him," she agrees. "When people do bad things, it's important that they're held responsible for their actions."

"Emory said that too. I thought I would miss my dad, but I don't really. He never really liked to be around me much. He liked Emory and Colt more."

Miss Willow looks sad. She moves closer to me and runs her cold fingers through my hair. "He doesn't deserve you. And you should know that it wasn't right for him to treat you that way."

"I know. Emory says sometimes men can be real jerks."

She smiles. "That's true."

"What's your dad like?" I ask. "Do vampires have dads?"

She hesitates before answering, "I wasn't always a vampire. I did have a dad. A long time ago."

"What happened to him?"

She turns me around slowly and guides me to a table with her hand on my back. I sit down, and she takes the seat across from me.

"It's a sad story," she tells me. "It's related to how I became a vampire."

"How did you become a vampire?"

I'm curious because some members of my pack have told me my whole life that vampires are all evil and heartless, but Miss Willow has only ever been nice to me. If she's nice, then maybe not all vampires are bad. Otherwise, she would have to be secretly evil, and I don't think she is.

"You're too young for that story," she reasons. "Emory will be upset with me."

"I'm not that young!" I counter. "I'll be a teenager before you know it. I'm not a baby."

Miss Willow contemplates telling me the story, looking into my eyes before giving in. "All right, but I'm not giving you all the details."

"That's fine."

Her eyes stare off into space, like she's remembering something, "Once upon a time..."

I give her a judging look. "That's the cheesiest way to start a story."

"This is how I want to tell my story. Do you want to listen or not?"

I mime zipping my mouth and throwing away the key.

"Once upon a time, back when this land was ruled by a different king, King Michael, he started hunting witches," she continues. "You see, at that time witches existed. They lived amongst the humans and had a tenuous relationship with the wolf shifters. But the vampires? They hunted the witches."

"Why?"

"King Michael thought the magic the witches wielded was danger-ous. He wanted to control the witches by preventing them from using their magic. When he started capturing them, he realized our blood itself was magical."

I lean forward wanting to hear more of the story.

"He discovered that if a vampire were to drink witch blood that they would be given an extra burst of energy–temporarily," Miss Willow explains. "Aside from that, witch blood is addictive to vampires. They like it more than human or shifter blood. Maybe it's the magic or just… the taste." She shivers as if she is thinking about a bad memory.

"And then what happened?"

"There was a young witch named Willow. She was from a small village to the south of here. Her father owed a debt to King Michael, so he sold off his only child to be a feeder at Castle Graystone."

My eyes widen in shock, and I ask, "Why would he do that?"

"He was desperate. Maybe he didn't care about her enough. She knew he was scared. If he didn't pay off his debt, he would have been killed along with their entire village."

"But you were his daughter!" I retort, hot emotion making my face feel like it is burning. "He should have fought for you!"

Miss Willow's cold hands grab mine in hers, and she tells me calmly, "It's all right. He's been dead a long time. This all happened long before you were born."

I feel tears making my eyes watery, but I don't want to cry. "He shouldn't have done that to you."

"I know," she agrees with understanding. "Just like I know that your father shouldn't have done that to you."

I go still in shock. "You know about what my dad did?" I feel ashamed. It doesn't feel good that other people know how cruel my father is. It's one thing when people in the pack know, but the vampires knowing it too makes me feel small. It's not easy to know that my father doesn't love me and never will.

If my dad loved me, he wouldn't have tried to sell me off to King Kane. He would have protected me. He would have fought for me. He did none of that.

Miss Willow nods. Her face looks solemn. "I know the story about how your sister ended up in the castle. The servants like to talk amongst each other. Some of them witnessed the bargain in the throne room."

"Emory saved me," I tell her. "I was going to be a feeder, but she stopped it. She's the only one that's ever loved me."

Emory fought for me. She stood up to our father and to the vampire king and told them they couldn't take me. Everyone else had kept quiet because they didn't mind losing me.

"And you're lucky you have a sister that loves you so dearly she was willing to sacrifice herself for you. Not many people have that privilege."

"I know."

I have always known that Emory loves me. Even when the rest of our family ignored me or said unkind things, I had Emory. When she was taken from me, I had to live with the Kincaids who were nice, but they couldn't replace my sister. I didn't think I would ever have to be away from her, but when it happened, it made me realize just how much I love her.

"What happened to you after you became a feeder?"

Miss Willow pulls away from me, physically and emotionally. "I've upset you enough. We shouldn't talk more about this."

"I want to know," I plead. "What happened to you when you came to this castle?"

She goes quiet, her eyes closing. I wait as she breathes in and out. Eventually, her pale blue eyes open, and she won't look at me as she continues with the story.

"Witches don't last long as feeders. Vampires often drained them dry if nobody stopped them. It was more common for vampires to go straight to the dungeon and take what they wanted at the time with no regulation. It was a nightmarish existence that could only be escaped through death. Since witches and humans could be turned, we had to be bled into a cup, but sometimes vampires would cut too deep and bleed us too much without thinking."

She's looking down at the oak table, her expression blank like she's just trying to get the words out.

"There was a vampire that fed on me the most. He was young, and he couldn't control himself yet when he fed," she says. "One time, he bled me too much. I should have died, but instead, I woke up, and I was… different. I'd become a vampire. I assume he must have bitten me when I passed out."

I take in the story. Miss Willow is quiet. She covers her mouth with a hand and looks upset. I want to hug her and make her feel better.

"Did that young vampire do it on purpose?" I ask. "Maybe he wanted to save you?"

She snorts, shaking her head. "It was an accident. He never cared about me. He never even looked at me again after he turned me. It was as if I never existed at all to him."

I frown. "That's not nice."

"No. It's not nice."

"What happened to him?"

"He continued living his life. We didn't cross paths much after that," she describes. "Once I became a vampire, I was no longer useful as a feeder, so I was released from the dungeon. I couldn't do anything about what I had become, so I worked at the castle. I was a maid, a cook in the kitchens, lots of things. My only reprieve was the library. The old librarian who worked here then was kind and would lend me books that I would read when I had free time."

"How did you become a librarian?"

"That librarian unfortunately died. He did something King Michael didn't like, and he was killed. It happened a lot back then, actually. They made me the new librarian since I was the servant that spent the most time here and knew how the place worked. And I like it here because most people avoid this place."

"Aside from me, of course."

Miss Willow smiles warmly. "Aside from an ever curious little wolf girl."

I get up from my seat so I can move closer to Miss Willow and hug her. "I'm sorry all that happened to you, but I'm glad you're here. You're the nicest vampire I've ever met."

"You're the nicest wolf I've ever met," she tells me. "I'm glad I got to meet you, too."

"Are we friends?"

"We can be."

"Can I call you Willow?"

"Of course, you may." She gets to her feet and holds my hand to lead me to a nearby bookshelf. "That's enough sad stories for today. How about we find you a happier tale to read?"

I smile as Willow starts to pull out books from shelves and tell me about each one. I'm glad I have a friend in the castle. Emory can't always be with me because she's busy as the Alpha, and I understand that. The castle is too big to not have a friend. It's too cold and lonely.

A DOZEN BITES

Emory

I hear about Lex being sent off as a hostage at Scarlett Thunder from my maids after he's already left. I don't get the chance to say goodbye. Lex and I may not have started out on the right foot, but I still feel bad he's essentially become King Peter's prisoner. I want to talk to Kane about what happened but hear he's in a meeting. I'm able to find Rainer who has a rare spare moment where he's not doing something for Kane.

"Lex said it's better this way," Rainer tells me. "It would have been an awkward scene if he stopped to say goodbye to you, and Lex doesn't find that entertaining. That chaotic little shit has a dramatic flair."

"I still wish I'd had a chance to say goodbye to him. It's not easy being a prisoner in a castle filled with your enemies."

I understand that feeling more than anyone. Kane treated me more like an honored guest rather than a prisoner, but I was terrified when I first arrived at Castle Graystone. Even when Kane brought me to a nice bedroom, and I got to wear beautiful clothes and jewelry, I didn't feel safe. I hadn't known who to trust, and I felt isolated and frightened.

"I can't imagine Lex is having a good time in Scarlett Thunder. His family is here," I remind Rainer.

He shrugs. "Don't worry about Lex. He has a remarkable talent for surviving odds. He's like a handsome, blonde cockroach that refuses to die."

I know Lex isn't completely helpless. He's a vampire, and he is still faster and stronger than any wolf shifter. How he will fare around other vampires, I don't know. He isn't a trained soldier like Rainer.

"Why would Kane send Lex to be a political prisoner?" I ask. "I know they've had their differences, but isn't this dangerous?"

"Someone had to go. Kane tried to dissuade him, but Lex really wanted to go for some reason. He chose this for himself. Kane did not push him into it."

"He volunteered to be a hostage?" I can't believe my ears.

"It shocked me too. I didn't know he had in him. I still think he has an ulterior motive behind all of this, but Kane seems to think his brother is being selfless and noble for once."

"Maybe he did it for Kane." I had sacrificed myself for my sister because I wanted to protected her above all else when nobody else would. Lex surrendering himself to King Peter in order to help Kane isn't as far-fetched of a concept to me as it is to Rainer. Lex could have done this for one simple reason–he loves his brother. And that is more than enough of a reason for me to believe that there is no ulterior motive.

Rainer frowns. "I can't believe that. The Lex I know is not that kind of man."

"Maybe you don't know him as well as you think you do," I point out. "And people can change, even vampires as old as dirt."

"Ouch." Rainer put a hand over his heart. "I'm not that old. I'm in my early hundreds, thank you very much."

"And that in shifter and human years is as old as dirt," I tease him. "Your bones would be dust if you weren't a vampire."

Rainer rolls his eyes before turning away to leave. "In that case, I'm going to go rest my bones before they disintegrate before your very eyes."

I'm about to tell him I'm only joking, even though he knows that, when Helga runs up to me. She looks harried.

I look at her in concern. "What's wrong?".

"You have to come, Princess," she says, urgently. "It's your father. He's been attacked."

The shock hits me like a lightning bolt. I've spent days trying to forget my father is even in the castle. The news that he's been harmed urges me to go find out what happened immediately. How is that possible when he's in the dungeon?

"Where is he now?"

"He's been brought to the infirmary," Helga answers. "Dr. Martin is looking over him."

I start walking briskly toward the infirmary. Helga follows me along with Rainer who stopped his retreat when he heard Helga's proclamation. The maid says she doesn't know any more details about the attack. She was informed by a guard who'd come looking for me in my room.

When I reach the infirmary, I find Bernard unconscious on a bed. Dr. Martin is giving him a blood transfusion. I have never seen my father look so pale. He's almost as pale as the vampire physician.

All my life, my father always looked big and tough. He was the strong, domineering Alpha that bowed to no man. It isn't until I learned who he really was, the greedy coward, that he became something else in my eyes. With him lying in that hospital, I can see how much weight he has lost in the dungeon. Bones poke out of his grimy clothes. He looks crumpled and brittle, like the doctor could break him easily if he isn't handled with care.

I approach the bed warily. Somebody had shaved his head, and they had done it badly. The loss of his hair makes it easier for me to see the bite marks on his throat. There are half a dozen bites. His arm is dangling off the edge of the bed, and there are bite marks at the wrist. This is the work of more than one vampire.

"Who did this?" I demand. "Who's been feeding on him?"

"I'm not aware of who it was," Dr. Martin answers. "You'll have to ask the guards."

I'm going to interrogate the guards to find out who is responsible and how they let this happen. If this happened to my father who is not supposed to be touched, then I worry for the feeders in the dungeons. The last time I was down there, it had been a hellish existence for the feeders. I thought I would be left to the same fate of living in squalor and being fed on until I died until Kane came to free me. And there are other abuses that happen down there, worse than just being fed on.

My understanding is that all of that has changed, but then, how did my father get in this shape?

I look at the heart monitor and see his heartbeat seems stable. "Will he recover?"

"He should recover with time and rest. He's lost a lot of blood, and he's malnourished."

"They weren't giving him enough food?"

Dr. Martin looks uncomfortable. "You'll have to ask the guards."

I have a lot of questions for the guards. The situation in the dungeons is meant to be different now. Kane had been furious when he saw how Clarke had been treating the feeders. I haven't gone to see if the changes he wanted had been implemented as I have been busy dealing with the pack and doing damage control, trying to right my father's wrongs.

I'm furious and ashamed. The feeders down there are wolf shifters, my people, and I had assumed someone else had taken care of the problems. I can't expect the vampires in the castle to suddenly be empathetic toward them after decades of bad blood. I should have done more to make their lives better and not left it to Kane to deal with the issues.

I turn to Helga. "Could you keep an eye on my father and call for me when he wakes up?"

"Yes, Princess."

Rainer understands without me saying anything that I want from him. He quietly follows my lead, and we head to the dungeons. When we arrive, we question all the guards about what happened to Bernard. While the feeders had been treated better since Clarke was no longer in charge of the dungeon, the same hadn't been applied to prisoners. The guards had largely left Bernard alone, forgetting to feed him for a day or two. Initially, he was loud and obnoxious enough to keep their attention. But after a week or two in his cell, he stopped being such a pain in the ass, and sometimes, they said, they forgot he was there.

The guards say none of them had been feeding on Bernard.

"Who was it then?" I demand, jabbing a finger at a short vampire with a long black beard. "You're the ones with easy access to him. The nobles and the staff don't come down here."

The guards look at each other, fidgeting under my glare.

"Well?" I exclaim. "Who was it?"

The youngest-looking guard stammers out, "I-It could have been the prisoner in the cell beside his. Another vampire."

"Who?"

"Jacob Maxwell."

My eyes widen, and I take off in a rush toward Jacob's cell. Rainer catches me before I can get too far. My impulse is to run and find Jacob Fucking Maxwell and punch him in the face. Rainer is stronger and grabs me firmly, but not painfully, by the wrist, tugging me back to his broad chest. I struggle against his hold, but he doesn't let go.

"I know; I know you're angry," he says. "But you can't attack that son of a bitch even if he deserves it."

When I think of Jacob, I remember his smarmy face laughing at me as his sister insulted me. I remember a fake note and a cruel plot. I remember his teeth biting into my throat. He had tried to kill me before, and I feel my blood boiling for retribution.

"Let me go, Rainer!"

"I'm sorry. I can't. Kane was very clear about how we must handle Jacob—especially since Lex is a hostage now."

The reminder of Lex makes me stop. My blood is still hot under my skin. I still want to punch something, but not being able to direct it at the right person frustrates me. I take a few deep breaths, willing myself to calm down.

"Are you okay?" Rainer asks.

I nod. He lets me go, and I walk away from the dungeon without a word. He follows after me as I run up the stairs and begin to make my way back up to the infirmary.

"Let me handle Jacob," Rainer suggests. "I'll break his leg again and make it look like an accident if I have to."

I don't want to talk about Jacob because I still want to run down to his cell and break his bones until he can never walk again. I am angry at my father, but he is still a member of my family, my pack, and I hate Jacob with all my might.

"Make sure he can't feed on anyone else," I say. "He shouldn't have been able to get to anyone."

"I can have the guards reprimanded and replaced–"

"Do what you need to do, Rainer." We reach the door to the infirmary. I turn to him and add, "You need to tell Kane what happened. If Jacob is able to get out of his cell, he might try to escape the dungeon next."

Rainer nods and turns away to go find Kane. I open the door and enter the infirmary. Dr. Martin is taking notes on his clipboard. Helga is seated by the wall, watching Bernard on the bed.

"How is he?" I ask.

"He's stable," the doctor answers. "However, another transfusion might be necessary."

"I could donate my blood."

He pauses before replying, "That might not be a good idea due to your condition. The vampire blood in your system would not help and could slow down his recovery. Besides, it could potentially take blood away from the baby."

I touch my abdomen. I forgot about my pregnancy. The doctor had also warned me about stress. It's bad for the baby.

"Pregnant women shouldn't be donating blood," Helga tells me, disapprovingly.

I'm about to reply to my maid when Bernard's voice booms out, "Pregnant?"

We all turn to see he's awake on the infirmary bed. He tries to sit up but is too weak and collapses back down on the bed.

"You're pregnant?" he questions in a raspy voice. "How are you pregnant?"

Dr. Martin comes over and tells him, "You must calm down. You've lost a lot of blood–"

"I know I lost a lot of blood!" he retorts, trying frantically to get off the bed. "That vampire has been feeding on me, and no one stopped it!"

Dr. Martin puts a hand on his shoulder to push him down on the bed, but my father snarls, "Don't touch me!"

"Father," I tell him sternly, "stop fighting the doctor, and calm down."

His grey eyes snap back to me. "Who's the father of the baby?"

"That's not important right now–"

"Who is it?" he yells. "Who's the father?"

I glare at him and answer, "Kane."

A WONDERFUL TIME

Emory

Bernard looks a mix of horrified and furious. His gray eyes are wide, and he stares at me dumbstruck for a full minute before he lunges. Dr. Martin and Helga grab him before he can get off the bed. They push him down, and Bernard is no match for their superior vampire strength. It doesn't help that he's lost a lot of blood and is malnourished.

"You have to get rid of it!" Bernard yells. "You can't keep that thing inside of you!"

"That is not your decision," I reply firmly. "This is my baby, and I get to decide-"

"It's going to be a monster!" Bernard's gray eyes look more scared than angry. "Whatever comes out of you, it's not going to be a shifter or a vampire; it's going to be an abomination."

My hand cradles my belly protectively. "No, it's not. My baby is going to be normal."

"Normal?" he scoffs. "It's going to destroy all of us. With Kane's spawn inside of you, it'll kill you as it tries to get out-"

The horrifying imagery makes me want to cover my ears. "Stop! Stop saying that!"

"Monster! It's going to be a monster!" he chants. "A bloodsucking monster!"

I remember all the folktales I read in the castle library about hybrids. Those books said they are mindless bloodthirsty creatures that decimated whole villages on their own. My baby won't become like that. I don't want to believe it.

A hand touches my back gently, comfortingly. I turn to see it's Kane. He wraps his arm around me protectively, and I want to let myself be lost in the safety of his touch. His anger is a cold fury that matches the blue of his eyes as he glares at my father.

"Bernard, I will not allow you to upset your daughter. She's carrying your grandchild." His steely gaze doesn't change as he pins Bernard to the bed with a look.

"That thing is not my grandchild! It's a crime against nature!"

Something inside me crumbles and dies. There has been this naïve part of me that still remembers Bernard as a loving father that thought he might be happy at hearing the news of his first grandchild. Instead, I have the reality of his disgust and outrage. What should have been a happy moment is twisted by his malice and distaste.

"We are done here." Kane turns me away from Bernard's ranting and out of the infirmary. "You don't need to listen to any more of this."

Rainer is waiting in the hallway. Kane tells him, "If Bernard is feeling well enough to act like an asshole again, he's well enough to return to the dungeon."

His friend doesn't disagree. The king keeps his arm around me as he leads me away from the infirmary. We walk through hallways, and I cling to him, needing his steady comfort. He takes us to his room, and we lie on his bed. My head rests on his chest as he cradles me in his arms.

"Are you all right?" he asks.

"Yes." After a second I confess, "I don't know. All that stuff my dad said was…"

"Don't listen to Bernard. He only wants to hurt and scare you.

Anything that comes out of his mouth is always for his own benefit. He's been known to twist truths into lies."

I know about my father's propensity for lying. He had our pack believe for decades that Kane had started the war between our species when it had been my father's fault for not paying a debt he owed. My father had attacked our neighboring packs to expand his power and territory only to fail. All that bloodshed and wasted resources, and what was it all for? Nothing.

My father built his ambitions on hubris and greed. And when his house of cards fell, he blamed everyone but himself.

I sit up, and Kane does as well. "I went to the library and read every book I could find on hybrids, and every story talks about terrifying monsters who only want carnage and destruction. What if the baby turns out like that?"

Kane cups my face in his hands. "Look at me, Emory. Those are just stories written by scared people from a long time ago. No one's seen an actual hybrid before. Not recently, anyway. No one knows what they're talking about."

"That means we don't know what we're dealing with. I don't know what's inside me–if it's a baby or some kind of monster."

"It's not a monster," he insists, gently. "It's a baby, *our* baby."

I let out a shuddering breath. My whole body trembles. My breath gets quicker, and I'm growing lightheaded.

"But *what* is it? Maybe it's a baby for now, but it won't always be that way. What if it grows up and becomes a monster?"

"Breathe, Emory," Kane tells me, firmly. "Breathe in and out. You need to breathe."

I inhale deeply and exhale slowly. Kane makes me repeat this until I don't feel lightheaded anymore.

"Our baby is not going to be a monster," he says. "And you want to know why? Because you're the child's mother, and that means that baby is going to be fine. Look at Lola. She's good and kind because of you."

I close my eyes, the panic and fear melting away to relief. He kisses my cheek, the tip of my nose, and my forehead. His mouth is gentle as he leaves sweet kisses on my face and neck.

He kisses me with such tenderness I hold still, afraid to break the moment.

"Whatever the baby is going to be, we'll take care of it," he concludes. "Our child will be loved."

I burst into tears. The shame of thinking the worst of my unborn child overwhelms me. Do I have such little faith? I have let old folktales and my father get into my head and make me doubt what I truly feel.

I know I love this baby. He or she is mine and Kane's. Whatever they may be—shifter, vampire, or something in between, they will be loved and cared for. They will never doubt whether a parent's love is real or unconditional. I will make sure of it.

Kane holds me and lets me cry on his shoulder. His hand rubs gentle circles on my back. He doesn't let me go until I fall asleep.

Lex

Opal is not feeling well that morning and is noticeably absent at breakfast. I don't care for her. I never have. When she was my brother's betrothed, I had no interest in her besides the physical.

Things are different now. She's pregnant with my child, and that is not insignificant. We're tied together in an irrevocable way whether either of us like it or not. I feel responsible for her.

Later that day, I still haven't seen her. Dinner is an unpleasant affair. King Peter mocks me to his courtier who jeers and snickers at my expense. It sickens me that I used to be like these fools who had nothing better to do than to look down on someone. I pay them no mind and leave as soon as the meal is done.

I make my way to Opal's room. No one stops me as I enter the suite. Opal is lying on the large bed. It is the most opulent room I've ever seen, more flashy than elegant. The furniture is made of the same dark wood like the rest of the castle's furnishings. The walls are painted a deep midnight blue but with sparkling stars sprinkled. As I move closer, I realize there are opals embedded into the walls. The large canopy on her bed has little opals sewn into the fabric. All this unnecessary expense is true to Opal's taste.

"Get out!" Opal yells at a maid, throwing a glass of blood at her. "Get the fuck out!"

Her maids scurry away and out of the room, not even bothering to clean up the mess that Opal just made. The mess has fallen on the carpets below, soaking them. Opal sees me and throws a pillow in my direction. I dodge, and the pillow hits the floor with a pathetic thump.

"Leave me alone!" she shrieks. "I want to be left alone!"

"You know, Opal, all that yelling is probably not good for the baby,"

She lets out an angry cry that reminds me of a pelican and turns away from me, covering her head with a pillow as if it could block me out. I look at the door and consider just leaving. She's made it clear she wants to be left alone but I can't leave until I know she's all right—for the baby's sake. I sigh to myself, lamenting how I got myself into this mess again.

My stupid cock. That's how.

Maybe I should take a vow of celibacy. Having meaningless sex has never done me any good. It's only more trouble than it's worth. I wonder if I have the fortitude for such a vow. I consider testing it.

I walk over to the bed and sit at the end of it. Opal keeps her back to me.

"I heard you're not feeling well," I say. "Is there anything I can do to help?"

"You can fuck off, Lex. I didn't invite you in here."

I ignore that and continue like nothing is amiss, "I talked to my mother about her experience being pregnant. She advised cold food. I know you like ice cream. I can get you some."

She turns to me and drops the pillow on the bed. Her sapphire blue eyes narrow in suspicion. "What the fuck are you trying to do?"

I sigh again and rub the bridge of my nose, wishing I was

anywhere else but here. I wouldn't mind living outside in the frozen tundra if it was far away from here.

"You're pregnant, and I want to help. It is my baby, after all, whether you want to verbally acknowledge it or not."

"It's not your baby," she hisses. "It will never be your baby."

I give her an unimpressed look. "Opal, we both know Kane never touched you. I came inside you at least a dozen times. You can keep saying it's his kid, but he will never acknowledge it as his own."

"That's his fucking fault for being so stubborn!" She throws a pillow at a wall. "If he would just marry me, we wouldn't be having any issues between our kingdoms!"

"We wouldn't be having any issues if you and your brother never attacked Emory," I point out. "If you would be honest with your father about the baby's parentage-"

"Why does it matter? It has Kane's family blood. That should be enough!"

"Kane will never accept your baby as his own because he despises you. You almost killed the woman he loves, and Kane has never been quick to forgive when someone hurts a person he loves."

She scowls. "All of this because of a werewolf? Is he really going to make a baby that's half-shifter his heir? Is he insane?"

The news of Emory's pregnancy had spread to Scarlett Thunder thanks to the diplomat, Lord Alistair, informing King Peter. Word of a royal hybrid being born is not just a salacious topic for vampires. The wolf shifters will be interested in the information too. I don't doubt the other kingdoms will learn about Emory's pregnancy soon enough.

"Kane is excited to be a father," I explain. "To Emory's baby, of course."

Opal hits me with a pillow. "I fucking hate you, Lex!"

I half-heartedly block her assault. She keeps trying to hit me in the head. "You aren't that sweet either, Opaline."

"Get out!" she screeches. "Get the fuck out of my room!"

I get to my feet and away from her reach. "Do you want ice cream or not?"

"No!"

"Fine." I turn to leave. "I'll try again tomorrow."

I walk out of the room just as a pillow hits the door behind me.

My mother is right. Pregnancy can be such a wonderful time. For other people, that is.

PERFECT PICNIC SPOT

Lola

I never see Willow outside of the castle, and I want to have a picnic, so I convince her to have lunch with me one day. She's reluctant at first because she doesn't like leaving the books alone, but I tell that the books will be fine for an hour. They can't get up and run away.

Emory isn't feeling well that day and is resting in her room. She tells me not to stay cooped up with her, so Nellie is there to make sure I don't get lost on the castle grounds. Sometimes, I get lost in the castle because it's way too big. Emory doesn't agree that we should move to a smaller castle or at least install an elevator in this one. I point out to her that she's going to have a tough time with the stairs once she gets a big baby tummy, but she just laughs at me.

Nellie carries a picnic basket with us as we make our way to the rose garden. She and Willow know each other as they used to work in the kitchens together. They are making idle chit-chat as I look for the perfect picnic spot. Once I find the best place, Nellie lays down a blanket for us to sit on. She opens the basket and takes out the food.

There are sandwiches, fruit, and a pitcher of freshly squeezed orange juice, as well as some blood for the vampires. Willow nibbles on some strawberries as I eat the sandwich Nellie had made. The sandwich is layered with chicken, bacon, veggies, and mayo. It's very tasty. I'm glad that Willow and Nellie eat some of the food and not just their blood. It's still gross to me to see people sipping on something that might've come out of someone just like me.

The weather is nice today, not too sunny and not too cloudy. It's a little windy which keeps the temperature cool. I want to climb some trees, but Nellie insists I finish my food first. She and Helga are very strict when it comes to food and cleanliness.

I'm halfway done with my sandwich when Rainer appears past the copse of trees. He's wearing his military jacket, but it's unbuttoned, revealing his white undershirt. Willow instantly stiffens when she sees him.

"Hello." He smiles a very charming smile at us, especially for a vampire. "Am I interrupting something?"

"We're having a picnic," I declare.

"I can see that. It is perfect weather for a picnic."

I'm wary around most vampires because they're mean, but Rainer is always nice. Emory likes him. She says he's a friend. He is always smiling and sneaks me sweets out of the kitchens.

"Do you want to join us?" I ask. "I think we have enough food."

"I am actually famished," Rainer replies. He takes a seat on the picnic blanket between Willow and I. Nellie hands him a sandwich, and he takes a big bite out of it. With a mouthful of food, he says, "This is really good, Nels."

Willow has stopped eating. She looks down at the picnic blanket and scoots away from Rainer. He notices and smiles at her. After swallowing, he leans closer and whispers something in her ear. She doesn't react to whatever he tells her and ignores him by pulling out a library book she brought with her and beginning to read it.

"What are you reading?" he asks.

She covers her face with the book so we can't see her expression. I can tell from how stiff she is that she's annoyed. Any time Rainer is around, Willow tenses up. I don't know why that is. I should ask her later.

After failing to get a response from Willow, Rainer looks to me and asks, "Where's your sister?"

"The baby's making her feel sick," I answer. "She's staying in bed today."

He looks worried. "Has she gone to see the doctor?"

"She has. The doctor says it's normal pregnancy stuff."

"That's good." He picks a blueberry from a bowl and bites it. A bit of juice stains his fingers. "You'll tell me if there's something unusual, right?"

"About Emory's pregnancy?"

He nods. "We all want to make sure she and the baby are healthy."

"Okay," I agree. "How would I tell you? You're usually busy."

"You can ask a servant to send me a message, or you could come to my room."

"That's inappropriate." Willow finally speaks again. "You can't have her going to your room. She's a child."

He waggles his eyebrows at her. "How about you show up at my room then, Willow? Or is that too inappropriate for you? I know exactly what inappropriate things I'd like to be doing with you–"

Nellie loudly clears her throat. "Maybe you shouldn't be saying such things around a child?"

Rainer gives an innocent smile that makes me think he uses that when he wants to get out of trouble. I've seen my brother Colt do the same thing back home.

"Lighten up, Nels," Rainer remarks. "Lola is too young to understand what I'm saying anyway."

"I'm ten," I tell him. "Emory already told me where babies come from."

He erupts into a coughing fit. "That's… that's good to know, Lo. Um, how about we don't tell your sister what you heard me say to Miss Willow over here?"

Willow hides her face behind her book. "Don't drag me into this. You were the one being inappropriate."

"I'm not supposed to lie to Emory," I point out. "But I could forget to mention it to her if you get me cake."

"Cake?" he repeats.

I nod. "Chocolate cake. The one with the raspberry filling that the cook bakes."

He offers his hand, and we shake on it. "A deal's a deal, little wolf."

Willow smacks him on the arm with her book. "Don't make deals with a child!"

"*She* made a deal with *me*," he says. "I just agreed to it."

"You're the adult," Willow whispers vehemently. "You're supposed to say no."

He winks at her. "I can't help that I'm easily persuaded, which you should totally take advantage of, Willow. I will not fight you for anything if you just ask."

Willow grimaces in disgust. "You're filthy."

"Not filthy enough yet. Just say the word, Wils. We can get filthy together."

Nellie loudly clears her throat and gestures toward me by nodding vigorously. "Again, the child is right there."

He points to me. "I know, I know. I'll get you the cake."

I giggle, amused at Rainer's behavior and Willow's annoyance at him. Curiously, I ask, "Do you like Willow? Is that why you tease her?"

He leans closer to me and whispers loudly so everyone can hear, "I like her a lot, little wolf. I don't think she likes me though."

We look at Willow, and she hides behind her book again.

"Maybe she thinks you have a girlfriend," I state. "Are you single?"

"I'm very, very single."

"Why? Do you not want to be with anyone?"

With a more serious tone he explains, "It's not that I don't want to be with someone, but I'm really busy these days. King Kane is dealing with a lot, and he needs all the help he can get. Ruling a kingdom is a lot of work."

"King Kane managed to fall in love with Emory while doing all that, so what's stopping you?" I ask him.

I'm not fully comfortable with the king yet. He is always polite and nice, but I can't look at him and not remember that bad day when my father almost sold me off to him. I can see how he takes care of Emory, and it makes it easier to not dislike him. And he's having a baby with her, so in a way, he's family now. I will have to learn to accept him eventually.

Is he part of the pack? I thought only wolf shifters could be pack members. I need to ask Emory.

Rainer rubs the back of his neck uncomfortably. "That's a good point, Lo. The king has always been good at multitasking. I'm a one task at a time kind of guy."

"Maybe you should tell the king you need more time off so you can get a girlfriend then."

He laughs, a boisterous sound that even makes Nellie smile. "You are so smart. Maybe you should be ruling a kingdom."

I frown. "Not if I have to live in a castle. They're too big. There's too many stairs. Not enough elevators."

"Those are all good points," he concedes. "But I do have to tell you that I enjoy my job even if it keeps me from dating. I like to be of service to my kingdom."

"You can be of service and find love. It can't be *that* hard."

I don't understand why adults have to make everything so complicated for themselves. They tell themselves they can't do something when they obviously can. They *won't* do something which is completely different. I think they should be honest with themselves more.

"I could try. Or maybe I just need to be more like Kane and fall in love with my own feeder-"

Willow gets up abruptly, nearly knocking over the pitcher of juice. "I have to go. Sorry, Lola. I'll see you later at the library."

She walks away quickly and is out of the rose garden before any of us can react. Rainer gets up and follows her.

RAINER

Willow moves faster than I expect. I have to run to catch up to her.

She doesn't acknowledge me, and is dead set on getting back in the castle before I reach her. She speeds up once I'm walking beside her, trying to lose me.

"What's wrong?" I ask. "Did I do something to upset you?"

"No," she answers, briskly.

"Are you sure? Cause it feels like you're trying to run away from me."

"I am not."

"Slow down then."

She doesn't. "I have to get back to work. Not all of us are close friends with the king and can do whatever we want."

Annoyance makes me speed up, and I block her path, preventing her from moving forward. "What is that supposed to mean?"

"Nothing," she replies, agitated. "Just let me get back to the library."

"If it's nothing, you wouldn't be acting this way, so it's clearly something."

She tries to duck past me, but I continue to block her way. I'm bigger than her in every way. She can't move around me that easily. "Willow, just tell me what's wrong so I can fix it."

"There's no fixing anything."

"Is the flirting too much? I can tone it down. Do you prefer courting? I can do that. Just tell me what you want."

I grab her waist to keep her still. She viscerally reacts and starts pushing me away, dropping her book in the struggle. "I want you to leave me alone!" she exclaims.

Her eyes are wide and terrified. Something about her expression feels familiar. I can't remember why. When have we done this before?

She takes advantage of my stunned silence and rushes around me. Her skirt billows around her as she makes her way to the castle and back to her safe haven. I pick up the book she dropped from the ground. Absent-mindedly, I wipe dirt off the leather cover.

I'm trying to catalog all my past interactions with this woman, and I can't remember anything significant. I avoided the library until recently, so it's not like we interacted much before her promotion.

When she had been a maid or a cook, she had mostly stayed out of my way and quietly did her work. She never drew any attention to herself.

She's a pretty face amongst a sea of pretty faces. With her brown hair, blue eyes, and red lips, she is undeniably attractive, but so are many of the female vampires in the castle. She had just been another face in the crowd until recently when I got to know her a little more. I only noticed her when Lola started frequently hanging out at the library. She's smart, helpful, and very good with Lola. All of those things make her attractive to me.

The question I can't find the answer to is what did I do to make her hate me? And why is she scared shitless of me?

SLIPPED MY MIND

Rainer

After trying to rack my brain for hours about how I know Willow, I decide to ask Kane if he knows anything. He's always had a better memory than me. He has a good head for remembering the smallest details. I've always been more of a bigger picture kind of guy.

I wait until after dinner to get Kane alone. We go to his room, and he pours us both a glass of blood mixed with whiskey. We have done this plenty of times before, so we don't rush into talking. We sit on the chairs by the window and are halfway through our drinks when I bring up the woman.

"Do you know the new librarian?" I ask.

"I haven't known a librarian since old Gaius."

Gaius had been the castle librarian before either of us had been born. He had practically been part of the wallpaper with how much of a staple he was in the castle.

"She's a pretty brunette. Kind of flighty. She likes to hide herself in the library."

Kane takes a sip from his glass. "I believe her name is Willow. Why are you asking about her?"

"Do you know where she came from?"

"Willow was part of the staff. She earned that position. Gaius had named her as a successor in case anything happened and he had to step down from his duties. Which my father saw to, as you know."

"And who was she before she was one of the staff?"

Kane stares at me. It feels like his blue eyes are penetrating straight into my soul. He asks, "You really don't remember?"

"I wouldn't be asking you if I did," I reply. "I can't remember anything significant I may have done to her."

He puts down his glass on the table. "Rainer, she came to the castle a long time ago as a feeder. Her father had sold her off to pay his debts."

"Human feeders aren't that valuable compared to shifters. Why was she considered substantial enough?"

Most human feeders don't last long in the dungeon. They can't heal like shifters, and there is a greater risk of them being turned into a vampire by mistake. It's why we mostly have wolf shifters as feeders now. They can't be turned even if we try.

"I have no idea. The deal was made with my father. He had a fondness for oral contracts which makes keeping track of every deal he made impossible."

This is a problem we don't talk about enough. The older vampires are set in their ways. They like to do things the old-fashioned way, no matter how impractical they may be. Kane is considered a progressively modern king by our kind's standards even if the other species still see us as archaic. King Peter is part of the old guard, which is a problem.

If King Michael would have made sure to leave a paper trail for all his contracts, life would be easier. If not more convenient whenever we have to look something up.

"But I do remember Willow because she was turned accidentally," Kane explains. "This was when my father was trying to control over-population within our species. He wanted to have her executed, but my mother pitied her and said that it wasn't Willow's fault she was turned."

Since most vampires can't procreate naturally aside from a few royal bloodlines, we add to our numbers by turning a human into one of us. It's not a complicated process, but it does make overpopulation a possible problem. King Michael was especially strict about who had the privilege of being turned into a vampire. Because of how long we can live and how we are superior in strength and speed compared to the wolf shifters and humans, a single vampire can cause a lot of damage, particularly if they have a weak personality to begin with.

"Queen Agatha saved her life."

Kane nods. "After that, Willow became part of the castle staff. Gaius took a shine to her and made her his unofficial apprentice."

"There's something you forgot to mention," I point out. "What happened to the vampire that turned her? Were they executed?"

"You don't remember that either? Don't you remember that time my father almost killed Lex because he turned someone into a vampire by mistake? It was Willow he turned."

The dots are connecting in my mind. I remember King Michael's fury at Lex for his carelessness. Lex had been a young vampire, barely in control of his thirst back then. Most vampires that disobeyed King Michael's rules were executed without mercy. Lex got off with a slap on the wrist due to royal nepotism. Being a prince, even the spare son, does have its privileges.

That explains Willow's behavior at the picnic after I made that thoughtless joke about finding my own feeder. Even if it has been a century, some wounds don't heal for the longest time. No wonder she looks so uncomfortable around me. She probably thinks Lex and I are friends. I need to apologize to her for my careless behavior.

I thank Kane for his help and leave him to look for Willow. It's getting late, but I have heard from the servants that she likes to stay late in the library most of the night. I'm not disappointed when I find her shelving books in a corner. She stiffens when she hears me coming towards her.

"Good evening," I say, contritely.

"Good evening," she replies, without looking at me. She focuses on shelving. "May I help you with something? I'm about to close up here."

"I came to apologize."

She stops, holding a book in her hands, clutching it like a lifeline. "What are you apologizing for?"

"I'm apologizing for my behavior earlier. I was careless with my words. It's no excuse, but I had forgotten about your past, and I didn't think about how my joke would land."

She finally looks at me, her blue eyes wide in disbelief. "You forgot my past?"

Embarrassment makes me want to hunch my shoulders like I'm some adolescent boy. I run a hand through my dark, curly hair

"I don't have the best memory," I admit. "I forgot you used to be a feeder."

"How?" she asks. "How could you forget?"

"I remember the situation with Lex, but I forgot the details. We never really interacted before recently, so it just slipped my mind."

"Slipped your mind?" She drops the book back on the cart. Her eyes close as if she is trying to control her emotions. "You just forgot everything?"

"Just the stuff with Lex turning you. I'm sorry. It must not have been a good memory for you."

Her eyes open, and they're twin blue flames of anger. "You forgot what you used to do to me?"

I blink. My mind goes blank in shock. "What *I* used to do to you?"

Her entire body is shaking, her voice rising as she exclaims, "You fed on me!"

"I did?"

"Don't you look and pretend to be so innocent!" she screeches. "You fed on me the most. You and Lex. Sometimes, you'd come down to the dungeons together, and you'd drain my blood into a cup and share it. You never took enough to kill me, but it was close. You were always on the verge of killing me, but neither of you had the mercy to end things and finally free me from that living hell."

I think back and I have faint memories of being blood drunk. I remember frightened hazel eyes and long, brown hair. I remember the taste of her blood. There's never been anything like it–before or after. Her blood tasted sweet and powerful with magic. I used to feel like I could fly when I had her blood on my tongue. It was the only time I'd ever go anywhere with Lex. Both of us agreed to put our differences aside for a taste of that magical blood.

I look at her face, glowing with anger and indignation, and all the puzzle pieces snap into place. "That was you?"

"Yes, Rainer," she spits my name like a curse. "That was me you fed on again and again until Lex got too careless and drank too much. He turned me into one of you, and then you both forgot about me like I never existed."

There are flashes of more moments–Willow in my arms as I carry her up the stairs to the healer, bite marks on her neck, her wrist, and her thighs. Her fair skin with a trail of bite marks. She lay still in a dirty gown, unable to move, her hazel eyes glassy with tears.

I struggle to say anything. I was the one who brought her to the healers to try to save her life. But I shouldn't have let Lex do that. I'd rushed in just in time to keep him from draining her. She must not recall that, and I won't tell her now. "I didn't…"

"Didn't what?"

"I didn't know that was you." I'd been under the impression that human had died.

Her pretty face twists into a sneer. "Well, now you know. And what are you going to do about it?"

Shame makes me want to run away and hide, but I'm not a little boy. I'm a man who faces my mistakes head on.

"I'm sorry," I say sincerely. "I'm sorry for everything I did to you. I wish I could take it back-"

"Don't!" She turns away, and her whole body shudders as she does her best to contain her sobs. "Just leave me alone. Apology not accepted."

I don't know what to say. I brought the book she dropped outside. I quietly put it down on the cart and move toward the doors. Willow's hushed cries echo in the large room. I ignore them and walk away as she's asked me to.

❄

Kane

Every day is just another day I have to put out another fire. The attack on Bernard is concerning as that means Jacob has been able to leave his cell. I have interrogated the guards in the dungeons, and the never-ending problem of them being swayed by bribes has not gone away. While the feeders are being treated more humanely, Jacob has been helping himself to the prisoners of war. Some have died, and their bodies have been disposed of.

I cannot sleep, so I decide to visit the current bane of my existence. Jacob sits on a thin cot in the corner of his cell, a far cry from the luxurious bedrooms he's used to. His leg has healed after Dr. Martin reset his femur in the right place. He is wearing an old gray shirt and pants that look like they've seen better days, and he smirks at me as I enter his cell.

"Your Majesty." He gives me a mocking bow from where he's seated on the bed, but he doesn't get up. He is chained to the wall, after all. "It's been far too long since you've graced me with your presence."

I don't dignify that with a response. I grab the chair nearby and take a seat. I'm in no mood for games tonight. I want the truth from Jacob even if I have to beat it out of him.

"Who bribed the guards?" I ask. "You don't have any money on you, and guards don't bother with promises of riches if they can't have their gold immediately."

He shrugs, still smirking. "Who says anyone bribed the guards?"

"Jacob, I could break your leg again and have Dr. Martin reset it. I could break both of your legs or your arms. As long as I have a doctor heal you afterward, I'm not in breach of the contract I made with your father," I tell him. "So I will ask you again. Who bribed the guards?"

"I did," he replies, unfazed with my threats. "I gave them my gold cufflinks and a watch. It's vintage. It's worth a lot."

"You didn't have anything on you when you were dropped in here."

"I hid everything up my ass. No one checked before leaving me here to suffer by my lonesome. Can you really blame me for trying to better my circumstances? A man does have to eat, Your Majesty."

I pull out the aforementioned cufflinks from my pocket. They're gold with the letter J written in diamonds. I have seen Jacob wear these before. The last time I saw them was the dinner before he and Opal attacked Emory in the library.

"The guards told me the same thing when I asked them what they were bribed with. It was almost word for word, actually." I just needed him to confirm it. It's a crime to bribe the guards in my kingdom. For both parties.

Jacob smiles wider, and it looks like he's baring his teeth. "I guess that means I'm telling the truth."

"Maybe you are."

I stare at him, waiting to see if he will break under my gaze. He fidgets slightly but keeps quiet. Eventually, I rise from the chair and walk away.

"Good night, Prince Jacob."

"Good night, Your Majesty."

When Jacob was imprisoned, I had his room ransacked. A maid had found the watch and cufflinks in his drawer which meant someone had taken them from his room and used the items to bribe the guards. I only had one suspect. A rat always sniffing for cheese is always close behind.

THE VIPER PIT

Lex

I had expected the court of Scarlett Thunder to be an unpleasant place to be trapped in, but I hadn't counted on *boredom*. For all the whispers behind my back and the fake smiles, the courtiers do not have the gall to directly harm me. As often as King Peter likes to throw threats in my direction, he has kept his part of the bargain with my brother. I get to skulk through the dark hallways of his castle and hide away in a comfortable suite instead of locked up in the dungeons with the other prisoners.

Opal vacillates between antagonizing me and pretending I don't exist. Her morning sickness still makes it hard for her to do anything but be miserable in her room. I try to visit her to make sure she's not dead, but she refuses to let me in. When she does decide to talk to me, it's only to shout insults in my direction before shutting the door to my face.

King Peter has forbidden me from leaving the castle to take walks on the grounds, citing that he doesn't want to give me the chance to run back home if the opportunity arises. As I feel cabin fever trying to settle into my bones, I find myself looking out windows and wanting to jump to my freedom several times a day, so maybe he's right about the escape attempts. The gloominess of Castle Blackmoor makes me feel like the literary wife trapped in the attic due to madness.

When I'm not bored, I'm lonely. It's hard to be trapped in a place you don't want to be in without an ally in sight. I can't even find someone I can converse with without being treated like the unwanted stepchild. Even the castle servants avoid speaking to me or even making eye contact.

During meal times, which I have to take with the rest of the court in the dining hall, I sit at the other end of the table from where King Peter is. I'm a pariah. If I'm not being mocked, I'm being ignored. Remembering how I had treated others similarly in the past makes shame settle uncomfortably in my belly.

King Peter is in a terrible mood this morning. Everyone stands as he enters the dining hall, almost holding our breath in anticipation. He stops when he sees me and barks, "Everyone but Lex, get out!"

The courtiers scurry away like panicked mice running from a vicious cat. I stand still, knowing I can't escape. King Peter looks murderous, and dread creeps up my spine. Whatever has made him angry, I am his chosen target for dealing with it.

When the last of the courtiers leave, the doors to the dining hall are closed by the footmen, leaving me alone with King Peter. He starts pacing like a tiger prowling the perimeters of its cage. If I had been in any other kingdom, with any other monarch, I would have said something witty. I would have tried to make him laugh, but King Peter is a notorious stick in the mud.

He stops and turns back to me, his red eyes gleaming with fury. "Did you know that your brother got that werewolf slut of his pregnant?"

The question makes me freeze. I truly had no idea that everyone else in the castle knew about Kane and Emory having a child together before King Peter. It was his own ambassador who came back with the news after all.

For whatever reason, he is outraged about this at the moment, so I decide to do what I do best and cover my own ass.

"I am shocked to hear that, Your Majesty," I say. "There had been no announcement when I was in Crimson Peak."

King Peter's eyes narrow suspiciously. "Why wouldn't Kane tell his own brother that he was having a child?"

"I would not dare question my brother's decisions."

"Is it because he doesn't trust you?" He begins circling me like a vulture waiting on its prey to die. "If he can't trust his own blood, then what use are you to me? If he values you so little, then there's no use in me keeping you alive."

I swallow as my heart is beating faster in my chest. I can't show King Peter any fear. He will smell it on me and see it as a weakness. Perhaps I've taken the wrong path by pretending not to know. I try to backtrack.

"I can assure you that my brother may have just been cautious before making a big announcement." I try to appease him with my most charming smile. "As we're all aware, pregnancies can be dangerous amongst our kind. I'm sure my brother was only waiting to make sure the pregnancy is viable."

"*Our kind?*" King Peter scoffs. "That thing inside of that werewolf bitch will only be half-vampire. The other half is a *wolf*. I never thought I'd see the day when such an atrocity occurs. Ancient bloodlines sullied in such a manner. Your ancestors are rolling in their graves."

I bite my tongue to keep myself from saying something foolish. "Knowing him, I can say my brother will love the child regardless of their parentage."

"He's been taking great pains to hide the existence of this child. He seems to care for it more than the child my daughter is carrying, a child of pure vampire ancestry."

My child, the petulant part of me wants to point out, but I ignore it.

"Kane has a fondness for children. That's why he spared the child who was offered to him and took Emory instead."

King Peter moves closer to me, menacingly looking down his nose at me. "I grew weary of your brother's constant disrespect. And are you still clinging to that fabrication of you being the father of Opal's child?"

"There is no fabrication–"

"Spare me," he hisses. "You expect me to believe my daughter who I raised to be a queen would sully herself with *you*, a second son who will never inherit anything?"

It astounds me how he denies the thought that Opal would be anything but pure as the driven snow. I had sex with Opal multiple times with other people. I had heard of her escapades in this very court from her own retelling. And I would bet my left testicle she has been sleeping around again.

"Perhaps she took pity on me?" I tell him, glibly. "Opal welcomed me with open arms and made me feel like I could be more than just the spare."

"My daughter would never lower herself to anyone less than what she deserves. She would rather die."

"If you say so, my Lord." King Peter will not listen. He refuses to see anything beyond his view of reality.

He is right in one aspect–that Opal will never settle for less than what she thinks she deserves. She is still dead set on marrying Kane and becoming Queen of Crimson Peak. She may have gotten pregnant on purpose in a bid to ensure the future she wants for herself, I had just been a means to an end.

"I want your brother to end this farce. He needs to marry my daughter and do right by her," King Peter demands. "I want that wolf whore and her offspring gone. He can drown the bitch and her pup for all I care. I will not stand for this."

Kane will never do it. Not only because he despises Opal but because he loves Emory, and I have seen how quickly she had become his world. I have a feeling not even a true war between our kingdom and Scarlett Thunder can change his mind.

"You must understand, Your Majesty, that my brother will never abandon his child–"

"He won't have a choice. I can't see him being able to keep his alliances with the other vampire kingdoms once they hear about this abomination Kane has fathered."

"There's no need to act so brashly–"

"I have been more than accommodating, but Kane has forced my hand."

King Peter walks over to the dining table and takes a seat. A servant comes over quickly and pours a glass of blood for the king. King Peter swallows a mouthful of the red substance, his pale throat bobbing. My mouth feels dry, but I don't move.

"If you are lucky, Lex. You may come out of this with your head attached. Your brother just needs to make the right choice."

He dismisses me after that, and I leave the dining hall quickly. I need to talk to my brother.

Kane

Correspondence with Lex is tense. We know that any letter or call will be monitored for information. We must be careful with our words. Too much is at stake to be reckless.

Lex calls me unexpectedly. He sounds more frazzled than I can remember him ever being.

"How is the weather in Scarlett Thunder?" I ask, casually. "Fair weather or cloudier than usual?"

"Cloudy as fuck," he answers. "I've heard weather reports about an unexpected… development. It could birth a real thunderstorm."

It takes me a moment to figure out what he's trying to say. This is my confirmation that Lord Alistair has definitely told King Peter about Emory's pregnancy.

"And what is the consensus toward the stormy weather?"

"Terrible," Lex replies. "The king hates the change. He's complaining to other people about it."

I pause before asking, "He's complaining to his friends?"

"He's complaining to anyone that will listen."

My allies will be getting this information soon. I have to get on top of this before King Peter manages to sway them over to his side.

"I should check on the weather reports here. Make sure we can deal with any upcoming storms."

"That would be for the best. I can't see any of this going smoothly."

"Thank you for informing me. I hope you're able to handle yourself through the harsh climate."

"I'm surprisingly adaptable to this environment. I didn't know I had it in me."

"I'm not surprised."

He sounds incredulous as he asks, "You're not?"

"No. I had hopes you would realize your own resilience without me having to spell it out for you."

"I might have learned about it sooner if you'd told me."

"Would you have listened?"

He concedes, "No." After a pause, he asks, "How is the weather over there right now?"

"It's fine as of right now," I tell him. That's true, though it sounds like things are about to get stormy here.

"And how are you liking the new flowers? Are they… permanent?"

I know he's asking me about Emory's pregnancy. "It's looking like they will be. I'm excited, honestly. They're beautiful."

He snorts. "Of course you are. You were born loving flowers."

"The same way I was born to be a king?"

"Yes," he says. "I have to live in the shadow of you being the world's best… gardener."

That makes me laugh. "You might be a good gardener too, Lex."

"I doubt it," he grumbles. "There are only weeds and dandelions to be found over here."

"You need to stop underestimating yourself."

"Why would I? When I can be surprised when I actually do well?"

"For the sake of your self-confidence."

"I…." He sighs. "I appreciate the advice, but I have a weather report to look at."

"What kind of report?"

"The developmental kind. I can't miss it."

"Tell me how it goes."

"I will, and you tell me how it goes for you too."

"I will. I promise."

The call ends, and I place the phone on the receiver. I sit back in my chair. It's a surreal thought to take in. My brother and I are going to be fathers. I never thought this would happen, especially around the same time.

I had thought for a while that Lex would die alone. The alternative is still complicated. If we were any other men in this world, we would both be celebrating without a care. Instead, I have to share news of my unborn child through the guise of talking about gardening.

My life couldn't be any more absurd.

OLD AND NEW

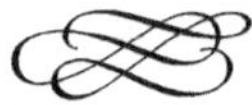

Lex

Opal is having her first ultrasound today. She initially refuses to let me come with her to the appointment. I manage to sway her into letting me be there since she has no one else to accompany her. Her brother is in the dungeon of Castle Graystone, and her father is too busy to give her his time for this.

"You're not the *real* father," she insists. "I'm only being gracious by letting you be here."

"Of course," I agree to whatever she wants to avoid any conflict. "I'm here as a supporting 'uncle' to your child."

Her blue eyes narrow in annoyance. "You *are* the uncle."

I blink innocently like a baby deer. "Of course, I am."

She would probably have cursed me out if the doctor hadn't started with the ultrasound then. He spreads a clear gel on Opal's stomach, moving the transducer probe over her skin gently. The image on the monitor looks like a grainy blob. I can barely make out any shape.

"And that's the head," Dr. Smythe says, pointing to the gray mass of something. "Would you like to know the sex?"

"Yes," Opal snaps. "Of course I want to know. Isn't it too early?"

"No, not at all. It's a boy," he replies. "That's his penis right there."

I squint and can't see it. "Are you sure?"

"I'm sure, my Lord. Would you like to hear the heartbeat?"

Opal rolls her eyes. "Don't pay attention to him. He doesn't matter. Ask me the questions."

Dr. Smythe only nods genially and asks, "Would you like to hear the heartbeat, Your Highness?"

"Just get on with it."

The sound of the heartbeat is quiet but steady. A noise that makes my eyes water from emotion. The grainy video makes it hard to see anything but the heartbeat makes everything feel real. There's a baby in there–*my baby*.

Opal looks annoyed and smacks my arm. "Don't fucking cry. You don't get to be emotional about this."

I sniff and turn away from her to wipe my eyes. The rest of the appointment goes smoothly. I take Opal back to her room, and she finds a seat on the bed, her legs crossed underneath her. I keep glancing at her stomach underneath her heavy gown. I can't even see the bulge now.

"Stop looking at me like that," she demands. "Just because I let you come to the appointment, it doesn't mean you get to act like this."

"I can't help it," I explain. "The ultrasound just put things into perspective for me."

"What perspective?" She glares at me. "You're delusional. You're never going to be this baby's father. Over my dead body."

This is supposed to be a nice moment. Other people probably get to be emotional and enjoy all this baby stuff. Unfortunately for me, the mother of my unborn child is a raging bitch. Opal can't let one good thing be genuinely enjoyed for once.

"No matter what, Opal, I'm going to make sure that child isn't raised by you," I tell her. "No kid deserves a mother like you."

I know that I'm right. Opal doesn't have the capacity to love anyone but herself. She will be a cold, monstrous mother. She will destroy this child, and he will have no chance.

Opal's eyes flash with hatred. "At least I'm going to be a better mother than that werewolf bitch. Whatever horror is coming out of her should be killed at birth."

I wince. "Don't say that."

The princess snorts. "Everyone thinks it, Lex, even you. We all know that we're better off with that baby never being born."

"Shut up."

I hate this woman. I hate her perfect face and her ugly personality. Velvet wrapped poison. She destroys everything she touches.

"Or what, Lex?" she dares, cocking her head in invitation. "What are you going to do to shut me up? Are you going to kill me?"

I can't hurt her, especially with the baby growing inside of her. Whether we like it or not, we will forever be entwined through this one thing. As soon as I heard that baby's heartbeat, I was truly trapped in every way.

"That's what I thought." Opal smiles like she's won. "Now get the fuck out of my room."

EMORY

Kane has to leave Crimson Peak to meet up with his allies. Unfortunately, but not surprising, King Peter has found out about my pregnancy and has been threatening to tell the other vampire kingdoms about it. Kane tells me not to worry and that he is going to get ahead of this before things can become a problem for us. One of Crimson Peak's oldest allies, Queen Olga of Sardania, insists the parley be in her kingdom, so Kane is going to be gone for a few days.

He has to leave at sundown so the morning is spent packing up whatever he'll need for the trip. He will be bringing a few of his men, with Rainer left in charge of the castle in his absence. The pregnancy makes it so that all I can feel is exhaustion even when I hardly do anything, so I sit on Kane's bed and watch him write letters while his maids pack. He is constantly writing letters and taking phone calls. Ruling a kingdom is a very taxing job, especially when the kingdom is at war.

"What's Sardonia like?" I ask, curious.

"It's in the highlands, surrounded by mountains and cliffs," he answers, not looking up from the letter he's writing. "It's freezing up there. It snows most of the year."

"And what's the queen like?"

"Queen Olga has been ruling since my grandfather's time. She's the longest ruling monarch in all of the vampire kingdoms. She's very wise, and her alliance with us has been helpful more than once."

"What do you *personally* think of her?"

He looks up, his expression cautious. "What have you heard?"

I shrug, smiling. "Rainer may have mentioned she gets a little handsy with you."

He puts down his pen and runs a hand through his dark hair. If he could blush, his pale face might have gone red. "People have said that she had a crush on my grandfather back in the day…"

"And?"

"I resemble my grandfather a lot."

"So now she's crushing on you?" He looks away, all but verbally confirming my thoughts, and that makes me laugh. "How old is she? She has to be ancient."

"Oldest living monarch," he points out. "She's over two centuries old, I think. She won't answer directly if you ask her about her age."

"You *never* ask a woman about her age," I tell him, remembering my mother teaching me that.

"Regardless, Queen Olga is an important ally, and I need her support now more than ever. She's well-respected by the other vampire kingdoms. Her word holds a lot of sway."

I sit up straighter, realizing how serious he's being. "If she doesn't support you over our baby, that's going to be bad, isn't it?"

His fingers drum a quick beat on his desk, conveying his inner nervousness. I'm getting good at reading all his tells. Kane is used to hiding his emotions, any vulnerability, behind a cool mask. I have to pay attention to get a glimpse of his true feelings.

"Queen Olga isn't irrational. As long as I explain things to her, I'm sure I can keep the alliance with her intact."

"If that fails, you can show her a little leg." He crumples up a piece of paper and throws it at me. It bounces harmlessly off my forehead. I giggle and tell him, "I'm joking!"

"I clearly can't take you with me. You might offend one of the royals with your witty remarks," he admonishes with no real heat.

"You can't take me anywhere."

He gets up from his chair and walks over to the bed, taking a seat on the foot of the bed so we are at eye level. "I am going to miss you anyway. It'll only be a few days, but I've gotten used to being able to see you every day."

I grab his hand and squeeze it, his touch mooring me like an anchor in the ocean. "I'm going to miss you too."

He leans down and kisses me softly, his tongue lingering in my mouth long enough to make excitement begin to pool between my legs. When he pulls away, I let out a sigh. "While I'm gone, stay close to my mother. She'll keep the nobles in check. And please have Rainer with you if you have to go outside."

"I'm going to be fine," I reassure him. "We are going to be fine."

He cups my face in his hands, his blue eyes staring intently as if he's trying to memorize my face. "I love you."

"I love you too." Then I tease him, "Please don't leave me for Queen Olga."

His dark eyebrows furrow. "She's old enough to be my grand-mother, even my great-grandmother. I have no interest in her. I never have."

"That doesn't mean she isn't crushing on you. And can you really blame her?" I run a hand down his magnificent chest. "You've got this insanely attractive kingly thing going on. Hardly anyone can resist that."

He rolls his eyes. "You're ridiculous. I don't want anyone else but you."

I'm not ashamed to admit that I melt like ice cream in the summer. He kisses me again and reminds me just how much he wants me.

His hand wanders up my side, cupping my breast. I lean into him, moaning as our tongues tangle. The ache between my legs continues to grow as his hands wander across my body. The maids know well enough to leave the room, but a few moments later, just when I'm about to tear his shirt from his body, there's a sharp knock at the door.

Kane pulls away. "Damn. I have to go."

I take a deep breath and nod. "I understand."

Kane

I've never had trouble leaving the castle for diplomatic trips. I haven't delegated the task to other people in the past aside from Rainer as I couldn't trust anyone else to have my kingdom's best interest at heart. Most monarchs only want to parley with an equal and not a subordinate, so compromising is easier in person rather than through a messenger. This way has less chances of misunderstanding each other's intentions.

However, leaving Emory behind for a few days brings a yearning ache that makes me want to stay and cancel my trip. Emory is looking at me with those wanton eyes, and it's physically painful to have to leave her in my bed. I kiss her forehead, her red eyebrows furrowing as I pull away from her touch. Her arms reach across the bed sheets as I get to my feet.

I take one last look at her face from my position by the door. I'm reminded that she's only twenty. She's young, but not naïve, having gone through so much these past few months. She has grown into a woman, an Alpha. People choose to follow her not out of fear but because they believe in her.

I stare at her pretty face and wonder how she can't see how extraordinary she is before I quietly leave the room.

The trip to Sardonia is long and arduous. It takes us days to travel up the mountains. We have to abandon our cars at a certain point where the easiest way to travel is on-foot. The higher we go, the colder and thinner the air becomes. We leave deep boot prints in the snow-covered paths.

The ambassador to Sardonia greets us when we reach the top of the mountain. He guides us inside to the city and to the castle carved into the mountain. Castle Whitehall is smaller compared to other castles from other kingdoms, but it is the oldest. Legend has it that the first Queen of Sardonia, Anastasiya, started working on the castle after the death of her husband. It took centuries before she finished, her descendants adding to the castle over time.

We enter Castle Whitehall and are led to the throne room. Queen Olga has her back to us as she's speaking with one of her men. The ambassador announces my name, "Presenting, King Kane of Crimson Peak."

"Queen Olga," I greet her. "You look well."

Vampires age exceedingly slowly, so while Olga isn't in the first flushes of youth, she is still an attractive woman with white-blonde hair the color of the now falling outside the window. Lines on her face around her forehead and mouth show her age only slightly. Her eyes are a piercing blue that remind me of frozen water.

"King Kane." She smiles. "It's been far too long."

ALLIANCES BE DAMNED

Kane

Queen Olga leads us to the adjoining throne room. At a long table sits the majority of our allies, old and new. Half of them have been ruling before I was even born, and the other half came into power with me around the same time. There are a few new faces, no doubt hoping to raise their cache through associating with more experienced monarchs.

I nod to several of the people at the table as I take my seat at one end. Queen Olga sits at the head of the table comfortable being in charge of this meeting. There is not much time for small talk. We launch immediately into discussing the war with Scarlett Thunder, the expense and potential casualties.

"I don't see why I have to help fund another war you're embroiled yourself in, Kane," King Matthias remarks. "That pointless battle of wills with the wolves didn't do you any good. It was a waste of time and resources."

King Matthias was a peer of my father's. He still tends to see me as the young king I used to be, despite my age. His kingdom is smaller with fewer resources than the others. I can understand his hesitance.

"I would prefer to avoid more bloodshed," I say. "If King Peter would agree to stand down, we can avoid having to lose more warriors and assets."

"Peter will not back down." King Cyrus speaks up. "He's stubborn as a mule. You'd have an easier time with an actual mule."

"As long as I have known Peter, he's never been good at compromising," Queen Olga agrees. "You will need to offer him something he can't refuse."

"I heard he wants you to marry his daughter and claim her unborn child as yours," King Matthias says, his blue eyes piercing into me. "I have also heard you've refused his demand and refuse to acknowledge the babe."

"Princess Opal's child is not mine," I explain. "As much as she claims that I fathered her baby, it wasn't me. I've never touched her."

"Why does it matter who's the father? You have an easy solution to avoid war. Marry the chit and play happy family with her. It's not difficult."

Telling them about Lex being the father of Opal's baby will not help me. It will only serve to show how I have no control over the situation. It's my word against King Peter's, and he truly wants to believe that I'm the father of his unborn grandchild.

"I heard you got another woman pregnant," Queen Desdemona joins the conversation. She's a younger queen, having come into power a few decades ago. "Is it true you impregnated a feeder? A wolf shifter no less?"

I stiffen and watch as the royals all whisper amongst themselves, a cacophony of noise that only ends when Queen Olga slams her goblet onto the table like a gavel, a bit of blood sloshing over the side. Her familiar blue eyes look into mine, and I can't make out what she's thinking.

"If you would answer the question, Kane," she says. "Is it true about the feeder?"

"She was never truly a feeder, more like a political prisoner."

"But she is still a wolf shifter?" Desdemona asks.

I can't lie, and I don't want to. I'm not ashamed of Emory, but I know the people at this table. Most of them were raised to distrust wolf shifters and only see them as a source of blood. Even the most tolerant of them won't consider a shifter as an equal.

"Yes," I answer. "She is the new Alpha of the Moonraker pack."

King Matthias's blue eyes are wide in disbelief. "Isn't that the same pack you've been at war with for the past decade?"

"I was warring with the previous Alpha, Bernard Moonraker. He is no longer in charge of the pack."

"And his replacement is related to him?" Matthias questions.

"Emory is his eldest daughter."

Whispers erupt amongst the royals again. I feel out of control, unable to find my footing in this landslide of accusations. None of them will understand about Emory as they hadn't been there to witness everything that had happened between us. From their perspective, I had shacked up with my former enemy's daughter and gotten her pregnant.

"How are we supposed to believe you when you say you never touched Princess Opal when you clearly can't keep your hands off any whore that comes your way–"

I move before I even think about it, getting up from my seat and rushing toward King Matthias to grab him by the neck and slam him against the wall. "Don't you dare call her that!"

King Cyrus grabs me by the shoulders and pulls me away. "Kane, don't."

I struggle in his grasp and another royal, King Basil, helps him keep me from lunging at King Matthias again. Anger makes my blood feel heated like it's boiling under my skin. I want to rip King Matthias's head from his neck.

"If you speak about Emory like that again, I'll kill you myself," I promise him. "Alliances be damned. You don't get to talk about the woman I love like that."

King Matthias rubs his neck, his face stony. "Alliances be damned then, Kane. You will not have my support from here on."

He walks away from the room, leaving without looking back. King Cyrus still hasn't released me, and he whispers in my ear,

"Calm yourself before you burn every bridge in this room. Don't be a fool."

I look at my uncle's familiar face, and I will myself to calm down. He has known me since I was born. If there is anyone in this room that has my back, it's him. I glance past him at the royals seated at the long table, their pale eyes of red and blue staring at me curiously. Some of them are looking at me in accusation.

"I apologize for my behavior," I say more to Queen Olga than anyone else. "It's been a tense time."

She nods and gestures to my seat. "I'm sure no offense is taken, Kane. Please tell us more about this Emory."

I take my seat again, trying to hide my discomfort. "I would prefer not to talk about her. I want to keep my relationship and my unborn child as my own business. My personal life has no bearing on the war."

Queen Desdemona raises a blonde eyebrow at me. "From what we've seen, Kane, this war started because of your personal life. If we as your allies are to continue supporting you, we need to know what we're getting into."

"We have our own people at stake," King Basil points out. "As much as I consider you a friend, Kane, I have to put my kingdom first, especially if this is going to be another senseless war."

King Cyrus nods. "They are right, nephew. Blood and gold runs dry for everyone eventually. And with no allies, this could mark the end of your rule."

"And that is why I ask you again to tell me more about this woman you are fighting a war over," Queen Olga tells me. "She must be extraordinary to be worth all the trouble."

EMORY

I wake up in the middle of the night. The room is shrouded in darkness, and it takes my eyes a moment to adjust. There's someone in the room. I sit upright and turn on the lamp on the bedside table to see who it is.

I let out a sigh of relief when I see it's Kane. "You scared me."

He walks over from where he's standing by the doorway and sits at the foot of the bed. "I'm sorry. I didn't mean to frighten you."

"You're back already?" I ask. "I thought you were going to be in Sardonia for the rest of the week."

"Plans changed."

The vagueness of his reply spurns me to ask, "Did something happen with the meeting?"

He takes my hand in his. "There's nothing you need to worry about. Everything is fine."

"And yet, you're back early so either everything went really well, or it all went really bad with the royals."

"I've been doing this for a long time. Things never go really well for me, but I succeed regardless of whatever happens." He brings my hand up to his mouth and kisses my knuckles. "You know what Dr. Martin said about stress. Please don't worry yourself over this."

I'm always tired or unwell. Some days, I can barely do anything but lie in bed. I feel like an invalid as my body betrays me. I'm not used to feeling so weak, and it frustrates me. "I keep wondering why I don't have that pregnancy glow they talk about," I tell him. "I feel like a wilting plant. I look like it too."

"You're beautiful."

"You need to get your eyes checked. I haven't showered recently. I haven't even brushed my hair."

He smiles and gently runs his hand through my messy red locks. "You're beautiful to me, always. Even when you don't feel like you are."

I swat his hand away and lie back down in bed. "It's unfair for you to say that. You look perfect all the time."

I glare at his handsome face. He always looks good whether he has just woken up or is sweaty from sparring with Rainer. He is even more attractive when he's in disarray, less god-like and touchable. If there is ever an example that the world is an unfair place, Kane's good looks are proof.

He looks amused as he lies down beside me, wrapping his arms around me. "I'm sorry?"

"Don't you dare apologize for being hot. That doesn't help anything."

He laughs, his warm breaths tickling my skin. "I can't help it."

"Whoever made vampires really made sure you could entice victims by being so pretty. It's ridiculous."

"We have to eat somehow."

I roll my eyes as he laughs again. I watch the mirth on his face and let myself bask in the relief of having him back with me. He was gone for less than two days, but I missed him like a widow whose husband had been lost at sea. Even Lola commented that I was moping around the castle.

"I missed you," I confess. "Never leave me again."

He smiles and kisses the top of my head. "I missed you too. My trip might've been better if you were with me."

"Are you allowed to take me with you next time?"

"Allowed?" he repeats. "I'm a king. No one 'allows' me anything. I can do as I please."

I roll my eyes and slap his shoulder. "You know what I mean."

"I'll take you with me next time," he promises. "My Uncle Cyrus wants to meet you. You'd like Cerise Port. It's a coastal town and very picturesque."

"Queen Agatha told me about her birth kingdom. Did you spend a lot of time there when you were younger?"

"My mother would take Lex and me to visit, especially in the summers. It's a smaller kingdom, and they're less formal there. We could be amongst the common folk without anyone batting an eye."

"You just got to be like everyone else," I tease him.

"It was nice. When we got older, I would send Lex there when he was being a bother here in court. Uncle Cyrus was good at keeping him out of trouble. Lex actually listened to him."

The reminder of Lex makes me wonder how Kane's brother is

doing at Scarlett Thunder. Kane has told me that Lex is keeping his head down, and I hope he is safe.

"You said your uncle wants to meet me," I say. "Does he know about the pregnancy?"

"He knows, and he's supportive," Kane replies. "We should go visit him soon. He's always been one of my most loyal allies."

I smile. "I can't wait to meet him."

MOTHERS AND DAUGHTERS

Emory

I am so sick of bed rest. I'm bored out of my mind, and I miss the outdoors. As I'm about to enter my second trimester, I feel worse by the day. Helga and Nellie hover and ply me with calming teas. They fluff the mountain of pillows I lie on and cater to every food craving I have no matter how absurd.

Lola has taken to following Nellie around the castle when she's not spending time with Willow in the library. She's made herself a favorite of the castle staff, who sneak her candy and snacks. She's been paying attention to the castle gossip as the staff is even worse than the nobles, and they know far more juicy information. Lola tells me about the gossip she's overheard in the afternoons as we have lunch at the small dining table in my suite.

Lunch today is light with a mixed fruit salad of strawberries, grapes, pineapple, and kiwi garnished with mint leaves and honey. There is a cheese platter with a selection of brie, camembert, aged cheddar, and gouda accompanied by prosciutto on baguette slices. For dessert, we have fruit tarts, a delicate pastry crust filled with cream and topped with fresh berries. We have a pitcher of fresh lemonade to drink.

"I heard that Thomas is planning to propose to Helga," Lola says as she takes a bite of the prosciutto and cheddar sandwich she's made. "He got a ring and everything."

"Don't talk while you're chewing," I tell her. "And who's Thomas again?"

Lola chews and swallows the large bite before answering, "He's one of King Kane's footmen. He's the tall one that looks like a bird."

"What?"

"He has a sharp nose. It looks like a beak."

I have no recollection of who she's talking about. "I hope you haven't said that to his face."

"I haven't," Lola counters. "Nellie says it's rude to point out how people look."

"She's right."

Lola takes a sip of lemonade then asks, "Are you going to get married too?"

That makes me pause. "Why do you ask?"

"Isn't that what people do? They get married when they like each other?"

"Liking each other is a start," I answer. "But there are other factors, like if you're compatible."

"Compatible how?"

"Lifestyle, values, interests—you could have all of those things in common and still have reasons not to marry."

I think of Darius and how we had everything in common growing up. I thought he would be my mate. The two of us together made sense on paper, but there was always something missing. This undefinable thing I didn't know I was searching for until I met Kane.

"Why not?" Lola asks. "How can you be compatible in all of those things and still not 'click'?"

"I don't know. If it's with the right person, it just works. You don't have to force it."

Lola looks thoughtful. Her gray eyes stare into her fruit salad as she mulls things over. She looks up and asks, "Is that what it's like with you and King Kane? Easy?"

"Nothing's ever easy, especially relationships. You have to work to keep things going."

"So it's hard work?"

"It is. It takes a lot of work."

Lola's blonde eyebrows furrow in confusion. "Then why do you want to be with him or in any relationship?"

I don't think I'm explaining things right. As Lola is getting older, she's asking more questions, and they're questions that are getting more difficult to answer. I don't want to lie to her, or not tell her anything at all, but I'm also aware of just how young she is. There are certain things I don't think she has the capacity to understand yet.

"It's nice to have somebody there, a person you can lean on so you're not so alone."

"Were you lonely before?"

"No, but things were different before," I explain. "I'm different."

"You're the Alpha, and you're pregnant."

I nod and reach across the table for her hand. "All of it can be really scary, so just having someone else there to go through it with me is a relief."

"You have me."

I smile. "Yes, but your job is to be a kid. That's all you have to do. I take care of you."

"King Kane takes care of you?"

"He does," I reply. "He's the king. He is supposed to take care of everyone."

I know that Lola still feels wary of Kane. I can't blame her, and I expect it's going to take time for her to be comfortable around him. I don't want to rush her. I want her to see that Kane is a good man without me forcing the idea on her.

"Does he love you?" she asks.

"He does. And I love him too."

"And you're having a baby together." She pulls away from my touch to continue eating. "Have you picked a name for the baby?"

"Not yet. Kane's been busy. Being a king takes up a lot of his time."

She bites into a strawberry. "The baby needs a name."

"I'll talk it over with Kane." Curiously, I ask, "Do you have any ideas for names?"

"Me?"

"You're going be the baby's aunt. Do you have suggestions?"

"Is it a boy or a girl?"

"We don't know yet. We'll find out at the next appointment with Dr. Martin."

"I hope it's a girl."

"Why?"

"Because boys are yucky." She makes a face. "Colt was always messy, and sometimes he smelled bad."

I stifle a laugh. "Do you have any girl names in mind?"

"I'll think about it." There's a pause before she asks, "Who picked my name?"

The question catches me off-guard. I try to remember when I first held Lola in my arms. I was not that much older than she is currently. I had been told her name and given no explanation for the name choice. I don't even know if Bernard had been the one to pick it.

"I'm not sure. It might have been your mother."

Lola has asked about her birth mother over the years, curious about the woman that gave her life but she never got to meet. I had been honest that Lola's mother had died shortly after she was born and no one ever wanted to speak about her.

"Who gave you your name?" Lola asks.

"Our father picked it, actually. It was his mother's name, our grandmother. She died before you were born."

"Oh."

She doesn't look upset, but she's become quiet. I wish I knew what to say to make her feel better, but I struggle with the words. "What are you thinking, Lo?"

"I wonder what my mom was like. Do you think I was like her?"

"Maybe. I know she had blonde hair like you."

Lola reaches up to touch her hair, running her fingers through it absentmindedly. "Do you think she would have loved me?"

"Lo, of course she would."

"Dad didn't really like me, so…"

"Your mother loved you before you were even born. And I loved you instantly when I held you in my arms. Lots of people love you, Lo."

Her eyes get glassy. She reaches for a napkin and wipes the tears away. "I don't want to cry. Babies cry. I'm not a baby."

"Don't grow up too fast," I tell her, trying to hold back my own tears. "Just be a kid as long as you can."

She blows her nose into the napkin. "I don't want to grow up yet. Everyone says it's not fun."

"There are more responsibilities to be sure," I agree. To cheer her up, I add, "You can pick the middle name for the baby, something that could work for a boy or a girl."

Her gray eyes light up in excitement, and she smiles. "Really?"

I smile back. "Absolutely, Lo. I'm sure you'll find the perfect name."

Kane

I haven't told Emory about what happened at Sardonia with the other vampire royals. I don't want her to worry, especially after Dr. Martin advised against stress during her pregnancy. There isn't anything Emory can do to help with the situation. She would blame herself for the opinions of people she doesn't even know.

Queen Olga wants to meet her. The old queen is fascinated with the woman that has managed to ensnare my heart. I've managed to hold off the vampire woman until after Emory gives birth as the trek up to her kingdom is a challenge for most people. I know I can't hold her off forever, but I will try as long as I can.

King Cyrus is a safer option. He's family, and Emory is going to be one of us if I have anything to say about it. She'll enjoy Cerise Port and what the smaller kingdom has to offer. My mother might want to come with us, and it will be nice to be away from court for matters outside of business.

I long for an escape outside the familiar walls of Castle Graystone.

My allies are split, half of them not wanting to support me after finding out that I'm having a child with a wolf shifter, and the other half are waiting out whether I can still be useful to them. They don't know the dire circumstances of my resources and how I lay awake wondering where I can find more blood and gold to fund this war. Queen Olga is right that I need allies more than ever, and I have come home with even less than what I started with.

All thoughts of war leave me when I enter Emory's room just as she's coming out of the ensuite bathroom. She looks a little green and more tired than I've ever seen her. Even after her father attacked her, she didn't look this exhausted. Concerned, I ask, "Are you all right?"

"Hey," she answers, weakly. She goes to take a seat on the bed. "It's just morning sickness. Dr. Martin says it's normal and should stop soon."

I walk over to the bed and sit beside her. "Is Dr. Martin sure this is normal? He hasn't treated that many shifter women."

"There aren't many shifter healers around here," she points out. "I'd have to get someone from my pack, and they're all still terrified to step foot in the castle."

I gently wipe the sweat from her brow. "Have you asked your mother? Were her pregnancies this difficult too?"

Emory's face crumples. "I don't know. She won't talk to me."

"What do you mean?" I question. "Why won't she talk to you?"

Emory sighs deeply. I can see the dark circles under her eyes. Her skin is sickly pale, showing the blue veins underneath.

"Colt says that my mother won't talk to me until I release Bernard from the dungeon, but I can't set him free because I'm afraid he'll just go off and cause trouble again. I can't trust him not to go back to his old ways."

"He'll try to start another war," I agree. "You've done nothing wrong."

"I know, but my mom is still loyal to Bernard even after everything he's done. And she's upset with me." Her voice cracks as she continues, "I really miss her. I have so many questions about all of this, and I wish she was here with me. I just want my mom."

I can't stand seeing her so upset. I pull her closer to me, and she cries into my chest. I stroke her hair and murmur reassurances into her ear. I'm reminded of how young she is. Strong, brave Emory who selflessly put her pack's well-being above her own is being punished by her own mother. It doesn't sit right with me.

"It will be all right," I tell her. "I will fix this."

"How? She won't even get on the phone with me."

"I will fix this," I repeat, determined. "She can't ignore me."

LOST AND FOUND

Lex

Something is happening at Castle Blackmoor. The servants are hard at work cleaning and decorating the entire place. Food is being brought in along with a new batch of feeders. The biggest significance is the large amounts of blood. I can tell when a party is being planned.

Opal has been feeling better this week, so she's ventured outside of her room. She's holding court amongst nobles during breakfast when I enter the dining hall. She's the only one that will answer a direct question from me, so my options to get answers are severely limited. Biting the bullet, I come over to her despite the disapproving looks from the nobles around us.

Opal scowls at me. "What do you want?"

"Is there going to be a party?" I ask, ignoring the sneers from the nobles. "What's the occasion?"

"Not that it's any of your business, but my father's having a masquerade ball. He's invited all the important families to come."

"A masquerade ball?" I repeat. "In the middle of a… disagreement between our kingdoms? This isn't really the best time for such things, is it?"

I have learned early on during my time in Scarlett Thunder that none of the people here think they are at war. Since there has been no actual bloodshed since the initial battle, even if the troops are on standby ready for more, it does look like a whole lot of posturing. A show of force is what they like to say their king is doing. The nobles in court wouldn't dare imply otherwise.

"Are you questioning my father's decisions?" Opal practically shrieks. "How dare you? He has done nothing but treat you with more courtesy than you deserve after your brother imprisoned his only son."

The nobles whisper to each other, and I look around feeling unmoored at knowing I have no allies in the room. No one will defend me or try to vouch for my innocence. I can feel the imaginary noose tightening around my throat. I'm always a step away from losing my head.

"You should be rotting in the dungeon like Jacob is in Crimson Peak," Opal continues. "An eye for an eye. My father is too merciful for the likes of you."

"Forgive me, Princess Opal," I try to appease her. "I would not dare cast doubts on the king's choices. For, he is wise and just. I was only curious about the upcoming party."

She scoffs. "It doesn't matter what you think. You're not going to be invited."

"Why not?"

'This ball is for friends of the kingdom. You are no such thing." Opal picks up her glass of blood and takes a sip. "My father doesn't even like you."

I can't help the wave of disappointment that comes over me. I have been bored as of late, and a party would be something to do. I've been to plenty over my long existence, and it's something I genuinely enjoy. Being excluded from anything always stings, and I've never liked the feeling.

I leave the dining hall and go back to my suite. I call Kane who picks up after a few rings.

"Hello, brother," he greets me. "How is the weather?"

"Terrible," I reply, leaning against the desk. "There's going to be a huge storm soon. It's coming from all over the place."

"A huge storm?"

"It's going to be a real show with all the rain and thunder that's happening very soon. Some people like that sort of thing and will gather around for miles to watch."

"I see," he says. "And will you be there to witness this?"

"Unfortunately not as I'll be stuck in my room and pretending it doesn't bother me to have to listen to the thunder through the walls."

"How bad do you think this storm will be? Is it to help with the upcoming drought?"

"Most likely. I don't know how much rain will fall."

"Is there a way you can sneak off and watch the storm?"

"It's an exclusive view that I am not privileged to witness."

"Perhaps if somebody took you with them as a plus one?"

I grimace. "I don't really have a friend like that over here."

"You've always been too charming for your own good," Kane tells me. "You could make a friend even in such a place with bad weather."

"If you're suggesting I'm a whore…"

"I would never say that."

"You're thinking it." The silence from Kane's end makes me roll my eyes. "I will see what I can do about making friends. It's not easy. I have to be careful with who I can trust."

"Blunt tools can have their uses. Bat your pretty eyelashes at them and see what happens."

I groan. "I miss the days when I was just useless in the castle, and you never cared about getting… weather reports from me."

"Those days are over." He sounds pleased with himself. "You're far too old to be hopeless and idle again."

"But I was so good at it."

Kane snorts. "I have to go. Be careful, brother."

"I will."

The call ends, and I rest my head on the desk. How have I managed to agree to spy for my brother? I never thought I had any skills that could actually be helpful to my kingdom. My one job for so long was to be the spare in case anything happened to my brother.

Now, I have to find a way to get into a masquerade ball nobody invited me to. I need to charm an idiot into taking me with them to the ball. The question is who. I bang my forehead on the desk and try to think.

Kane

It's been some time since I visited Moon Grove. The ancestral land of the Moonraker Pack is lush with trees and farmlands. My car drives by people tilling the fields and picking fresh fruit from trees. It's harvest season, and the land is bountiful.

Bernard tried to hide his deal with me, and he never invited me to come visit. The last time I set foot in Moon Grove was when my father was king. We came on a diplomatic visit to meet with Emory's grandfather, Colton. That was a long time ago, and I have seen the scars of war on this land. We drive past plenty of abandoned houses and graveyards.

I sent word of my trip ahead of time to Emory's young brother, Colt Moonraker. The young shifter is suspicious but can't say no to me. I promised to come unarmed and only with a handful of my men for protection. If they decide to attack me, I won't be going down without a fight, and I'll take a few of them with me.

The Moonraker ancestral home is a large four-story house. It's modest compared to Castle Graystone but nothing to scoff at. The town car stops, and one of my guards opens the car door for me. Colt and his mother, along with a few of their pack members, are waiting in front of the house.

"Colt, pleasure to see you again," to the young man.

Colt visibly swallows before nodding. "Welcome to Moon's Grove, King Kane."

I recognize some of the pack members. They were with Bernard when he attacked Emory. I ignore them and look directly to the former Luna of the Moonraker pack. Helena Moonraker stands tall, the only indication she's nervous is the slight tremble in her hands.

"I would like to speak with you privately," I tell her.

The shifters around us exchange worried looks, but no one protests. Colt leads us inside the house and what looks to be a study. I can smell his scent in the room and the faint lingering stench of Bernard. This must've been the former Alpha's office that Colt has taken over.

"I'll be nearby if you need me," he declares more for his mother's comfort than mine. "Please don't hesitate to call for me."

Helena gives him a reassuring smile. "I'm sure I'll be fine, son."

He hesitates before finally leaving us. The door shuts quietly behind him with a faint click.

Helena gestures toward the sofa in the room. "Would you like to take a seat? Do you prefer coffee or tea?"

"I would prefer to stand," I reply. "I'm going to cut to the chase if that's all right with you."

Helena stiffens, worry creasing her brow, and she nods. "What did you want to talk about?"

"I'm here on behalf of your daughter."

Her green eyes widen. "Is Emory all right?"

"She's pregnant."

"What?" Helena looks shocked. "With whose child?"

"Mine."

"That's not possible. Vampires and shifters can't have children."

"Nature has its exceptions. Emory and I are one of them. She's pregnant with your grandchild."

The shock has overcome her, and she takes a seat on the sofa. "Why didn't she tell me?"

"She tried. You won't speak to her."

"I… I had no idea." She covers her mouth. "Is she all right? Is she feeling well?"

"She's been having a difficult time with the pregnancy. Vampire pregnancies are risky, and I heard it's the same for shifters."

Helena nods. "There's a higher chance of miscarriages than for humans."

"That's why I'm here. Your daughter needs you. She's terrified of becoming a mother, and she just wants you there to support her," I declare. "You're punishing her for the mistakes your husband made. It was him that caused all of these problems when he went to war for no reason, and then tried to kill his own daughter for exposing the truth. He's imprisoned in the dungeon of my castle for all the damage he's caused."

The woman sighs. She looks smaller and frailer. "I know Bernard has made mistakes, but he is my mate. And I can't abandon him when everyone else has."

"You're going to abandon your daughter because of him? You're going to give up being able to know your own grandchild for him?"

She shakes her head. "You don't understand. I never had a choice in my mate. I've stood by him through so much. Even when he was unfaithful to me, through every humiliation and cruel word, I held on. For the sake of my children, my pack, I've done my duty."

"Your duty is fulfilled. Your pack has a new Alpha now. And your Alpha needs *you*."

Tears fall from Helena's green eyes. "Has she said that?"

"Yes," I confirm. "She wants her mom. Be her mom."

EMORY

Kane has been gone the whole day. He's not in any meetings in the castle. He left me a note saying he's off on business and should be back by dinner. Rainer has decided to keep Lola and I entertained by teaching us how to play poker.

I'm not sure if Lola is too young to learn how to play, but she's taken to it quickly. The card game passes the time, and by nightfall, Rainer leaves us in better spirits. Lola goes with Helga to clean up before dinner. I'm talking to Nellie about some castle gossip she's heard when Kane enters the room.

I smile. "Hey."

"Hi." He nods to Nellie who immediately leaves us alone. "I have a surprise for you."

"Is it a good surprise?"

He steps away from the doorway to show the person standing behind him. It's my mom. She smiles softly and says, "Hello, Emory."

I let out a cry like a child and run to her. I wrap my arms around her, and there's the familiar comforting scent of gardenias. She soothes me by running her hands down my back the same way she used to do when I was small. I can't help but sob in relief and joy because my mom is finally with me again.

"I'm sorry," she murmurs in my ear. "I'm so sorry."

"How?" I pull back. "I thought you were angry at me."

She wipes at my tears. "I am angry at your father. I'm sorry I took it out on you."

"It's okay." I laugh through my sobs. "I'm just happy you're here."

I look past her toward Kane. He did this. He brought me my mother because I needed her. I mouth to him, "Thank you."

This beautiful, wonderful man—what have I done to deserve him? He only smiles and steps out the door to give us privacy.

A FAUSTIAN BARGAIN

Kane

Emory has been in a better mood since I brought her mother to the castle. Helena has agreed to stay and support Emory through her pregnancy. Her experience as a midwife for wolf shifters makes her invaluable. The older woman is wary of the vampires in the castle, but she has been polite.

I usually find Helena with Emory in her room which gives me less alone time with Emory, but I don't mind it. I know that the mother and daughter need time to repair their relationship, so I give them space. I miss Emory. I've gotten used to having her sleep beside me, but I don't want to be selfish. Helena has to go home eventually, and I'll have Emory to myself again someday.

I am writing letters at my office when Emory comes in. "Hi," she says. "My mom's finally given me a break. She's on the phone with Colt."

I turn away from my desk to face her. "You two have been inseparable these past few days."

She comes closer and takes a seat on my lap. I place a hand on her back to support her.

"I know, and I'm grateful and happy she's here, but she's beginning to smother me a little. We didn't even spend this much time together when I was living under her roof. And besides...." She runs her fingers through my hair. "I've missed you. And I've actually been meaning to talk to you about something."

"What do you want to talk about?"

"Lola asked me if we've chosen a name for the baby. I wanted to wait until I was with you so we could discuss it."

I smile in delight at the topic. This is a lot better than having to figure out how to replenish my diminishing funds. "What names are you gravitating toward?"

"I'm not sure. Do you have any family names that you want?"

"My father's name was Michael. If it's a boy I'd like that to be at least a middle name."

She looks guilty and confesses, "I might have promised Lola she can pick the baby's middle name."

"That's fine. He could be Michael something."

"I like Michael," she concedes. "I also have other names in mind like Colton after my grandfather. I also like Connor, Lowell, and Alaric..."

I nod. All of those seem good to me. "What about girl names?"

"I was thinking Arianell, Tala, Zella," she continues. "Or maybe we can name her after our moms – Agatha Helena or Helena Agatha. What do you think?"

"I think our mothers would fight about which name goes first, so we should probably avoid doing that."

My mother has met Helena, and the two women don't care for each other. They aren't hostile, but they avoid each other like the plague. Giving the two women something to fight about would not be the best idea. We have to keep the peace at all costs.

"Good point." Emory asks, "What girl names do you like?"

"Selene."

"As in the Moon Goddess?"

"My kind used to worship her a long time ago. It's something our two species have in common. It feels right to give our daughter a name that belongs to both of our worlds."

"I didn't know vampires used to worship the Moon Goddess."

"As you know, we never cared for sunlight. We feel the safest at night, so we would pray to Selena for protection. I'm not sure why we stopped worshiping her. There's the ruin of an old church on the castle grounds that was built for her."

Emory smiles. "I like the name Selene. It'll remind us that we have more in common than what differentiates us."

I kiss her softly, my lips coaxing her into deepening in the kiss. She sighs dreamily, and we temporarily halt all talk of baby names. That can wait. We have more important things to focus on. I cup her breast and am about to pull down her bodice when there's a knock at the door.

We both sigh. Why are we always getting interrupted?

Lex

"What do you want?" I ask the skinny nobleman. He's young and not even a century old. "Give me a number."

The young vampire scratches the bridge of his nose. "My family's wealthy."

"And I'm sure you could always use more spending money. I'm bet there are some expenses your parents refuse to pay for. A nice car? A beach house?"

He shrugs.

"How about a girl?" I try again. "Is there a girl in court you're interested in? I can get her to like you."

"It's not that…"

"Girls? More than one? A guy? A variety of people you want to fuck?"

If the young vampire could blush, he might have. "You could make that happen?"

"I've made it happen. Many times, and my life kind of imploded because of it. Word of advice, condoms are not a one hundred percent effective form of contraception."

"What?" He sounds bewildered. "What does that have to do with me?"

I sigh and put my hands on his shoulder. "Look, Willard…"

"That's not my name. It's–"

"It doesn't matter," I cut him off. "I need to go to that masquerade ball. You have an invitation, and if you take me as your plus one, I will get you whatever you want."

"*Whatever* I want?"

I hesitate before nodding. "Within reason, Willard. Don't get too greedy."

"My name's not Willard."

"Give me your price, and I'll see what I can do."

He looks contemplative "Could I have time to think about it?"

"The ball is in three days. I need an answer quickly."

He shrugs. "It's not my fault you weren't invited. And you're desperate, so it's not like you have a lot of options."

I sigh, wishing I was doing anything but this. "I'll give you a day to think about it. I want your answer by tomorrow after breakfast."

"I'll give my answer when I feel like it," he counters. "You have no choice but to wait."

The little shit walks away, and I glare at the back of his head. This has been the response I've been getting from the majority of the nobles I've asked.

It turns out that the nobles in Castle Blackmoor are more scared of King Peter than anything else. Flattery, bribery, and even outright blackmail has not worked on any of the people I'm trying to persuade. All my roads seem to lead to one person, and I'm not pleased. There is only one vampire in this entire castle that can blatantly disobey King Peter and survive–his daughter.

Opal isn't in her room, and the servants won't tell me where she is. It's after dinner, and I'm searching through the castle for her. She's not going to be on the castle grounds at this time as it's raining, and Opal is vain enough to avoid ruining her hair. I can't find her in the usual places she likes to hang out with her gaggle of snooty nobles. It's pure accident as I'm walking back to my room that I hear the moaning.

Regrettably, I know what Opal sounds like when she moans. I close my eyes and tilt my head back as if I can escape what I'm walking into by praying to a merciful deity. No such luck. I walk over to where the moans are coming from and stare at the heavy wooden door before grasping the doorknob and opening it.

It's a parlor room I haven't been into before and there are people in all degrees of dress–from fully clothed to completely nude. They are everywhere: pressed against the walls, on the furniture, on the floor. Opal is on the couch in between two men who are in the process of unlacing her gown. No one has noticed me yet.

One of the men with Opal pulls up the skirts of her gown to touch her between her legs. The other one is simultaneously loosening her gown and getting it off her while trying to kiss her.

I clear my throat.

Nobody reacts.

Oh, for the love of everything good.

"Opal!" I call out. "Should you be having sex with other people while you're pregnant with my son?"

The princess freezes and turns to me wide-eyed. Her shock turns into fury. She grabs a throw pillow off the floor and aims it at my head. I dodge and it hits one of the couples who are busy against the wall. They stop temporarily before continuing unhindered.

"What are you doing?" Opal shrieks. "No one invited you!"

"I can see that." One of the men with her on the couch has unzipped his pants and his genitalia is hanging out. "Please put that away."

"Leave, Lex! No one wants you here!"

"I need to talk to you about something."

Opal's glare is so toxic it could kill a man. "Do I look like I care?"

"Fair point, but I digress. What did the doctor say about sex during your pregnancy?"

"That's none of your business!"

"It really is though." I grimace at the absurdity of my life. "I don't want it to be, but it is."

One of the men says, "This isn't really the time for talking. Unless you're going to join us, you can leave."

I let out a sad sigh. "See, Simon, a few months ago, I would have happily joined you, but I'm trying to change for the better, and that means no more orgies."

"My name's not Simon–"

"I want my older brother to be proud, and orgies make him very disappointed in me. I used to have orgies all the time. Ask Opal."

The princess has her face in her hands. I wonder if she's about to cry from frustration. I come over and pull her from the couch. She slaps my hands away, but I don't relent and lead her toward the door.

I apologize as we have to move around all the people who are on the ground. They ignore me. I almost step on someone's hair. Opal tries to escape my grasp, but I'm still stronger than her, and we're out of the room before I let her go.

I block the door of the parlor with my body, preventing her from going back to rejoin the orgy. "No, Opal. Bad."

"Don't talk to me like I'm your pet!" she hisses, furiously. "I'm a princess!"

"I know. And you should be in bed."

"I need to have sex!" She smacks my shoulder. "I've never been hornier because of all the hormones running through my body. All I want is to get fucked all the time, and it's your fault!"

"So we're acknowledging it's my baby now?"

She smacks my chest. "I fucking hate you!"

I grab her wrists so she'll stop hitting me. "What if I can help?"

Opal's blue eyes narrow in suspicion. "What do you mean?"

"Well…" I look to the heavens as if that merciful deity will finally free me from what I'm about to suggest. "I got you pregnant, so it only makes sense I help you with the symptoms."

"We're going to have sex?"

I look down at her pretty face and tell myself it won't be that bad.

We had sex before. I survived. Her evil vagina isn't going to melt my penis off.

"I'm still not sure if it's safe for you to have sex. I'll have to check with the doctor, but for now, we can do other things."

"Like what?" she scoffs. "Read poetry?"

"I'll eat you out as much as you want," I answer. "I'll keep going until you pass out from the orgasms."

Her blue eyes blink as she thinks this over. Then she nods and repeats, "As much as I want."

I remember that Opal is insatiable, but I'm resigned to my fate. She has a stamina that could kill a weak man. I don't trust any fool in this castle to be gentle with her while she's pregnant. And Opal is always nicer after she's satisfied in bed.

"Come on, Princess." I place a hand on the small of her back to guide her to her room. "Let's get you to bed."

DROP THE BALL

Lex

Opal breathes quickly, her chest rising and falling as she recovers from another orgasm. I rest my cheek on her thigh. I've set up shop between her legs. She is truly insatiable. If she could live on orgasms alone, she would do it.

"You're good at that," she murmurs, her voice drowsy. "How are you so good at that?"

I lazily crawl up the bed to lie beside her. "A *lot* of practice."

She glares at me, but there's no real heat in her gaze. "How many women have you eaten out?"

"I lost count," I answer glibly. "I could ask you the same thing. How many cocks have you–"

"You don't ask a lady that, Lex."

"You're not a lady."

"I'm a princess. And I can do what I want." She gets off the bed and goes to her vanity where she takes a seat and starts brushing her hair with a silver brush. "Why is it when men sleep with as many women as possible they're praised for it? But when I do the same thing it's wrong?"

I sit up and catch her gaze in the vanity mirror's reflection. "It's how the world is made, Opal."

"All this importance on virginity and limiting one's amount of partners," she continues. "Everybody has sex. That's how we continue on with the species."

I leave the bed to come closer to her. I take the silver brush from her to brush through her long, dark hair. "I agree. People should mind their own business. Why does it matter who and how many people you've had sex with?"

"It all goes back to our grandparents' generation. They wanted us all to be pure and innocent little dolls until they wanted us to continue the bloodline. And suddenly sex is necessary, and we should fuck until we give them heirs."

I snort. "That's why I'm relieved to be the spare. The burden of continuing the bloodline isn't solely on me. No one expects me to be responsible for that."

She scowls and continues, "My father cares so much about these things that he didn't even ask me if I wanted to marry Kane. Can you believe that? He just told me he had brokered a marriage for me and sent me to Crimson Peak without even considering how I felt. He shipped me off like I was a piece of furniture."

"Did you not like being engaged to Kane?"

"I didn't mind it. He's handsome and powerful. He's also not old enough to be my grandfather. I know that my father could have chosen a worse match for me, but I would have liked a choice, even just the illusion of it." She adds, "After he told me about the engagement, I decided to have sex with whomever I wanted. I needed to feel some semblance of freedom. I knew as long as I didn't get pregnant with anyone but Kane's baby that it was going to be fine. Since it's not possible for most men to get me pregnant, I wasn't worried."

I place the silver brush back on the vanity table. "Except I got you pregnant and ruined all of that."

She scoffs and turns around to tell me, "That wasn't an accident, Lex. I made sure you got me pregnant."

I've had some suspicions, but I didn't think I would ever get a confirmation from Opal. "Why?"

"I knew Kane didn't care about me. And after he brought that wolf whore into the castle, I knew I had to make sure he wouldn't leave me. I thought he would be honorable and marry me because as long as the baby was his blood…"

"You thought he would accept it as his own even though the baby is really mine?"

"I had it all planned out, and he still chose *her*." She shakes her head, perplexed. "I still don't understand it."

"Kane is in love. He would rather risk losing everything than not be with Emory."

"Love?" she echoes in disgust. "That's for fairy tales and commoners. *We* don't get that privilege."

I stop to really look at Opal and her perfect face. I have always seen her as petty and shallow. That's the version of herself she shows to the world. There could be hidden depths there she wouldn't let anyone see.

"Why are you looking at me like that?" she inquires.

"I just forgot how pretty you are." I turn her around in her chair so she can look at her reflection. "And somebody that attractive deserves to have an escort that can match her."

She snorts. "You still want to go to the ball?"

"Come on, Opal." I lean down to kiss her neck and her shoulder. "You know I'm a great dancer. And we'd look magnificent together. All the courtiers will be jealous."

She moans as I cup her breasts through her gown. "You do make a good point."

"Say yes," I murmur in her ear. "And I'll fuck you tonight. No more holding back."

She moans again as I suck at her pulse point. Sighing, she says, "Fine." I smile triumphantly and kiss her so she can't see the self-satisfaction on my face.

❄

Kane

Lex has managed to get his hands on the guest list. To my eternal dismay, almost all the vampire kings are going to be in attendance at King Peter's masquerade ball. King Myenas is my biggest concern. He has never cared for me, and an alliance between him and King Peter will be disastrous.

As the days go by, my allies doubt me and whether I'm worth supporting. If I'm the kind of man to wallow in despair, I might have done that. I can face off against Peter alone, but not Peter with the rest of the kingdoms by his side.

Rainer knows about the challenges I face, and he has one suggestion I shot down instantly.

"I can't make an alliance with the wolf packs."

"Why not?" Rainer questions. "There are wolf packs almost as wealthy as the other vampire kings. They can provide you with more blood and the forces you're scrambling to get."

"The wolf shifters still won't trust me after the war with the Moonraker pack, and I don't blame them. They stand to lose more than gain from allying themselves with me."

"And that's where Emory could come in and help. She's an Alpha now. She could smooth over any doubts the wolf packs have about you. They may not trust you, but they'll trust her."

I shake my head. "I can't put her in that position. She's a new Alpha, and her pack is recovering from a decade-long war. She needs to focus on rebuilding, not trying to help me recruit new allies."

Rainer looks put out and suggests, "You could still ask her how she feels about it instead of dismissing the entire idea. Emory wants to help."

"She's helped me enough. I can't add to her stress. There's the baby to worry about."

Rainer runs a hand over his face. "If only the solution would just magically appear to us, huh?"

I don't disagree with him. This whole thing feels futile. I feel like I'm pushing a boulder up a hill every day only to watch it roll back down so I can start all over again. Even in my frustration, I know I have to put Emory first.

Lex

The ballroom is filled with people. Women are dressed in elaborate gowns decorated with jewels and feathers. Even the masks are extravagantly designed to make it hard to see people's faces. I look across the crowd of people trying to see if I can recognize any of the guests but I can't.

There are tables filled with an array of food, more than a whole village could consume in a week. Goblets of wine and fresh blood are being offered by servants on a platter. A quartet plays soft music while nobles take to the dance floor. Opal's arm is tucked against mine as I move us through the crush of people.

She moves closer to me and says, "When the next song starts, dance with me."

I have always enjoyed dancing, and Opal is graceful on her feet. I accommodate her and take her to the dance floor for the waltz. We've danced together often before, so I easily lead her through the steps. We glide on the ballroom floor like we've been doing this for centuries.

The dance gives me the freedom to look across the ballroom as we twirl around the other couples. I find King Peter as he's still wearing his crown. He's talking to a man wearing a raven mask.

"Who's that?" I ask. "The man your father is talking to."

"King Myenas, I believe. See that stupid mask? He's obsessed with birds."

That confirms the guest list I found in Opal's belongings is accurate. I need to tell Kane. If King Myenas allies himself with King Peter, we will be in trouble. Before becoming king, Myenas was a warlord who accumulated land by wiping out entire kingdoms. He is a heartless butcher. And he has never lost a battle.

After the waltz ends, I try to excuse myself, but Opal isn't having it.

"You begged me to be my escort tonight," she says. "You can't jilt me now."

"I only need a moment. I'll be back soon."

"If you embarrass me by leaving me in front of everyone, Lex, I will never forgive you." Her blue eyes are serious behind her mask. "I'll never let you near me again."

My head begins to ache from stress and frustration. "Can't you amuse yourself for one moment? I promise I'll come right back."

"What's more important than me?" she challenges. "Is there someone else you're fucking besides me?"

I snort. "Don't be ridiculous."

"Am I being ridiculous? Really? Because you wouldn't have sex with me earlier, so it only makes sense that it was because you were getting it from somebody else."

"There's no one," I tell her, exasperated. "You are the only woman I look at. You've consumed my entire life."

She lets out a bitter laugh. "That might have sounded romantic from another perspective, but you don't care about me at all do you? Not even for a minute. Or is it just the baby inside of me you give a damn about?"

I can say something flattering and appeal to her vanity once more. I could lie and say that I care about her and maybe even love her. The truth is, I don't feel anything for her, and I don't think I'm capable of such emotions. I know she can't feel similarly about me.

We are alike in the worst ways. We mirror each other. What are we but two vain creatures needy for affection and willing to accept it from anyone? When I look at Opal, I see all the parts of myself I despise the most, the parts that I know make me hard to love. They make me hard to stand at all.

I choose honesty because I don't have the patience for lies tonight. I give her the unvarnished cruel truth. "The answer is obvious, Opal. Anyone can see it. Even you."

I see the flash of hurt in her blue eyes. Guilt blooms in my belly, and I ignore it. There is no point in letting her think we are anything besides two people that accidentally made a baby. It would truly be the worst thing I could do.

Opal closes her eyes and says, "All the men in my life always disappoint me."

The hurt and disgust in her tone is clear despite the cacophony of noise in the ballroom. Opal leaves the room, eager to get as far away from me as possible. She shoves and elbows her way through the crowd and out of the ballroom. People are staring at me, having watched the spectacle like the hungry vultures they are.

Standing in a room full of people, I have never felt so alone.

THE OLD RUINS

Emory

I can feel cabin fever settling in after being stuck inside the castle for too long. Being confined to my room doesn't help as there are only so many books to read and card games to be played. Even castle gossip is growing stagnant. I'm getting ready to climb the walls when my mother and maids finally agree to let me have lunch outside.

Summer is giving way to autumn, and it's beginning to get cold, so Nellie and Helga dress me in warmer clothes. The pregnancy makes me feel overheated more than anything, so I concede on a brown cardigan over a pale green sundress. I slip on a pair of brown sandals before quickly making my way out of my room and eventually out of the castle onto the grounds. Helga and Nellie follow with a large picnic basket.

My mother catches up to me before I can get far, chiding me for practically running down the hallways. "The doctor said light walks, not sprinting through the castle like the building is on fire."

I smile sheepishly, too happy at being able to be outside and breathe in fresh air. I close my eyes and breathe in deeply. The midday sun warms my face, and I open my arms to soak in the light.

This is what I had been missing. The forest grounds me like nothing else, settling something deeply inherent in my being.

I open my emerald eyes and glance over to my mother. She is smiling fondly.

"This reminds me of that time you broke your leg falling from that tree, and you couldn't go outside for a week," she says. "I had to practically restrain you so you didn't try to climb out of the window."

"I was eight," I reply. "And Colt and Darius were playing without me. It wasn't fair. I was bored."

"If I let you, you would have lived outside permanently. You and your brother were constantly getting cuts and bruises from running through the woods."

I shrug. "We healed."

"Your father–" She stops, her expression conflicted. Her face always looks so forlorn and torn whenever Bernard is mentioned. "He never cared what his children were doing. He was always so busy."

"Busy starting wars with our neighbors."

My mother gives me a reproachful look. "Emory."

"What?" I return. "Why are you still trying to defend him? He forced our pack into one useless battle after another."

"He's always been ambitious. Ever since he was young, he wanted to make something of himself. He wanted more for our pack."

"He didn't do any of it for the pack. He only wanted the best for himself. He was proud. An arrogant asshole who never listens to anyone, not even you."

My mother sighs, yielding, "Bernard could be his own worst enemy at times."

"More like all the time." I take my mom's hand. "It's a nice day. Let's not spoil it talking about Bernard."

My mother agrees, and we make our way to the picnic spot Lola had chosen weeks ago. Nellie and Helga arrive behind us and set up the large blanket before taking out the food and drinks from the basket. They have been trying their best to make my mother feel welcome in the castle. They ask the cooks to make her favorite foods and ensure her room smells like roses. My mother is living a more pampered life than when she was the Luna of the Moonraker pack.

We take a seat on the blanket as the maids serve us our food and pour us glasses of freshly squeezed lemonade.

"Kane told me there's a ruin of an old church on the grounds," I say to Helga and Nellie. "Do you know where it is exactly?"

Nellie nods. "It's by the gamekeeper's cottage."

Helga looks at me warily. "Are you planning on going there, Princess? The ruins aren't the safest place for you to be exploring in your condition."

I resist the urge to roll my eyes. Everyone is treating me like I'm made of glass. I'm a pregnant woman, not a china doll that will shatter if not handled carefully. If I'd let them, Dr. Martin, Kane, and everyone else would roll me up in bubble wrap and force me to stay in bed till I went into labor.

"I just want to take a look around," I reassure Helga. "I'm not going to try and climb the ruins."

"Why do you want to be running around the ruins anyway, Emory?" my mother asks. "What's so fascinating about an old church?"

"It's a church that was for worshiping Selene. The vampires used to revere the Moon Goddess like we do."

My mother looks genuinely surprised. "The vampires prayed to the Moon Goddess?"

I look at Nellie, who nods and explains. "A long time ago. It was before King Michael was even born. His grandfather used to worship the Moon Goddess. I don't know why we stopped honoring her."

My mother stabs into a piece of asparagus with her fork. "Is it because you didn't want to be associated with a Goddess wolf shifters worship?"

"I...I wouldn't know," Nellie answers, uncomfortably. "All I know is what I've heard in passing from the older vampires in the castle. They used to worship Selene but stopped."

"When it was no longer convenient?"

"Mom," I admonish her, "we shouldn't be questioning anyone's beliefs."

She doesn't say anything and focuses on eating her lunch. Lola and Willow join us. It's apparent Lola's been to the library because she's got a new book tucked under her arm.

My mother has been trying to be kinder to Lola. My sister is not unhappy with the change but is conflicted. It will take some time to heal old wounds.

I know my mother feels guilty for how she treated Lola in the past. She hadn't been cruel to Lola and had elected to ignore her instead. When Bernard had tried to sell off Lola as a feeder to pay his debts, my mother had gone along with the plan. She had even been glad to finally see her husband's illegitimate daughter be taken away. It's a betrayal we all have to work through and try to move forward.

As much as I love my mother and I know she loves me, it's hard for me to reconcile that she is capable of that kind of cruelty and direct it toward an innocent child. The entire situation is ultimately my father's fault, but my mother has never made the effort to be kind toward my sister. Lola has been made to feel she's an outsider in her own home. The damage that could do to such a young mind likely won't even fully reveal itself until she's older.

After we finish our meal, I insist that the maids take us to the ruins. The groundskeeper's cottage is on the other side of the castle furthest from Queen Agatha's rose gardens. We pass by the simple cottage and see the ruins nearby.

There isn't much to see. The temple has fallen victim to the elements for a long time leaving only a few stone walls. The roof, glass windows, and floors are long gone. The front façade is half of an archway covered in ivy.

I walk through the ruins and try to imagine what grand building used to stand there. I grew up going to the temple on Sundays and on special occasions to worship the Moon Goddess. The temple in Moon Grove is made of sandstone with high ceilings and stained glass windows. The stones of the ruins are the same shadow gray color of

Castle Graystone, and I assume the two buildings might have had the same architect.

"What's so important about the ruins, Emory?" Lola asks. "It looks like a giant went and stomped on this place. There's nothing here."

"This used to be a temple, Lo," I clarify. "The vampires used to worship the Moon Goddess, just like us."

"Why did they stop?"

"That's what people can't seem to answer for me."

"Maybe the Moon Goddess didn't like them as much as she likes us," she tells me in a loud whisper that the other women with us can definitely hear. "Miss Margaret told me we were the Moon Goddess's favorites."

I smile. "Is that so?"

Lola nods. "Yep. That's why we have two forms, so we will always be able to protect ourselves and our loved ones from harm."

"That might be it," Willow cut in with a conspiring tone. "We were too jealous of the Moon Goddess's favoritism, and we turned on her. Vampires don't play second fiddle to anyone. We're a proud lot."

Lola purses her lips. "Who do vampires worship now?"

"We don't," Willow answers. "After King Aeneas died, the practice of religion slowly went out of fashion."

"You don't believe in any gods?"

"I know some vampires worship other gods, but the vast majority of our kind have stopped praying to a monastic deity."

"What's monastic?"

"It means singular, only one."

Lola seems to accept that answer. She tries to climb the remaining stone façade of the church. Her little arms and legs cling to the rouge gray stones as she struggles to get her footing. I watch her nervously, and so do the other women. The façade is at least twenty feet high, and if Lola is to reach the top and fall…

"Lola!" I call out. "Maybe you should come down!"

She doesn't stop and grabs on the half arch of the façade to pull herself forward. "I'm almost there!"

"Be careful!"

My heart starts beating faster as her hand reaches for the stone above her, her feet perched on a ledge. I watch her fingers strain to grasp the ledge and miss. Her other hand slides off the stone, then her legs. Time slows down as she drops from high above us. Before I can even scream or move in that direction, I know Lola is going to hit the ground.

If she lands on her head, she might have a concussion or bash her skull on the hard ground. She could snap her neck. She could damage her spine and end up paralyzed. The best case is if she broke an arm or a leg because she can heal from those injuries.

I can only watch in horror as her little body flutters through the air.

Then she stops mid-air as if an invisible barrier is keeping her up. We all stare wide-eyed as Lola is slowly lowered to the ground by an invisible hand. Her feet touch grass, and she looks down at herself in surprise. She turns to me with wide gray eyes.

I run to her and grab her in a hug. I kiss the top of her blonde head, relieved she's in one piece before I pull away to check her for injuries and see there isn't a scratch on her. Lola begins to squirm in my grasp.

"Don't you ever do that again," I rebuke her. "You could have gotten seriously hurt or worse."

"But I didn't," she replies. "I'm fine."

"It could have gone all wrong. I told you to be careful when climbing."

"I'm *fine*," she repeats in a whine.

Miraculously, she is completely fine. This doesn't make sense. There had been that invisible force that caught her, stopping her fall. It had looked like magic.

I spin around to see what might have caused it. Nellie, Helga, and my mother are standing wide-eyed and look as shocked as I am. I know it's not me. Magic is beyond a wolf shifter's capabilities.

Real magic like that hasn't been seen in centuries. It's only been heard of in old folk tales of witches.

Witches. Could it be?

I look down at Lola and cup her face in my hands. "How did that happen?" I ask her, already feeling that I know the answer.

She points toward where Willow is standing. The female vampire's face has gone completely white. She looks utterly terrified, like a deer frozen in the face of a predator.

"Willow is a witch," Lola reminds me.

I turn to Willow, but she's not even blinking. I guess Lola scared her to death, too.

WHERE'S THE WITCH?

Emory

"Willow is a witch," Lola says like she's not talking about the impossible. I remember what Willow told me about her life before she was turned, but it's hard for me to grasp. In my mind, witches aren't real. No one has seen one in centuries. Growing up, I thought they were a fairy tale to make humans afraid to go into the woods at night–sort of like the hybrid stories I've read recently.

I tell myself that what Lola said can't be the truth, but I have also just seen Lola floating in the air with no other possible explanation. That had to be magic. It isn't something that can be easily explained away. I'm not the only one who saw it happen either.

Willow's blue gaze is filled with terror. She is still looking around like she's not sure what to do. I have known that kind of fear before. When I first arrived at Castle Graystone to be a feeder, I felt trapped and helpless in a place where I had no allies.

Willow turns to leave, but wordlessly, Helga and Nellie block her path. The brunette swerves away from them, trying to find another means of escape. I move closer to her, hands outstretched to placate her. She may not be as big and strong as Kane and Rainer, but she's still a vampire.

A vampire who is backed into a corner is going to snap.

"We're not going to hurt you, Willow," I tell her beseechingly. "I just want to talk about what happened."

"Nothing happened," she says quickly, panicking. "I have to go."

I try to keep my voice calm and steady. "You don't need to be afraid of us, Willow. We're all friends here."

"I can't stay here. I can't stay here." She keeps repeating the phrase. "I can't stay here."

"Willow?" Nellie says her name softly. "We worked together in the kitchen when we were younger, remember? I would sing songs to get us through the day."

Helga joins on. "We used to make fun of the nobles while we cleaned around the castle. You said Princess Opal sounded like a pelican when she would scream. Do you remember that?"

Willow nods, her expression looking less panicked. "I remember."

She nearly jumps when I try to move closer to her. When I reach out my hand to touch her, she flinches away. I stop, letting my hand fall. I manage to give her a friendly smile. "I'm your friend," I say. "You helped me find books in the library."

"And I'm your friend too!" Lola pipes up. "You recommend books to me, and you tell me stories. You're one of the nicest people to me in the castle."

The tension begins to melt away from Willow. Lola is as unthreatening as you can get. The little girl is as scary as a dandelion. Willow stops trying to run away, but she still looks terrified.

"It's all going to be okay," I reassure her. "There's nothing to be scared of."

"I'm not a witch anymore," she insists. "What happened is not what you think it was."

"Of course," I agree so I don't agitate her further. "I'm sure there's a logical explanation for what happened. You don't need to worry about it."

"It was magic," Lola speaks up. "Willow used magic to save me—" I cover her mouth to muffle out the rest of what she's saying.

"It's not magic," I emphasize with an imploring look to everyone.

"Willow is not a witch anymore. She's a vampire. Let's not harass her about it."

The maids and my mother look at me skeptically but don't say a word. I feel wetness in my palm and look down at Lola's narrowed gray eyes.

"Did you just lick me?" I ask, pulling my hand away. My palm is indeed wet with saliva.

"You wouldn't get your hand off my mouth," she returns defiantly.

I sigh at the thought process of a ten-year-old who can't seem to read the room. I look back to Willow who is slowly backing away.

"I'm sorry," she says. "I really have to go."

She turns and runs away, her blue dress billowing in the wind. I raise a hand to prevent my maids from following her. Willow is running away out of fear. Chasing her will not help the situation.

I know I have to tell Kane about this. Learning that one of the vampires in his castle is also a witch with magical powers is too great of a secret to keep. As much as I feel sorrow for Willow, this is too important to keep to myself. Even if I swore my maids and my mother to secrecy, there is a high chance Lola will tell someone. My little sister will sing like a canary if you offer her some of her favorite food.

I need to tell Kane soon. I just hope Willow will forgive me and that he'll promise to keep her safe. Willow is a good person, after all.

RAINER

Kane has summoned me to the throne room. Emory is there, and they have been talking about something serious. I can tell from the looks on their faces. Kane tells me, "You need to find Willow. She might have left the castle."

"Why would she leave?" I ask. "Did something happen?"

He glances at Emory and they share a meaningful look. Kane turns back to me and replies, "We'll explain everything once you find her and bring her back. It's important."

"Have the guards been informed?"

"I've given the order to prevent her from leaving the castle and grounds. She must not be harmed."

I nod and leave the throne room to begin my search. Time is of the essence. If Willow has just left the castle then I have to race to get to her before she can reach any of the borders. I think of which path she might be taking. She wouldn't head to Scarlett Thunder. She knows she wouldn't be given asylum in the middle of a war.

Willow could be heading to another of the vampire kingdoms or maybe west toward the lands belonging to the wolf packs. No matter where she goes, she's in danger. But Willow is smart. She has more will to live than most people I know. Guilt blooms in my belly as I remember her pale and frightened in a dungeon cell, and I push the memories away.

I make my way to the library. The librarian's quarters are nearby. Willow moved into them after the interim librarian's death. Her bedroom door is unlocked. I step into the room and look around the small space.

It's a sparse room with minimal dark wood furniture. The curtains, carpet, and bed sheet are a deep blue. Besides the bed, there's a dresser, a nightstand, and a lamp. The bay window has a reading nook with throw pillows. A book has been left there as if Willow has just stepped out.

I open the dresser and find there are still clothes inside. She must have packed in a rush, probably only taking one bag with her. Where would she have gone? I know the answers aren't in this room. I close the dresser and leave, shutting the door behind me.

Out in the hallway, I run into Nellie and Helga who look worried. Other servants are talking amongst themselves. Willow is their friend. She has worked alongside them for years. There is a loyalty and camaraderie amongst the castle staff that I have never been a part of due to my noble blood. I know I can never be one of them, but they are my only clue as to where she might go.

"Hey," I say. "Did you hear about Willow?"

Nellie and Helga share a wary glance. They both nod.

"We're all worried about her, and we want to bring her home," I continue. "Do you have any idea where she might have gone? Are there places that are significant to her?"

Helga shakes her head. "We have no idea. Willow liked to keep to herself. She never talked much."

"Hels, come on. I need to find her. It's important that we get her back before she gets hurt out there."

"Will you hurt her if you bring her back?" Nellie asks. "She didn't mean what happened earlier. She was only trying to help. She saved Lola."

I have no idea what happened earlier, and I wish someone had told me beforehand. I know asking about it now will only waste more time.

"I won't hurt her," I reassure them, sincerely. "I don't want anyone to hurt her, but we're in the middle of a war, and the wolf packs don't like us much either. There are not a lot of places she'd be safe outside of Crimson Peak."

The two maids share a look, communicating silently, before Nellie finally concedes. "She went west. There's that old hunting cabin near the border."

"I remember," I reply. "Thank you."

Helga grabs my arm firmly. In a serious tone, she tells me, "She's terrified. She won't come willingly."

I suspect as much. I nod in understanding before I leave. If Willow left on foot, I can still catch her by taking a car. We have some fast vehicles, and I don't mind driving fast and recklessly to find her.

I decide to go alone. If Willow is truly terrified then bringing men with me would only make her more anxious. She already doesn't like me, so the sight of me will not go over well. But I can handle her on my own. I'll just turn on the Rainer charm.

The old hunting cabin belonged to King Michael. He used to go on hunting trips to deal with the stress of running a kingdom. Neither Kane nor Lex has ever cared too much for hunting, so the cabin has remained unused since their father's death. It's in an isolated location deep in the forest with no neighbors to be found for miles.

I have to go off memory from the last time I saw the cabin decades ago. I speed along until I see the familiar turn and drive as far in as I can before I have to leave the car and go on foot into the woods. I walk through the thick foliage until I finally find the rustic cabin. It looks a little downtrodden after years of being left for the forest to reclaim. It's still standing despite the test of time.

I slow down my steps, trying to make as little noise possible as I approach the place. I don't know when she left, but I have a feeling she's here already. She must've had a good head start on me.

The windows are boarded up, so I can't look inside and get a glimpse if anyone is in there. I reach the front door and grasp the door handle. The doorknob is loose as if someone has already broken it to get in.

I open the door and find Willow on the other side of the room with a crossbow pointing straight at me. I stay still at the doorway of the cabin and wait to see what she'll do.

"One more step, and I'll fire," she hisses in a threat. "I'll do it, Rainer. I swear I will."

Her blue eyes are wide and terrified, but she's trying to hide it. Her hands are shaking. She's not a soldier. She doesn't know how to fight, but she is desperate and afraid. That makes her unpredictable.

"What's your plan, Willow?" I ask. "Are you going to stay in this cabin forever? Or are you going to run away to another kingdom?"

"That's none of your business."

"Unfortunately for you, it kind of is. Kane and Emory want you returned to the castle, and I'm not going back without you."

Her blue eyes narrow, her fear morphing to anger and indignation. "I won't go willingly. You can't make me."

"I'm only following orders, Willow," I say. "I would be glad to let you go off into the sunset if that's what you want. I suppose I owe you that for what's happened between us. But I can't. I have direct orders from the king."

"Just let me go," she begs. "You can say you never saw me, that you were too late. No one has to know."

"I'll know. And I can't lie to Kane. I swore an oath to serve him." I sigh as her jaw trembles as she struggles not to cry. "Why don't you put down the crossbow and we can talk..."

An arrow flies through the air.

A MAGICAL LOOPHOLE

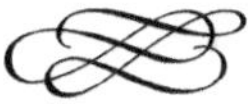

Rainer

An arrow flies through the air and embeds itself in the wall beside me, narrowly missing me by a few inches. It's chest level, so I know she was aiming for my heart. I stare at the arrow and then back at her in horror. She could have killed me.

Her blue eyes are wide in shock too as if she can't believe what she almost did, but when I move from the doorway, her shock morphs into panic as she scrambles to reload the crossbow. In the small cabin, I'm able to reach her in five steps. I yank the crossbow from her. She tries to keep her hold on it, but I'm much stronger.

Tossing the crossbow several feet away and out of her grasp, I hold her at arm's length. She grabs an arrow and tries to stab me with it. I catch her wrist and twist it until she lets the arrow go. I throw it far away, and before she can try to reach for another weapon, I pick her up by the waist and haul her over my shoulder. She fights me, kicking and flailing to try and escape, but I keep her locked on my shoulder with a heavy arm.

"Let me go!" she screams. "Put me down!"

I ignore her yelling and make my way to the door. I have to be careful slipping her through so that she doesn't hit the doorframe.

She gets wilder as we step outside the cabin, screaming like an angry, wild animal. She's going to scare any wildlife nearby.

The walk through the woods to the car is more bothersome than anything. Willow isn't particularly heavy, but she does not relent in her attempt to free herself, no matter how futile it is. I unlock the car and toss her into the backseat, slamming the door behind her and using the fob to lock it. She reaches for the button, and we have a showdown with me barely managing to get into the driver's seat and lock the doors again before Willow has a chance to get away.

"Don't." I glare at her through the rearview mirror as I start the engine. "You can't win, Willow. I'm stronger than you. Even if you get out of this car, I will find you again."

"There's no escaping you?" she says bitterly. "It's like I'm back in the dungeon all over again."

I swallow hard at her words. Guilt makes it difficult for me to look at her. I drive away from there and head back to the castle. Our shared past is a heavy silence that makes for a very uncomfortable car ride.

Kane

Emory bites her nails. She feels guilty for telling me about Willow and causing the female vampire to run from the castle. The truth of what Willow is would have come out one way or another. The fact that Willow has managed to hide it for this long is a wonder.

The throne room opens, and Rainer comes in, carrying Willow on his shoulder like she's a sack of potatoes. He goes to the table nearby and grabs a chair, depositing Willow on it without ceremony. He has rope with him and ties her to the chair quickly. Willow writhes against the restraints in an effort to get away. but Rainer has always been handy with knots. I imagine she's too afraid to use her magic again for fear I'll have her put to death.

I've always seen Willow as calm and unassuming. She never sought out notice, but right now, she is alive with anger and terror.

She bucks against the chair, causing it to move an inch forward. Rainer sighs and holds the chair still.

"Behave," he demands. "Don't make me get chains, Willow."

She shudders, trying to move away from Rainer, but she can't get far. Emory comes over and pushes Rainer aside.

"Hey," she says softly. "Are you okay?"

Willow shakes her head. She looks betrayed. "Why did you tell?"

Emory looks guilt-ridden, her brows furrowed. "I'm so sorry. I didn't know what to do. I thought it was best for the king to know. No one is going to hurt you, Willow. You saved my sister."

"I'm not a witch," she insists. Rainer's eyes widen; he didn't know. "I don't know how I did what I did, but it wasn't magic." She glares up at my best friend. "If I had magic, I would've used it against him."

"Then what was it?" I cut in, moving to stand by Emory. "What did you do?"

Willow blinks, her face panicked. "I don't know."

"You've been in this castle for a long time. You're old enough to have witnessed the witch hunts." Emory has already told me the story Willow told her about how she came to be here.

She shakes her head. "I'm not a witch any more. I swear it."

"I know you're scared to admit it, but you are not going to be harmed." Emory puts her hand on the librarian's.

Willow goes still. She looks down at the floor.

"No one will hurt you," I reassure her. "I only want to find out how you managed to keep your magic after being turned into a vampire."

She doesn't answer.

I gently tilt her chin up with a finger so I can look into her pale blue eyes. There's a fire there I haven't seen before, a simmering rage so unlike the placid librarian I know.

"I'll ask you again, and you will answer because I command you as your king," I continue. "How do you still have your magic?"

"I don't know," she replies through gritted teeth. "All I remember was being drained of my blood, and I woke up as a vampire. I didn't even notice that I still had my magic because I was too afraid to be discovered."

"When did you realize you still had your magic?"

"A few months after I was turned, I caused a bucket to levitate when I was cleaning in the kitchens. I avoided using magic as much as possible after that."

"And no one knew?"

"I didn't tell anyone. I couldn't trust anybody to keep it a secret."

"You told Emory and Lola you used to be a witch," I point out. "You told them how you ended up in this castle."

"I told them I wasn't a witch anymore. As for Lola, she's a child. I didn't expect her to actually believe any of it was a real story. No one would have believed her even if she told someone."

"But then you used your magic to save her from falling and people saw you in the act," I clarify.

Willow closes her eyes. She bows her head, defeated. She deflates like a balloon, all her anger and indignation evaporating in thin air. I watch as she swallows.

"Are you going to kill me?" she asks. "Burn me at the stake?"

"What?" Emory exclaims. "No!" The Alpha looks absolutely horrified at the suggestion. I put a comforting hand on her shoulder.

"A vampire with magic is an abomination," Willow says. "That's what your father believed. If we couldn't be food then we had to be disposed of."

I flinch, remembering my father's hand at decimating the witch population a century ago. "Times have changed. I'm not going to burn you at the stake."

Emory's green eyes bore into me. I will have to tell her about this shameful part of my family's history later.

Willow scoffs. "What are you going to do to me then?"

"I don't know yet," I admit. "I wasn't expecting something like you to drop into my lap. Nothing bad. I already promised you."

"I would gladly disappear and never be seen again if you will allow me to, Your Highness," she says. "I've never harmed anyone, and I don't want to." She looks at Rainer. "Well, almost no one. No one else has to know I have magic."

"I'm trying to understand why you have magic in the first place." I look at Rainer. "Is it because of who turned you?"

"Who turned her?" Emory asks.

"It was Lex," Rainer answers. "It was an accident. He was careless while feeding from her that one time. King Michael was furious with him. The king could have had Lex executed for his negligence, but since he was a prince, and his son, that didn't happen."

Emory looks back at me. "And you think that might have caused Willow to keep her magic?"

"It's the only theory I have," I reply. "Witches have been turned to vampires before, but they've always lost their magic."

"And why does that happen?"

"Our connection to nature lets us access the magic left in the earth. Leftover tools from creation," Willow clarifies. She looks exhausted. "When we are turned into a vampire, that connection is severed. At least, it's supposed to be."

"You managed to keep it," Emory declares. "Like some kind of magical loophole."

That makes me glance at her belly even though she still isn't showing. Nature has given us a loophole to have a child. It gave a witch turned vampire the ability to maintain her magic, which isn't that far off. Nature allows exceptions.

"The coven you came from, what were they like?" I ask Willow. "Did they practice any special magic?"

Willow shakes her head. "I was part of a small coven. We didn't do anything extraordinary. All we did were spells for a good harvest and potion salves for healing."

"It could be a combination of factors," I concede. "And if we figure out what those factors are, we might be able to replicate this."

"Replicate?" she repeats. "What do you mean?"

"We're at war. Vampires that can use magic would be helpful."

The shock silences Willow. I turn to Rainer and tell him, "If we can look into the coven she's originally from, we can start researching. If I was the one to turn them, it might work the same as when Lex turned Willow—if there are any left that my father missed."

Emory tugs at my arm. I look back at her, and she gestures toward Willow who is shaking in rage. The brunette has clenched her fists, and her pale eyes look like blue fire. I've never seen someone who looks like they wanted to kill me that badly.

"I will never help you with this war," she vows. "I will not assist you in taking witches and turning them into vampires just to be assassinated by your enemies."

"They wouldn't be assassinated by our enemies," Rainer claims.

"They would be soldiers in my army and given the highest honors should they survive the war."

Willow shakes her head. "Don't act like you're even giving them a chance to choose their own fate. You'll drag them into this damned castle and force them to become vampires whether or not they want this."

"I could offer them quite a bit in return–"

"What would you offer them, My Lord?" she mocks. "Once they have been turned, they are beholden to you. They will have no choice but to serve you. If you asked them to go to the battlefield without being trained, they would have to do so."

"I would not ask them to do that."

"No because you're a *good* king unlike your father who hunted and executed my people. You wouldn't dare take witches from their homes for your own agenda, would you?"

Anger makes me clench my jaw. "Bite your tongue, Willow."

"You wanted to speak with me, Your Highness. I am telling you the truth about what your family did. It's not a pretty story you can dress up to make it easier for Emory."

Emory's green eyes are staring into mine, pleading for me to explain. "Why was there a witch hunt, Kane?"

I can't lie to Emory. Willow is right. It's not a pretty story. I have never been proud of this part of my family's history. Admittedly, it's a time of brutality led on by paranoia. My father had been the kind of king to think ahead and get rid of any potential problems.

"It was my father's doing. He decreed magic illegal," I explain, helplessly. "And any witch that was seen practicing magic was executed."

"Hanging, drowning, or burning at the stake," Willow lists with a bitter smile. "And those of us who weren't caught practicing ended up as feeders in the dungeons because witch blood tastes the best, even better than wolf shifter blood."

Emory flinches. She looks at Rainer who turns away in shame. "Why would King Michael do all of that? Why did no one stop it?"

"Because he was the king, and no one questions what the king wants," Willow answers. "So if Kane decides he wants vampire witches in his war, he'll get them. He just has to give the command—and find them."

A HEAVY BURDEN

Rainer

A vase comes flying at me as soon as I step into the suite. I quickly step aside, and the vase hits the wooden door, ceramic breaking on impact and leaving shards on the floor. I will have to get a maid to clean that up later. At this point, we are going to run out of breakable objects for Willow to throw at me.

"Your aim is getting better," I say cheerily, knowing that will annoy her more.

It has been a couple of days since I dragged her kicking and screaming back to Castle Graystone. Willow has been in a bad mood since then, and she likes to take her anger out on anything breakable that can be found in the suite of rooms she is being held in, essentially as a prisoner. Kane wants her close so I can keep an eye on her and prevent her from escaping from the castle again.

The librarian's quarters are too far away and isolated, so I had to put Willow in the suite of rooms next to mine. With guards constantly standing outside of her door, and even below her window since that time she tried to climb down with a rope made of curtains and bed sheets, she's not going anywhere.

Willow is the most troublesome prisoner I've ever had to deal with, and that's saying something considering I'm the one who brought Jacob back here.

Kane wants her to practice using her magic again. So far, she's been levitating objects at me and set some curtains and bedding on fire. This leaves the maids having to keep replacing things in her room. As far as we know, Willow is the only vampire who can use magic at the moment, and that makes her valuable and a total pain in my ass.

"Have you thought about practicing your magic in other ways?" I suggest. "Like, how about doing something not so violent? Make the flowers bloom or turn water into blood?"

Willow's pale blue eyes glare at me in hatred. A pillow starts rising from the bed. It flies toward me, and I catch it with one hand. I toss it back at her, and she yelps as it bounces off her and lands on the floor.

"Hey!" she exclaims.

I shrug. "You started it."

"You're a child."

"You're the one that keeps throwing things," I point out. "I'm just retaliating after *days* of not reacting to your behavior."

"Oh boo-hoo, Rainer," she spits. "I was mean to you for a few days. How can you live with such treatment?"

"I don't know. You tell me." I give her a glib smile, and I can see it irritates her even more. She wants me to get angry so we can have a real shouting match. I abandoned such behavior in my youth. She's going to have to make do with frustrating cheeriness.

"Aren't you supposed to be trying to convince me to join Kane's war and betray all the witches?" she challenges, crossing her arms. "You're not doing a good job of it."

"My job is to babysit you and make sure you don't leave the castle." I take a seat in the chair near the window. "The convincing you to join the cause, thing is Kane and Emory's department. That's above my pay grade."

Willow looks disgusted at how blasé I am. "I find it so ironic you all want to use me for your own gain when a century ago my kind was being hunted just for having magic. Can't you see the hypocrisy in all of it?"

"We're at war. Desperate times call for desperate measures," I reply. "None of us could have predicted you were able to do this, which is something the other side doesn't have."

"And yet, I see no reason why I should be part of this."

I cock an eyebrow at her. "You're a vampire, and your king is asking you to. This is your kingdom and has been your home for a very long time. Whatever happens to Crimson Peak affects you."

"So I'm to raise the banners and come running?" she scoffs. "I will never do such a thing, especially after how the people of this kingdom have treated me."

"What happened with the witches was regrettable–"

"It was barbaric!" she argues. "We were never any threat to vampires. We didn't have the wealth or the organized strength of the shifters. We didn't even have the numbers of the humans. We were the weakest, and King Michael hunted us for sport."

Familiar guilt burns in my belly and crawls up to my chest. I swallow, unable to find anything to fight back with. Willow is in the right. Her people have been wronged, and I have no way of spinning it to make it sound better.

"The damage done is so bad that you all thought witches were extinct," she continues. "They hid amongst the humans, and they stopped practicing their magic to keep themselves safe. That is the legacy of your beloved King Michael."

I lean forward, and I can see all the pain and sorrow in her pale blue eyes. I want to soothe it away, but she won't let me touch her or even get near her.

"How do we fix it, Willow?" I ask. "What would you have us do with all this bad blood?"

"You can't fix it, Rainer. None of you have even bothered trying to apologize, because in some way, deep down, you still think it was justified. It wasn't, and it still isn't." She looks haunted, hollowed out.

"You didn't even remember how you benefited from it. All those nights you went down to the dungeon to feed, not even seeing our faces. Which is the same way you treat the feeders in the dungeons now…"

"That's not true," I begin, wanting to tell her things have changed for the feeders, but Willow turns away as if the sight of me makes her want to vomit. She walks to the ensuite bathroom and closes the door behind her, putting the necessary distance between us. I run a hand over my face, thinking about my past sins. Atonement is a hard road to walk.

Kane

I have told Emory all the gory details of the witch hunts, what I can remember of that time. She is horrified and saddened to hear about a war my people tried to erase from the world, not wanting anyone to remember our viciousness. Emory isn't completely shocked as she spent most of her childhood with her people at war with mine. She has some idea of the atrocities of war.

I haven't been able to speak to Willow since the interrogation in the throne room. Her unraveling of everything she and the other witches have endured unsettles me. I don't know what to say to her. All my excuses stay unspoken, as do the rest of my apologies since she never accepted the first one.

"Why did your father target the witches specifically?" Emory asks. "They hadn't done anything to provoke him."

"He was paranoid in his later years, and he became stricter with the laws he passed," I explain. "He saw potential problems and acted upon them before they could become a real threat. The witches were scattered and fewer in numbers, but magic was an unpredictable factor. It made them dangerous in my father's eyes."

"They could have never been a real threat to him unlike…" her voice trailed off. "Why is it he never started a war with my people?"

"The risk was too great for losses on either side. My mother convinced him to broker peace with your great-grandfather instead. It wasn't until Bernard forced my hand that I went against this precedent."

"We could have been wiped out like the witches," she concludes. "If the war between our species went on, eventually, you could have erased us too."

I shake my head. "Even I don't have the capacity for that. I knew Bernard would run out of funds eventually. I waited him out, and he caved as I'd predicted."

Emory turns to the window of my bedroom, taking in the view outside. I can only see her profile. "All those people, Kane. They were murdered. They have to be remembered."

"It's an ugly part of our history I had hoped to keep buried. I don't know how to make peace with what my father did and my part in not being able to stop it."

"No one tried to stop it." She sounds distant. It makes me ache to touch her and be able to connect with her. "And now we expect Willow to fight in a war for the people that have wronged her most?"

"None of it is fair. I wish I didn't have to ask anything of her after what she's been through," I agree. "But I'm… desperate. I'm running out of options."

She turns back to me, her green eyes filled with concern. "What is it? What's going on?"

"My allies have turned against me or are about to. We don't have enough gold and blood to bribe them all," I confess, all the weight I have been keeping in for months spilling out like wine. "I need Willow's magic if I have any chance of winning this war. I know she deserves better, but my options are limited."

"Why are your allies turning against you?"

I hesitate to answer.

"Kane?"

"They don't care for the idea of a child born between our species," I confess. "Intermarriage is unacceptable for most vampires. After they found out about the baby, they wanted nothing to do with me."

Emory steps closer to me, cupping my face in her hands. Her

gentle touch calms me, and I close my eyes, letting her comfort me. She asks, "Why didn't you tell me any of this?"

"I didn't want to add to your stress with the baby–"

"Don't be ridiculous, Kane," she admonishes. "You are my partner. We're supposed to lean on each other and work together. We don't keep secrets and suffer alone."

I lean my head against her shoulder and let out a ragged breath. "I know. I'm sorry. I'm not used to being able to rely on anyone besides Rainer and my mother. And even then, I've tried to handle most of it on my own."

"You're a king, not a god. You're allowed to need people. It's not a weakness." She lets out a sigh. "Look at me, Kane."

I open my eyes slowly. Her green gaze makes me feel naked, like she can see to the very core of my being. It should scare me, but there's a freedom to being seen completely as one is. Everything I am–king, vampire, man–melts away. I am only hers.

"Do you know the first thing shifters are taught? The lone wolf dies, but the pack survives. You can't do it all on your own. Let me be there for you." She kisses the corner of my mouth, softly. "I know we haven't known each other that long, but you've been the most dependable person in my life. You take care of me so I can be strong for others. I want to be able to do the same for you."

Long ago, I had hoped for a union like my parents had where they worked together as a team. I had given up that thought when I was betrothed to Opal. Then I met a wolf shifter who was willing to sacrifice herself for her sister and there was only one conclusion to that story. Love had hit me like a lightning bolt and there are times I still wonder how I was able to withstand it.

"You want to take care of me?" I ask. "It's not going to be an easy task. I'm known to be stubborn as a mule. And I always think I'm right."

She smiles. "We'll work on your massive ego, and I'm quite good at the caring part. Just ask Lola."

"Okay."

I give in because there is no point in fighting. I've been dealing with the burden of this on my own for too long. The promise of easing even a little bit of it makes me feel like I can breathe again. The war still looms over me and the impossibility of how to win it but for a moment, I am at peace.

UNDER THE SKIN

Emory

A potted plant flies across the room and stops halfway before reaching me. It falls to the floor, scattering glass, dirt, and tulips everywhere. I stare in shock at Willow who is standing by the window. I hadn't expected to have something thrown at me.

"Sorry," she says. "I thought you were Rainer."

"That's how you greet him?"

"He's annoying. He deserves it."

"Have you tried using words instead of breaking things?" I ask, moving around the mess on the floor to approach her. "There's less clean up."

"Talking with Rainer just makes me more upset. He lives to be the bane of my existence."

That's a title Rainer probably enjoys having.

I reach Willow and stop a few feet from her. "I'm sorry it took me so long to come see you. Kane and Rainer both thought you needed space after what happened a few days ago."

"You mean where I was dragged back here without my consent and forced to relive all of my trauma?" she offers sarcastically. "Why would I need time to process that?"

"I'm truly sorry about everything. I had no idea about the witch hunts, except for what you told me, and I wasn't sure how much of that was real," I tell her. "What you've been through is truly unspeakable. I am so sorry."

She crosses her arms over her chest, a sign she doesn't want to be held or touched in any way. "I don't know why you're apologizing. You and your kind have never done anything to me. All of that happened long before you were born."

"I know, but I don't know what else to say. I wish I could do something to make it better, but I know I can't."

She turns away, swallowing heavily. With her back to me, she sniffs as she wipes at her face. Her whole frame starts shaking as sobs overcome her. I watch helplessly, wanting to comfort her but not wanting to overstep Willow's boundaries.

"I haven't cried in decades," she says. "I tried to bury it deep down until I never thought about it, but it's all out in the open again."

"It makes you feel raw?" I ask. "Like you've had your skin peeled off?"

She turns to me, her wet eyes wide in disbelief. "How do you know how that feels?"

"I may not know exactly what you feel, but I've been through a war too. We lost good men because of my father's lies. There are losses we can never recuperate from. And no one wants to talk about it because it's too hard. I also know what it's like to feel betrayed and trapped."

She stares at me, unspeaking.

Not wanting to make this about myself, I conclude, "You're allowed to feel however you feel. No one can dictate that for you. It doesn't matter if it happened yesterday or a thousand years ago."

"I thought I had gotten over it," she explains. "I could pretend it was all just a bad dream. Then the reality of it all hit me, and it overwhelmed me."

"Have you ever talked to anyone about this?"

Willow shakes her head. "I was hiding what I was, remember? No one could know what I've been through, or I could be in danger."

"All those years of keeping all this hurt in can't have been healthy or easy."

"Now that I don't have to hide anything anymore, I feel so much. I feel too much. I'm angry, I'm sad, and I'm relieved–sometimes all at once. I don't know how anyone can feel all of this and not go insane."

"It's understandable if you go a little bit insane. No one will blame you."

"I think I have." She goes to the bed and takes a seat at the foot of it. "After I was first turned, I wanted to escape this castle and never look back."

"Then what happened?"

"I was too weak, at first, to try to run away. So I became part of the castle staff, and I got to know all of them. These people who I would have never have even talked to when I was a witch became my friends. I fell in love with all of them."

"I understand."

The same thing happened to me. When I arrived at Castle Graystone as a feeder, I was terrified and alone. Then I grew attached to the people, and I can't see this place the same way. Even when I felt like I couldn't possibly connect with anyone, they had snuck in and made me care about them.

"Gaius was like a father to me," Willow continues. "He was kind and patient. He let me borrow as many books as I wanted from the library. He didn't care that I wasn't a noble, only that I needed the escapism found in those books."

"I'm sorry you lost him."

I never met the former librarian, but from how Willow describes him he sounds like a kind soul. I'm sure she doesn't care for King Michael anymore knowing that he's the one who had him put to death.

"For many years, he could tell that there was something that upset me, but he never pushed. He wanted me to tell him when I was ready. I never told him about any of it, but I wish I had."

I take the initiative to go to Willow and sit on the bed next to her, taking her hand in mine. I don't mind her cold touch. She doesn't shy away from me.

"I'm here for you. If you ever want to talk, I'll always be willing to listen."

Her pale blue eyes look over my face, trying to find any insincerity. "Why do you care about how I feel? This isn't your war. You have no part in any of this."

"The people I love are part of this war, so it matters to me. You matter to me because you're a person I consider a friend," I say. "You will still matter to me even if you choose not to fight in this war. My friendship isn't contingent on it."

She shakes her head. "I can't fight for this kingdom, not after all I've endured."

"I understand."

"Even if you find more witches, they're not trained to fight. We will be slaughtered on the battlefield. And you can force me to fight your battles, but I refuse to drag any other witches into it."

"Anyone can be taught how to fight," I explain. "I've trained in combat tactics since I was a child. No one is unteachable with time and patience."

I watch as Willow's gaze sharpens, and she pulls her hand away. "You're an Alpha. Why don't you recruit the shifter packs to help with this war?"

"Kane hasn't asked for my help with recruiting the shifter packs. This is his war, not ours. I'm not sure he wants us to fight with him."

"Your people have the numbers and the resources to help," Willow points out. "Maybe you should start looking at home for what you need."

She has a point. I need to talk to Kane about it. Certain that she's all right to be left alone, I tell her goodbye and step over the mess by the door to take my leave.

Sometime later, I walk into the room I share with Kane to find him there. "We should ask Moonraker pack and our few remaining allies to help with the war."

"No," he says. "I don't want to drag you into this. Your pack has barely recovered from the last war."

I narrow my eyes at him. He's being stubborn as a mule. "What did I tell you about leaning on me? You need our help, and I want to provide it."

"You're directly involving yourself in this now. It's too dangerous."

"I'm perfectly aware of the danger, Kane."

"It's not that I haven't thought of this before, but I rejected the idea. This is a war the shifters are not a part of. You are not a part of this."

"Like hell I'm not. The man I love is at war. It definitely involves me. I will raise the banners myself if I have to."

He snorts and looks away.

I take his hands in mine, squeezing reassuringly. The coolness of his palms is a familiar comfort. "It's because of me your allies turned against you. They couldn't accept that you fell in love and are having a child with a wolf shifter. I can't just stand by and not do anything when I could help fix things."

"The prejudice of the royals is not your fault. I would rather have no allies than have those that would look down upon you," he declares, wrapping his arms around my waist and pulling me closer. "I am not ashamed of what you are. I'm not ashamed of our child. I have made my choices."

I melt a little under his adoring gaze. Is there a woman alive that can resist him when he is like this? He looks at me like I'm the center of his universe. It is intense, and I feel my body beginning to ache for him.

I manage to take a deep breath and return to reality. "That's all very romantic, Kane. But we still have to be pragmatic about this. There's no winning a war without allies. Bernard learned that the hard way, and look where he ended up."

I will be damned before Kane ends up imprisoned in someone's dungeon or worse. I don't even want to think about the worst alternative.

"I'm not going to be the most popular with the Alphas of the packs

Bernard went to war with," he reminds me. "Even the most tolerant of Alphas are still wary of vampires, and they have good reason to be."

"You won't have to win them over," I reply. "I'll do that. I'll hold a meeting with all the Alphas that I know and talk them into helping us."

His dark eyebrows furrow. "What would you say to persuade them to make an alliance with me? Most of them won't even come near Crimson Peak, for obvious reasons."

"You leave that up to me," I reply. "I can be persuasive when I want to be. With the assistance of the wolf shifter packs, you'll have the warriors and resources that you need."

His blue eyes stare at me like he can't believe I exist. "What did I do to deserve you?"

Wanting to lighten the mood, I joke, "Well, I volunteered to be your personal feeder, but you had other ideas. Now we're in love and having a baby. It's funny how life works out."

He chuckles. "I couldn't look away from you. You were terrified, but you were so brave and selfless. You loved that little girl enough to sacrifice yourself. I was smitten almost immediately."

"Smitten?" I repeat the old-fashioned word with a smile. "I didn't know you were smitten with me."

"Besotted, charmed, completely whipped," he adds with a smile of his own. "You know I adore you."

"I know. I just never get tired of hearing you say it."

I run a hand through his dark hair and pull him down for a kiss. It has been some time since we had sex. Dr. Martin hasn't forbidden us from being intimate, but I've been scared and prioritize being careful.

Kane has been so patient with me. He has never pushed or complained. He's waited tirelessly, and it makes me desire him more.

It's hard to remove a shirt I can't see so I stop kissing him and work on getting him naked. I struggle with the buttons, and Kane takes over, quickly peeling it off and throwing it on the floor. I run my hands over his alabaster skin, humming in delight. He reaches behind me to unzip my dress.

My bra comes off with a practiced flick of his wrist. I raise my eyebrows at him in surprise. "Where'd you learn that?"

If he could blush, his face would be red. "Let's not talk about my past."

"Just how many bras have you–"

He cuts me off with a kiss, distracting me with his tongue in my mouth and his hands pulling my dress down. The green silk falls to the floor and Kane lifts me up, guiding my legs to wrap around his waist. He carries me like I weigh nothing and gently drops me down onto the bed.

For a moment, he hovers over me, blue gaze sweeping over me like a caress. I resist the urge to cover myself and hide. My nipples harden from anticipation, wanting to be touched. After what feels like an eternity, Kane finally kisses me again. He pushes inside of me, and I moan in pleasure.

He's being careful, taking his time, moving with restraint. I know it's because of the baby, but I feel myself approaching the edge and urge him on a little, wishing he'd drive a little harder.

When I tug his perfectly sculpted ass, he lets out a little chuckle and increases the speed. His cock feels so good, stretching me in all the right places. I tip my head back and let the waves of ecstasy wash over me again and again until he grunts and joins me.

Breathlessly, I lift my heat to meet his eyes. "We are always better when we work together," I tell him.

"How can I argue with that?"

BEGGING YOU, PLEASE

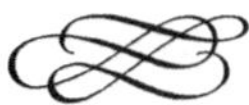

Kane

"Are you sure?" I ask Emory as I pull away from kissing her. Her green eyes are dazed like she's lost in a daydream. Her scarlet hair looks like fire against the black sheets.

It's been months since we've had sex. I've missed sharing this intimacy with her, but I haven't wanted to pressure her. She's been having a difficult time with the pregnancy, and her fears of losing the baby are understandable. I don't want to be self-centered and moan about not having sex when she is dealing with so much.

She smiles softly and replies, "I'm sure." She runs her fingers through my dark hair. "You've been so patient with me."

"I'll wait forever for you."

Her eyebrows furrow. "Not forever. I don't know if I could wait that long to be with you myself."

I chuckle in amusement and kiss her neck, my lips gently brushing over her pulse. I can hear her blood underneath her skin moving through her veins. I've promised never to feed on her, and I won't break that promise, but I'm momentarily distracted. I have not fed directly from the vein in a long time.

I've always considered it too intimate. Blood taken with a needle is impersonal. It's transactional. Taking blood with my teeth pressed into someone's skin is the opposite of that.

"Do you want to feed from me?" Emory asks. I raise my head, and she doesn't look afraid. She seems more curious than anything. "If you want to, I don't mind."

"I told you I would never feed from you. I intend to keep that promise."

"That was before we were together," she reasons. "I trust you not to go too far."

"It might hurt. Even if I take from you gently, it still may hurt a little. And the baby needs your blood, too"

I'd honestly heard that the bite could feel good. A little pain during sex makes the experience more intense. I've never indulged in it. Vampires sharing blood with each other is considered more intimate than sex.

"Would it be safe for the baby?" she asks.

"Probably not."

"Some other time then."

She pulls me down for a kiss, and I deepen it, my tongue tangling with hers. I kiss her until she shivers in my arms, needing to be touched. I lay kisses down her throat and the swell of her breasts. They're fuller now, her nipples a darker shade of pink. Her breath hitches when I take one in my mouth, licking and sucking until she moans.

I run a hand down the growing swell of her belly until I reach between her legs. I press a finger gently inside, feeling how wet she is getting. I slip in another finger, gently rocking them in and out of her. My thumb rubs her clit making her gasp.

"Please, please, please," she begs. "I need you."

"What do you need me to do?" I pull my fingers out, and she groans in frustration. "Tell me, baby."

Her emerald green eyes narrow at me, her cheeks flushed with desire. "I think you know."

I hum in reply and kiss the tip of her nose. Emory looks adorable when she's annoyed. She hisses at me like an angry kitten. I kiss her flushed cheek.

"Go on," I continue. "Tell me what you want me to do."

"Kane." I wait patiently and her face goes completely red. "I want you to fuck me."

"Since you asked so nicely..." I chuckle, and she grunts in irritation.

I position myself between her legs and thrust inside of her. She lets out a little gasp of surprise, her eyebrows furrowed and bites her lip, her eyes closing. The wet silk that surrounds my cock makes me want to groan.

I would have to be dead to forget how it feels to be inside of Emory. Bliss makes me lean my forehead against hers, my hot breath fanning her face. Her hands grasp my shoulders, nails digging into my skin.

"Are you okay?" I ask, even as I just want to get lost in the pleasure of it all.

"Yes," she replies, her voice breathy. "Don't stop."

I bury my face in her neck as I move, rocking into her gradually. She moans, her back arching as I find the spot within her. I take her leg and position it to wrap around my waist so I can thrust deeper into her.

"Kane," she gasps. "Please."

I move faster, and her hands move across my back, her nails leaving bloody lines on my skin. The smell of blood excites me, and I have to fight the urge to bite her. Her pulse is so close. I crave to know what Emory's blood tastes like.

Instead, I take her hand and place it over her clit. She instinctively rubs herself, mindlessly chasing pleasure. Her cunt squeezes my cock, and it nearly makes me stop, it feels so good. I thrust harder into her, and her hips meet mine.

"I'm going to come," Emory moans.

I raise my head so I can look at her. Her emerald eyes are the brightest I've ever seen. I kiss her as she comes, shudders traveling through her. I continue to move, wanting to join her.

I let myself go, lost into the haze of heat and desire. Emory looks dazed, her lips red from my kisses. I groan as I climax, my hips slowing down as I finish. I stop myself at the last second from collapsing into Emory, instead lying down beside her on the black silk sheets,

Emory cuddles closer to me. Her skin is slightly damp from sweat. Red strands of hair stick to her forehead and her neck.

"Are you okay?" she asks, almost shyly.

The question makes me laugh. "I was about to ask you that."

She smiles back. "I love you."

"I love you too."

My arm wraps around her, and I rest my chin on the top of her head. We stay like that until we fall asleep, lulled by the afterglow.

Lex

Opal is upset with me which is not a big surprise. Since the ball, she's been exceedingly moody. She either throws things at me or storms away angrily. In hindsight, I shouldn't have been that honest with her about the depth of my feelings for her and the lack of them.

Opal is emotional, vain, and deeply insecure. There is a deep-rooted need for her to be wanted. My rejection of her cut her deep. This is bad for me when I'm in a castle with no allies. Nobody wants to be associated with me as I represent my brother and my kingdom—their current enemy–and therefore, I am the scum of the earth to them.

I have no choice but to grovel so I can get back into Opal's good graces. Besides how useful she could be for my survival, there is the baby to think about. Opal has shown to be self-destructive even when she's pregnant so I have to curtail her selfish impulses. My child might not make it to term if I leave Opal to her whims.

I find myself carrying Opal out of a room where another orgy is going on even as she's trying to scratch at me. Her baby bump is beginning to show but is hidden by the voluminous skirts of her gown, so I have to be careful as I carry her in my arms.

"Put me down!" she yells.

"I will," I reply, exasperated. "Do you promise not to run back into the drug den?"

She grabs a hunk of my blond hair and pulls, trying to tear the strands from my scalp. I grip her wrist and force her to let my hair go.

"Opal," I chide, "stop being childish."

She scowls at me. "You don't even like me."

I raise an eyebrow at her. "What does that have to do with anything?"

"You don't like me, and you don't care about me," she says. "So why don't you just fuck off and let me be?"

"Because you were trying to consume enough drugs to do something stupid," I retort. "I don't want my kid to end up with a heroin addiction."

"All you care about is this damn baby. You don't even like kids!"

"That is not true. I just never bothered with the idea of having kids. Kane was the one who had to have heirs. I was going to be the cool uncle."

She glares at me. Her icy blue eyes are sharper than a knife. "What do I have to do to make you leave me alone?"

"Nothing, Princess. Like it or not, we're stuck with each other."

"We are not!" she insists. "You just can't accept that this kid isn't yours."

"Uh-huh," I reply. "Whatever you say."

We've had this argument many times. Opal refuses to admit I'm the father. I refuse to agree with her delusions. Rinse and repeat.

We finally reached the doors of her room. I open them with one hand and carry Opal inside, kicking them closed behind us as we enter the room. I finally put Opal down who proceeds to turn her back on me and go to her bed. She reaches underneath and pulls out a bottle of vodka.

For the love of everything good…

I run up to her and snatch the bottle from her.

"No, Opal," I chide her, pointing at her with a finger. "Bad. Bad Opal."

She smacks my hand away. "I'm not a dog, Lex."

"You're pregnant, Opal. You can't poison your body while you have something growing inside of you."

"You make it sound like a fungus," she grumbles. "And maybe it is. You and your entire bloodline are a scourge on this earth."

"You sound like your father."

King Peter's breakfast time hobby is throwing insults my way, mostly about how my family and I deserve to have been drowned at birth, and we're a shame to all of vampirekind. And then usually it's followed up by how all the troubles would go away if my brother would just do the right thing and marry his daughter. Funny how he was quick to say my family is a disease and at the same time still wants to be related to us through marriage. I will never understand King Peter.

"My father is very wise," Opal counters. "There is no better king out there."

"We'll agree to disagree, Princess."

Offended, she tries to slap me. I catch her wrist. As gently as I can, I push her to the bed, and she lands like a sad sack of potatoes. She glares at me.

I smile at her. I have to sweeten her up. If I want my unborn child to make it to term, I'm going to have to watch her like a hawk. I slide the bottle of vodka underneath her bed, making a note to grab it when I leave later.

"How are you feeling, Princess?" I ask in a saccharine voice. "Any aches? Your breasts? Your ankles?"

Opal must be tired because she just lies back and stares at the canopy of her bed. "My ankles are swollen."

"I've heard that can happen." I get her to move up so I can get on the bed. "How about a massage?"

"I am not sleeping with you, Lex!"

"Who said anything about sex? I was just going to massage your poor ankles. You've been on your feet all day. Let me help you."

Opal puts up some token resistance, but eventually, she gives in and lets me take off her shoes and stockings. I sit on the foot of the bed with her ankles on my lap as I massage her feet. I loosen her ankles by shaking them gently from side to side. Opal closes her eyes and lets me work, not even bothering to insult me.

I rub the top of her feet, upward strokes toward her heart for circulation. I do this for both feet until Opal is snoring in bed. When I'm sure she's dead asleep, I get off the bed as quietly as I can. Grabbing the bottle of vodka from underneath the bed, I make my way quickly out of the room. Fatherhood is shaping up to be a lot of work already.

COMING BACK HOME

Emory

I haven't been back to Moon Grove in months. Ever since my father tried to sell off Lola to Kane as a feeder, I've been staying in Crimson Peak. I haven't had the chance to return as I'm dealing with an unexpected pregnancy and trying to be there for Kane. Colt has been ruling the pack in my absence while keeping me updated on everything going on back home over the phone.

Kane and I talk about whether he should come with me or not but we ultimately decide that it would be better if I talk to the other Alphas alone. Rainer and my mother are coming with me for support. My mother will be accompanying me for the trip, but Rainer will be dropping us off before heading back to Crimson Peak.

I haven't had the chance to talk to most of the Alphas of the other packs since I became an Alpha, and I'm not sure how they will respond to me. I know that quite a few of them detest my father.

I watch the view outside of the car as we enter Moon Grove. Something in me relaxes as I see the familiar farmlands and forests of my childhood. A part of me will always consider this place my home. Too much of what I am has been made here.

My mother is glad to be home. She's tried her best not to show her discomfort while living in Castle Graystone, but being around vampires is deeply unsettling for her. She's lived her entire life being taught to fear them, and it's going to take time to unlearn those beliefs. Her moving into the castle to stay with me makes me appreciate her more.

My childhood home, the four-story mansion, comes into view. A bittersweet rush of emotions washes over me. Memories flood my mind, both good and bad. I reach for my mother's hand, and she squeezes reassuringly.

"It's going to be okay," she whispers to me. "The pack is excited to see you again."

I give her a smile, hoping it's convincing. The car stops in front of the house where Colt and several pack members are waiting. Rainer gets out of the front seat first and opens the door for me. I step out first trying to hide how nervous I am. My heart beats faster as I stand before my pack. They stare back at me expectantly.

Colt steps forward. He's gotten larger since I last saw him. He's over six feet, and he's gained muscle. My younger brother towers over me, and he's beginning to resemble a barn door.

What happened to that snotty kid who used to eat dirt? Who is this tall redheaded man that looks like he could fight a bear and survive?

Colt moves first, pulling me into a hug. The familiar scent of cedar trees, sweat, and sunshine greets me. I smile and hug him back. I'm genuinely glad to see my brother again.

"Welcome home," he says with a grin as he pulls away. "Alpha Emory."

"Welcome home, Alpha Emory," the pack repeats.

It still feels surreal to be called Alpha. I wonder if I'll ever get used to it.

"I'm glad to be home," I declare. "Thank you for all your hard work and caring for Moon Grove while I've been away."

My mother steps out of the car, and Colt immediately hugs her. She pats his back and then starts fussing over his appearance. She tries to fix his unruly red hair. Knowing Colt, he hasn't bothered even trying to comb it all day.

Rainer moves closer to me and asks, "Are you sure you'll be okay without me?"

I nod. "I'm surrounded by my pack. I couldn't be safer. Kane needs you more."

I don't tell him that the pack all look uneasy in his presence. He bows his head in agreement before sliding back behind the steering wheel. The car drives away, and I take a fortifying breath. I will be fine. I'm the Alpha.

I talk to the servants individually, asking them how things have been since I left Moon Grove. I know there are things that Colt has either forgotten to tell me or questions he simply wouldn't know to ask them. He's never known the servants the way that I do.

Colt warned me that there's a lot of healing that needs to be done for the pack after the war that lasted over a decade because of my father. He deceived everyone with his lies about why we had to attack other packs. Later we found out it was all for the sake of expanding our territory.

The Alphas of the other packs will be arriving soon, and the house staff is ready to receive them. Colt has readied guest rooms for the Alphas and their entourages who are coming from far away and would prefer to stay the night before making the long journey back home. There is going to be a modest, but delicious, dinner the servants have been working on for the last few days. Thank the Moon Goddess for the harvest has been good this year.

My mother goes to her room to rest and freshen up before the big meeting with the Alphas. Colt and I go to what used to be Bernard's office. My brother has been using the study and has made some changes by redecorating in small ways. He's changed the paintings in the room and switched the heavy leather chairs at the desk for newer office chairs. I can still faintly smell Bernard in the room, the familiar mix of cigar smoke and whisky.

As if able to read my thoughts, Colt tells me, "I can't get his scent out. It's sunk into the wood and carpets. I'd have to get rid of everything."

"It's just a room," I reply. "Besides, it was Grandpa Colton's office first."

"Do you remember him? Grandpa Colton?" Colt asks. "I was only a baby when he died, so I don't have any memories of him."

"I'm not that much older than you. I was three. I remember he had a beard and he smoked a pipe."

Colt goes to the mahogany desk and pulls out a drawer. He reaches in and takes out a pipe. "Is this it?"

I move closer to my brother to take the pipe from him. "This has been here all this time?"

"Dad–I mean Bernard–must have kept it."

Bernard has always admired his father. He spoke about Grandpa Colton with reverence. Colton Moonraker was a well-respected Alpha. He managed to even earn the respect of Kane's father, King Michael.

"You know what I don't understand?" I say. "How did Bernard turn out that way? Grandpa Colton was so different."

"I don't know," Colt returns. "Maybe Grandpa wasn't there enough for him, or Bernard was just born that way? We used to look up to Dad too, remember?"

I run a finger over the dark wood of the pipe. "Do you think Bernard was more like Grandpa Colton than anyone knew? And he was just good at pretending too?"

Colt shrugs. "We'd never know. No one would dare talk badly about the dead."

"We need to be better than those that came before us," I declare. "We owe it to our pack, to ourselves, to the future generations of shifters."

"I think we're doing okay, Em. We've inherited a shit show of problems, and we're doing our best to fix Bernard's messes. It's just going to take some time. Maybe a long time, but you've never been the type to back down from a challenge." He adds, "The pack has been happier since you took over. Although, it does take a lot to be worse than our father."

I laughed. "I know. And I appreciate you for all your help. I can't imagine trying to do all of this on my own."

"You don't have to do this on your own. We're a pack. We're supposed to work together." He pauses before adding, "And I owe you. After everything that happened before. I should have stood up to Dad sooner. What he tried to do to Lola, what he did to you–it was wrong, and I knew it."

I touched his shoulder. "Hey. you did the right thing eventually. You stood up to Bernard, and you had my back when I needed you the most."

"I wish I saw what Dad was doing sooner. We might have ended the war with Crimson Peak earlier, and things would be different."

I have been on this thought spiral of what-ifs before and know there is no point to it except to drive you insane. We can't go back in time and change things so there is no point dwelling on what we could have done differently. The only thing we can do is learn from the past to avoid making the same mistakes.

A part of me acknowledges that Bernard is too slippery not to have found ways of hiding his misdeeds even if he had been exposed sooner. I wouldn't be surprised if anyone that opposed him and got in his way has mysteriously gone missing over the years. I put very few things past my father.

"Bernard had us all fooled, but what's done is done. All we can do from now on is to rebuild the world for a better future. Bernard's mistakes will not be our legacy. I won't allow it."

Colt nods. He looks down at my stomach. I am showing now in my second trimester. The dress I'm wearing can't hide the bump. I'm not trying to hide my pregnancy but I haven't been announcing it to the world either. The other shifters will know by the change in my scent which has an added flowery musk mixed in.

"How far along are you?" he asks.

"I'm about four months, almost five."

"Is it a boy or a girl?"

"I don't know yet. Things have been hectic. I have a doctor's appointment once I'm back in Crimson Peak."

"You look bigger than four months." He winces. "Not that you look big. You just look bigger than other women when they're…. You know what? I'm going to shut up now."

I snort and punch him in the arm. "You're such an asshole."

He holds up his hands in surrender. "I didn't mean to offend you, Alpha. I'm just really excited about being an uncle."

Colt's green eyes are alight with mischief. I'm glad he knows now. He's been one of my most steadfast support systems these past few months. I trust him, and I know he wouldn't do anything to harm my unborn child, regardless of their vampire blood.

"I kind of already knew about the baby," he confesses. "Kane told mom when he came to visit, and I may have been listening in to their conversation."

"You mean you were eavesdropping."

"Which we used to do all the time," he points out. "Remember when Bernard had meetings in here, and we'd listen in from the other room?"

"I remember." We share another laugh before I ask, "You're not upset that it's Kane's?"

"Am I upset that my niece or nephew is half-vampire? It was a lot to take it in at first, but I've come around to it. No matter what, they're family." He looks guilty as he continues, "And after how this pack has treated Lola her entire life, treating somebody like they are less for what's beyond their control is kind of a dick move. There's no reason to treat someone innocent badly."

Colt was never truly cruel to Lola growing up. He mostly ignored her. He followed our mother's example on how to treat our half-sister. Seeing him learning and trying to be better makes me want to cry.

I turn away and wipe my tears. "Pregnancy hormones. Everything makes me emotional."

"Are you sure about the meeting with the Alphas? I know you said this is important, but we can postpone it if you're not up for it?"

"I'm fine," I reassure him. "I'm not the first, nor will I be the last, woman who has had to work through her pregnancy."

"Well, if you need anything, I'm here."

"I know. Thank you."

"So...." He gives me a look. "Am I going to be the godfather or not?"

"After you implied I'm fat? Absolutely not." We laugh, and I give him a hug.

ALL THE ALPHAS

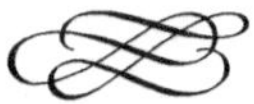

Emory

I have met the Alphas of other packs over the years. Some of them have visited Moon Grove and my father took the family with him to visit the other packs often. The visits grew less frequent over time as my father collected more enemies than allies. I know that our pack used to be on good terms with most packs during my grandfather's tenure as Alpha, but Bernard's unstoppable greed and ambition poisoned whatever good will Grandpa Colton had achieved during his lifetime.

I try to remain calm and hide my nervousness as the Alphas arrive at the mansion. They bring their entourages, believing in the power of numbers as all shifters do. I greet them at the front door, introducing myself as the new Alpha of the Moonraker pack. Most of them look at me warily, probably trying to assess how similar I am to my father.

I don't look much like my father, inheriting my looks from my mother's side of the family. Colt is as tall as our father, but his coloring is similar to mine. Somehow, neither of us inherited much of our father's appearance except for Lola who inherited his gray eyes.

It's not a bad thing this time as no one would look at me and be reminded of Bernard instantly.

Alpha Bastille of the Silvercrest pack arrives. He's the Alpha that assisted Bernard in trying to attack Castle Graystone. I don't hold any ill will against him as Bernard had tricked him into thinking Kane had stolen me from my pack to be a feeder against my will.

"Alpha Bastille," I say. "I'm glad you could come."

"Alpha Emory," he replies. "I'm glad to be here especially after the last time we saw each other. I'm hoping you don't hold what happened against me."

Bastille Silvercrest is known to be a family man with half a dozen daughters. If a vampire king had stolen any of his own daughters, he would have also marched off to war with his pack. No one could fault him for his sense of honor and duty.

"No at all," I reassure him. "Your heart was in the right place. And I hold no grudges for past events. I lay all the blame at my father's feet."

Bastille smiles in relief. "That's good as I do hope we can be allies if not good friends."

I smile, hoping that this is going to work lighting within me. "I would like that."

We have dinner first in the large formal dining room we rarely use except for special occasions and we had plenty of guests to accommodate. It's like Winter Solstice dinner with the spread of food on display. The shifters dig in, most of them starving from their long travels.

All of the Alphas are older than me and easily could be my parents or even grandparents. They've known each other for years, and the wine and good food put them into the mood for talking and enjoying each other's company. Soon, they're retelling old stories and laughing with each other.

To my right is the wife of one of the oldest Alphas. Luna Mary Claire of the Boldlight pack was childhood friends with my grandmother and told me about their youth.

"Your grandmother Emory, your namesake, was originally supposed to marry her father's Beta who was twice her age. That was until your grandfather swooped in and eloped with her. It was a big scandal. Your great-grandfather Elias nearly disowned her for it."

"Colton was a heartbreaker before he met Emory," her husband Alpha Silas interjects. "He left a long line of girls hoping to be his Luna crying before he settled down."

"I had no idea Grandpa Colton was like that when he was younger. How did he meet my grandmother?"

"That was me, dear," another older Alpha Nigel cut in. "Colton and I were friends from school. I knew Emory because I dated her sister Isobel. We all happened to be at the same party, and I made the introductions. It was clear right away they were fated mates."

"You have old Nigel here to thank for your existence," Mary Claire concludes. "And I'm sure he will never let you forget it."

Nigel winks at me. "You're welcome."

I share amused looks with Colt who is stuck listening to Alpha Gerald recount that time he and his brothers took down a grizzly bear when they were younger. It's an eventful dinner, and I am having a good time getting to know the Alphas. I'm by far the youngest Alpha at the table, and I know that the wisdom they can impart on me will be useful as I navigate learning to lead my pack.

As we are having dessert, I can see everyone is relaxed from the good food, drink, and chatter. Before I can bring it into the conversation, Alpha Silas beats me to the punch and asks, "My dear, I am curious, is there more to this dinner than introducing yourself to us?"

I nod, trying to hide my apprehension. "I've truly enjoyed getting to know all of you, but I do have another reason I wanted you all to be here."

The table goes quiet, and the Alphas and the dignitaries stare at me where I'm seated at the head of the table. I meet Colt's eyes who nods at me encouragingly. I look over the faces of our guests and take a steadying breath. I need to be brave.

"As you may be aware, I have an alliance with the vampire king of Crimson Peak. King Kane is one of my most loyal allies," I start. "You may also know about the burgeoning war between him and King Peter of Scarlett Thunder."

There's some grumbling as the shifters murmur to each other. I try to ignore the whispers and continue. "King Kane needs allies to aid him with this war. I'm fully committed to assisting him, but I cannot do it on my own. That's why I invited you all here. I'm hoping that you are willing to help us in any way that you are able."

A deafening silence fills the room. The Alphas stare at me then whisper amongst each other. Alpha Gerald slams his first on the dining table. Everyone is silent and looks at him.

"Let me get this clear," he says. "You want us to throw our support behind a vampire king your pack was at war with for years? Because of a war he is having with another vampire king, a war that has nothing to do with our kind?"

My mouth is dry. I swallow and reply, "Something like that."

There is another pause.

Alpha Gerald bursts into laughter. He reaches for his wine glass. "And I thought your father was the delusional one. Do you really think I'm going to help you after Bernard tried to take over my territory?"

Yet again, I want to punch my father in the face for all the horrible shit he has passed onto me to fix. If he hadn't been such a dick in the past, I wouldn't be having such a tough time trying to convince people to be my allies. It makes me want to go back to Castle Graystone and punch him in the fucking face.

"My father's past actions are regrettable. I am truly sorry for the harm he has caused," I say. "I'm trying to prevent more harm from being done by making sure King Kane wins this war. There is no world where King Peter being the victor will be good for any of us. I have heard he's allied himself with King Myenas."

That makes the shifters whisper more fiercely. King Myenas's reputation is well-known even among the shifters. He's a cruel king who makes King Peter look like a kitten. He's also rumored to be associated with sex-trafficking, particularly of young girls.

Shifter girls.

Alpha Nigel looks disappointed. "Have you thought this through, my dear? Getting involved with the troubles of vampires has historically never worked for us. It's only caused us more strife down the line."

"If you had said you were the one at war, we might have considered it," Alpha Silas agrees. "But to use our people and resources to aid a vampire king is unspeakable."

"We all have great respect for your grandfather, and that's why most of us have shown up today, despite our history with your father," Alpha Nigel explains. "Asking us to go to war for you is a big request."

"And from what I've heard, you and the vampire king are more than allies," Alpha Gerald adds in. He points to me. "I heard he's the father of your child."

My face goes red, but it's not from embarrassment. I'm angry. I try to recover and say, "King Kane and I do have a relationship. He is the father of my unborn child."

I'm not ashamed of Kane, and I'm not ashamed of our baby. I'll be damned before some Alpha makes me feel like I'm committing a crime for being in love.

"Are you sure?" Mary Claire asks. "Our kind and his have never been able to have children together before."

"There are myths about hybrids," Alpha Nigel's wife, Luna Angela, speaks up. "They're rare and tend to be omens of bad times to come."

A hand protectively cradles my swollen belly. All the folktales about hybrids being nightmarish monsters are always at the back of my mind. "My baby is not an omen. He or she will be just like any other child. And yes, I'm sure the child is Kane's. It couldn't possibly be anyone else's child."

"Your kid is going to be the heir to two territories. He will have claim to both Moon Grove and Crimson Peak," Alpha Silas points out. "Your child will not be like other children. The power they'll inherit alone will be substantial."

"And that should incentivize your cooperation," Colt jumps in, trying to help. "When Emory's child ascends the throne, you will be allied to a powerful king and Alpha. Are you really going to pass that up?"

Alpha Silas looks contemplative. "This child will be a ruler that will truly unite vampires and shifters as they'll be a part of both worlds. Not even a marriage alliance could have secured this."

"Isn't that what my grandfather wanted? He wanted us to live in peace with vampires. To work together with them instead of being at war." I look around at each of them, trying to drive my point home.

"It sounds like a dream," Alpha Nigel declares. "A far-fetched dream that is too good to be true."

"It doesn't have to be. We can have that future if you'll help me fight this war with Scarlett Thunder," I say. "And I promise you I will work on creating a future we all want. No more living in fear of being oppressed. We can finally co-exist with vampires."

I meet the eyes of everyone at the table, seeing their expression soften. I know I'm getting through to them. Alpha Gerald's face remains stoic. His facial hair really makes it hard to see if he's smiling or not. He finishes his glass of wine and immediately refills it.

"Are you fighting with me or not?" I question. "And if it helps at all, we have Bernard locked up in the dungeons of Castle Graystone. He'll spend the rest of his life there for trying to take over your territories."

Alpha Gerard laughs again. "I like you, girl. You've got spunk."

I look at the other Alphas. Alpha Silas raises his hands in surrender. "All right. I'm willing to listen. What do you need from me?"

Alpha Nigel grins. "Your grandfather would be proud. I don't think we've all agreed on the same thing in years."

The other Alphas join in after them, taking their cues from the older Alphas. I catch my mother's gaze, and she's smiling proudly at me. I smile in relief. The tight ball of anxiety inside my chest uncoils.

I have done it. I have my army.

I can't wait to tell Kane.

A CRUEL HISTORY

Kane

Emory has left for Moon Grove to persuade the other shifter packs into becoming our allies. I try not to be too hopeful that she'll succeed, not because I have no faith in her but because the enmity between our species has been around for far longer than Emory has been alive. It will take a lot of coaxing to get these old Alphas to want to fight on our side rather than be against us.

I have no choice but to let Emory move forward with her plan. I have to focus on what I can control. The information Lex has been able to provide me has slowed. King Peter is getting cagey which cannot bode well for me.

Rainer has not had progress with urging Willow to change her mind and join the war. The witch is prone to anger and has destroyed several pieces of furniture and other items in her room. Emory has also tried talking to her which went well enough but didn't change anything. Willow refuses to talk to me and actively hides when I try to visit her.

The guilt I feel over what happened to the witches follows me, haunting me with questions I cannot find answers to. My father is long dead. Trying to communicate with the dead is not something my kind has knowledge of. The closest I could potentially get to finding out what really happened during the witch hunts is to talk to my mother.

The queen is having her usual lunch in the gazebo. She's taken a liking to Emory's younger sister Lola and makes sure to have the little girl's favorite foods served during mealtimes. The blonde notices me first as I approach the gazebo by the rose gardens. She turns to my mother who whispers something to her.

Lola gets up from her seat and runs out of the gazebo. She stops in front of me and does a clumsy curtsy.

"King Kane," she greets me.

Before I can reply, she runs off. I watch her disappear from the gardens, her green dress blending in with the trees. I have tried to be friendly to the child since she's come to the castle, but she's still very skittish around me. Emory reassures me that Lola will eventually warm up to me, but I'm not sure if that will ever happen.

I enter the gazebo, and my mother is drinking from a goblet of blood.

"Are you hungry?" she asks.

"I haven't had the time."

She waves a hand and the servants place a goblet in front of me. They fill the goblet with fresh blood from a pitcher sitting on the end of the table. I take a long drink and savor the feeling of becoming reenergized.

My mother puts down her goblet. "When is Emory returning from her trip?"

"In a week," I reply. "She hasn't been back to Moon Grove in a while. She wants to spend time with her pack."

"I'm only concerned for her pregnancy. Traveling in her condition can't be good for her."

"She insisted on going."

"And you let her?"

I give her a look. "I'm not her jailer, and she's not my prisoner. You raised me better than that."

She gives me a pleased little smile. "She is too headstrong to be bossed around by anyone. You chose well. You'll have a true partner."

"Like what you had with father?"

"Your father seeking out my council was unusual in our time, and most rules still prefer their wives only bothered with producing heirs and keeping their silence the rest of the time."

I'm more than aware of how our society still values our women. Being raised by a political genius like my mother only showed me how much better my life would be if I don't underestimate the women around me. When it came to choosing a wife, I had chosen Opal for the political and financial gain she would bring to our union. I hadn't hoped to find a love match like my parents.

The bloodless way I chose a spouse came to bite me in the end. If I had chosen different criteria for my future wife, I would not be dealing with the mess with Scarlett Thunder. If I had waited until I found Emory, I wouldn't be in the middle of a war. It's a thought process that keeps me up at night.

"Father trusted you to always give him the best advice," I point out. "And you did. From what I've heard, you're the reason there was less bloodshed between us and the shifters."

"I never saw the reason to antagonize the wolves. While we may be stronger and faster, the tides can always change. There was a time when vampires were not at the top of hierarchy. We had to fight for our position."

"That's something I wanted to talk to you about." She waited for me to continue, her pale blue eyes focused on me. "I need to know about the witch hunts. Why did father feel the need to hunt down the witches to extinction?"

I watch as my mother's nail traces the rim of her goblet. "As you are aware, your father prided himself in his efficiency. He would quell any potential threats before they had a chance to even become a minor nuisance."

"I am aware of that, but from what I've also heard, the witches were never a real threat to us. They didn't have the numbers or the wealth. They didn't even have the ambition to try and overthrow us. They were the weakest of all the species."

"They had magic, and that was enough for Michael." my mother says. "Magic was unpredictable. We didn't know how to fight against it if the witches decided to overthrow us. One witch alone would be able to take down multiple vampires."

"They weren't trained for war. They focused on food and healing themselves."

"But for how long?" she questions. "How long before they decided to harness their magic for battle? How do you fight against such power?"

"They were physically weaker than us. And they would need a significant increase in population to even come close to something we had to worry about."

Queen Agatha turns away, her face showing more emotion than I'm used to seeing on her. Her composure is breaking. "Do you remember when you were a child and you asked me where vampires originated from?"

"You said we were created first before all the other species except for humans. The rest came after us."

"That's a lie." She pauses, taking a sip from her goblet before continuing. "The humans came first. That's true. That's why there're so many of them. They multiplied faster than all of us. From them, the witches came, humans that could harness magic."

I keep quiet, trying to take all this in. This isn't the story I've been told my entire life.

"The shifters came later when the witches harnessed their magic to change their forms for battle and hunting," she adds. "In their lore, they came from the Moon Goddess. We believe they came from witches. Either way, the shifters grew too strong, so the witches created a new species to fight the shifters."

"Vampires."

She nods. "That's why Michael feared the witches. They made us, and they could unmake us. Those of us who can have our own children are directly descendants from the witches. The others are turned humans. It's why he had to suppress their population. The less witches there were, the safer we would be."

I sit in silence, centuries of propaganda being dismantled in my mind. We had turned on our creators. The witches had been the most powerful of us. They had created at least one of the most powerful species.

"And you let father do all of that?" I ask. "To destroy so many lives in fear of what they could potentially do to us?"

"I never said it was right. Even I knew he was going too far, Michael was my king. His word was law."

"He was a tyrant."

"He did what he thought needed to be done," she says. "Our kingdom has managed to be stable and flourishing due to all his years of hard work. Crimson Peak would not be what it is if he had not sacrificed so much."

"And at what cost, Mother?" I demand. "I'm at war. I'm on the brink of losing everything. The only thing that might be able to save me is a witch, and she has no reason to want to fight for me."

She reaches over to take my hand. "Kane, you have to understand–"

"No." I get up from my seat abruptly, causing dishes and cutlery to rattle on the table. "I do not want to hear your excuses. We did monstrous things. There is no excuse for any of that."

I leave without turning back.

My mother calls out for me.

I ignore her.

She's not the one I need to talk to.

WILLOW

There is a knock at the door. I expect it to be Rainer, coming to annoy me again. I heard Emory has left the kingdom for business, so it can't be her. It might be Lola wanting to discuss books with me again.

Instead, it's the last person I expect to see. King Kane enters my room, looking more contrite than I've ever thought him capable of. I try to go to the bathroom and lock myself in there until he leaves. He raises a hand to stop me.

"Please," he says. "I just need to talk to you. I know I don't have the right to ask anything of you, but I need you to hear this."

I cross my arms over my chest, wanting to feel some kind of armor. I don't feel safe with him. I look at him, and I see King Michael. His father was a cold, cruel man. While the other vampires have always worshiped his memory, I know what the old king truly was.

"I'm sorry."

That makes me pause.

"I'm sorry for what happened to you and what happened to all the other witches," he continues, his expression pained. "What my father did was unforgivable. None of you deserved it. I should have stopped it. I should have said something, but I didn't because I was so young, and he was the king."

Of all the things I expect to hear from him, that isn't it.

"You're sorry?" I ask. "After all this time?" He'd made similar statements before, but now I can see he means it. He's not just trying to convince me of something.

"I tried not to think about the witch hunts because I was ashamed. I looked up to my father, but he did monstrous acts. I couldn't make peace with these two opposing sides of him. And I know it's not an excuse, but I need you to know, for all I have been a party to, I truly am so sorry."

I feel too much; the wave of emotions is threatening to break me. Anger, disbelief, sorrow, and a bittersweet respite that *finally* somebody is acknowledging what happened to my people.

But can I truly forgive them? Do I have it in me to be able to absolve all the wrongs against my people? Is it even my place to do so? I have lived longer as a vampire than a witch. Do I even have the say to give absolution for something I hadn't been for a very long time?

"You don't need to forgive me," Kane tells me. "Whatever you feel is yours to feel, and no one can take that from you."

A skeptical voice in me that has kept me alive warns me this is just a ploy to get me to be more agreeable. "Are you only saying this because you want me to fight in your war?"

"No," he replies. "I will not pressure you to fight for Crimson Peak if you decide not to do so. I owe it to you. You should have the power to choose for yourself."

"I…" I swallow the tears threatening to escape me. I will not cry in front of him. "I don't know if I can ever just let this go."

"That's fine."

"But thank you. I didn't know I needed you to apologize so sincerely."

He nods. "I will leave you to your privacy. And if there is anything you need from me, please let me know."

Kane leaves my room. As soon as the door shuts behind him, I collapse on my bed, my knees no longer able to keep me up. I feel hollowed out, all my emotions drained from me. I can't even cry.

HAPPY BIRTHDAY, EMORY

Emory

I don't immediately return to Crimson Peak. I take a few days to iron out the alliances with the other Alphas before they return to their villages. All the excitement from the previous days finally hits me, and I need to rest. My mother calls for a pack healer to come to the mansion for a check-up since the doctor I have been seeing is all the way back at Castle Graystone.

I have known the pack healer since I was a child. Collins was the healer that delivered Colt and I. And he and my mother have worked together over the years. Seeing a familiar face is a comfort despite my worsening health. He has no experience dealing with hybrid babies, but no one does.

The check-up seems to be going well until he starts asking questions. "How far along are you supposed to be?"

"Four months, almost five."

His dark eyebrows furrow. "Are you sure? From what I've seen, you're a lot further along than that."

That makes me look to my mom in worry. She comes over from where she's standing and places a comforting hand on my shoulder.

"What do you mean?" I inquire. "Is something wrong with the baby?"

"The child is larger than what it should be at four months. I won't be able to see clearly without an ultrasound, but the fetus being larger than it should be might point to underlying health concerns."

"Is it possible you're further along than you think?" my mom asks.

"It can't be. I was a virgin before Kane and I..." I blush, embarrassed I have to explain this to my mother. "There was no one else before him, and we hadn't been intimate until a little over four months ago."

"Could we have an ultrasound done?" my mom asks the healer.

"I don't have the machine with me. We could schedule you to come to the clinic soon."

"I'll be back in Crimson Peak soon," I explain. "I can have Dr. Martin do the ultrasound, and we can see what's going on."

Collins doesn't argue with me over that. He asks me more questions about my symptoms. He's looking over my chart and points out, "Your twenty-first birthday is this weekend."

Mortified, I cover my face with my hands. "I completely forgot."

My mother shakes her head. "I can't believe I forgot too. I gave birth to you."

"This year has just been a lot," I say. "The pregnancy, taking over as Alpha, and Scarlett Thunder..."

"It's all right. You've had to juggle a lot," Mom reminds me.

"The tiredness, the fever, and aches can be attributed to your body getting ready to shift," the healer explains. "The changes in your body could have worsened your pregnancy symptoms."

"Is there anything I need to do?"

Fear grips my heart as the thought of shifting while pregnant is taking over. Most miscarriages happen because of women shifting while pregnant. The body contorting and breaking is not good for the baby. Now that I know something might be wrong with my pregnancy, shifting feels like a death sentence.

"I can prescribe something to bring down your fever, but otherwise, lots of fluids and rest before you shift," he advises. "And if something happens during or after the shift, call me right away."

I follow the healer's advice and try to rest. It's hard not to worry as my birthday draws near. I tell Kane over the phone, and he wants to come be with me for the shift, but I prefer that he stay in Crimson Peak. He can't help me during the shift. It would be better to send for the doctor, but I won't. The healer will be my best bet if I need help.

My mother is going to be there with me for the shift. Colt and some of our pack members will be nearby to help if needed. I have been waiting for this day to come for years, eagerly anticipating meeting my wolf. There are a lot of benefits to finally shifting. Not only will being able to shift help me in battle, I should be able to heal more quickly once I have my wolf.

I'm glad I don't have to be alone for this. When my mother wasn't speaking to me, I thought I would have to be alone for my first shift. It's a terrifying and lonely thought. I'm relieved I'll be surrounded by my pack.

I spend the next few days in bed, trying to rest up and take the healer's advice. The morning of my birthday, Mother brings me the phone. I'm delighted to hear Kane's voice in my ear.

"Are you sure you don't want me to be there?" he asks.

"I'll have my mom with me. She's guided people through their first shifts before, and she'll call the pack healer if anything happens."

"I can't help but worry. I heard that it's especially dangerous when you're pregnant."

"I'm trying not to think about it," I confess. "It's not something I can delay or prevent from happening."

Shifting forms is a part of our biological makeup. Those that try to stop themselves from changing end up hurting themselves. There are tonics and what-not people have drank, but that will be even more dangerous for the baby. It's not a pleasant experience the first time, but it usually doesn't hurt.

"I wish I could do more for you," Kane tells me. "I feel powerless that I'm over here, and you might be over there in pain."

"I was always going to shift. It's what I am. What I need you to do is to just go through your day and trust that I'll be back in Crimson Peak by Monday."

He sighs. "I love you."

I grasp the phone with both hands wishing I could touch Kane instead. "I love you too."

"Happy Birthday, Emory."

The phone call ends quickly after that. I want to cry as I miss him so much. I do wish he was here with me as his strength and reliability have gotten me through so much this year. He has been my rock, and it's hard to be away from him when I am the most vulnerable.

I try not to focus on what's coming tonight and ruin my day. I'm going to do my best to enjoy my birthday. The servants prepared a nice breakfast with all my favorite food. My family and I spend the day together playing board games and recalling childhood memories.

The only one missing is Lola, but I would rather my sister stay in Crimson Peak instead of worrying about me during my shift. My family is there for me despite everything that has happened with Bernard. We have grown closer and prioritized each other over the incidents that divided us before.

After beating us in most of the board games, Mom brings out presents for me. I can tell which one is from Colt as it's the one wrapped messily with too much tape on it. There are a few from the pack and even from the Alphas. I'm surprised to see presents from Kane, Rainer, and the staff from Castle Graystone.

"King Kane had the gifts sent over this morning," my mom explains. "You should open them."

Colt has gifted me a personalized wax seal stamp with my initials wrapped in our family logo of a crescent moon. My mom's gift is a tennis bracelet that belonged to my maternal grandmother. Rainer has gifted me a dagger set in an ornate, bejeweled scabbard. The gifts from the pack and the Alphas are a mix of jewelry, clothes, and even money. The gifts from the Castle Graystone servants are more modest with hand knitted scarves and baby clothes.

I leave Kane's present for last. When I finally open it, I can't help but wish he was here with me. It's a set of emeralds that match my eyes perfectly. I lift up a set of pear shaped earrings and a necklace. They're beautiful. I can't help admire the light reflecting off the gems.

"King Kane has good taste," Mom remarks.

"He does." I give her and Colt my best smile, feeling full of gratitude but still sad about who is not here. "Thank you for today and the gifts. I'm glad I'm home."

My mom takes my hand in hers. "I've been waiting for years for this day. It's not how I had imagined it to be, but I am so proud of you."

Tears well in my eyes. "Thanks, Mom."

I plan to call Kane tomorrow and thank him for the gifts. I know I am too concerned with the shift that night to think about much of anything else. I'm too distracted to even eat dinner. Restlessness rumbles through me as I watch the sun go down from my bedroom window.

My skin feels overheated and tingly like ants are crawling all over my skin. My joints ache like I've been overworking my body. There's a thrumming in my blood as if something is waiting deep inside of me for what's to come.

I have always wondered about my wolf and what she will look like. Everyone's wolf is different. There are different beliefs about what influences our coloring and traits. Most say it's genetics, but it's hard to predict what a wolf will be like until it emerges.

When the moon begins to appear in the sky, Mom comes to my room. She stays by the doorway trying to be as strong and supportive for me as she can be. She asks, "Are you ready?"

"I'm as ready as I'll ever be."

I'm terrified, but there's no point focusing on that. I move toward the doorway, and my mom takes my hand, guiding me down the hallway and down the stairs. We make our way to the forests outside the house, the place I spent my childhood exploring. The forests are as much my home as the mansion.

Colt and the pack are nearby making sure we will be safe. But right now, I prefer some privacy. I look up at the moon and feel an involuntary shiver go through me. My heart beats like a drum in my chest. I want to run away, but there's no escaping my fate.

"It'll be all right," my mom reassures me as she helps me undress. "You are a Moonraker, descended from generations of Alphas. Those that came before you have shifted in this forest. You were born for this."

I hold onto my mother's words as I stand naked in the forest. The only light is from the mansion's windows far behind us and the moon above us. The waiting is terrible. All my nerve endings are anticipating potential pain. I'm more afraid for my baby than anything else.

The first jolt feels like I've been hit by a hot poker. My bones begin to break in unnatural angles, reshaping themselves into a new form. I hold my breath in terror, unable to stop what's happening to me. My mom urges me to lie down on the ground so I don't fall and hurt myself.

I claw at the dirt underneath me as I feel my nails lengthen and curve into claws. My skin feels like it's heating up. I can feel my spine protruding, my ribs expanding, and my legs beginning to bow.

It doesn't hurt too much, but it's such a strange sensation. I hold my breath.

I remember my baby. The child has barely lived, but might die as my body breaks itself.

"Mama," I beg. "My baby!"

She kneels beside me, her eyes worried and sad. "It'll be okay, Emory."

I close my eyes as my spine reforms itself, and I can't move, my face pressed to the ground. My body is taken over by natural forces, and there is no escape.

After several minutes, I can't talk anymore. My vocal cords have been rearranged, forcing me to endure the shift in silence or through the mind-link. All I can focus on is the dirt underneath me. How many different ways can my body wreck itself before it's done?

And then it stops.

WOLF LIKE ME

Emory

I open my eyes and stare up at the full moon. My senses are over-powered. I can hear and see things from afar. I smell everything from my mom's cloying perfume to the dirt coating my paws.

I look down at my new body. My paws are large and covered in white fur. I turn my head to look over the rest of my body. I am stunningly white with a fluffy tail.

"You're beautiful, Emory," my mother says with a smile.

I open my mouth to talk but only a wolfish whine comes out.

Mom only smiles and reaches into her purse to pull out a hand mirror. She holds it up for me, and I see a white wolf with golden eyes. I have a long snout. I'm larger than I expected and I hover over my mom. I expected to be red, like my hair. This must mean something.

"White wolves are rare," she says. "Your grandmother Emory had fur just like yours."

I nod in understanding, but I can't keep standing here. I want to run through the forest. I haven't had this influx of energy in such a long time. I know I shouldn't go far because of the baby, but I know these woods like the back of my hand. My mother must see my excitement because she gestures toward the trees.

"Go on," she encourages. "I'll be right here if you need me."

I don't need further encouragement. I run off, my paws kicking the dirt underneath me as I sprint into the trees. The cool, crisp air rushing through my fur feels amazing. I run so fast, I feel like I'm flying.

I have never felt freer. A joy and rightness overcomes me. This is what I'm meant to be. I stop running to let out a victorious howl.

Howls answer me, welcoming my wolf to the world.

Kane

I'm worried about Emory and her first shift. She told me that she's going to be fine, and she can handle it. I want to be with her, but I don't know how to help her if something goes wrong. I have never seen someone's first shift before, and I know the shifters regard it as sacred and intimate. I suppose having a vampire there would be offensive to her pack, no matter our relationship.

I'm unable to sleep the night of Emory's birthday. I stay up all night staring out of the window at the full moon. Rainer keeps me company, and we share a bottle of blood. We discuss his situation with Willow to keep our minds off Emory.

"Maybe you should look for another woman to pursue," I tell my old friend. "There are less troublesome prospects for you out there, plenty of fish in the sea."

Rainer takes a long sip of blood. "I want this fishy. I don't know why."

"I wonder if this desire is born from guilt." I say. "Perhaps you only want to make up for your wrongs against her?"

"This isn't that. Though I do want to atone for my past in whatever capacity she will let me," he explains. "I've been drawn to her since before our shared history was revealed to me."

"Because she's pretty?"

"She is. She's also intelligent, witty, and completely immune to my charms."

"A challenge can be exciting, my friend. But I do caution you to rethink how surmountable this challenge is," I add. "Willow is reticent out of fear and resentment. Giving her space might be what's best for all parties involved."

Rainer hands me the bottle and replies, "I would prefer you helped me rather than tried to discourage me, Kane."

"I only wish the best for our friend Willow. She's been through a lot."

"I know, and we are responsible for a majority of that."

"But?"

His pale blue eyes look down as if he's ashamed to let out the words. "I find it difficult to be away from her. I feel myself being drawn back in like a moth to a flame. Fighting it feels like I'm resisting something greater than myself."

I've never heard someone express how it felt to fall in love with Emory. Fighting fate was like losing a war I never even knew I was involved in.

I pour blood into my glass and hand the bottle back to Rainer. "Well, my friend, I wish you all the luck in the world."

I know he's going to need it.

EMORY

Collins checked me the morning after my first shift, and I'm fine. So is my child. It's a relief.

The difference in me after my first shift is profound. I have more energy. I don't feel so sick anymore. I'm able to be active and get work done without having to struggle through it.

Despite my growing belly, I feel agile. I'm still sensitive to smells, and my enhanced senses make my pregnancy symptoms worse, but it's not too bad. It will take time for me to get used to the enhanced hearing and sight. I can understand why shifters often hide away for up to a month after their first shift while they acclimate.

I'm eager to get back to Crimson Peak. I miss Kane, and there's still the war with Scarlett Thunder that can't be ignored for too long. My mom is not enthusiastic to go back to Castle Graystone, but she refuses to stay behind. She tells me she has no plans to leave my side until after I give birth. She probably won't leave until after the baby starts crawling. Her steadfastness is my gain so I don't fight her on it.

Monday morning comes, and Colt sees us out to the car. The servants load our luggage into the SUV.

"Are you sure you can't stay another week?" he asks. "Winter will be here soon. Do you really want to spend that in that freezing castle?"

"We'll be fine," I reassure him, pulling him into a hug. "You should come visit me after the baby is born."

He pulls away. "I've sworn never to set foot in Crimson Peak again, but for you, I'll brave it."

Mom goes to hug him. She kisses him on the cheek and tells him to take care of himself. She fusses over him, and he lets her. The driver opens the door for me, and I slide in. Mom follows me, and Colt closes the car door.

The driver starts the engine, and we drive away. Colt and the servants wave at us as we leave. I look back and watch the people I grew up with and my childhood home disappear behind me. A part of me will always belong to Moon Gove and my pack, but this isn't my only home anymore.

I'm going back to the other home I've found–Kane.

There is a relief when I see Crimson Peak appear before us. I enter the castle without any fanfare. It's the middle of the day, and the servants are busy working. The nobles are usually in important meet-ings, and I have no intention of running into them. My mother leaves to go unpack her luggage in her room while I go to find Lola.

I ask one of the servants where my sister is, and they inform me Lola is having lunch with Queen Agatha in the gazebo. I have servants bring my luggage to my room, and I make my way to the rose gardens. Sure enough, the Queen and Lola are having a pleasant lunch with tea and cake for my sister and the familiar goblet sitting in front of the queen. Lola sees me first and leaves the table to run toward me.

"Emory!" Careful of my belly, she hugs me. "I missed you!"

"I missed you too, Lo."

She pulls away and asks, "Why were you gone for so long? You said you would only leave for a few days."

"Well, Lo, I forgot about my birthday, so I had to stay longer."

Her gray eyes widen in surprise. "Do you mean *that* birthday?"

I nod. "Yes, *that* birthday. But I'm fine. I got through it."

"You met your wolf?"

"I did. She has white fur and golden eyes."

"Can I see her?"

I try not to wince at how vampires might react to my wolf form. While the servants have seemingly accepted me, the nobles are still another matter. I don't want to give them any excuse to attack me. Besides, I don't want to shift again until after the baby is born for safety's sake.

"Maybe some other time," I tell her.

Queen Agatha gets up from the table and approaches us. "It's nice to have you back, Emory. You're looking better."

Kane must have informed her about my first shift.

"The shifter healer gave me some advice to help with the pregnancy symptoms," I reply. "I still have an appointment with Dr. Martin today to make sure the baby is okay."

She glances down at my belly. Collins said I look bigger for how far along I am. Other people might be noticing it too. Even I can tell that I look further along than I should.

"Maybe you should go see him sooner rather than later," Queen Agatha suggests. "I'll make sure he clears out his schedule for you."

Kane

I wake up to Emory entering my room. She smells of the woods and sunshine. There's a new quality to her scent, the musky fragrance that I associate with wolves.

I sit up as she approaches the bed. "Hi."

"Hi," she greets me with a smile. She takes a seat on the silk sheets beside me. "Did you have a late night?"

"It's been hard to sleep without you. I tried not to worry, but it's been impossible."

She takes my hand and squeezes it reassuringly. "I called to tell you it all went well."

"I heard it's dangerous. I wasn't sure if you were just telling me what I wanted to hear."

"It was scary. I'm not going to sugarcoat that. I've never experienced anything like that."

My eyebrows furrow. "You're not making me feel better."

"I really am fine," she insists. "After I met my wolf, it was all worth it. I feel different. Stronger, faster, healthier. I'm not bedridden from the pregnancy anymore."

"And the baby is okay?"

"I have an appointment with Dr. Martin today. I would like you to be there with me unless you have important matters you can't get out of."

"Nothing is more important than you and the baby."

I lean closer to her for a kiss. I have missed the taste of her. I cup the soft silk of her cheek. I pull away, and her eyes open slowly. Her emerald eyes are bright with happiness.

"When is your doctor's appointment?" I ask.

"In about…" she looks at the grandfather clock at the corner of my room, "ten minutes."

I get up from the bed to dress. Emory stays seated as I open the closet door to pull out a shirt and pants. I inquire, "How did the negotiations with the Alphas go?" We haven't discussed this much because we've been concentrating on the baby.

"Each Alpha has a list of demands. We'll have to look over the contracts later to see what you're willing to agree to. There wasn't anything too egregious."

I slide my arms into the sleeves of a black shirt. "The treasury is a little sparse. We can't offer them gold."

"Most of them are actually hoping to marry off their kids or grandkids to our future child."

I raise both my eyebrows at her. "I thought shifters prioritized mates over arranged marriages."

"We do, but should our unborn child have one of their offspring as a mate, it would work well for all of us."

"There's no way you can choose a mate, right?"

She shakes her head. "No one really knows what influences the selection, but no. It comes from the Moon Goddess. That's what most of us believe."

I start buttoning the shirt I have on starting from the bottom. "What do you believe?'

Emory looks down. "I don't know, but I know I love you. If our child is as happy as I am with you, that's all that matters."

I smile at her, but I note she left out something important.

Did she find her mate?

FASTER THAN NORMAL

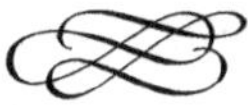

Emory

I try to stay calm during the check-up with Dr. Martin. He hasn't said a word as we started with the ultrasound. He is intently looking over the monitor to see the baby. We've had an ultrasound before, and everything had been normal. Our pack healer's concern is what's driving my anxiety for my baby's health.

"There's the head," Dr. Martin says. "And oh–did you want to know the sex?"

I look at Kane, and we both nod. "Yes," I tell the doctor. "We'd like to know."

Dr. Martin smiles. "It's definitely a boy."

I turn to Kane, and he smiles. "I told you we'd have a boy."

He grins back at me, and I can tell he's proud. "Maybe the next one might be a girl."

The next one.

My heart thuds happily at his words. He wants more kids with me. That means a future where we will still be together for years to come.

Dr. Martin pulls the wand away. He hands me tissues to clean the gel off my belly.

Mom's voice hesitates. "Is there anything abnormal about the child? Our pack healer was concerned about the size for how far along she is."

One of the nurses takes the ultrasound machine to put it away. Dr. Martin takes a seat on a rolling stool, his expression grave. "After looking at the ultrasound, the baby appears to be bigger than average for four months."

"Just a little bit bigger or significantly big?" I ask.

"You look closer to eight months along."

Startled, I turn to my mother who has gone white with shock. "Why would that be?" she asks.

"Simply put, I don't know. I have never dealt with a hybrid fetus before. Vampire babies may come a month early, but they often gestate the same amount of time as humans."

"Shifter babies are the same, though they're more prone to being born a month late," Mom adds. "Does this mean the baby could be born early?"

He nodes. "The baby could be born in a month or so."

"A month?" I repeat. "Will he be healthy?"

"I won't be able to tell for sure until after he is born. But if he's large because he's developing quickly, he should be just fine." He looks down and shakes his head slowly. "I wish I could tell you more, but this is beyond anything I've ever dealt with before."

Dr. Martin leaves to give us some privacy. My mother follows him to ask more questions. Kane wraps an arm around me for comfort. His touch steadies me even as the world feels fuzzy around me.

"It's going to be all right," he reassures me. "Maybe he's just so eager to meet us that he can't wait."

The folktales about demon children echo in my mind, a baby growing faster than normal because he's eager to inflict bloodshed and mayhem is a terrifying thought. What am I about to unleash into the world?

"What if something is wrong with him?"

"Who do you mean?"

I shake my head. "The books."

Kane grasps me by the shoulders and turns me so I can face him. His pale blue eyes stare deeply into mine.

"It's our baby," he says. "There's nothing wrong with him. We may not have the answers as to why he's developing so fast, but we are going to make sure that he is loved."

Scary thoughts that have less to do with monsters and more with the numerous health concerns for premature babies flash across my mind. I have tried to read as much as I can about babies and pregnancies the past few months and there are so many things that can go wrong. The baby could have long-term health issues. And who knows what kind of illnesses he could have from his ancestry.

"Emory," Kane coaxes me out of my thoughts. "Listen to me. No matter what happens, we'll get through it together. I'm your partner, remember?"

"Partners."

He pulls me into a hug, and I let him comfort me. Even with my cheek pressed against his shoulder, the seed of dread within me continues to grow. I have a baby coming a lot earlier than expected. No one can give me answers about why.

There's nothing I can do—and I am terrified.

Kane

Ever since the ultrasound with Dr. Martin, Emory has been preoccupied. She seems lost in her own world as the days pass by. The possibility of giving birth to our son so soon has all of us worried.

I'm also excited, though. I want to meet my son. Having children was a faraway concept for me before, but now it's a possibility about to become reality. I still have my doubts about whether I will be a good father or not, but I'm determined to try my best.

I inform few people about the accelerated pregnancy. Our mothers, Rainer, Lola, and Emory's maids are the only ones we trust with this information. I fear that people knowing Emory is about to give birth will incentivize attempts to harm her.

Then the most unexpected event happened.

Someone tried to poison Emory's food. If it hadn't been for one of the cooks smelling something odd, who knows what may have happened.

I'm doing my best to figure out who is behind it. My best guess is one of the nobles, but I can't start torturing them all for a confession. Rainer is working on finding out who did it, and we've put more protection in place. One of Emory's maids must watch her food being prepared. Emory thinks it's all too much, but I insist. She's in danger whether she wants to admit it or not.

Then a poisoned necklace arrived as a late birthday gift. Again, it was intercepted before Emory could be hurt. I've instructed all future gifts to be directed to Rainer to look over before they can even come near Emory. The lengths people will go to cannot be underestimated. I've weathered many assassination attempts over the years, and I am not taking a chance with Emory and our unborn son.

"Nothing goes to her without careful inspection," I tell a guard. He nodes, and I look up from where I'm seated on my desk to see Emory walking through the door.

"This is getting ridiculous," she says. "The food and the gifts are understandable, but what do you think they'll do with my mail?"

"They can line the letter with wolfsbane."

She scoffs. "Who would do that?"

"You never know. I've had several attempts to take my life over the year. One time, a servant died right in front of me from a silver tipped arrow."

She blinks. Her emerald eyes wide in disbelief. "That seriously happened?"

I nod, picturing the scene in my mind.

"Who was the cause of all of this?"

"An assassin hired to kill me from another kingdom. Rainer caught him, and we had him executed."

Emory shuffles uncomfortably. "All right. Maybe you do have reasons for being so paranoid."

I gesture for her to move closer to me. She walks over, and I urge her to sit on my lap.

"I'm heavy." She tries to decline.

I roll my eyes and pull her down. She resituates herself on my lap until she's seated more comfortably. I have a hand on her back to support her.

"You matter the most to me," I tell her. "I will do whatever I can to protect you."

"I just don't understand why they want to come after me. I haven't done anything to them."

"When you're in a position of power, people are either jealous, or they want to get rid of you to suit their own purposes. You are carrying my heir, and you are an Alpha who has managed to recruit other Alphas into being our allies. They feel threatened by you."

"I was brought up to be the Alpha of my pack. I never thought I'd have any modicum of influence outside of that. I never wanted this kind of power."

"You never wanted this power, so that makes you perfect to wield it. You want to serve your people rather than to fuel your own desires. You're noble." She smiles, pleased. I continue, "You choose to see the good in people, and you trust easily. I love those things about you, but it has caused you pain in the past."

She sighs. "I know it's naïve, but I don't want to live my life waiting for every person around me to try and screw me over. I hate having to doubt people's intentions. It's exhausting."

Her earnestness has always attracted me to her. Growing up in a viper pit was very different for me. But Emory wearing her heart on her sleeve is a refreshing and beautiful thing to behold. I take her hand and kiss her knuckles.

"You are a wonder," I say. "Don't change yourself to please others."

"I wasn't planning to," she replies.

I grin. I keep her hand in mine, swiping my thumb over her ring finger. "Marry me."

Her face crumples, and I know she's going to say no again. "I would love to. I really would but...."

The dreaded *but*.

"Bad timing," I offer. "The pregnancy and the war."

She nods. "But after? Definitely. Ask me again when we're not dealing with the world ending."

I hide my disappointment and agree. Cupping her pretty face, I capture her lips in mine. She responds immediately, kissing me back enthusiastically. Despite her large belly, she rocks on my lap trying to find friction. I feel myself getting hard, and I know I have to stop this soon. We have agreed not to take any chances with the baby.

She tries to unbutton my shirt. I grip her wrists to stop her. Pulling away from the kiss, I see the frustration in her eyes.

"Speaking of bad timing, we said we would avoid sex until after you've given birth," I remind her. "I don't want to take a chance with the baby."

She lets out an exasperated sigh. "Dr. Martin didn't ban sex."

"He's also confessed to not knowing how things work with a hybrid baby."

"Kane," she begs, "I'm so frustrated these days I can barely think. Can you not help me find relief?"

I can see the irony with Emory begging for sex instead of avoiding it now. This pregnancy has had some ups and downs. I don't know what I'm getting each week.

The pleading in her emerald eyes is hard for me to resist. I'm not made of stone.

"No penetration," I offer. "But I can help you find release."

Emory does not resist when I move her to the desk, shoving papers off the surface in haste. She spreads her legs wide as I settle between them. Lifting her skirts up, she holds them up as I slide her panties out of the way. She waits eagerly as I drop to my knees and kiss her folds, her breath hitching before I proceed to lick deep inside her.

I focus on bringing her as much pleasure as I can. I flick my tongue against her clit and then thrust my fingers inside her. I suck her most sensitive area until she makes mewing noises. She lies down on her back and moans with pleasure.

My cock is so hard, all I want to do is to thrust inside her and send us both plummeting into endless pleasure, but I have to be strong. I can attend to myself later when she's satisfied. I look up to see Emory's mouth wide open, her eyes closed as she continues to moan.

"Kane," she gasps. "Please."

I hum and she whimpers at the sensation of vibrating on her clit. She's squeezing my fingers like a vice as I continue to pump inside of her. I find that spot inside her that makes her scream my name, and then she comes undone.

MAMA DON'T PREACH

Kane

I'm having lunch with my mother at the gazebo. She insists that we spend more time together. Now that I'm about to become a father, she wants to make sure I'm ready for the responsibility as if I have not been taking care of an entire kingdom for over a century. I don't tell her this and just slowly sip my blood.

"The nursery is ready," she informs me. "I've had new baby items purchased. I saved several pieces from your childhood, but my grandson deserves his own belongings."

"What about Lex's baby things?" I ask out of amusement.

"If you can recall, your brother took pleasure in destroying his things. Most of his childhood toys were decapitated, burned, or melted."

I smile as I remember what a demon Lex was when we were children. He drove all our governesses into early retirement. Not even his angelic looks as a child could coax anyone into staying longer than a few months. The real problem began when Lex began to take pride in driving our nannies away. Not much changed when he reached adulthood.

"Have you chosen a name yet?" she asks. "The baby will be here soon. He needs a name, Kane."

"We have a list of names that we're choosing from," I explain. "I considered naming him Michael…"

My mother looks pleased. "After your father, of course."

"But after learning about the witch hunts, I can't burden a child with that history."

"He will be burdened with the history of his ancestors whether you name him after your father or not," she points out. "Your father is hardly the worst sinner in our family tree. The things your great-grandfather did would make your hair curl."

I studied the actions of my ancestors as part of my education as king. Some of them were great rulers, and some of them were madmen. As much good as my family has done for the world, we have also been the source of terrible things. I vow to be one of the great kings that history will be kind to.

"I would rather my son not carry the weight of those sins so readily," I conclude. "He will learn about what our bloodlines have done, and he can decide what kind of king he wants to be someday."

I want him to be a good king. I want people to look at him and not see the mistakes of those that came before him. It will be an uphill battle, but I will raise him to be strong. Emory and I will be there to weather the storms with him.

She takes a sip of her blood. "That is your choice. What other names are you considering?"

"I was thinking about Luther after grandfather but I don't want Lex to think I'm naming my son after him," I answer.

"Luther is a perfectly good name."

"I don't want to be dealing with Lex's inflated ego for centuries to come."

She waves my comment off like I'm being silly. "Your brother is not the only Luther in the family."

I ignore her and continue, "Emory also wants to pay tribute to her grandfather, Colton. She also likes Connor, Lowell, Alaric…"

Her lips purse. She disapproves.

"What's wrong with those names?"

"They're perfectly all right for other children, but those are shifter names, Kane."

I genuinely don't see the problem. "And my son is going to be half-shifter."

She sighs like I'm being obtuse on purpose. "My grandson is going to be king someday. He can't have a shifter name when he ascends to the throne."

"And why would that not be acceptable?"

She places the goblet down on the table. "It's simply not done, Kane. There is a right and wrong way of doing things for this family. We can't just start changing things because we feel like it."

I stare at her in disbelief. "I'm having a child with a shifter. I've already broken the unspoken rules, Mother. What's another one?"

"Names have power," she claims. "A name can dictate the kind of person somebody becomes, the life they end up leading."

My mother is clearly taking this more seriously than she needs to. A name is a name. We can even change it later if we want to. I have to make my mother understand how ridiculous she's being.

"What better statement is there to make than giving my son a shifter name because he is part of that world? He'll be of both worlds, the first half-shifter to become king of Crimson Peak."

She grimaces. "I see your point, darling. But must we name him Connor?"

"What's wrong with Connor?"

"It doesn't sound very… royal, does it?"

This is what it comes down to? It doesn't sound grand enough for her?

I roll my eyes. "Would you be okay with a shifter name if it sounded more *royal* to you?"

The queen picks up her goblet again and takes a dainty sip. "I could be persuaded with the right-sounding name."

"Lowell?"

She shakes her head. "Sounds like the name of a baron. The second son of a baron, to be precise."

This is unbelievable. My mother is going to shut down every name I suggest until I give in to what she wants. How am I going to explain this to Emory? She might like my mother, but she hasn't grasped just how domineering Queen Agatha can be.

"What about Alaric?"

"Keep trying, my love." She sniffs. "I'm sure you'll find a name that can work."

"Wolfram?"

"Are you even trying, Kane?"

EMORY

By Dr. Martin's estimate, I will be giving birth by next week. I'm completely terrified of what's to come. I've seen babies being delivered by my mother before, but being the one in labor is a new experience for me. I hadn't thought I would be having kids till much later in life.

I can barely eat from worry. I just move my breakfast around on my plate.

"You need to eat," Mom says. "You'll need your strength for the labor."

My fork clangs loudly as it hits the porcelain. "I don't know how I can do this. I don't know how any woman can do this."

"No one said childbirth is easy. It's one of the most painful things we can subject our bodies through."

I look at her in disbelief. "You did it twice, Mom. Why would you do that?"

"A woman forgets, and it's all worth it once you hold your baby," she explains. "The labor with you wasn't that bad. I was only in labor for a few hours. Colt was more difficult as he came out feet first. I was in labor for nearly a whole day."

The thought of giving birth to multiple children and being in labor for days might cause me to spiral, so I try not to go down that path.

"Your pregnancy is unusual, but that doesn't mean you won't be able to do this," she reassures me. "You're stronger than you think, Emory."

"What if I… what if I don't survive the birth?"

She takes my hand. "You can't think that way."

"If I die, Kane loses his allies. Colt is only helping because I asked him to. If Colt becomes the Alpha after me, he won't care about Crimson Peak and all the people here. And you may not like vampires, Mom, but I care about them."

She grabs onto my other hand. "You will survive the birth. And nothing will go wrong. You need to stop stressing yourself out. It's not good for you and the baby."

I want to start sobbing. "I'm scared, Mama."

"I know, I know," she replies. "I was terrified, too, when I was pregnant with you. I was barely older than you are now when I married your father. But when I held you in my arms for the first time, I felt a love I didn't know I was capable of."

I know that my parents met and married quickly. After they realized they were mates, my grandparents approved the match, and my mother moved to Moon Grove within a matter of weeks. I was conceived and born within their first year of marriage. My mother has been a wife and a mother since she was barely out of her teens.

I will be the same.

"When Colt was born, that love grew. You and your brother are everything to me," she continues. "I might not have been the perfect mother, but never doubt that I love you. You two are my greatest love."

There's something I've always wanted to ask my mother, but I've been too scared in the past to voice it out loud. Things are different now, and I want to know.

"Why did you stay with Bernard for all those years?" I ask. "He was unfaithful and cruel. He only cared about himself and his own ambitions. He didn't even try to fight for me when I took Lola's place as a feeder."

She closes her eyes. "I… I loved him. He's the only man I've ever loved. All my life, I was taught that my mate should come first, so I endured every humiliation and disrespect because I was told that was what I was meant to do." She opens her eyes, and they burn into mine as she continues. "When he left you in this castle, something inside me broke. How could he do this to my child? He had promised you and Colt would always come first."

"But that wasn't true." I don't bother to remind her he was willing to leave his other child behind–and she approved it. We've been through that before.

"No. It was just another one of his numerous lies." She shakes her head. "Some days, I think he began to believe the lies he told people. He stopped being able to tell reality from his made-up stories."

"Why didn't you leave?"

"The mate bond is absolute. There's nothing else like it. Trying to leave him felt like I was going to cut off my limbs. They told me the bond would always feel like a miracle. Instead, it was my prison for over twenty years."

There is brittleness to my mother's face, a bitter resentment I have never seen before. I long to make her feel better, but I don't know how. While I understand how it feels to be abandoned and feel unloved, it's never come from my mate.

My mate–is this pull I'm feeling toward Kane that or something else? Since I've shifted, I feel even closer to him. I have no doubt in my mind that the father of my child is my mate.

Mom interrupts my thoughts. "I wish I left him and took you and Colt with me. You might have been saved from his poisonous influence earlier."

"It wasn't your fault, Mom," I insist. "Bernard is the way he is. You did your best."

"And you know what's worse? A part of me still feels loyalty to him. This mate bond cannot be severed until one of us dies." She sighs. "I hope Kane doesn't turn out to be like him. You deserve somebody kind, brave, and true."

I know Kane is not like that, so I don't respond directly. "When I was growing up, I thought my mate would be Darius," I confess. "He was nice, handsome, and his dad was Bernard's Beta. It made sense, you know?"

"And yet he's not your mate?"

"I'm even surer than ever that he is not my mate. It's not him, and it never will be."

"Who is it?" Her eyes travel over my face as if she can see the name appear on my skin. "Is it someone I know?"

I smile. "You've met him, Mom." The realization is even stronger than it was before. How could I have ever doubted it?

"Well, then who is it?" When I don't answer, she nods as she's realizing something very obvious. "It's Kane."

I nod. "It is Kane."

"Are you sure?"

"When I first saw him that day in the throne room months ago, something in me woke up as if I've been waiting for him my entire life," I confess. "After my first shift, when I saw him again, everything clicked into place. It's him and it was always going to be him."

She pats my hand. "Then you should probably tell him that."

SURE AND STEADY

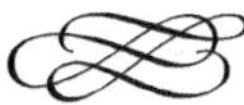

Lola

I knock on the door of Willow's room before entering. She is never in the library anymore, so I have to come visit her. She used to have a bedroom by the library until Rainer decided these rooms would be better. Her new rooms are larger and more comfortable so I guess that's why Willow never goes out anymore.

"Go away, Rainer!" Willow's muffled voice calls out.

"It's Lola," I reply.

Footsteps come closer to the door, and it opens with Willow's confused face appearing. "Lola."

I nod, smiling. "Hi."

"Hi." She looks around the hallway as if she expected someone to appear. "What are you doing here?"

"I was bored," I say. "And no one's in the library, so I didn't want to pick out books and make a mess."

Her eyebrows furrow. "There's no one in the library?"

I shake my head. "It's always empty. Very quiet."

"Rainer told me he would find a temporary librarian." She looks annoyed. "What did I even expect from that man?"

I wait, not saying anything. I don't know all the details about what's going on with Willow and Rainer. She really doesn't like him. I think he likes her. Adults are too confusing to try and figure out.

Willow seems to remember I'm there because she opens the door wider to let me into the room. "Sorry. You can come in."

I follow her into the room. The space looks sparser than the last time I was there. There's less furniture and decorations. No vases and statues. There are dents and scorch marks on the walls and floors.

I know Willow has been practicing using her magic again. I don't think it's going well from the condition of her room.

She notices me looking around the room and says sheepishly, "Turns out magic isn't like relearning how to ride a bike. There's a learning curve."

"Maybe you should practice outside," I suggest. "I don't think the servants are going to be happy if you damage the castle."

She lets out a snort and looks amused. "You're right. They will be very upset if I burn down the castle."

"I don't think you should practice near the rose garden either. Queen Agatha won't be pleased if you damage the roses," I add. "She'll purse her lips, and it'll make you feel really bad."

I've only seen Queen Agatha displeased once. I showed her my list of middle names for the baby, and she didn't say anything mean, but I could tell she didn't like any of the names. She pursed her lips like she was sucking on a lemon.

"I'll keep that in mind." Willow gestures toward the chair by the window, and I take a seat. She stays standing. "How are you, Lola?"

"I'm okay," I answer. "Everyone says the baby is coming any day now."

"How do you feel about that?"

"I'm mostly excited because everyone is so excited too. The baby is going to be my nephew which feels kind of weird because I feel like I'm too young to be an aunt."

Willow smiles. "Do you think so?"

"I always wanted a younger sibling, but instead, I'm getting a nephew," I explain. "I'm really happy for Emory because she wants this baby so much but..."

"But?"

"But I don't know if I'll like the baby. I've never been around babies much."

Willow takes the oak chair at the desk and pulls it closer to where I'm sitting. She sits and says, "When I was a little younger than you, my sister was born. I didn't know how I would feel about her either."

"You had a sister?"

She nods. "Her name was Bryony. She had brown hair and hazel eyes. She was a lot like you. Smart and sweet."

"Did you get along?"

"I loved her the moment she was born. I was the first to hold her. She was this tiny wrinkled thing. She was kind of ugly but I loved her."

I wrinkle my nose. "Ugly?"

"When they come out, babies are kind of squished," she tells me. "Being born is hard work."

That makes sense to me. I know where babies come from. Emory explained it to me last year when the stork story was becoming less and less believable. I've never even seen a stork at Moon Grove, so I know they couldn't be delivering babies in our area. Or if they did, they had been super sneaky about it.

Emory caved in and told me the details of how babies are really made, but I don't like to think about it. It's kind of gross. I don't know why adults bother. Surely, they should find a better way to create babies.

Pregnancies don't look that fun either. Emory's pregnancy had her bedridden most of the time. And before that, she was always throwing up. Pregnancy looks more like a really bad case of the flu.

"I was hoping for a girl," I continue. "Instead, we're going to have a boy. And boys are icky."

Willow laughs. "Boys are icky, yes."

"Like how you think Rainer is icky."

The humor on her face melts away. "Why do you think I find him icky?"

"You don't like being in the same room as him. You make this unhappy face when he's around."

"What face?"

"Like this." I mimic how she frowns whenever Rainer appears. "And when he talks, you roll your eyes." I roll my eyes and let out an exaggerated sigh. "I also hear you throw things at him."

"I-" she stops. "Who told you that?"

"The servants talk." I look around at all the dents on the walls and floors. "Throwing stuff at someone isn't very nice. Did he do something to make you so angry?"

She looks conflicted. "It's complicated."

"But did he do something?"

"A long time ago."

"Did he say sorry?"

"Yes." She turns away. "But it's not enough."

"What does he need to do to make it better then? Emory said that talking things over helps a lot of the time."

"It's not something that can be solved just by talking it over."

"But have you tried?"

"No." She sighs. "You'll understand when you're older."

I hate it when adults say that. What will I understand when I'm older? If it's so difficult for me to understand now then maybe adults just made things more complicated than necessary. Waiting things out will only make things worse.

Life is short. That's what everyone has always told me.

EMORY

After my conversation with my mother, I know I need to tell Kane how I feel about him. I'm sure more than ever of what he is to me. This isn't something I've ever doubted. It's a truth that is sure and steady, never faltering or diminishing over time.

Kane retired to his room after dinner. He is changing out of his clothes when I enter his suite. The sight of his muscled back makes me pause. He's always been handsome to me, beautiful even.

His alabaster skin is so fair I can see the blue veins underneath. He's not large like Rainer or any of the shifter men I know. He's leaner but not delicate, like a runner. Where Lex is pretty, Kane has a powerful and quiet allure.

He turns and smiles when he sees me. "Hey."

I feel shy all of a sudden. "Hey."

"How long have you been standing there?"

"Not long." My gaze traces the contours of his chest down to his abs. "It's unbelievable how good you look shirtless."

He grins, flexing his arms a little. "Do I?"

"Very distracting." I gesture toward him. "It's too much."

"I should cover up then?" he teases, reaching for the shirt on the bed. "Just so I don't distract you?"

"No," I reply. "That's worse cause I know what you look like underneath all that."

He drops the shirt on the floor and moves toward me. His hands circle my waist, my large belly preventing him from getting too close.

"I like you better naked," he says. "You're the one that's distracting."

"Because I'm the size of the moon and hard to miss. I practically have my own gravitational force at this point."

He laughs. "You're not big. You're pregnant."

"I'm still big. Does it matter why?"

He pushes the fabric of my shirt upward to reveal the skin of my rounded belly. "You're carrying my baby inside you. There's nothing sexier than that to me."

I look into his pale blue eyes to see if he is serious or not. "Is this a vampire thing or a Kane thing?"

"Me thing." He kneels down so he can kiss my stomach. "You're beautiful."

"Are you saying that to me or the baby?"

He looks up, his face bright with joy. "Both? Both is good."

I can't help but think that this is how Kane is meant to look. He looks happy. There's no haughty mask he wears in front of the nobles. He's not worrying about the kingdom. He's just completely himself.

I run my fingers through his dark hair. "You are a strange man, Kane."

"I'm *your* man."

I nod. "My mate."

He stills, his blue eyes staring up at me in surprise. He looks like he's trying to make sure he heard me right. Slowly, he gets to his feet, and now I'm looking up at him. He takes my hands in his gently.

"Are you sure?" he asks.

"Yes. Even before my first shift, a part of me always knew that it's you," I reply. "I've suspected it ever since we met that day in the throne room. And when I met my wolf, it just solidified everything for me."

"Why didn't you say anything before?"

"I was distracted with the baby and everything going on but I don't want another day to go by without you knowing." I pause, staring at his handsome face and memorizing the affection, surprise, and contentment I see there. "You are my mate, Kane. You are the man I was always going to be with. Nobody else."

His eyes close, and he leans down to rest his forehead on mine. "I don't know what to say."

"You don't need to say anything," I tell him, reaching up to wrap my arms around his neck. "I just need you to love me."

"I do love you," he declares. "I always will."

He dips down and kisses me. It's a soft, reverent kiss. I close my eyes and follow his lead. He deepens the kiss, and I feel the heat of desire rushing through me and between my legs. I'm getting slick, my body readying itself for his touch.

We undress each other, hands touching heated flesh. Kane lies down on the bed, pulling me on top of him. Taking his cock in my hand, I guide him to my entryway and slowly lower myself onto him. I close my eyes at the feeling of being full.

Kane lets out a pained groan. I move slowly, riding him carefully.

His hands on my hips help guide me. We're both eager. It has been too long since we last had sex.

He reaches for my clit and rubs it gently till I'm coming, convulsing around him. He continues to move me over his cock, his hips thrusting upward to meet me. His blue eyes are hazy as pleasure overtakes him. My back is killing me so I lie down beside him on the silk sheets.

We're both panting, our bodies slick with sweat. Kane turns to me and kisses me again.

"I love you," he says.

"I love you too."

We're wrapped up in the afterglow. I trace senseless patterns on his chest with my fingers. He closes his eyes, content and at peace. I'm drifting off to sleep when the pain in my back begins to intensify. I feel my stomach muscles tighten and realize this isn't just back pain. This is a contraction.

I'm in labor–the baby is coming.

TOO MUCH LABOR

Kane

Emory sits up, her face scrunched up in discomfort. I'm about to ask her if she's okay before she lets out a pained scream. I lean up, placing a hand on her back to comfort her. She's breathing quicker, her green eyes wide in realization.

"The baby is coming."

I nearly jump out of my skin. Fear has me by the throat. It's too soon. The baby isn't supposed to come for a few more days. Even then, that's earlier than we initially expected.

"Are you sure?" I ask.

Another contraction makes Emory grab my hand, squeezing my fingers as she breathes through the pain.

"I'm sure," she groans. "He's coming."

We get dressed as quickly and carefully as we can. It takes Emory longer as the contractions are coming quicker. We make our way to the infirmary. I bark orders at guards and servants.

Nettie runs to find Dr. Martin. Helga goes to get Helena to assist the doctor. Rainer and my most trusted guards are stationed outside the door, ensuring the clinic is the safest place in the castle. I help

Emory to lie down on a hospital bed, and she refuses to let go of my hand, holding onto me like a lifeline.

Dr. Martin appears and immediately looks Emory over. After timing the contractions, he says, "Emory should be ready to push in a few hours. We just need to wait for the baby to drop more."

"A few hours?" Emory repeats, her face in disbelief. "I'm in pain now."

Dr. Martin is professional as ever and replies, "You're not fully dilated yet. The contractions will be coming sooner."

He leaves to start preparing with the nurses. Helena appears and goes to her daughter, taking Emory's other hand in hers.

"Emory," she says, her voice warm with motherly affection, "it's happening."

"Not for a few more hours," Emory grumbles. Her face crumples through another contraction. "Mama, why did you do this twice?"

Helena kisses Emory's knuckles. "It'll be worth it when you hold your baby."

"We haven't even picked a name yet." Emory looks to me in concern. "He doesn't have a name, Kane."

"We have time," I reassure her. "When he's born, the right name will come along." I catch Helena's blue gaze and silently ask for her help. "Right?"

Helena nods encouragingly. "We- I didn't pick Colt's name until he was born."

"Why?" Emory asks.

"I couldn't decide," she explains. "Then I saw Colt's face, and the name came to me. It could also have been the epidural talking."

"Don't let me pick a name when I'm on drugs, Kane," Emory says. "I want to be fully sober when we pick a name for our son."

"Of course."

"Promise me."

I kiss her cheek. "I promise."

Emory leans back on the hospital bed as another contraction takes over.

It's going to be a long night. "Dr. Martin, when can she have an epidural?"

LOLA

I'm not allowed in the medical wing during the birth of the baby. Nettie and Helga say there's already a lot of people in there, and they don't want me in the way. I tell them that I'm not going to be in the way, but no one bothers listening to me. They're all excited about the baby.

Everyone in the castle is practically buzzing. The servants are huddled in the kitchen, waiting for any updates. I'm told that it has been a very long time since we've had a royal baby. They have been waiting many years for Kane to have an heir.

Emory hasn't told me what she's naming the baby. She let me pick the middle name, and I like the one I chose. Even Queen Agatha didn't protest when I revealed to her what it was. She's agreed to keep it a secret until the baby comes.

"What do you think they'll name the baby?" Thomas, one of King Kane's footmen asks.

"I'm not telling you a thing, Thomas Caldwell," Helga retorts, sternly. "I would never betray Princess Emory's secrets."

"It's not a secret if we're just guessing." He shrugs. "It's all for fun, Hels. No harm done."

Helga rolls her eyes, but she doesn't push Thomas away when he wraps an arm around her chair. I know Thomas has been planning to propose for a while. They really like each other even if Helga pretends like she can't stand him. Thomas is nice even if his nose is sharp like a bird's.

"Most probably they'll name the baby after King Kane," Nettie says. "Or Kane as a middle name. That's how royals like to name their children."

"Maybe after King Kane's father or grandfather," Thomas suggests. "Unless Princess Emory wants to name the baby after her family."

"Not Bernard," I pipe up, making them all look at me. "Our dad's not very nice, so Emory won't name the baby after him. Not even a middle name."

An awkward silence overshadows the servants before they try to laugh it off to break the tension.

"What are popular names for shifters, Lola?" Thomas asks. "Wolfgang? Wolfram?"

"No." I roll my eyes. "No one has names like that. Not unless they're super old."

The servants laugh again. I smile as they throw even more ridiculous names at me, trying to find the most outrageous name they can think of. They're all so silly. I'm glad I get to wait here with them.

Growing up, I was so alone. I couldn't play with the other kids as they either didn't like me or their parents wanted them to stay away. I never felt like I belonged with my own family, aside from Emory. This castle is filled with nice people who always make me feel I finally have a place that I belong to.

I never want to leave.

EMORY

The labor takes longer than expected. The pressure and pain in my back worsens as the contractions come closer and closer until I get the epidural. When Dr. Martin deems me ready to finally push, it's exhausting. My mom and Kane throw encouragements at me that I barely hear.

My body is sweat-soaked and overheated. I have to push along with the contractions. I want to scream. I feel like howling, wanting to sink my teeth into something, anything to help ease this.

"You're doing great," my mom says. "You just need to push more."

"I don't want to push more," I sob. "I want him out."

"I know. I know." Kane rubs my back, his hand squeezing the back of my neck in reassurance. "It'll be over soon. Just a little more, Emory."

"Why can't you do this for me?"

Kane snorts. "I would if I could, honey."

"Don't laugh at me!" A contraction makes me yell. "I hate this!"

"You need to push, Emory," Dr. Martin tells me, his tone infuriatingly calm. "I can see the head."

I suddenly hate Dr. Martin. I hate the medical wing. I hate this castle. And after this is over, I'm leaving and never coming back.

"Push, love," my mother reminds me. "You're almost there."

One big push, and the baby's head is out. He must have the world's biggest head for a baby. The rest of him feels deceptively smaller. He's covered in blood and fluid as Dr. Martin brings him over so I can hold him.

I burst into tears. He's wrinkly, and his little face is scrunched up like he's angry that he had to leave my womb. He's crying, howling like a little wolf. My heart feels like it's expanding to make more room for all the emotion I have for this tiny little human.

Kane's eyes are wet with tears, and he kisses my temple. My hair is sweaty and sticking to my skin.

"Thank you," he tells me, softly. "For him."

I don't even care about all the pain and exhaustion from the past few hours. None of it matters. All I care about is this little baby in my arms. His eyes open, and they're a pale blue just like Kane's.

"He needs a name," I say.

"What does he look like to you?" Kane replies. "Lowell? Alaric?"

"No." I only think about it for a moment, but I know what's the right name. "Michael."

Kane's eyes stare into mine, uncertainly. "Are you sure? That name has a lot of history attached to it."

"It's not all bad history. Your father tried to make peace with my father when other vampire kings wouldn't have even bothered. And he was your father. You loved him."

Kane swallows, his watery gaze focusing on the baby's face. "What about his middle name?"

"Lola picked Colton. Our grandfather was a good man and our

family isn't built just on Bernard's tainted legacy alone. There's a lot of history there too."

"Michael Colton," Kane tests out the name. "It's nice."

"Michael Colton Moonraker Alexander." I snort. "That's a mouthful."

"Royals have long names. It's tradition," he says. "Besides, no one should ever forget that he's part of two worlds."

"Hopefully, all the best parts."

We stare down at our son, and the world feels bright with hope.

RAINER

Helena comes out of the hospital wing doors to inform me that the baby and Emory are fine. I'm relieved, and I want to go inside and congratulate Kane and Emory. Kane is the brother I've never had, and I know I'm going to love that baby as a nephew and my godson. I'm about to enter the clinic when one of the guards runs up to me, urgently saying I need to see something in the dungeons.

"I'll be right back," I tell Helena. "Don't worry. I'm sure it's nothing."

Helena nods and reenters the hospital wing. I follow the guard to the dungeon, my heart thundering in my chest as I try to remain calm. The security in the dungeon has been a problem lately with us having to keep replacing guards. Too many instances of guards being bribed or abusing their power over prisoners and feeders make finding good men difficult.

I make my way through the maze of corridors that lead down to the dungeons. I stop at the sight of the two guards on the ground. A quick pulse check tells me they're both dead. I quickly make my way inside to the cells to find a dead body on the ground and a missing prisoner in the next cell.

This is not good. This is catastrophic.

The entire castle has been focused on the royal birth. We let our guard down for a few hours. The weasel of an ambassador had managed to slip in at the right moment, and my guess is that he's already out of the castle. I leave the dungeon and make my way to Alistair's suite. I burst in without knocking and find the room is empty, his belongings thrown around as he packed in a hurry.

Shit. This is really not fucking good.

It has to be today of all days. This day is meant to be a happy time. Instead, I have to deal with a crisis. Kane is going to be rightfully pissed.

I have no choice but to head back to the hospital wing. I pause right outside the doors, the guards nearby eye me warily. They must see the panic on my face, so I change my expression to be more neutral. It wouldn't do to have Emory worry. She just gave birth, and I'm not going to cause her any stress.

I walk to the hospital wing doors and pass through, going to the room I know Emory has been given and poke my head in. Emory is lying on the bed carrying a bundle in a blue blanket in her arms. Kane is seated on the bed next to her as they talk and smile over the bundle. The image is so sweet I feel more like an asshole for having to ruin this.

But I have a duty to this kingdom, and every second I'm stalling is time wasted.

Kane looks up first. "Rainer, what is it?"

"I need to talk to you for a minute," I reply. "Outside."

FIGHT OR FLIGHT

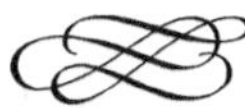

Kane

I don't want to leave Emory and my newborn son even for a moment, but the serious look in Rainer's eyes tells me that whatever he has to tell me is urgent. I have my most trusted guards right outside the door. Nellie and Helga are there along with Emory's mother. I know all these people would lay down their lives before letting anything happen to Emory and our son.

Emory looks exhausted. Her face is clammy with sweat. Michael is tiny in her arms. His scrunched up little face makes a fierce protective urge roar in me.

I lean down and kiss the top of Emory's head. "I'm sorry. I'll be right back."

Her green eyes are half-lidded. She looks half asleep. She gives a little nod. I make my way quickly to the door.

Rainer looks antsy. I immediately ask, "What is it?"

"Jacob escaped."

Alarm makes me want to start swearing. "What?"

"Alistair snuck into the dungeons while we were all focused on Emory in labor," he explains. "There were two guards on duty directly outside the dungeon door, and they're dead. There didn't seem to be much of a struggle, so Alistair must've gotten the jump on them."

I want to punch something. I can never get a moment of peace anywhere. "Where are Alistair and Jacob now?"

"I'm sure they've made it out of the castle. I was only informing you because I have to go after them before they can get to Scarlett Thunder."

Panic is setting in, but I try to remain calm. If Jacob reaches Scarlett Thunder, we lose our bargaining chip. There will be no reaching him. Lex will be in danger as King Peter will have little reason not to harm him anymore.

"Go then," I order. "Get Jacob back at all costs. You can bring back Alistair dead or alive."

I couldn't care less if Alistair comes back in one piece. I'm troubled with the turn of events, and even diplomacy won't keep Alistair safe once I have my hands on that rat again. He's a nuisance I want to get rid of as soon as possible. King Peter can get snappy with me for all I care.

"There's one more thing," Rainer says.

I almost close my eyes in dismay at the prospect of more bad news. "What is it now?"

"Bernard's dead. He was drained dry. I suspect that was Jacob's doing. He's going to need his strength for the escape."

I rub my temples with my fingers. This is meant to be one of the happiest days of my life. It seems the universe will not let me have anything for free. Too many things have happened, and I need to focus on what I can control.

"Get Jacob back," I reply. "He's the priority."

Rainer nods. "Right away."

He leaves, and I contemplate what I'm going to do. I glance back at the door to Emory's room. I will have to tell Emory about Bernard's death, but she has just gone through labor, and she needs to rest first. Helena will need to be informed about her mate's demise, but I want to see the condition of Bernard's body first.

I make my way to the dungeons, alerting more guards to come

with me to see the mess Rainer described. The two dead guards are still lying right outside the doors. Their bodies are slumped against the wall, blood pooling around them. Their severed heads tell me nothing about how Alistair managed to get the jump on both of them. It's possible he had help from one of my own servants.

The doors are unlocked, but none of the other prisoners seem to have escaped. They're still in their cells. I walk past the prisoners to Bernard's cell and find his limp body on the ground.

His skin is pale, indicating all the blood has been drained from him. There is a large gash in his neck where Jacob bit him, and the wound is gaping. Jacob wasn't gentle as he fed on the former Alpha for the last time. Blood drips down Bernard's collarbone to the front of his gray tunic.

He has lost a lot of weight. The plain food in the dungeons and no access to sunlight has taken its toll on the shifter. Even if he tried to fight Jacob off, a weakened vampire is still stronger than a healthy shifter. In this leaner state, Bernard stood no chance.

Bernard's gray lifeless eyes stare off into nothing, his face frozen in an expression of shock. I've never cared for this man. I've had even less respect for him. But he's still Emory's father. Before the truth of who he truly was had been revealed, she'd worshiped him.

Reaching down, I close Bernard's eyes. Moving closer to the cot near the wall of the cell, I pull off the threadbare blanket and drape it over his corpse. I'll need to have his body removed from the dungeon and Helena will need to be consulted on how she wanted to bury him. I don't know much about the burial traditions of shifters, so I'll leave that for her to decide on.

It can wait a day. I tell the guards to make sure the body is undisturbed. The past few days have been long and wearing on all of us. As important as this is, Bernard's grandson is waiting for me to return, and I need to tend to my family.

RAINER

Alistair and Jacob are unable to steal a vehicle which is a saving grace as it makes it easier for me to chase them. They've had to go on foot, and I can gain on them in a fast car. Even vampire speed has its limitations. They're nearing the border when I see them running as fast as they can toward their freedom. Unlike his first attempt to escape, he had a huge lead on me, but this time I was wise to pause to grab a car.

Jacob is slower than Alistair as months in the dungeon with drops of blood and lean meals has made him a gangly mass that lumbers ungracefully. His leg took a while to heal as it was left unattended too for so long. He didn't have the chance to exercise his newly healed bones and muscles, and the consequences are obvious. Alistair has to slow down to make sure the prince isn't left behind.

The older man sees me as he turns back to check on Jacob. His pale blue eyes widen in panic as he urges Jacob forward. Alistair spreads his arms out, sacrificing himself as a shield for Jacob's escape. Grimly, I step on the gas and swerve the car to stop it right behind Alistair. I'm barely out of the car before he launches himself at me, trying to slam my head into the car window.

I'm stronger, and I fight him off by grabbing his arm and twisting him around till I have him in a headlock. He tries to buck me off, kicking at the ground and clawing at my arm around his neck. He reaches up to claw at my face, but I move my head away, keeping my arm around his throat until he finally goes limp in my arms.

I drop him to the ground like a sack of potatoes. I have to resist the urge to twist his head off. He will get his punishment, but that'll be for Kane to decide. I have bigger fish to focus on.

Jacob shifts directions, attempting to go around me, but he's still within sight. I look around me for anything I can use to stop him and regretfully realize what I have to do. Damn it. I like this car.

I pull off the back car door, the metal giving way under my superior strength. Pulling my arm back I aim and throw it like a frisbee. It spins in the air, the metal door large and shining under the moonlight. It hits Jacob in the back, knocking him to the ground.

Quickly getting into the e car, I shift into drive and head straight to where Jacob lies flattened on the ground. He's clearly in pain and struggling to get out from under the door. He's gasping as I stop the car and step out to loom over him.

His pale blue eyes gleam with hatred. "Fuck...you..."

"I missed you too, Jake." I lean down and grab Jacob by the shoulders, hauling him up like a limp marionette. "Come on, princess. I'm taking you back to the dungeon."

"No!" The threat of being imprisoned again brings the fight back to Jacob, and he pushes me away. He's full of shifter blood and has the strength he wouldn't have had otherwise. "I'm never going back there."

"I have orders to bring you back alive," I tell him. "Don't make this difficult for the both of us."

He bares his fangs at me, reminding me of a cobra about to strike. He lunges, but I'm ready for him. I catch him by the shoulders and slam him to the ground. The earth rattles from the force, dirt flying into the air from the impact.

He snarls and kicks out my legs, knocking me to the ground. He crawls over me landing a punch to my face and pain blooms in my jaw. He lands another blow to my nose and blood gushes out. Snarling, I punch up and hit him in the eye causing him to yelp like a wounded animal.

Kane wants Jacob alive, but he never said the prince has to come back unharmed. We tussle for a moment, exchanging blows until I've had enough and grab Jacob's injured leg. I pull hard and the bone snaps again. He screams in pain, and I manage to knock him off me, scrambling to my feet.

I grab him by his remaining arm and start dragging him toward the car.

"I'll rip off your other arm if you keep fighting me, Jacob," I threaten. "I will do it. Don't test me."

"I'm going to kill you. You are the scum of the earth!" He kicks my shin, but it's no use. He can't fight me off with only one arm and a broken leg. "Once my father knows what you've done to me, he's going to chop you into tiny pieces, and he'll feed you to the dogs!"

"Isn't that some lovely imagery?" I quip.

I open the door to the passenger side with one arm and toss Jacob in. I'm about to slam the car door when something hits me in the back of the head. I fall forward, my face hitting the car. My scalp feels wet.

Jacob slips out of the car and kicks me in the ribs with his broken leg, wincing in the process. "You filthy, stupid peasant!"

"Prince Jacob, you must get to Scarlett Thunder." Alistair pleads. He must've woken up during the struggle with Jacob. "I'll take care of this. You have to save yourself."

Jacob kicks me in the ribs again. "I'm going to kill this fucker before I go!"

"Prince Jacob, please! Your father is waiting!"

Jacob snarls and kicks me in the stomach. I cough up blood.

"I'll get you next time," he growls.

I dig my hands into the ground, trying to get up. I wince as I struggle to get to my feet. There are black spots in my vision.

Alistair looks panicked and exclaims, "Prince Jacob, go! I'll hold him off!"

Jacob limps away without looking back as Alistair lunges at me, but I push him back, hard. He hits the hood of the car. I wrap my arms around his throat and squeeze. He reaches for my face, hands grasping at my nose and mouth. I resist the urge to bite off his fingers.

He grabs at my hair and tries to pull. The sting at my scalp reminds me of the head injury I have. I need to end this. I twist his neck, and it snaps like a twig. He stops moving.

Jacob is gone.

PRODIGAL SON RETURNS

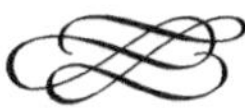

Lex

There is a commotion that evening when an unexpected guest arrives at Castle Blackmoor. No one will tell me who it is at first, but I'm able to guess the identity from Opal's reaction. She only cares about a few people in this world. When she runs to the medical wing in her nightgown with no care about her appearance, it all but confirms to me that Jacob is back in Scarlett Thunder.

I'm not allowed near the clinic, so I listen in on gossip around the castle. King Peter is not at breakfast. I need to speak to Kane to tell him about what's going on, but I can feel eyes on me wherever I go. I don't know if Jacob has been returned or he escaped. Either way, I wasn't informed about this beforehand, and it makes me nervous.

If Kane was planning to return Jacob to his father, surely, he would've told me and made arrangements to get me out. My safety is dependent on Jacob being held prisoner in Crimson Peak. Without that leverage, King Peter has little reason not to kill me. I spend the day anxiously watching my surroundings, trying not to flinch any time the guards pass by.

It's not until the next day that King Peter appears in the dining hall. He takes a seat at the head of the table, and all the nobles wait with bated breath for him to speak. I hunch over myself, trying to be as inconspicuous as possible. I've learned the hard way that any time King Peter is happy it's going to be bad news for me.

"I have good news," King Peter declares. "Wonderful news for all of us. My son has come home."

The nobles start whispering to each other as Prince Jacob enters the dining hall limping. He's missing an arm, but I know that happened the first time he tried to escape. Jacob looks a lot skinnier than the last time I saw him, his hair not as shiny. His time in the dungeons of Castle Graystone has left its toll.

Opal is with him, her arm clinging to his remaining arm like a vine. I know the two have always been close. As self-involved as Opal may be, she does care about her brother, and he cares about her. They make their way to the head of the table and take a seat next to their father.

King Peter raises a glass. "Welcome home, my son."

Jacob reaches for a wine glass and his hands shake a little as he raises it. "I'm glad to be home, father."

They sip their wine, the other nobles following their lead. I cannot even touch my glass. I feel too on edge, waiting for the attention to fall on me and spell my doom. I stay as still as I can, hoping I will not be noticed.

"Now that Prince Jacob is back, Your Grace, does that mean the *disagreements* with Crimson Peak are in the past?" one of the noble ladies asks. "Have matters with King Kane been resolved?"

Before King Peter answers, Jacob cuts in, "Fuck no."

The nobles whisper furiously amongst each other.

Jacob continues. "King Kane did not set me free. I escaped with the help of our trusted dignitary Alistair, may he rest in peace. They kept me trapped in their filthy dungeons for months. They starved me and abused me." He looks over all the faces in the dining hall, his face ugly with anger. "His general ripped my fucking arm off!"

None of this looks good for me.

"We are not going to make peace with Crimson Peak," Jacob

declares. "We're going to crush them in this war. I want Kane's head on a pike along with that werewolf bitch he knocked up."

King Peter nods. "Of course, they must pay for what they have done to you. They treated my son, my heir, abominably. They will have to pay in blood!"

I need to get out of there, but I can't leave without being noticed. I have no choice but to stay in my seat until dinner is over. I escape as the nobles are leaving for bed, trying to get lost in the sea of perfumed and bejeweled bodies. Managing to make it to my room, I lock the door behind me and finally let out a deep breath.

I go to the desk and reach for the landline. The line is bugged, but it's better than not communicating with my brother. I sit down at the desk and bury my face in my free hand as I wait for Kane to answer. He finally answers after a few rings.

"What's going on?" he asks.

"Weather report," I answer. "A new hurricane came in."

"How bad is it?"

"Terrible. It's going to get even worse because it's headed your way."

"Do you know when?"

"I don't know the exact time but probably soon," I reply. "Get ready, Kane. This might be the worst storm we've weathered yet."

"I know." He sounds solemn. "How are you doing over there?"

"I'm fine for now, but I don't know how long before they remember I'm here. If you don't hear from me after this, you can assume I'm somewhere I can't reach a phone."

"Lex, I should have never sent you there."

"You did what you had to," I counter. "And I volunteered. This was my choice. Don't take my sacrifice away from me."

"I wouldn't ever do that to you. You're braver and stronger than I ever gave you credit for."

"We'll see how true that is soon enough." I swallow my fear that is trying to choke me. "Kane, if this is the last time we get to talk, I need you to know that I-"

The phone is taken from me and thrown against the wall. It

smashes into pieces as it hits the hardwood. Jacob snarls down at me, and I get to my feet, backing away as he advances on me.

"Missed me, Lex?" he growls. "While you got to live in this nice room, your brother kept me in a cold cell with barely enough blood to keep me alive."

I raise my hands up in surrender, trying to placate him. "I'm sorry about what happened to you, Jacob. I never wanted you to suffer–"

"You don't know what suffering is, you stupid prick!" he yells. "You don't know what it's like to have your leg unable to heal because your brother refused to let me see a doctor! You don't know what it's like to have your arm ripped from your body!"

I continue to back away, and he throws a chair to the wall.

"If it wasn't for you, none of this would have happened to me! You chose loyalty to that werewolf bitch over your own kind!"

"Jacob, I didn't–"

"Shut the fuck up!" He lunges at me and knocks me to the floor. Even with one arm, his anger gives him the strength to keep me down. He punches me in the jaw, and my mouth begins to bleed. "It's all your fault!"

He throws another punch, and it hits me in the ear. There's a ringing in my head that makes me wince. He tries to throw a hook, but I block him, pushing him off me. He lands on his bad leg and yelps in pain.

"Fuck you, Lex!"

"What happened to you wasn't my fault," I argue. "You attacked and almost killed an innocent woman because your sister was jealous. All of this was of your own doing."

"And you think you're any better?" he snarls. "How many cruel games did we play on other people, Lex? We had fun together because you're just as bad as I am."

Shame prickles my skin. The reminder of the kind of company I kept and the petty games I played in the past makes me feel lower than low. As much as I want to deny it, my actions were similar to Jacob's in the past. That's what attracted me to him when he first arrived at Castle Graystone with his sister. I saw reflections of myself in both of them.

"I'm nothing like you now," I tell him. "I'm better. I'm trying to do good."

"By spying for your brother? How much have you really helped as you ate our food and slept in a soft bed?" Jacob taunts. "You're still the same needy little bitch that got on his knees and begged to suck my cock because, at the end of the day, Lex, you will never matter. You're nothing more than a fucking spare!"

My face feels hot from anger and humiliation. Memories of orgies where I had let myself be used by this scum of a human being disgusts me. I've never felt shame when it came to sex before, but now, all I want is to scrub myself clean. Looking at him now, Jacob's handsome face has lost all its appeal. All I see is the ugly creature underneath.

Jacob gets to his feet, clumsily as he has to do it with one arm and a leg that looks to still be healing. He looks down at me, his pale blue eyes icy. "Do you honestly think you're better than me? I'm the heir, Lex. I'll be king of this kingdom someday. And you will always be the second son wishing his brother would die so he could be king instead."

"I've never wanted Kane to die."

"Bullshit!" Jacob exclaims. "If there was a way for Kane to drop dead tomorrow, you'd suck anybody's cock to make that happen. You'd suck a hundred cocks, you dirty whore."

Not wanting to hear any more of his taunts, I get to my feet. "Maybe if you spent less time caring about whose cock I'm sucking, you could actually make your father proud."

Jacob's eyes flash in fury. "Shut up!"

"We're both fuck-ups, but at least I'm not meant to rule a kingdom. Your father tried to mold you to be the perfect little prince and instead you're pathetic."

"You shut your mouth, or I'll have your tongue cut out!"

"If he really cared about you that much, he would have gotten you out of the dungeon sooner. Instead, he was willing to let you rot in there. Maybe he hoped you'd die so you could finally be useful to him, and he could have a better reason to start a war with my brother-"

"Shut up!" He throws a punch, and I feel the crunch as my nose breaks.

Despite the pain, I laugh. "Looks like I hit a nerve."

"Shut up!" he screams, throwing an uppercut at my jaw. I hear another crack of bone. "Shut up! Shut up!"

He hits me in the eye, and I go down. I let out another laugh. He kicks me in the stomach, and I bowl over in pain. He continues to beat me as he yells obscenities at me. I try to laugh despite the pain until I can't anymore.

I keep my eyes closed as guards come in and drag me from the room. They're not gentle as they push and pull me through the castle. They toss me into a room, and I land on a cold stone floor. My ribs ache which makes me think they must be broken.

Opening my eyes, I watch as the guards lock the cell door, preventing me from escaping.

"Get comfortable," one of the guards mocks me. "You'll be here awhile."

I look around the cell with one swollen eye. It's dark with barely any light. There's no windows. I'm in the dungeon.

An acrid smell permeates the stone walls and floors. I haven't smelled it since I was much younger and we would sneak down to the dungeon to take from the feeders. The smell of death is unmistakable.

Am I going to die here?

I honestly don't know.

Someone is coming for me.

They have to.

FORGIVE AND FORGET

Rainer

I make it back to the castle despite the head injury. Dr. Martin wants to keep me in the hospital wing overnight for observation. My ribs aren't broken, but I have bruises on my torso. This makes it hard to lie down in any position besides on my back.

I've had worse injuries. Nothing a little rest can't fix. I'll be out of commission for a few days as Dr. Martin doesn't want to take chances on disrupting my recovery. I'm more bored than anything else as I have to command the guards from a hospital bed, and I have to trust the guards to be giving me accurate information.

Kane strolls in looking disheveled and worried, though he's smiling. "You look like hell."

"You don't look much better," I tell him.

He shrugs. "I haven't slept in two days, but I have a beautiful baby boy."

I grin at him. "I bet that makes up for everything else."

"He's got my eyes," he says. "He's bald, but Helena says there's a chance he'll have red hair like Emory."

"He'll grow up to be a looker like his mom then," I quip. "To off-set your ugly genes."

"You're lucky you're injured, or I would punch you," Kane tells me, but there's no heat in his voice. There's no hiding how pleased he is about the baby.

"Fatherhood suits you."

Kane nods and sits next to me in a chair meant for visitors. He's been my first. "I never really thought about what being a father would mean. It always seemed like a faraway concept."

"And to think you originally planned to have children with Opaline." I shudder. "She would probably eat you after conception like a black widow."

Kane grimaces at the visual. "I'm more than aware of my previous folly when it came to choosing partners."

"Aren't you glad Bernard Moonraker was such a cold-blooded bastard that he had no problem selling off his daughters to you?"

He rubs the back of his neck. "I hate to say this, but bless Bernard Moonraker's soul for being such a heartless monster."

"May he suffer endlessly in whatever horrible afterlife he ended up in," I conclude. "Cause without him, you would not have Emory and little Mikey in your life."

He shakes his head. "Don't call my son that."

"Mikey? It's a nickname. He's too small to be a Michael at the moment. Once he's taller than me, he can earn the right to be called whatever he wants."

Kane knows when to quit a losing battle, so he drops the discussion and changes topic. "Speaking of Bernard, I haven't told Emory and Helena yet."

"Why not? It's been days, Kane."

"I know, but Emory's still recovering from the birth, and we've all been so occupied with Michael--"

"Mikey."

"--that I felt it was best to wait. I don't want these first few days with him to be tainted with the memory of Bernard's death. Even though he's my son's grandfather, he would have preferred Michael was never born. I don't want the first week of my son's life to be tangled up in the death of a man who would have never cared about him."

"I don't even know who would actually grieve Bernard. Did he have any real friends?"

"None that I know of. He made more enemies than allies during his time as Alpha. I'm sure Helena will be upset, though. She's his mate. I'm surprised she hasn't felt the bond break."

"If you think about it, he's a really sad person," I point out. "He couldn't make a real connection with anybody, not even his mate, and in the end, he was all alone with nobody there to save him."

"I'm not evolved enough to feel sorry for Bernard Moonraker." He touches my shoulder. "Get better, and we'll tackle all the problems coming our way. I need you by my side."

"I would never abandon you," I say firmly with the weight of our shared history. "My loyalty has first and foremost been to you."

"You mean to the crown."

"No, to you."

Kane smiles, his gratitude at my loyalty clear on his face. "Once Dr. Martin lets you out, come visit Emory and your godson. Mikey is the cutest baby you'll ever see."

I laugh because he called him Mikey. My charm works on everyone. "He's cute thanks to his mom's pretty genes."

Kane rolls his eyes. "Fuck off, Rain."

He leaves and I try to rest, but I'm still bored. All I do in the hospital wing is sleep and eat. Any time I've tried to leave the clinic to take a walk or speak to one of the guards, one of the nurses ushers me back in. Dr. Martin does not play around and has threatened to tie me to the hospital bed if I don't behave.

I close my eyes and try counting sheep. The more I rest, the faster I'll be released from Dr. Martin's prison of healing. The soft clicking of the door closing makes me open my eyes, thinking it's Kane returning because he forgot to tell me something. Instead, Willow comes toward me dressed in one of her prim high-collared dresses.

"Willow," I say. "What are you doing here?"

She crosses her arms under her chest. Her mouth is pursed, and she reminds me of an angry school teacher. "I haven't seen you in days. The staff told me you were injured."

I grin. "Did you miss me?"

She scoffs. "Like the plague. I wanted to make sure you really were dying and not faking it for attention."

"I don't need to fake injuries for attention," I argue playfully. "I can get attention with my charm."

"What charm?" she returns. "I've yet to see it."

That makes me grin again. "I missed you and your razor-sharp tongue."

The sight of her in her conservative dress reminds me of the many times I thought about ripping off her clothes to see what's underneath. I can feel myself hardening under the blanket on my lap. If she looks down, she'll recognize just how happy I am to see her. If she comes closer, I'll be able to get a whiff of her vanilla and parchment smell.

"I didn't miss you," she replies, waspishly. "But the guards refused to let me out of my room due to your orders. I was only let out because I was coming to see you."

"My evil plan of giving you cabin fever is working then." I discreetly reach for a pillow behind me to cover my lap. "Next step, you fall madly in love with me."

"That's not possible. I would *never* fall in love with you."

I pause to stare at her pretty face, trying to find all her little tells. "Why did you really come to see me, Willow?"

"I told you. I wanted to make sure you were dying. I would hate to miss the sight of you taking your last breath." She narrows her eyes. "Why are you looking at me like that?"

"Like what?"

"Like you're sad." She sputters, "I won't fall for it. This poor-me act you have going on. I know what you're really like deep down."

"I'm the monster that haunted your nightmares for years," I say with no guile. "And I couldn't even bother to remember what I had done to you."

She nods, her eyes watering despite her efforts not to be emotional. "You're the worst."

"I truly am sorry, Willow. For everything I did. I'm not excusing it. And I understand your anger, but I want you to know that the last thing I want to do is hurt you again."

She closes her eyes, tears escaping down her cheeks. She wipes them away furiously. "It doesn't erase any of it."

"I know."

"Even if you're sorry, it doesn't mean I have to forgive you."

"Of course not."

"But...." Her blue eyes open wide, and she looks conflicted. "No matter how I've tried to fight you, you never gave up on me. Why?"

"I don't know," I answer. "It's like I've been daydreaming throughout my life, and then I woke up, and I saw you. And you're the only thing in color."

She's quiet. Her mouth quivers, and I watch the play of emotions on her face–sadness, anger, longing, joy, and finally, acceptance.

"I've tried to fight this," she tells me. "I fought as hard as I could, but you got underneath my skin."

"I know, sweetheart." I coax her to move forward. "Come here."

"I'm not ready to go there."

"I would go there, but any time I try to leave this bed, a nurse appears out of nowhere like a poltergeist and scolds me. I'm convinced Dr. Martin is some kind of necromancer, and all his nurses are summoned from the underworld."

Willow shakes her head. "You're an idiot."

She doesn't leave. She moves closer to the bed and takes a seat near my knees. I reach for her and throw the pillow to the floor so I can have her sit on my lap. Her blue eyes widen as she can feel my erection rubbing against her through her long skirt and the blanket.

"Have you been like this the entire time?" she asks.

"Since you walked into the hospital room," I answer. "Now, I don't know how much time we have before Dr. Martin checks on me again. We might have to make this quick, and we have to be quiet."

"If you think I'm going to do anything with you on this hospital bed, you're delusional-"

I cut off the rest of her sentence with a kiss. She instantly melts against me, kissing me back as if we have been lovers for centuries. Worried that we'll be caught, we don't fully undress. I unbutton the high collar of her top so I can push up her white bra and see her breasts. The pink tips are practically begging for my mouth so I have to kiss and suck on them till she's moaning and begging me for more.

"You're not winning," she says, stubbornly. "Just because I'm letting you touch me doesn't mean you've won me over."

"Of course not, darling." I push down the blanket and sleep pants I'm wearing to free my cock. She eyes my substantial erection. *"We're winning."*

It takes a little bit more maneuvering with pushing her skirt and panties out of the way so she can sink down on my cock. She's so wet, there's not much resistance. Once she's fully taken all of me, she closes her eyes as she rocks back and forth looking for a rhythm she likes. I keep still, letting her chase her own pleasure.

A certain angle hits the right spot, and she lets out a loud moan. I kiss her to silence her, eyeing the door that leads to Dr. Martin's suite. When no one comes rushing to spoil our fun, I grab Willow's hips to find the right spot again. When I find it, she shudders and starts moving against me.

There's no more talking after that. Willow kisses me to muffle her moans, her teeth biting my lower lip till I taste blood. It's not a slow and gentle coupling as we're rushed for time, but it doesn't make it any less good. I know with how perfect she feels around me, sex will only get better from here.

"I'm close," she whispers, panting.

I guide her hand to her clit and watch as she touches herself, her pussy fluttering around my cock as she begins to come. With her blue eyes drunk on pleasure, moaning out my name, Willow isn't just pretty. She's beautiful. Sexy.

I turn her over so I'm on top, an athletic feat on this small hospital bed. I encourage her to wrap her legs around my waist so I can thrust deeper into her. I'm not going to last. This thing between us has been building up for months, and no fantasy can compare to the reality of her.

I bury my face in her neck, chest to chest, it's like we're one creature. Sex has never been this good. I can't remember it ever coming close to this.

"Come for me, Rainer," she whispers in my ear.

I obey her command. There's no losing in this regard.

BABY OF MINE

Emory

Michael won't stop crying. I don't know what he wants. I've fed and burped him and changed his diaper. Nothing seems to work.

Even with my mom and the maids help, I'm exhausted and not getting enough sleep. No one can figure out why the baby won't stop crying. During a check-up at the clinic, Dr. Martin says he thinks it might be colic. He suggests a list of soothing techniques to help but none of them work.

After the end of a very long week, I want to start crying, too, but my mom cautions me not to. "You can't show babies fear," she tells me. "They can smell it."

I don't know if she's kidding or not. "I just want him to stop crying," I reply, practically begging. "Why won't he stop crying? What am I doing wrong?"

I'm rocking Michael as he wails, walking back and forth in the nursery. My mom is seated on the rocking chair that hadn't worked on soothing Michael. Nothing seems to calm my baby. I think he is angry that I pushed him out of me, and he wants me to know it.

"Colt had colic too," my mom says with a faint smile. "He cried for almost a month straight, kept everyone in the house awake. The servants all wanted to stay away from the house at that time so they wouldn't be bothered by it."

My brows furrow as I try to recall any events. "I don't remember any of that."

"You were barely three, and you were the lightest sleeper. Your Grandma Emory picked you up and took you to the hunting cabin. You had your grandparents all to yourself. You were ecstatic."

The memory of my grandparents does bring me some nostalgic joy even as Michael continues to scream his unhappiness. "What helped with Colt's colic?"

"Your father took him outside to the woods. Something about being outdoors soothed Colt, and he would go to sleep as soon as he was surrounded by the trees."

We both share a look of bemusement as that hadn't worked on Michael. Back rubs and warm baths hadn't worked. I could walk the length of Castle Graystone and back, and that wouldn't soothe Michael. I'm truly at a loss on what he wants from me.

My mom looks at her watch. "It's time to feed him again."

She gets up from the rocking chair and rocks him as I unbutton my dress and the maternity bra underneath. She hands him over, and I bring him closer e so he can latch on, but he refuses. He turns away from my breast as if I've offended him with my offer. We keep trying to get him to feed before giving up.

She takes him to the rocking chair and tries to sing a lullaby to him. I button up and stare in dismay at my little baby as he seems determined to starve himself now too. My growing fear that I'm just a terrible mother makes me want to cry even more.

"Why won't he eat?" I ask. "Is there something wrong with my milk?"

"He could still be full."

I go to the bed by the crib where I've been sleeping for a week and plop down, feeling like a massive failure. "Maybe I'm doing everything wrong."

"You're trying your best," my mother assures me. "You're not going to fail at being a mother, Emory."

I sigh, burying my face in my hands. "It feels like I am."

"Michael might just want some baby formula." She holds him up so she can look at his red, angry face. "Is that what you want? You want to have something else?"

Great. My baby prefers formula to my own milk. Is my breast milk not good enough? Am I not producing what he wants?

My mom's blue eyes widen in realization. "Maybe he wants something else."

"Yeah, formula." I get up and walk to the table in the corner where we have a supply of baby formula, water, and bottles at the ready in case he never latches on again. "I'll make him a bottle."

"No," she says. "There's something else we haven't tried.

"What?"

"Michael is half-vampire. We haven't tried giving him blood."

I blink as I remember Dr. Martin explaining that vampire babies are fed blood along with milk usually along the six month mark. Due to Michael's hybrid nature, we haven't been sure if he would require blood at all. Shifter babies are like human babies. All they need is breast milk or formula.

"What if it's too soon?" I question. "Dr. Martin said that blood from the feeders could make him sick."

Blood from other people could be infected, and Michael's immune system isn't fully developed yet, leaving him vulnerable to contracting something.

"What about your blood?" she suggests. "He's used to taking milk from you."

"Right."

I have never given blood to anybody before. The thought hadn't occurred to me that my baby would want my blood. I feel almost stupid that my half-vampire baby might've wanted blood all this time, and I have been unknowingly depriving him.

I look at the blade I received as one of my birthday gifts. The blade is sharp. I could use that to cut myself.

"You're not thinking straight," Mother says calmly. "Get one of the doctors to take it from you like they do the feeders, honey. With a needle."

I roll my eyes at my own stupidity. One of the maids uses her mind to call a nurse in, and a few moments later, I'm hooked up to a blood bag. Scarlet liquid leaks out, and once we have enough, we pour it into a baby bottle. It's not that much, and we mix it with the breast milk I pumped earlier. The milk in the bottle is a very pale shade of pink.

My mom and I share a look of hope and near desperation as we give Michael the bottle. He latches onto the nipple and quiets down. We both stare in awe as Michael has finally gone quiet as he drinks from the bottle. When it's empty, his pale blue eyes close, and he goes to sleep.

For a few minutes, neither of us moves, scared that it will wake Michael, and he would return to crying his lungs out. When he doesn't stir and appears to finally be truly sleeping, Mom gets to her feet and carefully takes him to the crib to put him down. Making sure he's swaddled, we stare down at his peacefully sleeping face. The silence around us is the most beautiful thing I've heard in such a long time.

"Oh thank the Moon Goddess," I whisper.

"He just needed a little bit of blood," she whispers back with a smile.

"I can't believe I didn't think of that."

"None of us thought of it." She rubs my back soothingly. "Don't be hard on yourself."

I rest my head on her shoulder. "I'm so tired."

"Why don't you take a nap?" she tells me. "I'll wake you when he needs to feed again."

"Thank you, Mom."

I am so grateful I have my mother with me in the castle. I can't imagine not having her here to support me. She has been my tireless rock as I navigate being a new mom. I would be lost without her.

❋

Kane

Michael has been dealing with colic all week. His loud cries echo throughout the castle. The nobles have moved to a wing on the opposite side of the castle to get away from the noise. Some of them have even grumbled about leaving the castle altogether and returning to their properties which I think is a fantastic idea, and I don't dissuade anyone from trying to leave.

The silence that greets me when I go to visit the nursery concerns me. It puts me on edge as I open the door and enter the room expecting the worst. Emory is sitting in the rocking chair with Michael in her arms. He drinks from a bottle greedily, making happy little sucking noises as he does so.

Nellie is cleaning up around the nursery, putting away clean baby bottles and straightening diapers. She bows as I move closer before departing to give us privacy. Emory doesn't look up when I stop in front of her to gaze down at Michael's sleepy face. She looks less frazzled than the last time I saw her.

I feel guilty at having to leave her to the brunt of caring for Michael. I want to be there more for them, but I still have a war to deal with. Now that Jacob is back at Scarlett Thunder, I expect King Peter to launch an attack any day now. The birth of my son has added a new fear to my life–the fear of losing him in this war.

I am more determined than ever to find solutions to help me win over this conflict. I have more to protect now.

"Did he tire himself out from crying?" I whisper, trying not to disturb my son who looks ready to fall asleep.

"No," Emory answers. "We found out what was wrong. He just needed a little bit of blood."

"Did Dr. Martin suggest that?"

She shakes her head. "He didn't think the baby would need blood until Michael is six months old like most vampire babies."

I can't fault the doctor for not knowing how to handle a hybrid baby. We all have to play it by ear when it comes to my son. He is something new entirely. All rules go out the window when it comes to how things will go with him.

Michael's pale blue eyes close, and Emory gently pries the bottle from his mouth. She wordlessly hands it to me, and I put the bottle down on the table nearby. We spend a moment watching Michael sleep in Emory's arms. He looks like he doesn't have a care in the world.

Sleeping in his mother's arms, Michael looks like any other baby. No one would know from looking at him that he's a hybrid. All those terrifying folktales sound so silly when I look at this sweet, little baby. This is no creature of nightmares.

I can't help but chuckle at the thought. Emory looks up, her green eyes bright with affection. "What's so funny?" she asks.

"It just sounds so ridiculous now that we were ever worried about what he would be," I say. "Look at him. He's a baby. He's *our* baby but definitely not the big, bad, scary hybrid."

Emory snorts. "The thought of him rampaging through villages when he can't even hold his head up is pretty funny."

"He's too cute and small to scare anyone."

"Except when he cries," Emory says with a grin. "Are the nobles still threatening to leave the castle?"

"Yes, and I am not trying to persuade them to stay at all. If they decide to never return, I won't shed a tear."

Emory coos at our baby. "Look at that, Mikey. The nobles are already living in fear of you, and you can't even crawl yet."

"An astounding feat for any future king," I agree.

"Imagine when he's finally able to speak. The nobles will never feel at peace again."

"That would be for the best. They've been too comfortable this past century. A little fear will do them some good."

Emory shakes her head. "You silly man."

My heart fills with tender fondness at the sight of the woman I love with the child we created together. It's not the first time I wonder what I've done to be so lucky. Everything I've never known I needed is here, and my world is as it should be at this moment. All my worries melt away in this little oasis of contentment.

"I love you," I declare.

I have the privilege of seeing a new version of Emory, the strong and loving mother. Like any part of her, it's easy to fall in love with. She doesn't even have to try.

"I love you too," she replies. When Michael moves in his sleep, she adds, "And we love you, Mikey."

I'm truly the luckiest guy in the world.

A HOSTILE HOMECOMING

Rainer

As soon as Dr. Martin discharges me from the clinic, I'm back to duty as if I've never been gone. A lot can happen in a week's time, especially since we're on the verge of a war that could annihilate our way of living. With our leverage against Scarlett Thunder gone, we're anticipating King Peter's next move any day now. The air practically crackles with tension as everyone in the castle knows something is about to happen.

With Kane and Emory busy with Mikey, I have to step up so that they can take the time they should be spending together as a family. If I can lighten the load for Kane in any way, I will always do so. My old friend has a way of trying to shoulder all the burdens of the world. I've taken on the work of trying to help him for as long as I've known him.

I visit the nursery to meet my godson as I have promised to Kane. Mikey is awake and sucking on a pacifier. Emory hands the baby over to me and shows me how to hold him. She instructs me to support his head which feels a little too big for his body.

His face is all scrunched up like an elderly man. He's completely bald. The homeliness somehow manages to make him look cuter. This fragile bundle in my arms is the hope of two species.

Pale blue eyes stare up at me, and I can't help but smile. "Hey, Mikey. It's me, your Uncle Rainer."

Kane snorts, but I ignore him. I continue, "I've known your dad for a really long time. Don't worry. I'll teach you all the fun things he won't let you do."

"Don't you dare, Rain-"

"Like all the fun places in the castle to explore, how to sneak out without any of the guards knowing, the best place to meet women."

"If you teach him anything inappropriate, I will make sure you regret it-"

"I'm sure you're going to be a looker like your mom because we all know your dad has a face only a mother could love."

"-and with the blatant disrespect, I could have you thrown into the dungeon!"

Emory hides her laugh behind her hands. "He's just teasing you, Kane."

"It's too early to be losing your sense of humor," I remind Kane, making funny faces at the baby. "If you can't laugh at my jokes, how are you going to survive Mikey when he reaches puberty?"

Kane rolls his eyes and only grunts when Emory pokes him in the side to try and get him to lighten up. He knew I was joking, but he's in a foul mood, it seems.

"Don't you worry, buddy," I tell my godson. "Uncle Rainer will always be here for you."

Holding this tiny baby, I feel more responsible than ever. I have to make sure our kingdom is safe from King Peter and anyone else that wishes us harm. The next generation, and their futures, need to be protected.

If I don't do my part then who will?

WILLOW

Things have irrevocably changed since that day in the hospital wing when Rainer and I became intimate. He's a very affectionate man, constantly wanting to physically touch me, whether it's playing with my hair or rubbing the back of my neck. After a century of trying to avoid people, Rainer's touch is going to take some getting used to. Holding hands feels both endearing, sweet, and oddly wholesome for people our age.

Rainer drives with one hand while he holds my hand in the other. We're making our way from Castle Graystone to the village that used to be my home. After a century away, I don't know how much the area has changed. If there is still a trace of my former coven, I won't know until we get there.

I'm nervous. I don't know how the witches will react to me. I still remember being brought up to fear vampires and how we had shunned witches that had been turned regardless of whether it had been their choice or not. My father had sold me off to be a feeder, caring more about paying off his debts than how the coven would judge him for his actions. I haven't heard any news of what became of my coven after I was brought to Castle Graystone all those years ago. All I know is that King Michael wanted all the witches destroyed.

Rainer parks the car, and we step out of the vehicle. We're in the middle of a clearing where there are only trees and the ruins of old stone cottages to be found. The place looks like it was abandoned a very long time ago. My heart sinks as I try to look for any trace of the coven I used to be part of.

"Is this it?" Rainer asks.

"It should be."

I can only smell the woods; no human scents to be found. I don't know where the coven could have gone. Had they left by their own choice to restart elsewhere? Or worse, had they been wiped out, and this is the last trace of them ever existing?

I step forward and nearly stumble back as I hit an invisible wall.

Rainer is quickly on high alert. "What's wrong?"

I raise a hand and feel for the barrier. The magic hums in my hand, almost burning my skin. "There's a protection spell."

"Can you break through it?"

"That depends on how far this wall spreads."

A little glimmer of hope begins to burn through me. This kind of magic requires maintenance. If whoever had cast it left this place long ago, the magic would have eroded over time until only faint traces of it was left behind. Whoever cast this spell has to still be around or left fairly recently.

I put both hands on the barrier to trace the magic, following it with my eyes as it spreads for miles around us. A barrier this large takes more than one person to cast. It would require a whole coven working together. Excitement makes me almost giddy. I began to move with my hands on the wall, Rainer behind me and concentrate on trying to find a weak spot over the blanket of invisible magic. Relearning my magic these past few months brought back old knowledge of how to detangle and deconstruct spells.

It takes a while to untangle the different points of magic intertwining until I find the spot that holds it altogether. I cast a few spells to try to break through, but it holds strong against my assault, refusing to untangle itself. Frustrated, I take my hands off the barrier. I glare at where I know the magical knot is high above the trees.

"What's wrong?" Rainer asks.

I raise a hand, signaling for him to wait as I work on this problem. Rainer quietly watches me pick up a stone the size of my palm. The rock glows a bright purple as I pour my magic into it. Pulling back my arm, I throw the rock high into the air, it hits an invisible ceiling before the magic shudders, and the air shimmers as the magic dissipates around us.

As the barrier unravels itself, Rainer's blue eyes widen. The image of the abandoned village gives way to a more modern town with houses and buildings. People are standing still, their faces watching us warily, too afraid to breathe loudly. Their fear is palpable; I can practically taste it in the wind.

At the front of the crowd is a dark-haired woman with hazel eyes.

She's wearing a red gown, her hair partially covered in a red shroud. She stares defiantly at us, using her body as a shield for her people. There is no mistaking from her clothing that she's this coven's high priestess.

I place a hand on Rainer's arm, preventing him from moving forward. I shake my head at him, urging him to stay silent so I can take the lead. He brought me here because he knows I will have a better chance of reaching the witches than he does. These used to be my people after all.

"What business do you have here, vampire?" the woman in red demands. "If you do not let us be, we will be forced to take action to protect ourselves."

I raise a hand, trying to appease her. "We have not come here to harm you."

"If you've come to take us to be feeders, we will not come willingly. We will fight to the death rather than waste away in your dungeon."

"That's not why I've come," I insist. "My name is Willow. I used to be part of this coven. I was sold off as a feeder by my father, Asher. I had a sister, Bryony-"

"High priestess Bryony?" the woman asks.

That makes me pause. "I didn't know she became the high priestess."

"After her sister was sold off as a feeder, Asher was shunned by the coven. He was forced to leave the village. High Priestess Morgana took in Bryony and raised her as her own, and eventually, Bryony named as her successor," the woman in red explains. "Bryony was my great-grandmother. I'm Ivy, the current high priestess of this coven."

With the stubborn eyebrows and those familiar hazel eyes, she looks so much like my younger sister Bryony. The family resemblance is unmistakable. I never thought I'd see my sister again, and yet, here is proof that she survived and had a family. There's still something left of Bryony in this world, living in this woman.

"Ivy." I repeat her name, emotion catching in my throat. "You look so much like Bryony."

"She thought you were dead." Hazel eyes look over me critically. "I guess she was half right."

I'm self-conscious of my pale skin and eyes. There is no mistaking what I am now. There is no hiding it. Even with the revelation of the family connection, Ivy doesn't look all that welcoming or glad to see me.

"Why have you come back?" she questions. "Why return to this coven after all this time?"

"I am in need of your help."

Ivy crosses her arms over her chest defiantly. "And what does a vampire need from us? More feeders for your dungeon? Kindling for your bonfires?"

I wince at the reminder of the witch hunts. "Crimson Peak is at war. We need your assistance in order to win the battle that is to come."

The villagers murmur among themselves, their outrage and disbelief unmistakable among the cacophony of voices.

"After what has been done to our people, why should we fight for you?" Ivy stresses. "After what was done to *you*, how can you fight for them?"

I look over the angry faces of the villagers. Rainer is strong and fast, and should the witches attack us, he won't go down without a fight. But bloodshed is the last thing I want to happen. I don't want to hurt any of them.

"May we talk in private, Ivy?" I ask. "At least hear me out before you reject me completely. It's what Bryony would have done."

Ivy looks conflicted. She turns toward her people and then back to me. I don't know if she ever even met Bryony or if they were close, but I'm hoping that the familiar connection between us gives me enough advantage that she will listen to me. I know what's at stake if I fail here today.

Women come forward and whisper to Ivy. My superior hearing lets me catch what they're saying. They're all telling her to not listen to me and demand I leave. They have to recast the barrier and protect the village.

Ivy takes in their concerns, and I wait with bated breath. I grab Rainer's hand and hold on, needing his strength to get me through this. I have spent a century hiding myself, and now I must be seen as I am. No more hiding.

Finally, Ivy turns to me and makes her decision.

AN UNLIKELY ALLIANCE

Willow

"Bryony never stopped hoping you would come back. And it's because of her, I will listen to what you have to say," Ivy declares. "We will speak alone in my home."

Relief washes over me. "Thank you, Ivy."

She raises a hand to stop me. "Only you. *He* can't come into the village."

Glancing down my intertwined hand with Rainer's, I give him an apologetic look. He whispers in my ear, "I don't like this. If you're in danger, yell for me, and I'll fight off the hoard to get to you."

"I'll be fine," I assure him. "Try not to piss off the witches any more than they already are."

His blue eyes bore into me. "Be careful."

"I will."

I squeeze his hand reassuringly before moving away from him. I feel the weight of dozens of stares as I follow Ivy into the village. We walk past buildings until we reach the largest house. It's a two-story limestone building covered in foliage. Vines wrap around the metal railing of the balcony on the second floor. It makes the house look like it sprouted from the earth.

Ivy opens the heavy oak door and lets me in. She leads me into a kitchen which has dozens of labeled jars. Herbs, spices, and other ingredients that I recognize are used in potions. There is a large pewter cauldron on a table that looks well-used.

Ivy puts the kettle on the stove to boil water for tea. She takes out two delicate china teacups and saucers and carefully places them down on the round kitchen table. I watch as she makes tea like my mother used to, placing mint leaves into the kettle. When the whistle blows, she takes it off the stove and pours us each a cup.

I wait for the tea to cool before even attempting to touch it. Gingerly, I pick up the teacup and take a small sip. The minty taste reminds me of a life I was taken away from a long time ago. This kitchen that smells of herbs reminds me of a home that doesn't exist anymore.

Ivy hasn't touched her tea. Her hazel eyes feel like they're piercing straight to my soul.

"Well?" she prompts. "How are you going to convince me that fighting your war is a good idea?"

I place the teacup down. "For what it's worth, I didn't want to involve the witches in this at all."

"Then why did you come?"

"I'm here because Crimson Peak has become my home. There are people I care about there that I want to protect. If I don't do anything to help in this war, they're as good as dead or imprisoned should King Kane lose the fight."

"I still don't see how this is any of our business."

"Do you really think King Peter's going to stop at Crimson Peak? Once he's conquered one of the largest vampire kingdoms, what's to prevent him from marching forward and claiming your territory?"

Ivy glares at me. "You truly have become one of them, trying to intimidate us into doing what you want. What will you do if I say no? Hunt down every person in this village?"

"We won't hurt anyone," I insist. "But you must see that Crimson Peak is the only thing standing in the way of Scarlett Thunder taking over land in the north."

"That may be a possible problem in the future," she counters. "It still isn't enough of an incentive for us to risk our lives for the very people that hunted us down not that long ago. Besides, without a witch, they won't get past our defenses."

"I know what happened. I was there," I remind her.

"What they did can't just be forgotten."

"No, but we can move forward," I say. "King Kane isn't like his father. He's had a child with a shifter woman. He would be open to forging an alliance with this coven if you would give him the opportunity."

"An alliance?"

I nod. "An alliance could prevent any more witches from being hunted ever again. You would benefit from an arrangement like that. You would be equals."

Ivy's fingernail traces the rim of the teacup, her expression contemplative. "What else would King Kane be able to offer for this alliance?"

"The man that came with me would be able to tell you more," I explain. "He is King Kane's right hand man."

"And you are *friends* with this man?"

If I could blush, my face would be red. "We are friends."

She raises a dark eyebrow at me. "More than friends?"

I clear my throat, trying to hide my embarrassment. The last thing I want to do is have to explain my relationship with Rainer to my long lost relative.

"It's not important," I say. "Are you willing to speak to him?"

"I will hear him out."

This has gone better than I expected. I'm about to thank Ivy when she reaches across the wooden table to touch my arm. She turns my hand over with calloused fingers to trace the veins on my pale wrist. I know my body temperature runs colder than a human's, almost like ice.

"How did you break the barrier?" she asks. "A vampire shouldn't have been able to do that without the help of a witch."

"I still have access to my magic. My father's expertise was in warding magic. He taught me how to create and unravel spells of that nature."

Her dark eyebrows furrow in confusion. "How did you keep your magic even after becoming a vampire?"

"I don't know," I answer. "I thought it would have disappeared after I was turned, but somehow, I can still access the magic in the earth."

Witches are taught that losing their magic is a sign of a lost soul. A witch unable to access the magic in the earth, the leftover tools from creation, means she is dead in all the ways that matter. A witch turned vampire that has magic shouldn't be possible at all. And yet, here I am, proof against those beliefs.

Ivy nods, her hand slipping away from me. "Bring your friend here. I would like to listen to his offer now."

Kane

I tried not to be too hopeful when I sent Rainer and Willow looking for her old coven. I know trying to find witches that will be willing to ally themselves with us in war is not going to be an easy task. So when I receive word that, against all odds, Willow and Rainer have succeeded in granting me an audience with the high priestess of Willow's former coven. I have no time to waste, and I make the trip to the village in the north.

I bring only a handful of guards with me, knowing the reception from the witches will not be warm and welcoming. There is a lot of bad blood between our species. I can't blame them for their distrust and anger. I have to leave my guards outside the village, only escorted by Rainer and Willow.

They lead me to the house of the high priestess. I expect an old crone, but the woman I find looks barely twenty. I can see the resemblance to Willow in the shape of their eyes and their noses. Ivy is a child compared to me, but the defiance in her hazel eyes reminds me that she is only young but not naïve.

"King Kane," she says when I enter her living room. The simple furniture and herbal scent of the house is exactly what I expect her home to be like. "I have heard a lot about you."

"All good things I hope," I reply, trying to be charming.

She doesn't smile. I try not to let it get to me. I have dealt with difficult royals and nobles my entire life. I'm able to hide any discomfort I'm feeling easily.

Ivy carries herself like a queen. We sit at her kitchen table and discuss terms for the alliance. I agree to relinquish my ownership of this land back to her coven as well as a certain amount of gold. This village has plans for expansion, and that always requires money.

In return, Ivy will recruit witches from her coven and the ones she is associated with to give us the numbers we need for the upcoming war. Despite her youth, Ivy is a skilled negotiator and is able to sway people to her side. She would make a formidable enemy. I'm glad she is on my side instead of against me.

Rainer presents the contracts we've written, and we sign them, Ivy using her magic to make sure I cannot back out of her terms even if I want to. Her magic pricks into my skin like needles. I force myself not to wince until she finishes casting the spell. When all is done, there is a chain of glowing runes around my right wrist.

An identical chain of runes appears on Ivy's wrist. She asks, "How quickly do you need us to fight?"

"Sooner rather than later," I answer. "I will send word when you and the witches are needed."

She nods, getting up from the table. I follow her to the kitchen cabinet where she pulls out a bottle of bourbon and two glasses. She pours and hands me one.

"To a long alliance." She raises her glass. "And to not dying in this war."

"To a long alliance—and long lives." I clink my glass against hers.

We both swallow and the burning sensation of the liquor down my throat helps unwind the knot of tension in me. After months of failed alliances, I've finally succeeded in my efforts, and this can turn the tide for us. With the shifters and witches on our side, suddenly our chances don't feel so dismal. The most unlikely of alliances might be what saves my kingdom from ruin.

"I heard you had a child with a shifter woman," Ivy says. "Is that true?"

I nod. "I have a son with Emory Moonraker. She's the Alpha of the Moonraker pack."

"I've heard of her father." She frowns. "He wasn't a pleasant man to deal with."

"You met him?"

"My mother did. She didn't like him."

"Not a lot of people did," I agree. "His daughter is different. She's selfless and puts her pack first."

She looks contemplative. "How did a vampire king and an Alpha shifter end up having a child together?"

"It's a long story."

"Perhaps you'll tell me the story someday."

I nod. "When there's time, I'll be glad to do so."

Even with the more genial air in this house, I can't ignore the heavy ball of guilt I've been enduring since the bloody history with the witches was brought up. I'm very much aware that each person in this village has been affected by the actions of my family. I can't brush everything under the rug and never acknowledge what my own father did to these people.

I put my glass down on the kitchen table. "I would be remiss not to bring this up. For what my father has down to your coven, to your kind, I am truly sorry. And I know there's nothing I can say that will make up for the grave wrongs that were done to you, but this is me trying to try to make amends."

Ivy is quiet, clutching the half-empty glass of bourbon in her hand like a lifeline. Finally, she replies, "I grew up terrified of vampires. I heard the stories about the witch hunts, and I can feel the pain and sorrow of those that came before me. Their suffering cannot be wiped away with just an apology."

I nod, expecting this reaction. "I know."

"But...." She glances over to where Willow is standing with Rainer. "We can move forward to a better future. For the sake of my people, I must create a better path for them."

Ivy's hazel eyes stare into mine as she concludes, "I appreciate the apology, but actions speak louder than words. Keep yours, and we'll be allies for a long time. Break your word, and you'll wish we'd never met."

I look right back at her. "I believe you."

MORE MAGICAL LOOPHOLES

Kane

A few days after the alliance with Willow's former coven is finalized, Ivy is going to meet up with the high priestesses of covens she is associated with. Surprisingly, she's taking me with her. When I ask her why she wants me there, knowing how the witches will not positively react to me, she points out, "This war is your mess. You should be doing half the work of trying to convince them."

I don't really have an argument for that, so I call Emory to inform her I'll be gone for a few more days then make the drive to the meeting point the high priestesses agreed on. We drive even further up north, my guards along with Willow and Rainer tailing us. It's even more remote here, no buildings and people to be found for miles. When we reach our destination, we step out of the car, and Ivy guides me toward stone steps that lead up a hill.

The steps are steep and have been carved into the stone. There are no railings for support. I look around at this desolate place and wonder what we've done to the witches to make them live this way. I owe them a lot already, and they haven't even started fighting with us.

On top of the high hill, forty bluestone standing slabs are positioned in a circle. Each monolith is over six feet tall and has to weigh over two tons. In the center of the monoliths stands a bluestone slab altar. Some stones are stacked on top of the vertical stones to form a triangle. The wear of the stones indicate that they have been here for a long time.

"We used to gather here for ceremonies," Ivy explains as she lights torches with her magic. "At least until our gatherings made your kind too nervous."

Familiar shame makes me want to wince. Ivy has made it known she doesn't care for my apologies, so I don't say a word. As we walk closer to the large stones, I can see runes have been carved into them. Considering my father's crusade in trying to cull the witches' power, I wonder how this place managed to stay untouched.

As soon as we enter the ring of stones, I feel the hair on the back of my neck stand up as ancient power ripples over the area. Even with my ignorance of magic, I can feel it beneath the earth and in the air. This place is older than me. Centuries of magic has been cast here, and traces of it can still be felt.

"They don't mind you bringing me here?" I ask. "The other witches?"

"It's not the first time vampires have tried to come up here," she explains. "And when they come with their poor intentions, the magic reacts accordingly."

The magic around us feels like a hundred eyes are watching me. It almost makes me shudder. The guards stand outside the circle of stones, not daring to move closer. Willow and Rainer circle the monoliths, the former touching the stones reverently.

"If you are insincere in your intentions of making peace with the witches, the magic will strike you down where you stand," Ivy continues. "You may lie to my face, but the magic can read your heart clearly."

I look up as the sky darkens, thunder booming above us. I stand still, waiting for judgment. Ivy's hazel gaze is steady on me as she stands by the altar. Lightning flashes above us for a minute before the clouds slowly clear and show us the night sky again.

"That's a first," Ivy says. "I've never seen the magic actually tolerate a vampire."

"Maybe I'm special," I reply, trying to hide how nervous I am with a joke. She thought I was about to die and didn't warn me? I guess I can't blame her, but I'm also not sure I can trust her.

The high priestess shrugs. "Special? If you say so, King Kane."

"I've come to learn that nature has loopholes," I tell her. "Perhaps you can clarify something for me."

She leans back against the altar, her hands on the bluestone behind her for support. "What is it you need clarification on?"

"I've had questions ever since I met Emory and felt the undeniable pull between us. When she became pregnant and she learned that I'm her mate, it seemed to go against everything we know about our two species."

"It is true that a vampire and a shifter usually don't have romantic relationships. At least that's what I've heard."

"Our relationship goes beyond that. I'm her fated mate. Why would nature allow something like that to happen?"

"Trying to make sense of why nature and magic do things can drive someone insane."

"I have no one else to ask about this," I admit.

Ivy purses her pink lips. She looks contemplative before answering, "Nature values survival, not strength. Perhaps nature thinks a child of two species will benefit the survival of both."

I remember how the shifters decided to align themselves with Crimson Peak after learning about Michael. His existence alone assures me that I have Alphas to fight for me in this war. This is not a feat I would have accomplished on my own. The vampire royalty feels differently about my son, but maybe in time, they will change their minds.

"Magic is finicky. Vampires were created using magic, so whatever ancient magic is within you could be to blame as well," Ivy adds. "It could also have to do with your bloodline."

"My bloodline?"

"Haven't you ever wondered why some vampires are born?

Unusual for a species that can create more of you with just a single bite, isn't it?"

"What do you mean?" Of course, I've wondered about that, but I want to hear what she has to say.

"Part of the reason we shun witches that are turned into vampires is because we learned they're still able to get pregnant. All vampire royals have a witch ancestor or two somewhere in their bloodline. Ironic, isn't it?"

The answer to a mystery I've wondered about my entire life is so easily given to me, I'm reeling trying to process it. My father's actions feel more shameful considering we're descended from witches. This magic has been in my blood for millennia, probably waiting for the right catalyst to create something new.

Maybe falling in love with Emory and having Michael is all part of some grand design.

A gasp makes us both turn to where Willow is standing. She has gone shockingly pale.

Ivy gives her relative a bland smile. "You should probably use some protection just in case, Auntie Willow."

WILLOW

The witches arrive about an hour after we reach the top of the hill. I have only been to a few of these ceremonies, when I was a child. It was before my mother died of a fever one winter, and my father started drinking to cope. Bryony was only three the last time we went. After that, meeting up in large masses like this became too dangerous.

The high priestesses don't come alone. They are all wearing shrouds in different shades from bright colors of red, green, and yellow to dramatic dark blues, purple, and even black. They have come with other witches who are carrying lit torches to guide the way. They all look suspiciously at the vampires. Kane's guards keep their distance, sensing they are unwelcome in this place.

Once the high priestesses enter the circle of stones, they get straight to business. Kane and Rainer negotiate their terms for an alliance with each coven. It's a long process that requires bargaining and some level of posturing. My inexperience with politics and diplomacy makes me useless in this process. I step away to give them space and make my way down the hill. My superior eyesight makes it easy for me to navigate the darkness.

I find more witches below. They have set up tables overflowing with food and drink. Dozens of lanterns illuminate the area. They stop and stare as I approach.

I try to smile reassuringly. "Hello. I'm Willow. I come in peace."

The witches exchange glances. One of the younger witches with brown hair asks, "Do vampires eat food?"

"We do," I answer. "We need blood to survive, but besides that, we eat plenty of food, even though we don't need it."

Food is a safe, neutral topic and we discuss the differences and similarities in the food we eat. Vampires usually have access to more expensive food while witches make do with more hearty and filling meals. It's a conversation not much different to the ones I've engaged in with the staff at Castle Graystone during a boring week. When they learn I used to be a witch, their curiosity gets the better of them, and they ask me more personal questions.

"Do vampires have sex?" one of the men asks. "Or is it all just biting each other and drinking blood?"

"We can do both if we want," Rainer answers easily with a grin. He walks toward us and stops beside me, wrapping his arm around my waist. "It depends on how kinky you are. I don't judge."

I dig my nails into his wrist, quietly admonishing him. The witches around us have gone red.

"Where are Kane and Ivy?" I ask. "Are they done negotiating?"

"They're making their way down for the feast."

He nods toward the group of people walking down the stone steps with torches. I see Ivy and Kane at the front. We all wait for them to reach us. It seems we are going to share a meal together.

I don't think witches and vampires have ever done that. This must be a first. Negotiations must've gone well since the mood is light. The witches aren't making small talk with the vampires, but they seem to have relaxed as we sit and begin eating, grabbing from the food and drinks at the long tables.

"How did things go?" I ask.

Ivy is drinking wine and eating a plate of baked fish. "Better than we expected, actually. King Kane charmed those mighty women with his silver tongue."

Kane shrugs, a pleased smile on his face. "Turns out my pretty words work better on the other high priestesses."

Ivy snorts. "You'd think these women wouldn't be fooled by a handsome face."

"We all have our weaknesses," Rainer points out.

His gaze meets mine, and it makes heat and desire pool in my belly. It's annoying how easily he affects me.

"Some of us are weaker than others," I counter.

His only response is his hand on my knee. No one will see it under the table, but I try to keep my face straight as I feel his fingers travel higher until he's dangerously close to my inner thigh. This man is shameless. All the while, he looks like nothing's a miss as he eats grapes from my plate.

Kane goes to the high priestesses at some point and makes them giggle and fluster by plying on the charm thick. Ivy speaks to witches closer to her age and leaves me alone with Rainer. He leans closer to me and murmurs, "Do you want to get out of here?"

I glare at him. "Seriously?"

He smiles boyishly like he's never done anything bad in his life. "Will you *please* come with me? Pretty please?"

I roll my eyes and make a show of being annoyed with him as I get to my feet. He takes my hand and practically carries me away from the feast. He takes us to the nearby woods, deep enough so we're hidden by a crop of elm trees. My back is pressed against the solid trunk of a tree, and I let out a squeak as Rainer pulls me up so I can wrap my legs around his waist.

"I've been thinking about this all day," he says before he kisses me.

The kiss is hot and deep. His hands are everywhere, pulling up my skirts and unzipping his pants. He's deep inside me before I can even protest–not that I want to. All I can do is moan and follow his lead.

Maybe I'm just as shameless as he is.

THE LONG WAIT

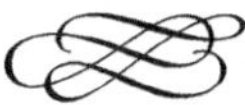

Lex

The days blur together in that dark cell. I can barely do anything but sleep. Somebody brings me blood on occasion. My ribs are broken, and they are trying to heal, but I need more blood.

My nose has healed, and it feels crooked, which will mar my looks forever if I don't have it reset soon. There are bruises on my torso that make it hard to rest. Whenever I move in my sleep, the broken ribs and the bruises awaken me with pain. I've never been this uncomfortable in my life.

I pay attention to what I can in my cell. The tiny window is too high for me to reach, but it's the only thing that can tell me about the passage of time. The guards change a few times a day, and that's usually when a servant brings me a pitifully small goblet of blood. No one wants to talk to me, and they place the tray with the goblet on the ground before closing the cell door quickly.

I try to bribe the guards, but they laugh at me. I offer the expensive watch Kane gifted to me for my twenty-first birthday, but they merely took the watch and ignored me. The servants won't look me in the eye. I am stuck waiting for Jacob to add to my injuries or be forgotten here to die a slow, painful death.

After a week, the guards begin murmuring to each other. Most of them are being assigned to leave the castle. Some are excited, but others are wary for their safety. They mention Crimson Peak, and I know this means the war is truly starting.

If Kane loses, will I be stuck here in this cell forever or executed? I don't know which fate is worse. I'm lying on my back, trying to take shallow breaths to ease the pain in my ribs when a visitor arrives. There are barely any lights in the dungeon, certainly not any in the cells. It's night time, so not even the few beams of light from the sun that sometimes make their way through the window are there to help. A female silhouette unlocks the cell door and enters, closing it behind her.

The woman pockets the key and moves toward me. She doesn't have a goblet of blood with her. That's a shame because I'm thirsty. Her scent makes me pause.

She kneels down on the ground beside the thin mat I'm lying on. My superior eyesight makes it easy to make out her features. She's plain with dark blonde hair and brown eyes. She looks young with a round face, maybe nineteen or twenty. She's unmistakably human with her olive complexion, and after a week of not having enough blood, my eyes trace the veins on her exposed neck.

"Your Highness," she whispers. "I'm here to help you."

"Escape?" I ask almost in disbelief. "I don't think you'll be much help against the guards."

She shakes her head, taking the key out of her pocket. She shoves it underneath the thin mat I'm lying on.

"You'll get your chance to escape soon. The battle is about to begin," she says. "You must not try to escape before then. You will not get another chance."

"How do you know this?"

"I was sent by a friend to help you."

I sit up too quickly, my ribs making me grimace in pain. "I appreciate your help, but I can barely walk. Even if I get out of this cell, I won't be able to fight anyone off."

I won't go down easily, but I know I'm too weak for a prison break. If only Jacob hadn't broken my ribs. If I had just stopped myself from provoking him and his fragile ego, I would be strong enough to get myself out of here. I can practically hear Kane admonishing me for my impulsive, bad choices once he hears about this.

"There will be a car in the woods by the north tower waiting for you tomorrow. You must get out of Scarlett Thunder," she says.

I stare at her suspiciously. "Who sent you?"

"A friend," she answers.

"Who?"

She doesn't answer, and she pulls out a needle from her pocket and begins to attach it to a bag. "You need your strength for tomorrow. You need to feed."

"What-"

I watch in shock as she places the needle in her vein, and crimson blood starts dripping into the bag. When it's full enough, she offers it to me, and the hunger spurs me on, practically burning my throat. I take the bag and drink, her blood salty and vibrant. After starving for days, her blood tastes better than even the best food in the world.

I empty it and then lick the blood that has dripped down the bag. I want more. I'm still hungry even though the bag is empty. I have to be careful not to take too much from her, though.

"Who sent you?" I ask again.

"It doesn't matter," she replies. "You only need to focus on getting stronger."

I should ask more questions, but all I can think of is tasting more of her blood. The meager portions they've been serving me will not give me the strength I need if I want to escape this castle alive. Even with the mouthful of blood I've taken from her, my ribs are already trying to heal themselves. My flesh is stitching itself together, and the bruises are fading away.

She offers me some more, and I don't hesitate before I ask her to fill the bag again.

RAINER

The nobles have left Castle Graystone, hiding away in their own properties after Kane tells them that King Peter has ordered his armies to march into Crimson Peak. It's almost amusing to watch the snooty nobles running out of the castle, yelling for servants to bring their luggage with them. They pile into their expensive cars and drive away with no care about what might happen to their king. I have no doubt that they will leech onto whoever wins this war.

Kane and I discuss the best strategy for the battle. The Alphas will be arriving with their warriors soon. Emory went to meet them in Moon Grove where Helena will be staying with the baby. Ivy and the witches are already in the castle, waiting for Kane's command.

Willow has not left Ivy's side since her relative's arrival at the castle. The two women have been trying to get to know each other in the short time since they've met. I know that connecting to the last of her family is important to Willow, and I give them the space they need. I shadow Kane around the castle, trying to gauge his moods.

We have been through a lot together, me and my old friend. We have managed to avoid war until now.

"It's not too late to leave," Kane tells me as he stands by the window, watching the view outside. "If you decide you don't want to die for me, I won't be offended."

"And miss out on all the action?" I quip. "You want me to hide away while you get to have all the fun?"

"I'm serious, Rainer. You don't need to follow me into this. Not this time."

I have followed Kane's lead for as long as I can remember. He's the leader, and I'm the loyal second. He makes the choices, and I help execute his wishes. I have never had any desire to change that.

I snort, moving closer so I can stand beside him. "Don't be so dramatic, Kane. I'd be more offended if you sent me away."

He continues as if I never spoke. "You can just grab Willow and go. Run far away where King Peter can never find you."

"And what kind of existence will that be? Living in hiding? Willow has already done that for a long time. I won't force her to live like that again."

"If I lose this war, neither of you will have any sort of life," he argues. "If you're not executed, you'll be prisoners or enslaved."

"*If* we lose," I remind him. "You're thinking only of the worst case scenario. There is a chance we can win this war, and none of those possibilities come to fruition."

He buries his face in his hands. "I never wanted people to risk their lives for me like this. I never wanted this kind of violence and bloodshed on my conscience, but there's no avoiding this. King Peter wants my head on a pike, and everyone else is collateral to him."

I shrug. "He's a prick. Always has been."

"Even if I win and I lose you, I don't know what my life will be like without you, Rain. I don't trust anyone else. I can't. You have been my one true friend."

I feel my throat closing up as unexpressed emotion makes it hard to speak. Damnit. Kane wants us to cry our feelings out. I guess becoming a father has made him more emotional–the bastard.

"Kane," I say, seriously, "my place has always been here by your side."

He turns to look at me, slowly nodding.

"I'm your friend," I declare. "I'm with you until the end of the line."

Emotion flashes through his blue eyes, and he swallows hard. "Thank you."

We have known each other for years. It goes beyond my duty to the crown. My loyalty has always been to Kane, the first friend I ever made when I became a vampire. Whatever is coming for us, we will get through it like we have our entire lives–together.

It's hard to fall asleep when you know a battle is about to begin. I know I need to rest, but my mind keeps me awake, buzzing away at the possibilities of what's about to happen. Clairvoyance has never been my expertise as a witch, so I can't say all my worries are premonitions of the future. They're anxious thoughts that will not leave me alone.

I leave my room, hoping a walk through the castle will help. The hallway is empty. The staff have been given the choice to stay in the castle or leave. Most have opted to stay, feeling the castle will be safer than anywhere else they choose to hide.

For most of the staff, this castle is their home. Like them, whatever home I had before coming to this place no longer exists. The house I grew up in burned down decades ago. On top of the land, another house was built, and it eventually became an apothecary.

Like so many people here, I have nowhere else to go. Visiting the village I was born in made that more clearer to me than ever. This realization doesn't make me sad like I thought it would. I accepted long ago that the person I used to be has long been dead, and my life before that is not something I can return to even if I wanted to.

I can navigate the castle in my sleep. I don't think about any specific path, only focus on taking in the sights of the castle like gazing at an old friend for the last time. I find myself back in the library, opening the big oak doors and walking between the shelves. My hands absentmindedly touch the books, my dearest friends through the hardest times.

My desk hasn't been touched since I last came to the library. It feels like yesterday that Lola and Emory showed up in the library wanting to hear about old folktales. I open the desk drawer and see the fountain pen that my old mentor Gaius gifted me for my birthday. I smile just thinking of him.

"There you are," Rainer says as he enters the library. "I've been looking for you. You weren't in your room."

I close the desk drawer. "I can't sleep."

"That's understandable. I can't sleep either," he replies. "I find that I'm getting used to sleeping beside you even if your hands are always cold."

"My hands are not always cold," I argue, waspishly.

He grins and makes his way toward me, pulling me into an embrace. "I don't mind. I'll always keep you warm."

I relax in his arms. "Could you promise me something?"

"Anything."

"Don't die tomorrow."

He pauses, his blue eyes staring into my face as if he's memorizing me. Finally, he answers, "I'll try."

I wish he'd be less honest. I would rather have heard his bravado declare he couldn't die. Delusions of invincibility would have been more comforting. In the end, Rainer decides to not lie to me.

It's both cruel and kind.

I kiss him anyway.

WOLVES OF WAR

Emory

My mother tells me about what happened to Bernard before we arrive in Moon Grove. His body is transported in a separate car as we make our way back to my hometown. I'm too numb from shock and the millions of things I need to focus on other than my father's death. Bernard, until the end, is causing problems for me.

I don't have much time to give attention to this so I let my mother handle most of the arrangements for the funeral pyre. All Alphas are traditionally cremated outside while their family and friends look on and tell stories about the life the Alpha lived. Bernard's public disgrace makes this a small affair. It's just my mom, my siblings, and I. We were the closest to him, and still, none of us had really known him at all.

It's sundown by the time the funeral pyre is ready. I was only three the last time I saw an Alpha's cremation when Grandpa Colton died. I move mechanically through the funeral. My mom says a prayer to the Moon Goddess, and we stand under the moonlight quietly.

Colt has been the one to help set out the pyre, but I have to set it ablaze as the new Alpha. He lights a torch with a lighter and hands it to me. I approach the pyre made of wood, straw, and kindling.

Bernard's body is covered in a white sheet hiding his face from view. His body has begun to rot, and the smell of death burns my nostrils.

"From the light of the moon we serve," I say, "and away from the light, we rest."

It almost feels like an out of body experience as I lower the torch and set the funeral pyre on fire. I step back as the fire spreads and devours everything in its path. The fire grows, and the heat warms us as we stand there. I rest the torch on a poll nearby, and Lola holds my hand for support. My mother is on my left, her blue eyes grimly watching the growing fire.

The smell of burning flesh isn't pleasant, but none of us say anything. No one wants to break the silence.

My mother, ever dutiful to a mate who never deserved her, takes on the responsibility and speaks first. "I didn't like Bernard the first time I met him."

All of us turn to her in surprise, I reply, "What? But you and Dad always said it was love at first sight."

She snorts which is more shocking. My mother never snorts. "Maybe it was lust at first sight on his end," she says. "I wanted to marry a boy from my father's pack. I had gone to school with this boy, and felt I knew him better. And even at that time, Bernard Moonraker already had a reputation."

"A reputation for what?" Colt asks.

"Going through girls like a hot knife through butter." She sighs. "Then he turned twenty-one and declared I was his mate."

Lola, who looks unsure if she can even join in, questions, "And you fell in love?"

My mother's eyebrows furrow in contemplation. "I tried to love him, forced myself to for the sake of the family we built together. It was never enough for him, and I tried to fool myself that it was enough for me."

"I never knew that, Mom," I tell her. "I wish you'd told me sooner."

"I didn't want to speak ill of him in front of his children, even when he probably deserved it."

I take my mother's hand and squeeze it reassuringly. "I'm sorry he never loved you like you deserved. He wasn't right for you."

"He gave me you," my mother tells me tenderly, looking between me and Colt. "You two are the loves of my life. It was all worth it because of that."

She pulls us both closer, kissing Colt's cheek and my temple, the warmth and strength radiating from her is a calming balm. I glance at Lola who stands outside the triangle we've created. I tug on her hand and pull her closer, wrapping an arm around her shoulders. She relaxes beneath my touch.

"He gave us you, Lo," I add. "That's another good thing he did."

"In spite of himself, Bernard managed to make good kids," Colt says. "We're his legacy. The best thing he's ever done."

My mother nods. "He's wronged many people and made many mistakes. People will remember him for what he's done and not the man he pretended to be. But all of you don't need to live in that shadow."

She looks us all in the eye, even Lola, and concludes, "You will all live bright, beautiful lives away from his memory. This pack will remember the things you achieved and the good you brought to the world. That is the Moonraker legacy, not Bernard."

We are all in agreement that Bernard Moonraker has a list of sins that could go on for miles, but the one thing he took for granted is his best achievement–his family.

We watch as the funeral pyre continues to burn. The forest is quiet as if giving us the space that we need. As the night gets colder, we slowly retreat back into the warmth of the house. We leave Bernard and his memory behind us where he deserves to be.

Kane

I wait in a tent for news of warriors expected to arrive soon. The only updates I've had so far are from the other side of the field where King Peter's troops are growing by the number. He's called on his allies, and King Myenas seems to have an endless supply of men. I don't see the banner men of my former allies, at least, so I know the other royals haven't completely turned on me yet.

Rainer is outside talking to our soldiers, trying to keep morale up. There has been no word from King Cyrus or Queen Olga about sending more men and supplies. Emory and the wolf shifters haven't arrived yet. I'm stuck sitting here staring at a battle map and feeling like a fool.

A fool about to lose everything.

I know I cannot fall into despair. The battle hasn't even started. I am not completely without allies. Ivy and the High Priestess have upheld their end of the alliance and have sent witches to fight. There are at least fifty of them outside which could be considered a small amount, but their magic cannot be underestimated in combat.

The witches are physically fragile, so I will need my men to protect them as they cast their spells and curses. If we have a good defense, the witches can throw magic from a safe distance away and still take out numbers on the other side. Yet, there are still so many on the other side of that damn field.

Rainer's estimate is that there have to be at least five thousand men. I have a quarter of that amount with me. It's still not enough, even with the witches' numbers. Once they break through the soldiers and get to the witches, this battle will be over quickly.

I'm interrupted from my spiraling thoughts as Emory enters the tent. Her bright smile is like moonlight in a dark cave. Her red hair is in a high ponytail, showing off her graceful neck. I get up from my seat to go to her. Having her in my arms again feels right. She's my anchor in the sea of chaos around me.

"I missed you," I say. "Where's Michael?"

"At Moon Grove with my mother and Lola," she answers. "I missed you too."

I cup her beautiful face in my hands and kiss her, the time we spent apart feeling like years instead of days. She kisses me back, and there's a desperation from both of us. The looming battle and the possibility of never seeing each other again gives a bittersweetness to the kiss, like this will be the last time we get to do this. She opens her mouth, and I deepen the kiss, savoring the taste of her as if I could stay in this moment and keep us here forever.

Emory pants slightly when she pulls away. "The other Alphas are outside along with the men."

"How many?"

"Around two thousand."

I close my eyes in relief. I can work with those odds. We might win this war after all.

"I love you," I tell her. "And not because you brought me an army."

She smiles. "I know, and I love you too."

We have to leave the tent so I can greet all the Alphas. I've met the older ones through our mutual alliance with Emory's grandfather Alpha Colton back in the day. I knew the parents of the newer Alphas, and it's easy to see the resemblance among most of them. Emory is the youngest, and it's never clearer as she stands beside them.

She's got her whole life before her, but she's about to fight in a war. I pull her away to talk to her, further enough that the vampires with their superior hearing can't eavesdrop on us.

"Are you sure about this?" I ask. "You can go back to Moon Grove and stay with Michael."

"I told you I'm not going to leave your side," she argues. "We're in this together."

"If something were to happen, Michael should have at least one parent to take care of him…." I swallow hard. "I've been around a lot longer than you have. You've got so much of your life left to live."

She pokes me hard on the shoulder. "Stop doing that."

It doesn't really hurt, but I rub at the spot anyway. "Doing what?"

"Your martyr King Kane act again," she replies with an eye roll. "I'm going to fight by your side, and you can't stop me. I will claw and bite my way out of whatever cell you put me in."

I sigh and look across the field. "There are eight thousand warriors on that side by our latest calculations. We have around four thousand. The odds aren't terrible with the witches, but they're not that good either."

"Your grandfather went to war at Ruby Rivers with a thousand men against an army of four thousand and still won." At my surprised expression, she explains, "I read up on the wars your kingdom has fought in during my pregnancy bed rest. I got bored."

"I'm not my grandfather. He was an exceptional general."

"Then be an exceptional general," she counters. "You've done what no king before you has ever done, Kane. You've united vampires, shifters, and witches to fight for you. No matter what happens, they're going to write books about you."

I look around us at the different faces. Three different species have come together for a common cause. This is an unprecedented event. I'm living history.

"Okay." I feel the weight of a future I am writing on my shoulders, an homage to the crown I've been wearing for decades. "Let's do this."

"Together."

"Together."

I've seen wolf shifters transform before, but I haven't seen Emory shift yet. It's quick. She kicks off the brown boots and plain grey dress she has on. She's naked for a brief second before she leaps into the air for her body to mold and stretch itself into another form. Fur grows out of skin and limbs elongate into claws in split seconds.

A white wolf appears in Emory's place. I look into her golden eyes and can still see Emory in there. I cautiously lift my hand to touch her, and she bumps her wet nose against my palm. She wags her tail excitedly.

"You are beautiful," I say in awe.

Emory gives me a playful bark before she turns away quickly, running toward the other wolves. They stand at attention, waiting for orders. She's the Alpha, and she'll be leading them into war. Hope shines brightly within me like a beacon.

THE GREAT ESCAPE

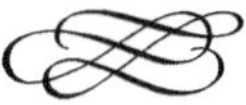

Lex

The girl lies limp on the dungeon floor. I've drank more than I meant to this time, and I feel her blood running through my system. Since she first started to visit me a few days ago, she's returned several times, and my body has begun to heal itself. My ribs still feel tender as the bruises fade around my torso. I haven't felt this strong in weeks.

I gingerly get to my feet, stretching my limbs. I try not to glance at her. The faint beat of her pulse echoes in my ear, so I know she's still alive. This time, she insisted I drink straight from her. She said she was willing to sacrifice herself for my cause. I have no idea why. So… if she doesn't die from blood loss, she'll become a vampire.

I don't have time to dwell on that now. Most of the guards around the dungeon are gone as she said they would be. They have left the castle to fight in the battle against Crimson Peak. Knowing my chance will never come again, I reach for the key in my pocket she gave me and unlock the cell door.

It opens, and adrenaline pumps through me, urging me on. I glance back at the girl on the floor and decide to leave the cell open.

She saved my life, and I can't leave her trapped in there. I can't take her with me as she'll slow me down.

"I'm sorry," I say. "And thank you."

I have no time to waste. I walk quickly through the dungeon finding the staircase. After months of living in this castle, I've discovered all its little hidden hallways that the servants use to not be seen by the nobles. I make use of them now as I duck into hallways to avoid the remaining guards in the castle.

I could bump into any of the servants, but I'm hoping most of them are huddling together in the kitchens while trying to weather this out. They'll be the ones who will want to be informed of any changes. There are still some servants doing their chores around the castle. Work is work whether there's a war going on after all.

I make my way to the laundry room to change into something else. The women are hard at work, washing and drying clothes. My bright platinum hair is eye-catching, so I grab a knitted cap along with clean pants and a shirt from a clothes line. Ducking out quickly before anyone can see me, I go into a broom closet and change clothes.

Keeping my head down, I exit the broom closet, avoiding eye contact with two passing guards who are distracted talking about the battle. I find myself in the kitchen. The cooks are chatting about the battle, too. I'm on a mission, and I can't afford distractions. Grabbing a bowl off the table, I use it to cover half my face as I pass by a group of servants hurrying toward the dining hall. The nobles haven't left the castle and still expect to be served their meals on time.

I walk quickly past the hallway leading to the dining hall, trying to avoid the swerve of nobles coming in to eat. They expect me to move around them, and I roll my eyes as I have to swivel like an eel to pass. I manage to make it down the hallway and turn the corner toward the north tower. The hallway is empty, and my freedom is close.

I turn around and see if the coast is clear and drop the bowl on the ground before I make a run for it. There are footsteps behind me, and the clunking of armor alerts me that it's the guards. I reach the door leading to the north tower and turn back to see them looking down at the discarded bowl on the ground. I slide into the north tower and lock the heavy wooden door with the deadbolt.

Out the window, I see the gardens below, so I head toward the stairs and make my way down, cursing the numerous steps. I'm slightly out of breath when I reach the first-floor landing, but I don't stop. I open the door that leads to my freedom and to the outside.

The eastern gardens are filled with grotesque antique statues King Peter's ancestors had commissioned or taken from other kingdoms they conquered. They are covered in vines and moss, largely forgotten by the gardeners, some of which are trimming hedges and tending to flower bushes at the moment.

I sprint past them, and they don't pay any attention to me. I can see the crop of trees where a car should be waiting for me. I just need to reach it and drive out of here. By the time anyone notices, I'll be home where they can't reach me.

"Lex!"

I stop. I don't know why I do that. I should keep running, but the desperation in Opal's voice forces my feet to halt. Turning around warily, I see her dressed in a white muslin gown, looking more innocent and sweeter than she's capable of being.

The knit cap I'm wearing has flown off in the chase from the north tower to the gardens. My hair is exposed for everyone to see. I absently run a hand through my dirty locks as I look at her.

Opal's blue eyes are wide, pleading. "Don't go."

"I can't stay," I tell her. "We're at war, Opal. I have to get home."

"That's why you should stay," she insists, stepping closer to me. "If something were to happen, you'd be safer here."

"I am not safe here. Your father and brother both want me dead."

She shakes her head. "They want Kane dead. You were just the closest thing to him."

"I'm done being their proxy for my brother. I have to go, Opal."

"Lex, please!" she exclaims, her face crumbling. "Kane is going to lose this war, and my father will want him dead at all costs. When that happens, my baby won't have a father anymore."

Opal has a hand on her belly, and I can see the rounded shape of it through the thin muslin. That protective tenderness makes me want to stay and take care of her. That baby inside of her is innocent and is already being used as a tool in this mess. It's not fair to this kid who hasn't even been born yet.

"I need you to stay so this father will have a baby," she continues. "I'll persuade my father to make you the king of Crimson Peak, and we can rule together. We could have everything."

The suggestion rings through my ears like a gunshot.

"That is Kane's throne, not mine," I retort. "It was never mine. I will not take it from him."

Opal bursts into tears. "Lex, please. I can't have this baby alone. I don't know how to be a mom. I don't know what to do."

She starts sobbing, ugly wet tears. Opal hates looking less than perfect, so she covers her face in her hands. I move closer to her and pull her into my arms. She sobs into my chest as I try to soothe her.

"Everything is going to be okay," I assure her. "No matter what happens, I'll take care of the baby. I promise you, Opal. We'll get through this together."

She sobs harder. "I was supposed to be married by now. Not pregnant out of wedlock like some cheap whore."

"Well…"

"Will you marry me?" She looks up, her face wet from tears. Her eyes move back and forth frantically as she contemplates her next desperate move. "You were right. It's your baby. You want to do right by this child, don't you?"

I stare at her in disbelief. She's finally acknowledging the baby is mine, and she wants me to marry her. I'm very uncomfortable with all of this. I'm not sure whether to believe Opal is serious or if this is some kind of a terrible joke.

"We don't like each other," I point out. "We have nothing in common but sex."

"That's better than most arranged marriages."

I don't want to entertain this insanity more than I already have. I place my hands on Opal's shoulders and tell her, "I will be there for the baby, but I have to go now."

She grip my shirt with her sharp nails. "Don't go. My father's men will hunt you down like a dog."

I pull her hands away from me. "Not if I get out of this cesspit of a kingdom first."

"Lex!"

We both turn to see Jacob walking briskly toward us. He's carrying a sword in one hand. *Oh shit.* Now I really had to go.

"We'll discuss co-parenting later," I say to Opal, kissing the top of her head and gently patting her belly. "Hang in there, Junior. Papa is coming back."

I make a run for it, but my wounds haven't healed completely, and I'm slower than usual. Jacob reaches me and tackles me to the ground. He buries his sword into my shoulder, and the sharp pain of metal cutting through skin and muscle makes me hiss in pain. Jacob keeps me pinned to the ground with the sword buried in the earth up to the hilt.

"Did you really think I was going to let you get away?" he snarls. "You owe me an arm."

"Rainer."

"What?"

"Actually, it's that Rainer owes you an arm. I had nothing to do with you losing a limb even if you did deserve it."

He pulls out the sword, dirt and blood flying into the air. He raises the sword and aims for my heart. Jacob isn't a bad swordsman. I would be dead if Rainer hadn't taken his dominant hand.

Jacob isn't as sure while wielding a sword in his other hand. I push his arm away, and he stumbles to the side. Without his other arm to steady him, he falls to the ground beside me. His blue eyes are wide in shock and humiliation.

"I hate to knock down a man with one arm and a shattered leg, but sometimes exceptions have to be made," I quip. "I really do have to go, Jacob. You understand."

I move to leave, but Opal grabs my arm, her nails digging into my skin again.

"Don't go, Lex. You have to stay. You're going to make things worse," she insists.

"Opal, let me go!"

Jacob hobbles to his feet. He raises his sword at me. I look between him and Opal and decide whether he could hurt his own sister. Without thinking about it, I pull her behind me and out of harm's way.

Jacob snarls. "Did you really think I would hurt Opal? I let myself be captured for her."

"I don't know. Maybe you lost your mind in the dungeon."

Jacob gestures to the side angrily. "Get away from her. We'll fight like real men."

"Fight like real men?" I repeat in disbelief. "I don't have a weapon!"

A shovel seems to fly out of nowhere and land on the ground in front of me. The gardeners who have become my saviors are nowhere to be seen. Great. I'm bringing a shovel to a sword fight.

It's better than nothing.

I move away from Opal, and she looks like she's about to cry again. I grab the shovel and raise it against Jacob. He scowls at me and then lunges. The sword collides with the shovel with a metal clang.

Jacob raises the sword again, and I parry with the shovel. The shovel is heavier and clumsy to use. If Jacob was fighting with his other hand, he would have made quick work of me by now.

Sword meets shovel. Our faces are only separated by his blade and the garden tool.

I raise an eyebrow. "Give up?"

"Never."

He pulls back then lunges again.

THE FINAL BATTLE

Lex

The sword hits the wood of the shovel, digging into the weathered wood. Jacob's blue eyes glare into me. I don't think I've ever had someone hate me this much before. The ferocity with his attacks tells me that he truly wants to kill me.

This isn't just a mean boy wanting to pick on someone. Jacob wants me dead.

The wood begins to break under the weight of the sword and Jacob's strength. I step back, and he takes the opportunity to swing again. The blade catches me in the arm, easily slicing through the thin layer of fabric I'm wearing. I hiss as my arm begins to bleed, staining the white shirt red.

Jacob swings again, and I dodge, opting to tackle him to the ground. The sword flies out of his hand as I force him on his back. I drop the shovel and wrap my hands around his throat, cutting off his air. He scratches at my arms with his one hand, his legs trying to kick me off, but I sit on his torso to steady myself.

I have never truly wanted to kill anyone. I never thought I had the stomach for it, but looking down at Jacob and thinking of all the shit he and his family have put my people through, my grip tightens on his throat. At this moment, his father is marching into my kingdom and spilling the blood of my people. This is the same man who threw me into the dungeons to die.

"Lex!" Opal cries out. "Let him go!"

I ignore her. Jacob begins to turn blue.

His sister is at my back, trying to pull me away. "Please let him go! Please!"

I shake her off, and she lands on the ground. I instantly regret it and get off Jacob to check on her. Opal has landed on her hands, breaking her fall. I fuss over her, hoping I haven't truly harmed her or our child.

"I'm sorry," I tell her, checking over her for her wounds. "Are you okay?"

Opal slaps my hands away, impatiently. "I'm fine. The baby is fine."

From my peripheral vision, I can see Jacob has recovered. He's on his feet. He picks up the shovel I discarded. I look around me for any weapon and see Jacob's sword a few feet away. I crawl toward it as fast as I can.

Jacob is walking briskly toward me, ignoring his sister's pleas to stop. My hand grips the handle of the sword, and I turn around just as he raises the shovel to strike. I lunge upward and the blade goes through his chest, piercing his heart. His blue eyes widen in shock before he goes down, the sword sticking out between his ribs.

Opal lets out a horrified scream and runs toward her brother. He's gone completely still. I've done it.

I've killed Prince Jacob.

RAINER

Kane has changed into his armor. It is custom built for him so he's able to move in it easily while still having protection. He holds his helmet in his hand. The only difference between his and mine is that his has a symbolic crown engraved on top. We walk toward the amassed troops.

"There is still no word from either your uncle or Queen Olga," I tell him. "King Basil has decided to stay neutral."

"And the others?"

"Most have also declared neutrality although King Matthias has pledged his allegiance to Scarlett Thunder."

Kane hisses out a curse. "I should have known Matthias would do that. His ego has been bruised and he wants his pound of flesh."

"Perhaps we should have worked on being more diplomatic with Ruby Rivers?"

"I don't want anything to do with that kingdom," Kane retorts. "Matthias and Ruby Rivers have made their view of me known. They've chosen their side."

I'm not feeling that charitable to our former allies either, so I don't push the topic.

Kane puts on his helmet and swings on top of his steed. The black stallion Aramis is large and fast. My horse is his brother Porthos who is of a similar build. A squire hands Kane his shield. We are faster than horses when we run, but we may as well save our legs while we can.

"What are the odds, Rainer?" he asks.

"They could be better but they're not dire now that we have the shifters with us. We have the strategy with the witches which gives us an advantage."

"Hold the fort."

I nod. "Hold the fort."

I leave Kane to mount my steed. Porthos is calm and steady underneath me, but I pet his neck, trying to hide my nerves. I am no stranger to battle, but it has been some time since I've been in a war of this magnitude. Our last encounter with King Peter was nothing compared to this.

I direct Porthos toward our frontline. We will need to hold in order to give the witches time to cast their spells. Shifters and vampires stand side by side waiting for my command. I turn to where King Peter and King Myenas sit across the field on their horses. Even from the distance I can see the smug looks on their faces as if they've already won.

King Peter turns to his men and nods.

"Charge!" one of the soldiers shouts.

Hundreds of vampire warriors charge forward.

"Archers!" I yell. "Pull!"

Our archers who have been at the ready pull back their bows and dozens of arrows fly into the sky and fall down on Scarlett Thunder's army. Some hit their marks. The rest continue forward. I pull out my sword and rush into the fray.

"Charge!" I shout.

The frontline lets out a welcoming war cry as they follow me. We greet Scarlet Thunder's forces in the middle of the field. Swords clash, and shifters knock vampires to the ground. I use my shield to block an axe coming my way and the weight forces me off Porthos.

I land on the muddy field, rolling to get on my feet quickly. A vampire from the other side flies at me, but I dodge him. A shifter behind me lunges at the soldier and bites his neck clean off his body. Before I can thank the shifter, arrows descend on us, and I have to use my shield to block them,

Dozens of arrows hit the shifter, and I watch as he tries to move forward until the weight of them forces him to collapse to the mud. Porthos is unharmed and has returned to my side. I quickly mount him again and charge forward to slash at a nearby group of soldiers that have cornered another shifter. It gives the wolf enough room to escape as our men move forward to help.

I turn back to where the witches are casting their spells.

"Ivy!" I shout. "How long?"

I can barely hear her response through the thrashing around me. "Get out of the way!"

Magic has a distinct smell. It is sunlight mixed with a sweet flowery scent. As Willow and the other witches cast their spells, the other vampires on the other side halt, attempting to figure out what's happening before several dozen of them immediately burst into flames.

"What the fuck was that?" King Peter asks loudly enough that I can hear him from where he sits at the back of the battlefield

"Magic," I shout. "Don't fuck with witches."

Despite the danger, more vampire warriors advance from Scarlett Thunder's side. I watch as more of our men fall. Shifters and vampires drop to the mud, never to get up again. A fresh wave of enemy soldiers comes into view in front of us. I look to the right and left and see them advancing from there as well. Did Peter just get reinforcements in from another kingdom?

I look for Kane, but I can't see him. I'm sure he's attacking the vampires on the battlefield somewhere.

The witches need time to recharge, and we are getting hemmed in from all directions.

Porthos panics and kicks his front hooves into the air. I try to calm him, but the steed is terrified. He rears back, and I leap to the ground. As my horse disappears, I take note that Scarlett Thunder's forces are circling closer and we're huddled so close together it's hard to breathe.

Fuck. This is not how I want to die.

I hear Kane's voice through the madness and turn to see him, slightly bloodied. "Hold," he says. "Hold your line. No one retreats."

A shout from behind us draws my attention. I turn to see King Cyrus on horseback with his banner men behind him. Sardonia has come in our time of need. They rush forward and break through Scarlett Thunder's forces trapping us on three sides.

The witches are recharged, so they begin to throw spells at our enemies again. Some burst into flames and body parts implode inside their armor. It's brutal but effective. A soldier knocks a male witch to the ground and bites at his neck, tearing off his head in the process.

I run to slice the soldier through with my sword, but Willow beats me to it. She grabs the soldier by the face, and I watch as all the blood vessels burst from the vampire. He drops to the ground in a bloody heap. Willow rams her boot into his chest.

I grab her by the soldiers. "Are you okay?"

"I've been better," she replies. "Have you seen Ivy?"

A booming explosion makes us turn. Ivy stands near the middle of the field next to a gaping hole she just created. Dozens of Scarlett Thunder's forces scream as they fall to their deaths, their shouts echoing off the walls of the sinkhole.

Ivy stands there covered in mud and blood.

We stare at her in shock.

"What?" she says.

"Nothing," Willow and I both reply.

I look around the battlefield frantically. Where did our king go?

"Has anyone seen Kane?"

Kane

King Peter has not joined the battle. King Myenas ran off with his personal guard a few moments after Cyrus showed up, but Peter remains, watching. His smug face makes my blood boil as I fight through the hundreds of soldiers to get closer to him. Emory is by my side and we work as a unit.

My wife knocks a soldier to the ground, and I thrust my sword into his chest, past the chainmail to pierce his heart. He grows still and we move on. A soldier with a war hammer comes lunging forward, raising it to hit Emory. I intercept him and take the brunt of the force with my shield.

She moves around me to get to the soldier, jumping on his back to bite at his neck. He tries to shake her off, but her fangs dig into his flesh until she reaches his spine. There's a snap as his neck breaks. I step backward and let his body collapse to the ground.

Emory's white fur is filthy. Her muzzle is covered in bright red blood. Her claws are caked in mud. She's a sight to behold.

As if she can read my mind, her tail wags, and she pushes me forward with her muzzle. I turn around, and King Peter is only a few feet away. His men surround him, preventing anyone from moving closer. I spread my arms to get his attention.

"King Peter! Let's settle this once and for all," I declare. "We fight man to man. Stop the bloodshed between our warriors."

He dismounts from his horse. The battle behind us grows still as if they can sense that their fighting is not necessary anymore. He does not move forward but stares me down like I'm an insolent child.

"Are you scared, Kane?" he questions.

"What say you?"

"Blood has already been spilled. Are you scared to lose more than you already have?"

I shake my head. "I'm not afraid of you."

"Very well," he replies. "Let's make this field famous. This little muddy plot of land shall forever mark your gutless shame."

BETWEEN TWO KINGS

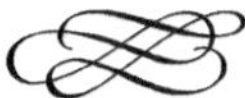

Kane

Troops from both sides surround us with bated breath. The battle is mostly over. This duel between King Peter and me will determine the outcome of the war. It is the culmination of months of posturing and preparation.

"Here are my terms, Kane Alexander of Crimson Peak" King Peter says. "If I win, you will marry my daughter and make her your queen. If you do not, I shall have your head and place her on the throne, and your child will be next in line to reign."

I don't correct him when he calls Opal's child mine. He will not accept any other reality than the one he has in his head.

"If I win, you will return my brother to me unharmed and surrender your children to be punished for hurting Emory Moonraker," I reply. "I will not claim Opal's child as my own, but the child will be taken care of."

King Peter snarls. "I agree to your terms."

We circle one another for a few moments. I half expect him to pull out a weapon, like a coward, but he doesn't. After several minutes, he lunges first.

We exchange strikes and parries, exchanging blows, trying to get to one another in the most sensitive areas. King Peter is older but more experienced. He was fighting in battles long before I ascended to the throne.

My youth is an advantage. I'm faster and stronger. I stand my ground as he bears down on me with his fangs exposed, and I force him back, nearly knocking him off his feet. He slips on the mud but recovers.

I take the opportunity and strike, knocking him to the ground. He hits his head on a rock and looks up at me, dazed.

I can see the panic in King Peter's blue eyes. I place my foot on his neck and crouch down so that I'm looking directly into his face. With him in this position, it will be easy enough for me to grab him by the head and twist.

"Surrender," I command.

He spits on the ground. "I'd rather die than to surrender to you."

"Surrender," I repeat. "Think of your men, your kingdom."

"I will never concede to a pathetic excuse of a man that consorts with wolves and witches. You are a blight on our kind."

I glance at where Emory is standing. She's changed back to her human form and has gotten dressed.. Her face is streaked with mud and blood. She looks at me grimly as if she knows what I'm about to do.

"You could have been a better man and king," I state. "Instead, you will be known in history as a stubborn fool."

I grab hold of the sides of his head and twist. He lets out a billowing scream. I toss his head aside, and it lands in the mud. His blue eyes are wide open, and his mouth hangs open in a soundless scream.

I turn to face the troops of Scarlett Thunder. "Your king is dead," I tell them. "Surrender."

Without question, they bend down to kneel, their heads slumped forward in defeat. I won, but I don't feel like cheering. Exhaustion washes over me. My men rush over to me cheering, relieved that it's all over. They lift me up, and I find the strength to cheer along with them.

Once they sit me down, the crowd parts for me. Emory smiles softly as I go to her. Her hand caresses my jaw. My shoulders slump as all the worries I've been carrying for months dissipate.

"Let's go home," she says.

I wrap an arm around her waist, and we walk forward. The soldiers around us continue to part. There's still much work ahead of us, but I know we can sort through the terms of surrender when we do it together.

EMORY

After the Battle of the Red Field, as we are referring to it, there are negotiations to be made for what happens now between the two kingdoms. We were stunned to return to the castle to find Lex already there. He told us how he killed Jacob while he was trying to escape. While we're glad he's back and alive, now we have to figure out who will sit on the throne the lands we've conquered. We could merge them into one kingdom, but that also would be problematic.

I'm secretly glad Jacob will not be ruling anything.

A royal council is quickly put together to help with negotiations.. It's a collection of vampire royals and the nobility of Scarlett Thunder. Kane is in charge of the council, and I am also included. There's some disgruntled protests from some of the council members at having a shifter on the council, but Kane silences them.

Kane is the conquering ruler. He can do what he wants. Him even putting this council together is his desire to be diplomatic. He believes in fairness, and I love him for it.

We sit in the war room of Crimson Peak at a table so long, I can hardly see the other end. Kane sits at the head of the table, and I'm on his right with Rainer on his left. Queen Olga is at the other end of the table, the oldest ruling vampire. I've met her since the battle, and she seems very curious about me. I don't know if that's good or not.

"King Peter has no other heirs, except for Opaline," Queen Olga says. "It would make sense for the throne to pass to his daughter."

"From what I've heard of Princess Opaline, she isn't fit to rule," King Cyrus counters. "She is too emotionally unstable to be queen. She cannot be trusted to keep her kingdom's interest at heart."

"That's true," I agree. "I personally know how Princess Opaline is. She'll start another war if you leave her in charge."

Clark's snooty voice points out, "Scarlett Thunder has always been patriarchal as well. Changing that would be imprudent."

Queen Olga rolls her eyes. "And look where that got them. A woman on the throne would do them some good."

"Not this woman," Kane says, shaking his head. "Opal is unfit to rule. The throne cannot go to her."

"Isn't she pregnant?" King Cyrus asks. "I've heard it's going to be a boy."

Rainer nods. "Lex has confirmed it with her physician."

"And he is the father as well?"

"He is the father," Kane answers.

The council members whisper amongst each other.

"The throne should go to the boy," Clark declares. "Opaline can be the regent until he comes of age."

"She can't be the regent. It's the same problem," Rainer retorts. "Why are you even here? All your ideas are terrible."

Clark glares at Rainer through his spectacles. "I was invited to be on this council by His Majesty. If you have a problem with me being here, take it up with him."

Rainer looks to Kane who sighs deeply and says, "It seemed like a good idea at the time."

Rainer gives Clark a smug look, and the other vampire scowls. I bite back a smile. I don't like Clark, and I never will, so I couldn't care less if his feelings are hurt. I don't know why Kane invited him to be on the council. It might have just been temporary insanity.

"Since Lex is the father, he could be the regent," King Cyrus suggests. "Of course, he and Princess Opaline will have to marry to legitimize the child."

Kane frowns. "You want to force my brother to marry a woman he doesn't care for so he can rule a kingdom where he was held as a prisoner?"

"It's not an ideal circumstance, but it's not much different than any arranged marriage, King Kane," Queen Olga beseeches. "Your brother would be a better ruler than Princess Opaline, and with your nephew as the next king of Scarlett Thunder, you'd be in a better position than anyone."

Kane looks at me. I hesitate to say anything. Forcing Lex to marry Opal for political reasons feels abhorrent to me, but somebody has to rule Scarlett Thunder. If it were Lex, that would ensure peace between our two kingdoms.

"It should be Lex's choice," I assert. "It's his life we're asking him to modify."

"He will be doing duty to the kingdom," Clark drones. "Duty must come before personal desire. Always."

I shoot a pointed look at Clark. After this meeting is over, I want him back in his suite where he can't annoy anyone.

Kane takes my hand under the table. I squeeze his fingers reassuringly. He seems to be mulling over the decision. I don't envy him having to make this choice.

The royal council can agree and disagree on matters, but Kane still has the final say.

"I will take all of this under advisement," he declares. "And I will inform all of you when I've made my decision."

Kane

After the meeting with the royal council adjourns, I leave the war room and go outside for some fresh air. Emory comes with me, keeping an arm around my waist. Her touch is comforting and an anchor in the chaos of my thoughts.

When we reach the rose gardens, I let out a deep sigh and run a hand over my face. The heavy pressure of having to make a decision I don't enjoy closes around me. Emory doesn't let me go and rests her chin on my shoulder. Her emerald gaze doesn't judge.

"What are you thinking?" she asks.

"I'm thinking I'm about to ask my brother to give up his freedom again," I reply. "This time for years. His son won't be old enough to rule till he's at least twenty-one. That's decades of Lex's life he'll be trapped in Scarlett Thunder."

"He'll be the regent, not a prisoner this time. He'll be in charge."

"He'll be in charge of a kingdom that views him and our entire kingdom as the enemy. Bad blood won't disappear overnight."

"Lex can help ease the tensions. His child will be of both kingdoms," she points out. "Like how our son is helping bridge the gap between our species."

The shifter Alphas have a new respect for me after they fought with us in battle. They have a new respect for Emory as another Alpha, and she's proud that she's able to have better relationships with the other packs. Bernard's legacy will not haunt her. She's making her own name and her own destiny.

"I hate to ask him, but it will ultimately be Lex's choice." I turn and cup her face in my hands, staring deeply into her eyes. "What would I do without you?"

"Keep putting questionable people on your royal council like Clark?"

I wince. "I thought Clark would have some good advice. He does have some wisdom that's been useful in the past."

She snorts. "Maybe before I was born. Has he had a good idea in the last decade?"

I laugh. "I suppose not."

The bright smile remains on her face. The stress from the war continues to melt away, and she kisses me. I return the kiss, enjoying this moment of peace. We've been so busy dealing with the aftermath of a war that we haven't had that much time to be together.

I've missed her. I've missed us.

She pulls away from the kiss and rests her forehead against mine.

My eyes remain closed, and I breathe in his feminine scent and the fresh garden air.

"I love you," I whisper softly like a secret. "None of this would matter without you."

She smiles and opens her eyes. "You've changed my life, you know? From the first moment I saw you, I knew that nothing in my life would be the same."

My eyebrows furrow. "Aside from you offering to be my personal feeder?"

She snorts. "Before that."

"Of course."

"This year has been the most hectic and wonderful year of my life," she continues. "I became a feeder, I fell in love with you, then I became an Alpha."

"You got pregnant and gave birth to your child," I add. "We fought and won a war. This year has felt more like a decade."

"That's true."

What a life.

I cup her jaw again and ask, "Will you finally marry me, Emory Moonraker?"

I have asked her to marry me before. She held off because it wasn't the right time then.

"In this moment I know with everything in me that my path forward will always be by your side."

The rightness of it is overwhelming.

And much to my relief, she answer, "I would love to marry you, Kane Alexander. As soon as possible."

THE QUIET AFTER

Kane

Despite Emory's urging that we get married as soon as possible, I want to do this right. I only plan on getting married once, and I'm not going to have a rushed wedding. I've been asking her to marry me for months, and I want us to have the wedding of her dreams. Besides, planning a wedding is less stressful than preparing for a war.

A smaller, more intimate wedding would have been ideal for us, but we both understand that our union is a declaration. After centuries of bad blood, a vampire king is marrying a shifter Alpha. This is going to ruffle feathers, and we are going to face everyone opposing our union head on. We've fought a literal war to be together, and we know that there will always be people that think our love is an abomination.

As I'm getting ready for the wedding, I feel calmer than I've ever been. There's a sense of rightness to this day that any cold feet aren't going to ruin. I'm changing into my clothes for the wedding when Lex enters my suite. He walks taller and with more purpose these days.

My little brother who has always felt lost and looking for his reason to exist has risen to do his duty. When I spoke with him about marrying Opal and becoming regent of Scarlett Thunder, he accepted it with grim resolution. Lex knows what I asked him to give up to ensure peace between the two kingdoms, and I am grateful that he agreed so easily.

"How are you doing?" he asks.

I struggle with my tie. "I'm good. How have you been?"

"Opal is about to pop any day now, so I'm just trying to wrap my head around being a father when the baby is finally here."

"You'll adapt faster than you think."

He nods. "I suppose so, though I don't think I'll adapt as fast as you."

"Why not?"

"You were born to be a father. You've been wanting to take care of everyone even before you were king."

"I was raised to be that way."

"You took to it naturally." He pauses before admitting, "Unlike me."

I stop and look at him, really look at him. There's an agitation there that's new. It's not from restlessness but from the pressure of being responsible for so many lives. The first few years adjusting to being a king is not easy, especially when you have the responsibility of rebuilding after a war.

"How are they treating you over there?" I ask. "Are they treating you badly?"

"No, but they don't trust me. They won't say it to my face, but the nobles can't stand that I'm the regent, and they have to fawn over me now. And Opal..." He grimaces.

There was a quick wedding between my brother and Opal after the royal council insisted on it. Held in the throne room of Castle Blackmoor, only a few people, including myself, stood as witnesses. Opal was still red-eyed and grieving her brother and father as she said her vows. Lex hadn't looked enthusiastic either but had gone through the whole thing without complaint.

He hasn't spoken about his marriage, but I doubt it's a happy one. The guilt I feel intensifies.

"I'm sorry, brother," I tell him. "I wish you could have married for love or at least to someone you could like."

"Opal is not that bad," he tries to assure me unconvincingly. "Maybe after the pregnancy hormones aren't making her so moody, she'll lighten up and throw less pillows at my head."

I doubt that. I almost married Opal, after all, and I know what she's like.

I put a hand on his shoulder. "Perhaps after your son takes the throne, we can arrange for a divorce."

He snorts. "Royals don't divorce."

"We don't marry shifters either, but here I am."

Lex snorts. "Enough about me. This is your big day."

He picks up the blazer off the chair and helps me into it, declaring, "Let's get you hitched."

We leave my suite and make our way to the ballroom where dozens of guests are waiting. Most of the vampire royals have come. We didn't bother inviting King Matthias and King Myenas as I have no desire to bother with diplomacy with them for a long time. All of the shifter Alphas showed up, and I nod to them as I make my way to the altar.

Rainer is there to stand beside me as my best man. Willow stands on the other side as Emory's maid-of-honor. The dress she's wearing has an empire waist, effectively hiding the swell of her growing belly. We found out recently she and Rainer are expecting a girl. No one knew that Rainer was capable of having children since he wasn't born a vampire, but then, Willow is a witch, so she has a lot of power.

This year has been fruitful when it comes to babies. All our children will be around the same age.

I glance over the crowd and see Queen Olga, Uncle Cyrus, and a few of the other royal vampires. Some decided not to attend as they still can't accept that my bride is not a vampire. I'm going to remember who didn't show up. The insult to my future wife is not something I can't just swallow.

The ballroom is fully decorated in white and gold, the designers opting for elegance over opulence. Everything is lovely.

The pianist starts playing music as Emory appears in the doorway of the ballroom. She's dressed in a tasteful wedding gown. She's chosen a long train over a large poofy skirt. Her shoulders are bare, and the sleeves are long and reach her elbows.

Embroidery of white leaves and flowers decorate the bodice down the skirt. Emory wanted a reminder of the forests where she grew up, a reminder of who and what she is. Her long red hair has been styled in loose waves, contrasting against her gown. The tiara she's wearing is modest compared to the crowns the other royalty is wearing. The golden metal work is shaped like vines wrapped around gemstones.

She looks beautiful, and I can't take my eyes off her. Her emerald eyes catch my gaze, and she smiles brightly. Her face lights up, and I know this is the woman I'm meant to be with. I'm so lucky she walked into my life when she did and saved me from Opal.

Rainer looks closer to whisper in my ear, "You're a lucky man."

I smile, agreeing wholeheartedly.

Lola is the flower girl. She tosses white petals down the aisle. Helen and Colt escort Emory down the aisle. Helen wears a simple sleeveless green gown. Colt tugs at the color of his suit and rolls his shoulders, obviously uncomfortable.

They finally reach the altar and hand Emory over to me. Helen kisses Emory's cheek, and Colt nods at me before they leave to take their seats. Helen takes Michael from Nettie and places my son in her lap. He is wearing a suit, but it's made of more comfortable material. He squirms in his grandmother's lap, already bored with the events of the day.

Emory continues to smile as I take her hand, and we face the officiant. We only have eyes for each other as we recite our vows. It has taken us a long time to get here, but all of it has been worth it. I feel like the luckiest man in the world.

EMORY

The reception feels like it's never going to end. Feeding so many people and having to mingle with them so we're not rude takes a lot of time and effort. It's my first time meeting a lot of the vampire royals, so I try my best to make a good first impression. Most of them seem curious about me more than hostile.

The constant stares at Michael have me feeling protective, so I tell Nettie to retire him early to the nursery. Kane feels the same way I do as he has extra guards watching over our son that night. We both know that even with the smiles and polite chatter that there are still people that wish our son harm. They will never accept the existence of a hybrid, let alone one who is going to become a king someday.

We would rather be safe than sorry when it comes to protecting Michael.

Kane leads me around the dance floor smoothly for our first dance. I have endured months of dance lessons for this. Kane has years of experience, and he puts it to show as we glide around the room. Dancing with him is like a dream.

"Why don't you dance with me more?" I ask

"You never ask," he replies. "And we're both usually too busy for dancing."

"Well, we should pencil in more dancing in the future. We can make the time."

He smiles in agreement. "We'll make the time."

People join us for the second dance, but then Kane smoothly directs us to the balcony for some fresh air. The cool night air feels good on my skin. This gown I'm wearing is exquisite but overly warm. I place my hands on the marble of the balcony railing and take a deep breath.

There's a full moon tonight. I look up at it, thanking the Moon Goddess for Her blessings. I've felt Her watching over me through this tumultuous year. I've done a lot of growing up recently changing from a girl into a woman and a woman into an Alpha.

And through it all, I found the love of my life. The father of my child. The other half of me.

We started in the most unconventional of ways, but we found each other even in the most unusual of places. What I thought would be the end of my life was actually the beginning of a new adventure. If I could go back in time and tell that scared twenty-year-old girl how her life was about to change, I don't think I would have believed myself. And there are somedays I can't believe everything that I've experienced and survived.

Life is too vast and random to ever predict.

Kane's hand wraps loosely around my waist. I rest my head on his shoulder and breathe in his familiar masculine scent. I will never get sick of how he smells and what it invokes in me—desire, love, and contentment.

"Willow and Rainer are having a girl," Kane whispers.

"I know."

They have asked us to be godparents to their unborn daughter. I know the two are planning on eloping soon as neither of them want the pomp and circumstance of a big wedding. It suits those two. They're not the type to want to do things conventionally.

"I was wondering if you'd want to have a daughter someday."

I raise my head to look at his face. He seems unsure. His blue eyes are filled with hope and affection. "Are you asking me if I want more kids?"

He nods and says, "It will be lonely for Mikey to grow up as an only child. Even as annoying as Lex was, it was nice to have a brother."

"I feel the same way about Colt, but Mikey is still breastfeeding. Having another baby with our packed schedules is going to take a lot of work and prioritizing."

"We'll have help."

"We'll need a whole village."

"We have a whole castle," he points out. "And you know it'd be nice if they were closer in age. I'd actually like to have more than two kids."

"Hold your horses, Your Majesty," I assert. "Let's just get Mikey talking and walking first, and then we can discuss giving him a baby brother or sister."

"Deal."

"Deal," I agree, resting my head on his shoulder again. "Best deal I've ever made."

Except for when I decided to take Lola's place as the vampire king's feeder.

I wonder if our adventures are over. Something tells me they're just getting started.

ALSO BY BELLA MOONDRAGON

The Alpha King's Breeder series:

Bought by the Alpha: The Alpha King's Breeder Book 1

Loved by the Alpha: The Alpha King's Breeder Book 2

Lost by the Alpha: The Alpha King's Breeder Book 3

Luna of the Alpha: The Alpha King's Breeder Book 4

Legacy of the Alpha: The Alpha Kings's Breeder Book 5

Daughter of the Alpha: The Alpha King's Breeder Book 6

Descendants of the Alpha: The Alpha King's Breeder Book 7

Shadow of the Alpha: The Alpha King's Breeder Book 8

Son of the Alpha: The Alpha King's Breeder Book 9

Spare of the Alpha: The Alpha King's Breeder Book 10

Claimed by the Alpha: The Alpha King's Breeder Book 11

Atonement for the Alpha King: The Alpha King's Breeder Book 12

Rejected by the Alpha: The Alpha King's Breeder Book 13

Abducted by the Alpha: The Alpha King's Breeder Book 14

Wolf Shifter Fairy Tale Retellings series

Beauty and the Alpha Beast

Sleeping Beasty

Tangling With the Alpha

The Luna's Vampire Prince series:

The Culling

The Kingdom

The Conquered

Pregnant With Four Alphas' Babies

Chosen As the Breeder

Mated to Four Alphas

Threats Against the Breeder

At War for the Breeder

The Stolen Breeder

Four Alphas, Four Babies

Becoming the Luna Queen

Descendants of the Breeder

Desired by the Devil series

Whispers of the Devil

Banter of the Devil

Murmurs of the Devil

The Mafia Kings series

Indebted to the Mafia King

Loved by the Mafia King

Claimed by the Mafia King

Secrets of the Mafia King

Burned by the Mafia King

Kidnapped by the Mafia King (coming soon!)

Dark Stalker Romance series

Tempted by Sin

Fated to Sin

Secret Billionaires series

Finding the Secret Billionaire by Olivia Bhelle Kildare

Falling for My Secret Billionaire by Bella Moondragon

Driven by the Secret Billionaire by ID Johnson

Wolf Shifter Alpha Kings series

Ravens and Ruins

Sundrops and Shadows

Snowflakes and Sabotage

The Vampire King's Feeder series

Claiming the Alpha's Daughter

Loving the Alpha's Daughter

Finding the Alpha's Daughter

Bewitching the Alpha's Son (coming soon!)

Writing as B. Moon

The Boy Who Died

Sign up for Bella's newsletter here.

Or get a free novella from The Alpha King's Breeder series when you sign up here:
The Beta and the Maid

Follow Bella on Facebook here.

Follow Bella on Bookbub here.

www.ingramcontent.com/pod-product-compliance
Lightning Source LLC
Chambersburg PA
CBHW060616300726
48975CB00005B/1582